DELTA SIERRA

A novel of the Vietnam War

LARRY R. FRY

DELTA SIERRA. Copyright © 2018 by Larry R. Fry

All Rights Reserved

Printed in the United States of America

Cover Painting: "PICKLE THE LOAD"
Copyright © 2017 by Nathan Ostrow
Used by permission

Base Map on page vii: Department of Defense

This is a work of fiction. Names, characters, places and incidents either are the product of the author's imagination or are used fictitiously, and any resemblance to actual persons, living or dead, entities, events or locales is entirely coincidental.

ISBN 13: 978-1475009989
ISBN 10: 147500984

Dedicated to all those who flew North

And to the memory of

Ken Bell, Brigadier General, USAF

Jack Broughton, Colonel, USAF

Michael Cooper, Lieutenant Colonel, USAF

Harold "Lem" Heydt, Master Sergeant, USAF

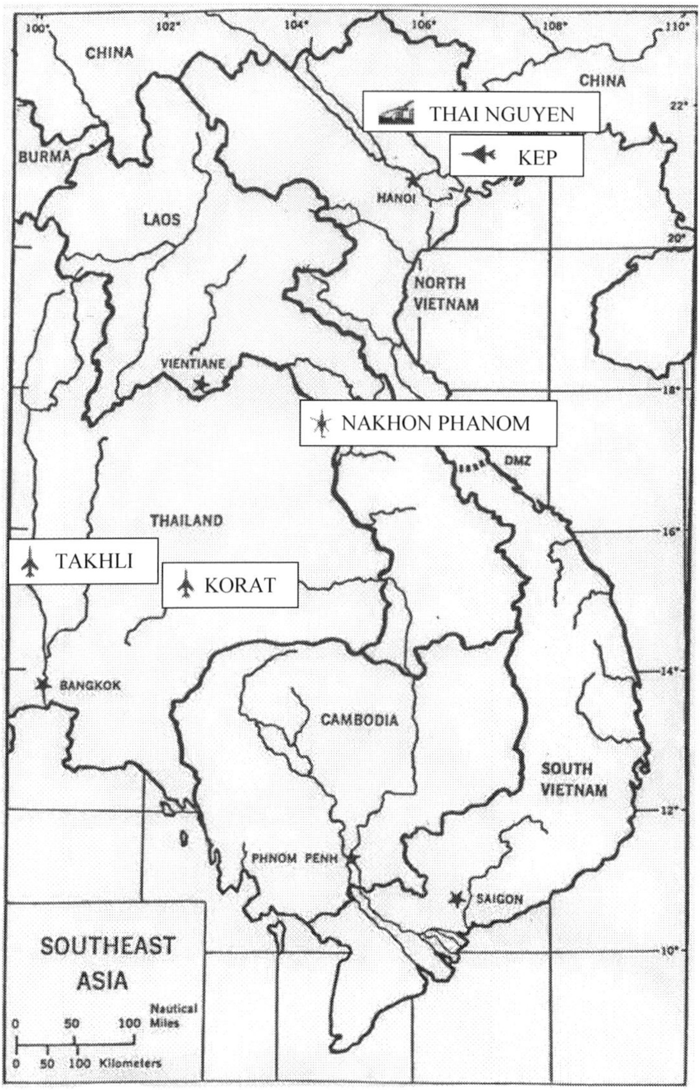

100°
102°
104°
106°
108°
110°
22°
20°
18°
16°
14°
12°
10°
CHINA
CHINA
THAI NGUYEN
KEP
BURMA
HANOI
LAOS
NORTH VIETNAM
VIENTIANE
NAKHON PHANOM
DMZ
THAILAND
TAKHLI
KORAT
BANGKOK
CAMBODIA
SOUTH VIETNAM
PHNOM PENH
SAIGON
SOUTHEAST ASIA
0 50 100 Nautical Miles
0 50 100 Kilometers

PART 1

In war, truth is the first casualty.

—Aeschylus, Greek Playwright

DELTA SIERRA*

They say it's the only war we have.
"So push the edge. Do your best.
Get your ticket punched.
Fear not. Be brave."

Those on the ground mouthing such words,
which don't mean a thing
to those who fly the Thud,
the air machine of war.

Hoping we aren't caught
in the enemy's sparkling fire
as we zoom down,
leaving flame and steel on the land.

Most return with great bravado
bearing crooked sweaty smiles.
except for those captured by hell's fire,
now in Delta Sierra.

From the combat diary of Gary Bishop Deale, First Lieutenant, United States Air Force, 2 March 1967

*DELTA SIERRA (Military Phonetic)—Deep Shit
  (or to the pilots, Dog shit)

BUICK 4

_____ 1

Gary Bishop Deale, First Lieutenant
United States Air Force
In Flight Near Hanoi, North Vietnam
14 July 1967, Counter Mission Number 76

AS GARY BEGAN his dive toward the target, the sky filled with red and orange flashes from enemy shell bursts.

Multiple Surface-to-Air Missiles (SAMs) blasted from the ground aiming at Lieutenant Colonel Foxe's formation.

We're screwed, Gary thought. An experienced pilot, with seventy-five bombing missions over North Vietnam, he had never seen this many SAMs in the air at one time.

Lieutenant Colonel Foxe figured it out first. "Take it down! It's a SAM trap!" he radioed.

Gary pushed the control stick forward. His F-105 bucked and rattled from the violent maneuvers. Maps, papers and dust flew about the cockpit. Sweat poured from his body, fogging his eyesight. Blood pounded in his ears.

He weaved between the SAMs flashing by. Flying telephone poles, his pilot friends called them, like a thirty foot spear with a flaming tail. Gary slammed his stick to the left and then to the right. Missiles exploded ahead of him. Blast concussions jarred his plane.

Two SAMs aimed directly at him. His eyes widened. He gulped oxygen through his facemask. The missiles kept coming straight and true.

"Take it down! Turn! Turn!" Lieutenant Colonel Foxe screamed.

Gary slapped the stick against his left thigh trying to turn into and behind the SAMs. He steepened his dive, pushing the left descending turn.

Two thunderous blasts bounced him from one side of the cockpit to the other. A fusillade of shrapnel struck the F-105, like a softball-sized hailstorm. His plane yawed and slid out of control.

"Buick 4's hit hard," Gary shouted. Smoke filled the cockpit, blocking his sight. Sucking oxygen, he fought to save his plane. His nose and throat burned from the acrid fumes.

The F-105 rolled in an uncontrolled dive. Trying to level his plane, he punched the button to drop his bombs and then jettisoned the external fuel tanks. The fighter dropped lower as the speed increased.

Finally, the plane stabilized. The controls and throttle seemed to work. He breathed a sigh of relief. One second later, another SAM blast struck his plane. I'm truly fucked, he thought. In his gut, he knew the end had arrived.

Flames filled the cockpit. His flight suit began to burn. Searing pain hit him like a shock wave.

"4's on fire," Gary yelled as the plane began disintegrating.

Fire swirled under his helmet visor. Reaching for the left handle to fire the ejection seat, Gary realized that arm wasn't working. Piercing pain. Fire. Burning. "Fuck," Gary screamed, convulsing in terror.

"4's done," Gary yelled, grabbing the right handle and pulling.

"Allison," Gary screamed as the canopy blew off and the ejection seat fired.

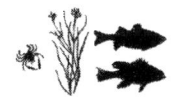

MEN IN BLUE

———————————————— 2

Allison Faith Deale
Newport River Estuary, Beaufort, North Carolina
Eighteen Hours Later, July 14, 1967

I PULLED THE slimy trawl net into the skiff, hand-over-hand, on the port side. Carmen de Ramieres, my close friend and fellow marine biology graduate student, kneeled on the starboard side doing the same thing.

Our boat drifted in the middle of an underwater grass bed, a prime nursery for juvenile finfish and other creatures. The net quivered with thrashing fish. We had to identify and measure each one.

Bile filled my throat. I leaned my head over the side rail and puked.

"What's wrong with you, Allison?" Carmen asked, touching my shoulder.

"I'm fine." I wiped my mouth with a towel. I hesitated, wondering if I should tell her the full truth.

"OK. You need to drink water."

I took several swallows from my canteen. "You count and I'll record."

"¡Bueno!" she said. "Striped bass, 30 centimeters; red drum, 25; blue crab, 11."

Carmen worked quickly, freeing fish from the net and calling out the names and sizes of the animals. Our skiff bounced in the wake of a passing boat. I leaned over the side and vomited, again. My hair cascaded into the water. Cupping my hands, I rinsed my mouth. Plunging my head beneath the waves, I tried to cool my brain and slow things down.

After wiping my face and wrapping my hair in a towel, I lingered a moment, trying to regain equilibrium. The sun's rays sparkled in the waves. Underneath the surface, small fish flashed through the remnants of my lunch.

"Allison, really, what's wrong with you?"

"I'm fine, but I'm slightly pregnant." This was the first time I had said those words to anyone. I had known this for a week, holding it inside. I couldn't tell my husband, face-to-face. He was far away. Who will I tell? I had wondered. Carmen was my dearest friend. I trusted her. I felt happy, relieved at telling her first.

Carmen grabbed me in her arms. "Are you serious?"

"Yes!"

"Have you told Gary?"

"I sent a letter. He should know by now."

Gary, my husband, flew Air Force fighters in Southeast Asia. SEA, he had called it before he departed on his assignment, refusing to say anything specifically about the location. And, never mentioning the pilots killed or missing in action.

He flew bombing strikes into North Vietnam. I knew he was in great danger. We had had long conversations about the missions during his leave in Hawaii, seven weeks before.

Carmen jumped up and down in the boat.

"Don't do that!" I clutched my belly.

She grasped me closely, her hot-blooded Cuban personality shining. Never one to miss a chance to dance and celebrate, Carmen had almost swamped us.

"I don't feel anything," she said, maneuvering her hands around my belly.

"I'm only seven weeks."

Carmen squinted, calculating. "Hawaii?"

I smiled.

"You are blessed," she said, holding me in her arms. "I'm so happy for you."

I am blessed, I thought. One of my college friends had tried repeatedly to have a child, with no success. Virtually on my first attempt, I found myself pregnant.

We finished clearing the net and began stowing our field notes and gear.

Two skiffs turned out of the main channel and headed directly toward us. Strange, I thought. No one ever came near us when we were conducting research. I could tell there were a number of men in the boats. A feeling of fear overtook me.

Glare from the intense sunlight nearly blinded me. By squinting and placing my hand over my sunglasses, I barely identified the occupants.

Dr. Pointer, my adviser from the Duke University Marine Lab, and two men in Air Force blues rode in the first skiff. Jacob and Samuel Craven, my two neighbors in Seven Springs and retired Air Force officers themselves, stood in the second boat, also in uniform.

My body turned cold as ice. I began shaking. Sickness overtook me.

"No, not Gary!" I cried, gagging and heaving over the side.

"Allison," Carmen gasped, *"¡Madre de Dios!"*

PART 2

The essence of war is violence and moderation is imbecility.

—Lord Thomas Macaulay, 1831

WHERE?

Years slid by
preening, smiling, dancing,
screwing, hoping and waiting.
Taking chances,
running risks
and stumbling in the darkness
of unrequited love.
The question arises.
Where have you been?

From the diary of Gary Bishop Deale, Second Lieutenant, USAF, 7 January 1965

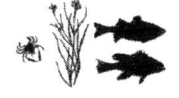

ALPHA

_____ 3

Allison Faith Seaford
Friendship Airport, Baltimore, Maryland
Thirty Months Earlier, December 28, 1964

MY PARENTS DROPPED me off outside the United Airlines entrance at Friendship Airport. They had planned to go on this New Year's skiing trip to Colorado but cancelled due to an important business meeting in Baltimore at the Maryland Savings Bank. Their loan application to expand our family's motel in Ocean City, Maryland, had been approved. They were meeting with the bankers to finalize the deal.

Their small motel needed to be enlarged to satisfy the demands of the summer vacationers from Washington and Baltimore. After construction of the Chesapeake Bay Bridge near Annapolis in 1952, the number of visitors increased with each year. Previously, tourists from the cities had to use a ferry to cross the bay. The bridge cut hours off the journey and opened up Maryland's Eastern Shore, as we called it, to increased business opportunities.

The Eastern Shore, also known as the Delmarva Peninsula, had been a sleepy agricultural area until that "damned bridge," as locals called it, opened the land to large-scale development.

Mom and Dad and Uncle Bill were business partners on our farm and also with the motel. My parents named it The Wight Sands Motel, located on the beachside boardwalk at 21st Street in Ocean City.

I checked my bags at the United counter and proceeded down the concourse.

Stopping by a snack shop, I purchased coffee and a pastry and made my way to the gate. People crowded the lounge area, but I found a seat near the window overlooking the runway. Piles of snow lined the nearby taxiway. Across the ramp, an American Airlines jet backed away from the gate, pushed by a small tractor. Peeling away bits of pastry, I dipped it into my coffee and savored each bite.

Next to me a woman sat, glancing anxiously up at the clock on the wall and then checking her watch. She shifted in her seat and checked the time again.

Digging into my carryon, I found the dog-eared copy of *To Kill a Mockingbird* and picked up reading where I had left off the night before.

After turning a page, I sensed this presence beside me and then felt a tap on my shoulder. That touch changed my life forever.

"Excuse me, but aren't you Allison Seaford?" a voice that I did not recognize asked.

"Yes, I am," I said as I turned to see an attractive young man dressed in a strange blue uniform. "And who are you?"

"You probably don't remember me, but my name is Gary Deale," the newcomer said. "I followed you on the concourse and thought it was you, but I wasn't sure."

"Yes, it's me," I said as I stood, holding out my hand. I didn't remember the face of the stranger, but his name brought back memories from Stephen Decatur High School. I vaguely recalled something about him and the football team. He was my height and very handsome. Realizing that he was much thinner than in his high school days, it finally dawned on me that we had been in classes together.

"Small world! I thought it was you," he said, shaking my hand. "What are you doing here?"

"I'm on my way to Denver and then on to Vail," I said. "What are you doing here and what is that uniform?"

"I'm also going to Stapleton. I'm returning to the Air Force Academy. I graduated in June."

"The Air Force Academy. Wow! I remember you had been admitted to one of the military academies, but didn't know which one."

"I'm returning early to prepare calculus lectures for the spring semester."

"What's the gold bar?" I asked, touching his shoulder.

"I'm an officer, a second lieutenant, the lowest rank." Gary flushed. But he proudly stood there in his crisp blue uniform.

"Oh, I don't know anything about the military."

"I love it. Are you going skiing?"

"Yes."

The lady sitting next to me closed her book, stood and walked away. Gary sat down beside me.

We ended up trading information. I told him about my classes in marine biology at Washington College in Chestertown. He told me about flying in the back seat of a jet fighter and how much he wanted to be a pilot, sit in the front and be the man in charge. We talked about skiing—we both loved it.

The agent at the desk called for the first passengers and a wave of people began lining up. By the time they announced our seats, we'd decided to ask a stewardess if we could sit together.

As the crew began closing the airplane, Gary and I took two empty seats near the back door.

"Cool," I said, "we can talk over old times."

STAINED GLASS
_____ 4

Gary Bishop Deale, Second Lieutenant, USAF
Air Force Academy Cadet Chapel
Colorado Springs, Colorado
7 January 1965

GARY SAT IN the chapel in a quiet corner looking at the stained glass window looming above him. This was one of the few places on the academy grounds where he found peace and solitude. Multicolored shafts of light beamed through the chapel as the sun began to descend toward the front range of the Rockies. He lifted his head in the sun rays, soaking in the warmth.

He didn't consider himself to be a deeply religious person, but found solace and comfort in the chapel. While thinking about his written orders to Randolph Air Force Base, Texas, for undergraduate pilot training scheduled to begin in June, Gary said a silent prayer of thanks. His lifelong dream had come true. He had previously received a verbal commitment. Now the actual papers waited on his desk. Primary flight training took one year. Gary hoped to move on to jet fighters, but he would cross that bridge when he came to it.

Somehow, an innocent airport conversation with a young woman he had known in high school led to one of the happiest weeks of his life. He had questioned his decision to tap Allison on the shoulder at the time, but now he was glad he had taken the risk.

Using leave days, previously saved for spring break, he skied with Allison at Vail. He wanted to be with her.

Gary thought of their days together in the mountains, covered in white and with a pure blue sky backdropping the towering peaks.

While skiing on the second day, it began to snow as they rode the dual chair lift to the top of the 11,000 foot mountain. Allison placed her gloved hand on his shoulder. "Isn't this beautiful?" she asked, pointing at the snow covered fir and pine trees.

"It is," he responded, "even more so with you here."

Allison leaned toward him and kissed his cheek. Their first kiss, such as it was, and the first of many.

Pure powder on several of the days provided perfect skiing conditions. While he considered himself an excellent skier, Allison matched his skill level. They gradually moved from the intermediate to the advanced slopes as the week progressed.

After a full day of skiing, Gary and Allison jogged the darkening streets of Vail, working out the soreness from the twisting and turning on the slopes. It was striking; snow covered fir, stark aspen stripped of their leaves, evergreen Christmas wreaths decorating small cottages with candles sparkling in the frost covered windows. Ice covered the small stream which wound through the village.

Allison's uncle had assigned Gary to his guest room in the chalet, warning him of the restricted area on the loft where Allison slept. Gary took him seriously at first, but then realized that Uncle Bill, as she called him, was only joking.

Gary and Allison kissed and hugged each other over the week, but that's as far as it went. He thought things might have gone further if he had really pushed himself onto her, but he had decided to proceed slowly. She hadn't really resisted his advances. They both had had previous relationships. He didn't want to hurt her or himself.

Allison turned out to be an attractive, sensuous and smart young woman. One clear vision of her remained. On New Year's Eve, Gary and Allison had prepared dinner at her Uncle Bill's chalet for the two of them. This was their first meal alone. Bending over the oven, Allison checked the sizzling steaks to see if they were medium rare. The smell of broiling meat filled the room. Gary opened a bottle of red wine to let it breathe and lit the candles on the table while Allison put the sour cream on the baked potatoes. As she plated the food, Gary studied her closely. Allison's red silk blouse clung to her body. Her top two buttons were open, revealing brief glimpses of her cleavage as she moved through the kitchen. It became clear that she wasn't wearing a bra. It took tremendous willpower to avoid staring.

As they ate their meal, Gary savored each bite. "The steak is excellent," he said.

"I'm glad you like it."

As they finished, Allison served dessert, hot fudge sundaes. She leaned over him, serving the chocolate covered ice cream. Gary got a full view of her breasts. Grabbing her and taking the next step entered his mind.

Rethinking those days with Allison was pleasurable. Consumed by her, he began writing a poem in his head, trying to capture his feelings. While he had done some preliminary outlining, the poem needed more work.

One thing he knew for sure. The young lady from Maryland captivated him. She had stolen his heart.

GOING TO THE CHAPEL
_____ 5

Allison Faith Seaford
St. Martin's Church, Bishopville, Maryland
Saturday, June 11, 1966

I HAD OFTEN wondered if the right man for me even existed, but good fortune, luck, grace and happiness comes into our lives in various forms and at random times.

Somehow, the stars aligned for us and our hopes came true. Both of us ended up in North Carolina. Since July of 1965, I had been enrolled as a graduate student in marine biology at Duke University.

At the same time, Gary attended undergraduate pilot training at Randolph Field, Texas. He had only recently been issued orders assigning him to a jet fighter replacement training unit at Seymour Johnson Air Force Base near Goldsboro, North Carolina.

We had enjoyed holidays and long weekends together over the previous year. I flew to Texas several times, and Gary ventured to North Carolina on cross-country training flights from Texas as often as his instructors allowed.

Gary had surprised me on Christmas Eve. We were both spending the holidays with our parents, who lived about twenty miles apart on Maryland's Eastern Shore. While taking a walk with him on my family's farm in a snow shower, Gary paused by a grove of white encrusted holly trees. "Allison, you know that I love you very much," he said, dropping to one knee and opening a small box. The words, "Will you marry me?" buzzed in my ears. He had caught me unawares. I didn't pause before saying "Yes!" through my tears of joy. He slipped the ring on my finger and gave me a knee-weakening kiss. When I asked him how he had determined my ring size, he said that he had asked Carmen, my best friend.

SIX MONTHS LATER, we were both home again in Maryland. After thunderstorms the previous night, small white tufts of clouds sailed across the stark blue sky. Riding along the dirt road with Carmen and my parents in their antique horse-drawn carriage, I recognized that a new life began for me on this day. Our pair of draft horses, which we kept for special occasions and for the county fairs in the local area, plodded along. Throwing their heads proudly and neighing, almost showing off, the horses pranced, throwing up clods of wet sand. Uncle Bill drove the team, singing a song from somewhere in his past. "*Make way, make way, for the fair maiden approaches!*"

Raising myself from the seat, I adjusted my dress. Carmen and I had made my plain strapless white sheath with a lace bodice over the past four months. She had also made her own similar dress in yellow. After visiting bridal shops in Raleigh and Durham, Carmen and I decided we could make our own. The design emerged as we leafed through stacks of bridal photographs and magazines.

Uncle Bill then switched to a bawdy ballad, which made me blush. "*There was a young tart from Siddon. She liked to ride, rather than be ridden.*" My mom squirmed in her seat. I thought he was making it up on the fly. As the verses went on, the song got saucier. Then it turned, twisting into a parable of true love, with really funny lines. Always ready to sing, Carmen said, "I would sing along if I knew the words." My dad laughed and slapped his knee. I giggled and then broke into laughter, followed by Mom. Uncle Bill turned and smiled.

When I later asked him about the song, Uncle Bill said it derived from an obscene poem he had learned in a pub in England in World War II. He had served and fought in the Army's Tenth Mountain Division. "We needed comic relief on the carriage ride," he said, "otherwise everyone would have been crying."

As the carriage rounded the last curve, St. Martin's Church appeared before us. The red brick Georgian building, constructed in 1764, nestled nearly hidden in a grove of pine trees. My parents had been married in the church. This is where I had been baptized and confirmed.

Our local community spent the past few years slowly restoring the structure to its eighteenth century appearance. A plain country church, it followed the colonial tradition of simplicity. Constructed of red brick, with two windows on each side, there were no exterior embellishments.

Inside, peeling white stucco walls helped lighten the interior. Three bays of light-colored wooden box pews, one against each wall and one in the middle served as seating for the congregation. The floor consisted of rough and worn red brick. Not really having an altar, per se, the front chancel railing enclosed tall wrought iron candelabras and a plain table. A high parson's roost in the left bay provided the lectern and sermon mount.

Still singing as we approached the churchyard, Uncle Bill switched to another song, "Going to the Chapel," made famous by the Dixie Cups. That tune provided a more relaxed atmosphere, especially for my mom.

A stiff breeze rippled through the trees, bringing with it the smell of the ocean and the nearby marsh.

Uncle Bill tied the horses to a hitching post, which must have stood by the church for two centuries. He helped us down from the carriage and escorted my mother through the newly painted doorway. Carmen hugged me and slowly stepped into the church.

At this great transition in my life, going from a daughter to a wife, melancholy filled my heart. Sad, but yet excited, I felt the blood roaring through my body. Flushed and sweating, my hands felt like ice.

Giving me a hug and then offering his arm, my father said, "Are you ready for this, Allison?"

My heart fluttered. My throat choked. I croaked, "I've been waiting for this day all of my life."

Taking each measured step, we walked into the sanctuary. The string quartet began playing the traditional "Here Comes the Bride."

The tall trees outside decreased the amount of natural light and the building had no electricity. Fortunately, thunderstorms the previous evening had brought with them a cool front reducing the Maryland heat and humidity to a pleasant level.

Candles, mounted on long wooden holders, flickered at the end of each family box pew, casting shadows across the wall. Carmen and I had spent the past month making white bows now anchored to the side of the stiff-backed wooden benches. Mounds of white hydrangeas covered the front rail, backed by a meadow's worth of wildflowers, creating a rainbow in the background. A sweet scent filled the air partially masking the musty smell emanating from the old brick building.

Holding fast to my father's arm, I stepped carefully on the uneven and rough bricks. As I passed by each boxed-in row of pews, I smiled at my family and friends.

Turning the corner, I shifted my eyes toward the chancel for the first time. I saw Gary dressed in his formal Air Force blue uniform with Blaine Steffan, his best friend from the Academy beside him. They both smiled as I read Gary's lips, "She's beautiful."

Of all Gary's friends in the Air Force, Blaine was the only one who could make it to the wedding. Other classmates and friends, spread across the United States or in Southeast Asia, a military code for an assignment to fight in the Vietnam War, found themselves unable to attend.

As I turned to Rev. Showell, he began, "Dearly beloved, we are gathered— — "

PART 3

No one starts a war—or rather, no one in his sense ought to do so—without first being clear in his mind what he intends to achieve by that war and how he intends to conduct it.

—Carl von Clausewitz, *On War*, 1832

SEA CIRCUS MAXIMUS*

A fight for freedom and
our nation responds.
War restrained
by books of rules.

Seeing cobras, honey pots, *Klongs*,
multicolored silk sarongs,
non-such tits
and horizontal slits.

Witnessing
blossoms of fire and steel
in the air
and on the land.

Flying through twisting contrails
of smoke and death
yielding war's rewards—
absent friends and empty chairs.

Another fine day
in SEA.

From the combat diary of Gary Bishop Deale, First Lieutenant, USAF, 1 April 1967

*SEA—Southeast Asia

YURI
_____ 6

Yuri Vaskilev, General Lieutenant
Soviet Troops of National Air Defense
Near Chkalovskaya Airbase, East of Moscow, USSR
28 September 1966

YURI HEFTED A pitchfork full of straw from the back of the wagon as Sergeant Komarvsky scraped more toward him. The two men worked hurriedly without speaking. Snow was in the air, the first of the season. They had to get the carrots and turnips covered before the clouds opened up.

Having worked together as comrades in arms since the massive tank battle of Kursk during the Great Patriotic War, as the Soviets referred to World War II, talking fell away as the men labored in the garden.

Grunts and curses filled the air as the two men carried the straw and began spreading it over the rows. Placing a thick layer over each crop provided insulation to prevent the root vegetables from freezing until they could be used in stew.

Yuri paused to look across the garden at a fox, eyeing his rabbit and chicken pens. He waved his arms and the fox scampered back into the woods. Another job to do, Yuri thought. Trees needed to be thinned out in his woodlot. Seasoned logs awaited splitting and stacking for winter fuel.

After years of close friendship and with his wife's approval, Yuri had talked Sergeant Komarvsky into moving into a separate small cottage at his *dacha*. Once Sergi, Yuri's son, had married, another house had been constructed. Sergi and his wife were both medical doctors at the local clinic.

The two men finished with the straw and walked to the woodshed. Lifting a maul, Yuri began splitting, while his friend cut the logs into sections with a bow saw.

This had become their daily ritual. After work at the nearby airbase, the men labored in the garden or woodlot, trying to get ahead of winter. It was a losing proposition, as the snow always came early here.

As the darkness settled around them, Yuri called it a day. "Enough work," he said. "It's tea time." Sergeant Komarvsky grunted and nodded his assent. Yuri filled their mugs with hot sweet tea from his thermos and then poured in a generous shot of vodka. His wife's thick rabbit stew simmered in the oven, their evening meal.

The two men sat on a bench, huddling against the cold. Stark leafless trees surrounded his *dacha*, granting privacy and a source of fuel. An owl called from the nearby swamp; otherwise it was still and quiet.

"Are the electro-optical sights for the *Dvina* missile working?" Yuri asked. Using quiet moments like this to work through problems and to brainstorm, he quizzed his friend, turning back to their primary mission of Soviet air defense.

"Somewhat," Sergeant Komarvsky said, wobbling his hand with a wishy-washy motion. "The problem is slaving the missile guidance system to the video signal. If we can get that to work, it will defeat the American countermeasures on the radar."

"Keep working. What about the special apparatus?"

"Same kind of problem, linking the radar to the gun controls. More worries."

"Will the system be ready for our journey south in the spring?" Yuri asked, taking a long slug of doctored tea. "I think I have the ministry convinced that we need to test it in the field."

Yuri relied on Sergeant Komarvsky for his technical expertise. No one understood radar, missiles and computers better than him.

At first a few flakes, and then an avalanche of snow cascaded down on the two men. "Fuck your mother," the sergeant said, "here comes winter."

WAR!
_____ 7

Gary Bishop Deale, First Lieutenant, USAF
Seymour Johnson Air Force Base
Goldsboro, North Carolina
28 September 1966

IN THE OFFICERS' Club Stag Bar after that day's training mission, Major Hooper summarized his critique of the flight. He was a bear of a man, heavily built. Gary wondered how the major fit into the cockpit of an F-105, but he did so every day. "Do y'all have any more questions?" Major Hooper asked in a heavy Texas drawl. Brushing huge fingers through a severely cut flattop, the major stared at his three students.

Gary had lots of questions but he was too intimidated to ask. He thought he would get his answers in due time.

Not receiving any inquiries, Major Hooper switched to his favorite topic—the Vietnam War. "After Castro and his lot took Cuba, Washington became afraid of its own shadow," the major said, slowly drawing out each word. "The Godless Communists were only ninety miles from Florida and that scared the shit out of the movers and shakers up in DC. After Ike's humiliation of watching Fidel climb out of the jungle and into the palace, nobody wants to be the next American president to lose another country to the Red Horde. Hence, JFK and then LBJ began putting our butts into the *SEA Circus Maximus.*"

Gary loved to hear the Texan speak. When he had first arrived at Randolph Field, a year previously, he thought that he was in a foreign land. Not being able to fully understand the local folks' speech or cadence, Gary slowly adapted. Now he understood every word. Naturally, the way most Texans will, Major Hooper embellished each story.

The four men who had flown the mission sat in the Stag Bar chewing their burgers and sipping beers. Sitting at a booth with one of the few windows, Gary could see the sun beginning to slide to the horizon.

After flying and partying together, the four officers had become friends, at least as much as senior officers and instructors can be with their underlings. Each one had Thailand in their future.

Sitting next to Captain Bradley Mims, a fellow student, Gary listened to the two majors, trying to keep up, concentrating on their words, but thinking that he missed important points. Major Hooper and Major Tracey sat opposite.

Brad had been a T-38 Talon jet trainer instructor pilot in Oklahoma. Flying the F-105 was his first experience with a combat aircraft. Tanned and fit, he described himself as a California surfer guy. He often told Gary that nothing beat California girls.

Taking a puff on his cigarette, Gary watched the stream of smoke merge into the blue cloud hanging above the bar. He now allowed himself three cigarettes a day, one right after a flight to calm his nerves, and the others at the club. If Allison found out about his habit, she would wring his neck.

Major Hooper had received orders to transition into an F-4 Phantom replacement unit at Seymour beginning in January. After completing training, his next assignment would take him to an operational squadron in Thailand. With the alarming number of planes shot down over North Vietnam, F-105s faced extinction. The number of Phantoms headed to the war increased each day, replacing F-105s shot down by the enemy.

"The falling dominoes theory is that the Red Horde is first going to take Saigon and then Bangkok, Singapore, Manila, Honolulu, San Francisco and Las Vegas," Major Hooper said, dragging out the words with his slow Texas cadence. Pausing to take a drag on his cigarette, and a drink of beer, he continued. "We can't have them taking over Vegas and ruining sin city, so we have to stop them now. At least, that's the theory. I mean nobody here wants the Supreme Soviet running the whorehouses in Vegas, do they?"

Gary thought the major exaggerated the falling dominoes theory with his rhetoric, but recognized the employment of comic relief when he saw it.

Hooper paused, finishing his burger. "Some guy once said that the first victim in war is the truth," he said. "What really happened in the Gulf of Tonkin incident? Why are we even over there? What is the truth?"

"The truth is an elusive motherfucker in this war," Major Tracey, the third student pilot, said. "The Godless Commies have their truths and we have ours. Never the twain shall meet."

Major Tracey was a sharp contrast to Major Hooper. While the senior instructor was a hulk, Major Tracey was a thin lanky native of New Hampshire. His soft New England accent fit his compact frame.

"If the Commies indeed do unify North and South Vietnam, will that mean the end of world democracy?" Hooper asked, employing a Texas style rhetorical question. "What we have in the SEA is a proxy war, the Soviets staking North Vietnam and Laos, while the U.S. backs South Vietnam. Do we have any business being in a war of national liberation as the Red Horde calls it, or do we contain Moscow and its client states in Vietnam?"

"That decision's way above my pay grade," Captain Mims said, daring to break into the conversation between the two majors.

"I don't know about the bigger truths, but I do know what's going on in South Vietnam," Major Tracey said, twirling his wedding band with the fingers on his right hand. Gary knew he had flown 157 combat missions over the south in an F-100 Super Sabre out of Danang during his one-year tour. "We can't secure the average peasant in most villages. Those poor people go with the flow. All they want is to be left alone to make babies and grow their rice."

"Are you going to finish that burger?" Major Hooper asked, squinting his eyes and staring at Gary's plate. The major handed his now empty plate to a waiter, just passing by.

"I'm working on it," Gary said, trying to keep up with the conversation and eat at the same time. Following the ebb and flow, he tried to take notes in his flight diary, things to think about later. Listening to the two majors talk about their experiences, he realized that he knew nothing about the facts on the ground in the Vietnam War. Even though Gary read extensively, none of the books or news articles disturbed him as much as these conversations. The ignorance he felt during the bull sessions made his head spin. He thought he knew much more than he did about the politics of war. He knew nothing.

Major Tracey paused, waiting for the senior instructor pilot to sneak up on the six-side of Gary's plate and strike. The blind spot at the bottom of Gary's plate offered a wide-open target for Major Hooper to attack. It had happened before. "The ARVN, the South Vietnamese Army, is supposed to be protecting the peasants, but for the most part it's corrupt and unwilling to fight. With the exception of a few elite units, the ARVN avoids the enemy at all costs."

Gary stretched his arms over his head and put his hands behind his neck, massaging his neck muscles. He closed his eyes for a few seconds to help absorb what was being said. This offered a grand opening for Major Hooper's advances on his plate. When Gary opened his eyes, the major sat demurely, munching French Fries, which had appeared out of nowhere, and looking out the window at the sun going behind the trees.

Tracey took a sip of his beer and a puff on his cigarette before continuing. "The United States has 485,000 soldiers over there, but that's not enough to secure the people and make them safe in their villages. You know what our grunts say, the men doing the fighting? They say, 'It don't mean nothin'.' Can you believe that?"

"Nothin'?" Gary asked, mouth full, munching on his burger. He wondered about the men doing the fighting. Did they really believe that the war doesn't mean anything? How could that be?

"Yeah! Just that."

The waitress cleared away empty mugs. "Do you want another round?"

All four men raised their hands.

Major Tracey took a cigarette from his pack lying on the table and flipped open his Zippo. "You talk about truth in war—we have a huge problem with the whole fiasco about body counts. The Pentagon measures our progress by the number of enemies killed. We know precisely how many of our grunts died in Vietnam thus far, 16,839. There's no way in hell we can figure out how many VC are killed in action in the bush. Yet the Pentagon craves the number of enemy KIA, like that's how we know we're winning."

Tracey finished eating the last morsel of his burger and took a long sip of Bud. "Whenever we did an airstrike in South Vietnam, the first question we had to ask the air controller was, 'How many dead enemy VC?' I can't imagine how many lies are being told with that whole body count farce."

Newspaper articles Gary read about the fighting in South Vietnam seemed to feature the number of enemy soldiers killed during each battle. It appeared to be the lead of the story. But this was the first time Gary had heard body counts as being a farce.

The waitress arrived at the booth, lighting candles as the evening grayness darkened the room. "Thunderstorms moving in," she said, piling the empty plates and carrying them away.

"Gentlemen, a question for you," Major Hooper said. "Are we at war? I mean we, as fighter pilots."

"Yes," the group agreed, saying so and nodding our heads.

"Long ago, another famous guy said that violence is the essence of warfare and moderation is imbecility," Hooper said, strumming his fingers on the table. "If we're at war, we should be operating a sustained bombing campaign against North Vietnam with everything we have, including B-52 strategic bombers. If the U.S. really wanted to end this fiasco, we would have done that years ago. This war would be over already." The major's voice had risen as he spoke. His hands clenched, his face reddened, the veins bulging in his neck. He stared at each of the men intensely, seemingly testing their loyalty to him.

Gary wondered about this man, whom he knew had fought in two wars. How did Major Hooper come to be his instructor? Was it fate or chance? The man was teaching him everything he knew to help Gary survive his upcoming combat missions. He felt young and naïve compared to the major.

Major Hooper took several deep breaths and leaned forward, placing his elbows on the table and resting his chin on his palms. He continued. "What we're actually doing is sending messages, trying to coax the North Vietnamese to come to the peace table. News reports state that the president and chain of command approve each and every North Vietnamese target. LBJ says that the military can't bomb a North Vietnamese outhouse unless he says it's okay."

Hooper smirked. "All we really have is a half-assed campaign known as Rolling Thunder, with its bombing pauses, surges, critical targets that are off-limits, and restricted areas. I ask you again, are we at war?"

The group offered a mixture of yes, no and curses.

This was the first time Gary had heard Rolling Thunder referred to as a half-assed operation. Half-assed operation, Gary thought. His impression from reading newspapers was that Rolling Thunder was an all-out effort to vanquish the North. Sending messages, what the hell does that mean? Gary wondered. He had just heard unfamiliar words, shaking his belief in the war.

"There you have it, boys and girls, one swirling Charlie Foxtrot after another," Hooper said.

Gary smiled at the major's use of Charlie Foxtrot, a military Phonetic Expression, as a code to disguise the true meaning—Clusterfuck. It was one method the pilots used to cover up the intended words, especially in mixed company. Civilians simply didn't understand it.

"Thus ends this church service," Hooper said. "It's time to go home to our families."

WAR?
_____ 8

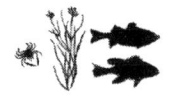

Allison Faith Deale
Seven Springs, North Carolina
October 10, 1966

GARY AND I sat at the picnic table on our screened porch. Having just finished a late afternoon meal of meatloaf and baked sweet potatoes, we lingered over glasses of red wine.

I loved our small house, our first home. After Gary had received orders for Seymour Johnson, I drove through the countryside around the base searching. Only by accident did I stumble across this small brick rancher located near the village of Seven Springs. The house, tucked away in pine woods with a For Sale sign, exceeded my desires for a natural setting with privacy. Our offer was accepted and the property had become ours four months before.

"Where are you going to be stationed?" I asked, already suspecting the correct answer.

"SEA," Gary responded.

"But, where specifically?"

"You know I can't tell you that, it's classified!"

"Is it in Thailand, to be exact Takhli or Korat?" I asked, having heard those bases mentioned in stories told by pilots at squadron parties.

His grin spread from ear to ear.

"No answer to that one, huh?"

He smiled.

But, I knew the base, Takhli. I also knew that the very thought of sending Gary off to fight in a war in SEA as he called it frightened me.

"Why?" I asked.

"Because, I have been ordered to go."

"Not that! Why are we fighting in Southeast Asia?"
Why are we in this war? I wondered. This question came into focus two days previously when I was walking across the main campus in Durham. While making my way toward Allen Hall to drop off paperwork from Dr. Pointer, my graduate adviser, I approached a group of protesters. I heard them before I saw them, yelling slogans about the war. Large posters showed the maps of South Vietnam, Laos and North Vietnam. Large bombs had been painted over each country. Photographs of napalm explosions and burned children were displayed near their booth. Pamphlets rattled in the wind. I paused and then hurriedly walked away.

I knew that universities in the south did have demonstrations, which in no way compared with the turmoil in the north and west. When I walked on the main campus the other day, I heard the chants: "Hey, hey, LBJ, how many kids have you killed today? Make love, not War! One, two, three, four, we don't want your fucking war! All we are saying, is give peace a chance! Hell no, we won't go! and Eighteen today, dead tomorrow!"

At the time, I didn't know what to think. My husband was preparing to go fight in this war. Meantime, students were doing all they could to end it.

Gary leaned across the table, kissing me. "Shall we?"
"Of course, later."

We carried the dishes inside and placed them on the counter. As I cleaned food scraps from the plates, Gary began washing the glasses.

Turning my way, he kissed my neck, his hot breath filling my ear, tingling against my throat. My belly began to quiver. His lips lingered. "Now?"

"Not now! Later!" I said, pushing him toward the sink. I wanted time to think about us, about our future. But I also wanted to hold him.

As Gary's training had progressed over the previous few months, I asked questions and learned answers to the basic questions of who, what, when and where. A satisfactory response to why, the most troubling question, eluded me.

Gary's upcoming assignment to Southeast Asia or SEA, as he called it, and to be more specific, Thailand, even though I had never been officially told that, loomed before us. With only two months as a student pilot remaining before his departure, I wanted to find answers to the unknowns in our future.

I listened to their stories at squadron parties and socials and picked up facts that Gary never directly told me. Thailand, for instance, was his destination rather than the generic SEA. The Air Force utilized Royal Thai Air Force Bases to conduct bombing missions over North Vietnam. Takhli and Korat were used by F-105s whereas F-4 Phantoms were based at Udorn and Ubon.

Answers as to why we were there evaded me. It seemed to me that many American citizens asked the same question, and the issue remained unresolved and unsettling.

Questioning the war's legitimacy created other problems. Anyone posing such questions immediately came under attack as being a Communist, hippie or a Peacenik.

Of course the other side exemplified by a group known as the hard hats also shouted their own slogans: "Love our Country! America, love it or leave it! Long Hairs and Hippies suck cock! and These colors don't run!"

My country divided itself into the hawks and the doves, pro-war and antiwar. Strong feelings existed on both sides. Some took action by burning their draft cards or even the American flag. Many young men turned their draft cards over to peace groups. Vietnam vets attempted to return their medals and awards to Congressional authorities. Sit-ins and teach-ins disrupted normal college life. Draft-age men contemplated departing for Canada or Europe. Many fled, fully recognizing the fact that they might never be able to return to the United States.

Antiwar actions grew and spread. Hard hats, not a timid group, participated in counter-demonstrations, with a little head-bashing of the unwashed Red Filth, as they referred to students, thrown in to teach bloody lessons.

I found myself trapped, a student at a large university with a husband in the military.

While dirty dishes remained piled on the counter, I wrapped my arms around Gary's shoulders. "Now," I whispered.

TERRA FIRMA
_____ 9

Gary Bishop Deale, First Lieutenant, USAF
Near Seymour Johnson AFB, North Carolina
26 October 1966

SWEAT DRIPPED FROM Gary's brow and nose, but he had no way of doing anything about it as a flight helmet, oxygen mask and visor enclosed his head. His flight suit was drenched.

Gary's hands trembled with fatigue as he adjusted the throttle with his left hand and steadied the flight control stick with his right, trying to maintain his correct position in the group of four F-105D Thunderchief jet fighters.

He flew in the rightmost position in the formation as the wingman to Captain Mims, whose plane was just to the left of Gary's wingtip. The two F-105s made up the rightmost element in the flight of four planes. These two aircraft always remained together even in combat. Gary's responsibility was to remain on the wing of his element leader and to watch behind the planes for enemy aircraft, known as checking-six.

To their left, the second element consisting of Major Hooper and Major Tracey completed the four-plane flight. Usually a major or colonel commanded each flight of four aircraft. On this mission, Major Tracey commanded, while Major Hooper, his wingman, observed each pilot.

Much of the two-hour training flight had been flown in a finger-four formation with the fighters in the same relative position as the fingertips on a right hand.

Gary piloted the rightmost plane, the most difficult flying slot. He struggled to fly in the correct position just off Captain Mims' wingtip, constantly adjusting his throttle to hold the proper airspeed.

Maintaining situational awareness, or Sierra Alpha, as the pilots called it, meant that Gary had to anticipate maneuvers by the flight and element leaders. While doing that, he also had to monitor and control his own airplane, known as staying ahead of his fighter.

Even though his aircraft location on the opposite side of the formation from Major Hooper made observation difficult, Gary felt the senior pilot's eyes on him the entire time. Following the course syllabus for this flight, number twenty in Gary's logbook, the F-105s had taken off, refueled in mid-air from a KC-135 jet tanker, fired the fighter's internal 20 millimeter (mm) cannon at targets on an air-to-ground range on an island off Georgia, refueled again and headed home to Seymour Johnson.

Major Hooper always added a few maneuvers over and above what the outline called for. Each mission flown had included a few moments of air combat simulation, what pilots referred to as dogfighting or bust-your-ass time, and aerobatics.

No doubt about it, Gary had mastered the basic course objectives and learned something on each flight. But thus far, he had been unable to impress Major Hooper in the extracurricular flying. He never figured out how to shake off the other fighter in a chase, never found the other plane when they were in a dogfight looping about, and never maneuvered behind the major's plane into what pilots called the dead-man or six position. But, he had learned new tricks. On some flight soon, Gary hoped to bust the major's ass.

Landing the F-105 meant a transition from following the leader in the finger-four formation to each man putting his airplane on the runway. Every movement was a test. Gary found landings to be much more difficult than any other maneuver, except for refueling. On his first flight in an F-105, he had wondered how he was going to land such a big airplane on that little airfield.

Most of the time, Gary did fine. Every now-and-then he screwed up and there was hell to pay during the debriefing. Today's flight hadn't been too bad, but one maneuver had gotten away from him.

As the formation approached Seymour Johnson, Major Tracey received permission for a tactical overhead landing. Using this procedure enabled the planes to land in a minimum amount of time in case one of the pilots had fuel difficulties.

Just after passing over the east end of the runway in the finger-four formation, Major Hooper pitched up his fighter and broke away in an ascending left turn.

Following at short intervals, Major Tracey and Captain Mims peeled out of formation until it was Gary's turn. He eased the stick back to the left, depressing the left rudder peddle to begin a sweeping and ascending left turn.

Gary saw and followed the smoke trail from Captain Mims' F-105. He lined up about one mile behind him on the downwind leg before landing. Squinting through the sweat in his eyes, Gary peered south through the haze, searching for Major Hooper's plane. The major had turned outside the other pilots, lining up to observe the landings. Gary rocked his wings, letting the major know that he had a visual. I'm gonna' catch hell for not seeing him sooner, Gary thought. Major Hooper's aircraft wobbled, acknowledging Gary's sighting.

Centering his stick, Gary eased back the throttle. His aircraft descended gradually as the four aircraft proceeded in trail, like ducks in a row, one behind the other on the downwind leg parallel to the runway and one mile southeast. Time moved very quickly. Gary swept the sky with his eyes to make sure no other planes were near him. The airspeed wound down slowly. With the throttle at minimum power, the engine made little noise. Gary crossed over U.S. Route 70, a major three lane road, lined with North Carolina BBQ restaurants.

Major Tracey, piloting the lead plane, began a 180 degree descending left turn taking him through the base leg to final approach. At short intervals, each pilot duplicated the first plane's maneuver.

By the time Gary completed his turn onto final approach, Major Tracy's plane had touched down throwing up a cloud of blue smoke. Captain Mims landed next. Crossing over the airfield fence, Gary eased back on the throttle allowing his plane's airspeed to decrease from 220 knots. Focusing on the spot on the runway where he wanted to touch down, he eased back on the stick, raising the nose. Gary sucked in oxygen, fighting the tightness in his chest. His right arm strained, trying to hold the stick steady.

Gary tuned his senses to the F-105's movements and didn't detect any negative messages. His fighter passed over the end of the runway, briefly floating along in ground effect. The runway rushed toward him. Settling toward the ground, just beyond the number 26 painted on the runway, the main gear touched down throwing off a mist of smoke. He eased back on the stick, holding the nose in the air, bleeding off airspeed, and popped the drag chute. Gary had hoped to land near the numerals and succeeded in doing so. Gary was on *terra firma*.

Taxiing toward his parking spot, Gary prepared for the intense two hour debriefing, knowing he would catch hell for his botched Cuban Eight maneuver. He had nearly completed it, but his airplane got ahead of him and slipped out of the descending turn in the second loop.

The pilots debriefed in the squadron planning room. Gary sat on a metal chair, elbows resting on the table. He wiped his face with a sweat-soaked towel, listening as Major Hooper panned the mission. Using both hands to simulate maneuvers, as any fighter pilot would, the major talked the three students through their flight. Next, Hooper sat with each pilot, going over their performance.

Being the lowest ranking officer, Gary's turn came last. He took the major's commendations and recommendations seriously, asking questions, taking notes and drawing diagrams.

"What was the F-105 designed for?" Major Hooper asked, his Texas drawl stringing out each syllable.

"Sir, straight and level flight," Gary responded.

"For what mission?"

"Delivery of nuclear weapons."

"Kerblam," the major said, forming a mushroom cloud with his hands. "Now, tell me how the F-105 is actually being used."

"We use it to drop conventional iron bombs on North Vietnam blowing up rice paddies, Communist trees and other such worthwhile targets as directed by, with all due respect, the Commander in Chief, President Johnson."

Gary had listened to Major Hooper's lectures and diatribes enough to be able to sing the song. The major had recently returned from SEA. He carried grievances after watching some of his friends get blown out of the sky while bombing questionable so-called strategic targets in North Vietnam.

Major Hooper was an excellent pilot and Gary had learned so much from him—including the major's personal vision of the *SEA Circus Maximus*, as he called it.

"That's good, now let me walk you through that botched Cuban Eight. You have to feel what the airplane is doing." Hooper looked around to see if anyone was listening to his description of maneuvers outside the syllabus for that day. "That's why we do these things. Straight and level, you aren't going to feel a damned thing, other than a nudge when you blast through the sound barrier. Maneuvering, that's when the bird talks to you. Understand?"

"Yes, sir."

"What are the short stubby wings for?"

"Speed and speed alone, sir."

"Sierra Alpha! Sierra Alpha!" the major said, slapping his hand on the map in front of him. "You have to keep working on your situational awareness with each flight.

You're much better now, but you must constantly improve it."

"Yes, sir."

"This is what you did wrong," Hooper said, using his hands to demonstrate Gary's mistake.

Later, the critique continued in a corner booth in the Officers' Club Stag Bar. The pilots ordered beers and burgers. By the time the four men arrived, the lunch crowd had already departed. Blue smoke drifted above the long bar. Dark wood paneling added to the gloom. Gary lit his second cigarette of the day.

Once Major Hooper had exhausted himself on the flight, he switched to telling war stories, which Gary eagerly anticipated after each debriefing. Such stories were often mixed with sadness and remorse. This day offered no difference. The waitress delivered the Buds. Each man took a hearty slug.

Today's story was about a mission in the Route Package 6 area in North Vietnam. "Four of us were assigned to flak suppression, spread out about a thousand feet apart, way up north in Pack 6 heading toward the Kep Railyard, a very 'stra - te – gic' chokepoint," the major said, emphasizing the word by stretching the syllables.

Gary knew all about Pack 6, the target area in North Vietnam located north of Hanoi. The North Vietnamese, with assistance from the Soviet Union and Red China, had set up the world's most extensive air defense system in Pack 6. Pilots referred to missions around Hanoi as Going Downtown.

"Colonel Hock was the flight leader and I had the element," Major Hooper said, waving his cigarette around leaving a trail of smoke. "We were trolling around just above a heavy cloud layer hunting for a hole to drop down through. Talk about being dumb shits, flying around with our asses hanging out! But the colonel was the leader."

Gary shifted in the booth, his back and butt aching from the two hours sitting on the ejection seat.

"Here's a lesson for you," Major Hooper said, pointing his mug in Gary's direction.

While delivering the burgers and fries, the waitress took orders for refills.

Hooper went on to tell how a new pilot had called out a warning for a Surface-to-Air Missile. While alerting the formation that a SAM was headed their way, he didn't say where the missile was.

Major Hooper paused, taking a bite of his burger and a gulp of his beer. "Boom!" Hooper yelled, slamming his hand on the table.

Gary felt as though he had been punched in the chest. He took a deep breath and leaned back against the booth, closing his eyes. After opening his eyes, he wondered why Major Tracey smiled so broadly. Captain Mims chuckled. Gary also wondered why Major Hooper, who had already eaten all of his fries, suddenly had a pile on his plate.

Hooper described how his leader's F-105 had been struck by a SAM and disappeared in a red flash. He led his wingman diving into the clouds, taking their airplanes down into the murk. It had been a Hobson's choice. After emerging from the dense whiteness, they searched for the missile site.

There in that moment, Gary saw clearly how fate and chance merged, probably snuffing out the life of a seasoned pilot. As the major described the scene, it seemed to happen so suddenly. Boom, and it was over. If catastrophe struck this pilot with years of experience, Gary wondered how he could prevent it from happening to him.

Hooper paused, eating the pile of fries on his plate. "Tally Ho, the LT yells, at three o'clock. Sure enough, I see the contrail and dust cloud from the SAM. I lead him in and we drop our bombs on it and get the hell out of Dodge."

Gary leaned against the table, his hands covering his face. How can I do what the major just described? he wondered. How can I go nose-to-nose with a SAM site? How can I be so brave?

"A sad story ends here," Major Hooper said, rising from the booth. "Sharp eyes that LT had. Another good lad wasted. He got his bombing a 'strategic' truck ferry."

After signing the chit for his food and drink, Gary followed the other pilots outside into the bright afternoon sun.

Allison had written out a grocery list for him. Gary picked up the things they needed at the commissary. He stopped at their local Mom-and-Pop mart for a case of cold beer and snacks.

Gary carried with him orders he had received earlier that day at the squadron for his next assignment to SEA scheduled for February—providing he finished F-105 training. He and Allison knew the assignment was coming beforehand, but seeing it on paper overwhelmed him. When reduced to English, the orders meant one year in SEA or one hundred missions North, whichever came first.

That is, if he made it that long. Gary immediately put such thoughts out of his mind—Bad Karma.

Driving near his home, Gary mulled over the orders and Major Hooper's story. He checked the carport for Allison's Mustang, but she hadn't made it home yet from the lab in Beaufort. He pulled his truck off the road and onto a neighbor's fallow field.

Gary parked with the rear of his pickup facing west. The sun inched toward the horizon. Clouds floated by, so he decided to wait and see what happened. He dropped the tailgate and had a seat, popping the cap off a bottle of Bud with his church key. A murder of crows flew over him, cawing and squabbling among themselves. Six deer stood at the edge of the wood line across the Craven brothers' field, where bright orange pumpkins peeked out from green vines. A flight of four F-105s, beginning a night training mission from Seymour Johnson, flew by at low altitude, roaring along above the Neuse River headed toward the coast. Gary raised his beer in salute.

No fighter pilot ever admitted being afraid, but thoughts of flying missions into the maelstrom of North Vietnam scared Gary. The record spoke for itself. One-hundred-and-two F-105 pilots had been killed or were missing in action, shot down while flying bombing missions over North Vietnam.

Fear, the unmentionable fifty ton elephant in the room, lurked over each pilot's shoulder. Gary knew each one of the men paid open homage to the pucker factor, the tightening of the rectum in dicey situations. They never discussed fear or being afraid.

Major Hooper had said that it was statistically impossible to complete one hundred missions North and survive. Yet, he had done so.

The bottom rim of the sun kissed the horizon. Looking behind him to the east, a sliver of a waning moon had risen. As the rumble of the passing jet fighters died away, a sweet stillness settled over the land. A stiff breeze swept across the field pushing bits of golden straw. Now chilled, Gary walked to the front of his pickup and pulled his flight jacket through the open window. He slipped his arms through the sleeves and returned to the tailgate.

On some bombing missions, the North Vietnamese shot down two or three planes. The numbers went against the pilots. Gary tossed all of this over in his head and was glad he was alone. Facing Allison at that moment was impossible.

Fighter pilots believed that they were invincible. I'm the best pilot in the world and nothing bad is going to happen to me became the mantra of each man. But the numbers didn't lie.

Gary had known pilots who were flying along without a care in the world and one second later, in big trouble. Delta Sierra—Deep Shit—the pilots called it. Survival in such desperate situations seemed to be random. Some made it and for others, life was snuffed out in an instant.

Slowly, the western sky turned pink, purple, orange and red as the sun disappeared, its day's work done. Zipping his flight jacket, he pulled the collar up to his ears. He rotated his head, stretching his stiff neck. Taking a sip of beer, he watched as the colors of the sky flashed and merged, turning darker by the second.

Gary accepted and welcomed his duty as an Air Force pilot. Realizing the dangers yet ahead, he eagerly anticipated his upcoming assignment in Thailand, or rather—*SEA Circus Maximus*.

In the gathering darkness, a coughing John Deere cut across the field toward Gary. He recognized the sound as coming from the Craven brothers' ancient machine. Jacob drove the tractor and Samuel perched on the fender. A wagon piled high with firewood trailed behind. Jacob, thin and wiry, stood a good six inches taller than Samuel, the more muscular brother.

Gary saluted the brothers and they returned the greeting. Both were retired Air Force officers who had begun their careers at Tuskegee Institute in the early 40's. Jacob had been a pilot while Samuel was a maintenance officer. Jacob flew P-47 and P-51 propeller driven fighters with the Red Tails during World War II and then F-86 jets during the Korean War. Both had witnessed the progression of the Air Force from the days of segregated units during World War II. The two men retired before the Vietnam War turned hot.

Jacob stopped the tractor and the two brothers ambled toward the pickup. Gary pulled three beers, popped the caps and offered each a bottle.

"Quite some sky this evenin'," Jacob said.

"It is," Gary said, raising his beer to the west in salute.

"Allison told us y'all were low on firewood," Samuel said.

"We are," Gary said, "but I don't think we need that much."

"We'll throw some off," Jacob said.

"Send a bill to my attorney," Gary said, knowing the Cravens never did such a thing.

The farm had been in Craven family hands since reconstruction and recently morphed into a truck farm growing produce in addition to row crops. Gary helped in the fields in his spare time. The manual labor helped keep him fit and the brothers appreciated his work. Currently, harvesting pumpkins filled the brothers' days.

Pastel colors in the west began turning darker and fading. The brothers and Gary sat there, silently watching. Gary trusted the Craven brothers. He felt a sense of gratitude that he and Allison lived by them. They would be there to look after Allison and make sure she was safe while he was gone.

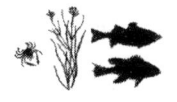

JUST A DREAM

_____ 10

Allison Faith Deale
Seven Springs, North Carolina
October 26, 1966

"I'M HOME," I yelled, pushing open the door with my hip.

After seeing his pickup parked in the driveway, I thought Gary must be in the house. Not hearing a response, I dumped my folders and notes onto the dining room table and proceeded to the kitchen. As I glanced out the window, I saw him and the Craven brothers sitting at the picnic table on our screened porch. Gary waved his hands through the air, obviously telling another airplane tale. One or the other of the Cravens proceeded to wave their hands about in response.

I noticed that the woodpile had greatly expanded. That explained the three men sitting at the table in near-darkness.

Standing there, I watched and wondered about the stories being told. Nothing in my life matched what they did. Gary flew jet fighters. Jacob had done so during the Korean War. Before that, he piloted a propeller driven plane during World War II. Samuel had also been there with Jacob, although he didn't fly.

A short line of dead soldiers, a term I picked up from Gary, marched across the picnic table. A lighter flared in the darkness as Gary lit a cigarette. He had fallen off the wagon again, smoking wise. At least he wasn't smoking in the house. That was one rule I hoped he would obey. The men looked as though they needed reinforcements, so I walked to the fridge and picked out four beers. Loading a bowl of pretzels and chips on a tray, I went to join them.

The three men rose as I approached the table. "Good evenin', Miss Allison," Jacob said, doffing his hat.

"I brought more," I said, as Gary put his arms around my shoulders and kissed me.

"Hello, darling," Gary said, his arms lingering.

"You shouldn't have done that, Miss Allison," Samuel said, "we're just fixin' to leave."

"But since you're here—," Jacob said.

"We might as well drink up," Gary finished.

I lit several candles and passed the bowl of pretzels and chips.

Sitting on the bench, Jacob resumed his story of flying an F-86 Sabre Jet over North Korea and being jumped by a lone MIG-15 fighter. "Scared me half to death," Jacob said. His eyes were wide open and his face bore a look of terror, reliving the attack.

Samuel moved his hands and finished the story of how his brother eluded and then shot down his third enemy plane.

Listening to the three men talk about their exploits made me very happy that we had bought this property. Jacob and Samuel Craven and their families had openly welcomed us into their small community. We loved our house, isolated in the country by ourselves with the Cravens living across the road. Gary and I often jogged to the nearby Cliffs of Neuse State Park.

We finished drinking our beers and the Cravens wished us goodnight. Coughing and backfiring, the John Deer started. Chugging away, the tractor turned the corner around our house and was gone.

I cleaned the picnic table while Gary stirred the burning logs in the fire pit. Steaks and foil-wrapped potatoes waited on the kitchen counter.

"Do you want another beer?" I asked.

"I think I'll open a bottle of red wine," Gary said.

"Pour me a glass, please."

"OK, did you have a good day?"

"Keypunching all day long," I said, shaking my fingers. "We had rain this morning, so we didn't go out in the boat. Did it rain here?"

"It stopped before we took off."

"Where did you go? What did you do?"

"We refueled in air and then did air-to-ground gunnery on the range off of Georgia. Major Hooper liked what I did, but I messed up on a Cuban Eight. I got chewed out for that."

"I'm sorry," I said, knowing how Gary was a perfectionist who hated to make mistakes.

"I'm learning," he said, "I'm learning."

"The coals are almost ready," I said. "I'll do the steaks and potatoes if you make a salad and set the table."

"You've got a deal."

Later, we ate our steaks, each describing our day. I learned more about flying a jet fighter as each conversation passed and Gary heard more than he ever wanted to know about nekton, water quality and salinity.

"What are you doing later?" Gary asked, running his bare foot up and down my leg under the kitchen table.

"I have about an hour's work to do on data plots. Why, do you have something in mind?" I teased.

"Yes, I do. Nothin' like a little lovin' to top off the day."

Gary and I had such good times here. I wished it would remain this way forever. But I knew that was just a dream.

IRON BOMBS

_____ 11

Gary Bishop Deale, First Lieutenant, USAF
Dare Bombing Range, Coastal North Carolina
1 December 1966

THE FLIGHT OF four F-105 Thunderchiefs had taken off from Seymour Johnson at dawn on a mission to the Dare Bombing Range near Pamlico Sound on the North Carolina coast. Their plan called for a quick flight, one hour from takeoff to touchdown.

Major Tracey, the flight leader, confirmed low level flight clearance with air controllers. They flew over the North Carolina swamps at three hundred feet above the ground in a finger-four formation. Below, pine trees and bare hardwoods cast long shadows. Small black tannic streams meandered through the brown swamps. Gary's left wing tip nestled ten feet from Captain Mim's plane.

After clearing the coast, the four F-105s orbited in a hold position in a restricted Military Operations Area thirty miles out over the Atlantic. Except for the rumble of their jet engines, all was silent. Below, two fishing trawlers had their nets spread. Major Tracey turned wide circles above the two boats, waiting. He controlled all maneuvers by issuing hand signals, or by certain aircraft movements. Making one sweeping turn after another, the four fighters circled low over the ocean as the range controllers cleared the airspace.

Major Tracey's F-105 wobbled as he leveled out of the turn, dropping in altitude. Major Hooper, rolled his plane off to the left and lined up well behind Gary. Hooper would follow the flight to observe the students as they dropped bomb loads.

Now in trail formation, Gary followed the two planes in front of him as they streaked over the coastal barrier island. The small fishing village of Ocracoke flashed by off the tip of Gary's right wing. He pushed the throttle forward and out, into the afterburner detent, causing injection of a raw stream of fuel into the engine exhaust. After checking-six, the visual scan of the blind area behind the formation looking for enemy or unknown aircraft, he gradually pulled back on his control stick and began a pop-up climb.

As his F-105 roared upward near the top of his roll-in altitude, Gary flipped the fighter upside down to keep his target and the planes in front of him in sight. Gary hung from the straps, his belly doing flip-flops. For just a second, he felt woozy as he adjusted to this abrupt change in position. He concentrated on their target, a group of five clapped-out cargo trucks arranged in a wide circle.

Ahead, Major Tracey began the roll-in for his run down the chute, the sixty degree angle used for dive-bombing. This attack method provided the most accurate delivery for iron bombs. Captain Mims followed.

Gary neared the peak of his climb at 10,000 feet. Gently pulling back on his stick the nose began to drop, and he arced over the top. Weightless for just an instant, he floated in mid-air. His plane began to drop with increasing speed. Pulling his throttle back out of the afterburner position, the plane dived at about 450 knots. He rolled his F-105 upright and began his run down the chute. The brown marsh below rushed at him.

Placing his aiming pipper (crosshairs on the target aiming device) on the bull's-eye in the exact center of the circled trucks, Gary scanned the cockpit dials and warning lights one last time. He made a slight adjustment with his left rudder as the pipper drifted off the aim point. Once centered, he punched the red button on the control stick and felt the plane lurch as six inert bombs weighing a total of 4,500 pounds dropped off the ejector rack under the fuselage of his aircraft.

After Gary punched the red button to pickle the load, the six bombs released and dropped away, flying free. Gravity, friction, airspeed, dive angle, wind and, at times, misfortune took over as the concrete-filled dumb iron bombs screamed toward the ground. Gary had no control over where the bombs went after they dropped off the rack.

Pulling back on the stick, he fought to flatten the fighter's dive toward the ground. Dropping below 5,000 feet in a combat situation was very dangerous. Enemy gunfire easily knocked planes down at this altitude.

G-forces pushed him down into the parachute and survival kit. In a matter of seconds, Gary had gone from Zero-G at the top of his climb to Six-G at the bottom. The many hours running and lifting weights at the gym helped him fight off the effects of pulling G's, which squeezed his internal organs and disrupted normal blood flow. Gary felt as though an elephant had sat on him, smashing his chest and belly. He huffed oxygen from his facemask trying to fight the pressure. As many times as he had executed this maneuver, the gravity forces pushing against his body still surprised him. Gary squinted his eyes and shook his head, trying to clear the fog from his brain.

Pulling excessive G's caused blackouts because blood pooled in lower extremities. The G-suit leggings Gary wore squeezed his legs, helping force blood from his thighs and calves to the core of his body. Another side effect was bleeding hemorrhoids. He did not want to think about that.

Up until this flight, Gary's missions had used small practice bombs, which made a white puff of smoke upon hitting the ground. Today's drop was the first with a full load of six M117 750-pound bombs, albeit inert ones filled with concrete. Before the course ended, Gary knew he had to drop actual bombs filled with high explosive Tritonal.

Gary rolled the plane and watched the bombs strike the ground, burying themselves, throwing up clouds of sand and water and plowing up the marsh. He hoped there weren't any creatures down there. He shuddered to think of what Allison might think about the damage he did to the swamp.

At the speed he was going and the distance away from the target, the impacts looked reasonable. He hoped the strike film showed him to be correct.

With each flight, Gary's situational awareness improved. He anticipated his flight and element leaders' maneuvers correctly. He had an easier time flying the F-105, with no problems staying ahead of his airplane. No matter how well Gary thought he had done, Major Hooper reminded him after each mission—Sierra Alpha! Sierra Alpha!

After the bomb run, the planes circled off the coast waiting for clearance to the low level route they planned to take back to Seymour. Gary anchored his plane beside his element leader's fighter. Once again in the tail-end-Charlie position, Gary scanned the sky behind the formation, checking-six.

Just as he turned his head, he spotted a flash of silver, dropping out of the sun behind them. Gary rolled his plane to the right and looked again. He called out a warning, "Tulsa Lead, 4. Boogies at five o'clock in the sun, dropping behind us."

Gary's first job responsibility consisted of following his element leader at all times and getting his bombs on the target. Secondly, he checked-six to ensure the airspace behind them contained no enemy fighters, or in this case, friendly hotshots trying to jump them.

"Burners, take it down," Major Tracey radioed as his plane dropped toward the ocean. No other fighter had the ability to keep up with F-105s in level flight. Gary's flight descended and skimmed along, less than a hundred feet above the ocean's waves.

Gary looked again. Four F-100 Super Sabres, which the pilots called Huns, lined up behind his flight. As the speed of his airplane increased, the Huns fell further behind.

"Four Huns, well behind at six o'clock," Gary radioed.

"Myrtle Beach cowboys," Major Hooper called out.

"Huns, break it off, we're at minimum fuel and headed for home," Major Tracey said.

As the four Huns broke away, Major Tracey wobbled his plane, turning toward the barrier islands.

"Good eye, Number 4," Major Tracey radioed. He raised his right hand with four fingers extended, then pointed his thumb straight down. All four pilots repeated the same motion. Air controllers had given approval for their low level flight home.

The four planes roared over the barrier island and headed inland, passing just above the pine woods of eastern North Carolina. Gary kept his plane in tight formation as they porpoised over the rolling sand hills of the coastal plain, just clearing trees. Farms with barren fields of brown corn stubble flashed by in a blur. Off his right wing, a small derelict area of cotton plants with their white balls still hanging appeared and then was gone. Two men fished from a small rowboat in a stream in a swamp. Gary flew directly over top a brightly painted red barn. On the Neuse River above New Bern, a colossal wood and stone mansion zoomed by, with people actually swimming laps in the pool. Not bad for December, he thought.

The pilots executed a tactical overhead landing. As far as Gary could tell, he had flown an error free mission.

During their debriefing in the squadron planning room, the pilots watched the strike films. Gary flinched as the bombs he had dropped hours before struck the ground. Five of the bombs went true and hit within the circle of trucks. One bomb, albeit a dumb iron device, apparently had a mind of its own, as it went wide, left.

"Look at that rogue son of a bitch go," Major Hooper said, pointing at the screen.

The errant bomb hit way out of the circle. "Fuck," Gary gasped, raising his hand to cover his mouth. "What happened?" He was shocked and embarrassed. His stomach tied in knots. What had he done wrong to cause this?

"Shit happens," the major said, pointing his finger at Gary. "You checked the tailfins on each bomb during preflight, right?"

"Yes, sir, I did," Gary said.

"It happens," Major Hooper said, raising his hands, making a gesture to indicate 'so what.'

"How do you rationalize that innocent civilians may be killed when bombs go astray like that?" Captain Mims asked, with a puzzled look on his face.

Gary had thought of this very question many times. The rogue they had just looked at on the film hammered true the point that bad things happened when bombs dropped from an airplane.

"Your mission in *The Circus Maximus is* to put bombs on target," Major Hooper said, pointing at an enlarged aerial photograph of the circled trucks they had attacked. "That sounds nice when you read the Rules of Engagement, but it's much different when the people on the ground are shooting at you. Sometimes unplanned events happen."

Major Hooper pointed to Gary. "How do you think of your target?"

"A target is a point on the ground, an enemy objective to be destroyed, sir," Gary said, almost by rote, looking in Major Hooper's eyes. He knew that was the official answer given in a previous Rules of Engagement briefing. But underneath that, Gary knew that enemy soldiers and civilians were probably also at or near that chosen point on the ground. When he bombed that enemy position, blood was going to be shed.

After watching actual film from Rolling Thunder strikes over North Vietnam, Gary knew the destructive power of one M117 750 pound bomb filled with Tritonal. Multiply that by the six bombs carried on each plane.

"Pre-cise-ly," Major Hooper said, using his slow Texas drawl. "Obviously, people are going to die when those bombs detonate. Those who die are your enemy." The major spoke in a matter-of-fact tone, as if to say, "This is reality, folks." He continued, slowly, saying what needed to be said. "I have no doubt that civilians are being killed over there. On an average mission, there are sixteen F-105s with six M117 bombs each. That's ninety-six 750-pound bombs. Thuds are being shot at, SAMs are in the air and thousands of rounds of Antiaircraft Artillery shells are flying around. All of that, bombs, SAMs and shrapnel from Triple-A has to hit the ground. Innocent people get hurt. We call it collateral damages—civilian houses and people being blown up. We're at war! Shit happens in war!"

Major Hooper let his statements about collateral damage sink in. "This was your first mission with a full fuel and bomb load at takeoff. Everyone made it off the ground okay, we didn't get lost on the way to the target and all the bombs except the rogue the LT dropped went true. But, the LT saved us from being embarrassed by the Huns, so good Sierra Alpha with that."

Hooper waited for questions. "Soon we'll carry real bombs that go BOOM! Then you'll really see the dirt fly. Let's go get lunch."

Gary drove his pickup to the Officers' Club, thinking about what the major had just said. War is war. People die in wars. He wondered how he could explain any of that to Allison.

While the other three pilots ordered burgers, Gary decided on a turkey and ham Colossal Club with a side platter of fries. He lit his second cigarette of the day and looked around the room. The window by the booth the men sat in provided the only natural light source in the room, the one way to check on the weather outside. In summer, the officers had used it to keep tabs on the women at the pool in their two-piece bathing suits. Across the way, by the bar, darkness merged with the cloud of blue smoke. Conversation turned to their upcoming assignments and *The SEA Circus Maximus.*

"We do one more mission with inert bombs, then switch to the real thing late next week," Major Hooper said. "On our last week we go to Nevada for nuclear qualification."

"Why do we have to do nuclear, when none of us are going to be doing that mission?" Captain Mims asked.

"Because it says so in the syllabus," Hooper said. "None of us know where we will be going after SEA. Some of you may end up in England, Germany, Turkey or South Korea where that will be your assignment. If the balloon ever goes up, your mission will be executing Emergency War Orders. That means laying a nuke on an enemy airfield."

Me, flying an F-105 containing a one megaton nuclear weapon, Gary thought. Jesus! He knew that the F-105 was designed to deliver tactical nuclear bombs. He had never thought about actually dropping one himself.

"It's not a pleasant thing to think about," Hooper continued, slowly and softly, "because if you don't get shot down and survive the approach to the target you may get blinded by the flash or knocked down by the shock wave. There probably won't be a place left to come home to because the Godless Communists will have done the same thing to your base. Literally, it will mean the end of the world."

There it was, for Gary and all to see; plain and simple. The end of the world. That was the bottom line in a nuclear war. Gary, Allison, their parents, friends and family all gone in mushroom clouds. What are we doing to ourselves as a civilization? Gary wondered.

The food order arrived and Gary placed his water glass, ketchup bottle, beer mug and napkin holder around the outside edge of his plates to fend off Major Hooper's raids.

"You guys did good today," Major Hooper said. "Those trucks were arranged in a five hundred foot radius and all of your bombs struck within it except for the LT's rogue. That circle of trucks is there for a purpose. It designates the accuracy we're getting over North Vietnam, even with the enemy shooting at us. We call it CEP—Circular Error Probable. CEP means 50 percent of the bombs dropped fall within that circle."

"We're doing much better than the B-17s did during World War II," Major Tracey said, with his soft New England accent. "They had a CEP of 3,000 feet."

"I studied strategic bombing by B-17s during World War II at the academy," Gary said, daring to speak out.

The two majors at the table snorted and wrinkled their faces in disgust at his mention of the Air Force Academy. Both came out of ROTC programs and held the "ring-knockers," as academy graduates were called, in low esteem. Captain Mims, who also graduated from the academy, smiled at the two majors' exhibit of displeasure.

Gary continued, "In 1943, two raids with a total of 513 B-17s bombed the Schweinfurt Ball Bearing Plant and ninety-six were shot down. That's 960 men."

"There you go," Major Hooper said. "B-17s were not as accurate as we are. Plus, ten men went down with each plane. When an F-105 gets it, there's only one of us."

Gary looked at his plate. There's no way in hell, he thought. How did that happen? One-fourth of his sandwich had disappeared.

Numbers, Gary thought. Five hundred feet, 3,000 feet, one man per F-105, ten men per B-17. He knew that over one hundred F-105 pilots had been shot down, missing or killed over North Vietnam. Soon, he would be flying strike missions there. No matter which way he looked at it, war meant suffering and death. Will I end up killing civilians? Gary wondered. If so, will I even know?

CARMEN

_____ 12

Allison Faith Deale
Marine Lab, Pivers Island, Beaufort, North Carolina
December 8, 1966

"HOW MANY MORE are there?" Carmen asked, typing away on her keypunch machine.

"Stacks of them," I said, loading more blank punch cards on my machine.

Sitting in our office in the rustic building used by grad students, I looked across the courtyard at the Salt Box style dining room. All of the structures at the lab looked the same, weathered gray split cedar siding and roofs. My belly growled, soon it would be time for lunch.

I punched another card and leaned back, stretching my neck. "This is a pain in the ass," I said, trying to wipe the boredom from my face.

"This is true," Carmen said. "But just think how it all comes together when we run the actual data plots."

"I know. It all becomes clear."

Punching holes in the cards was a rainy day job. Carmen and I were compiling facts on species collected in our research site, the Newport River Estuary. For each specimen found, we keyed a data record on a separate punch card. Each card contained information about the animal; date, location, zone, method used, a six-character code for the scientific name, a code for the common name, water temperature, specific gravity and salinity.

The data plots we obtained after all the cards were punched and sorted would be the capstone. Then we would see the species distribution by salinity zone.

The winter cold and bad weather had kept us off the water except for monthly water quality tests, so we organized our field notes and entered data onto IBM punch cards. We then sorted the cards and tabulated data in categories using other machines.

As graduate students in marine biology, we were assessing the recovery of the Newport River Estuary after the area had been ravaged by Hurricane Hazel in 1954 and again by Donna in 1960. With each massive storm, winds exceeding one hundred miles per hour and a towering storm surge devastated the estuary. Our research on the body of water concentrated on the recovery and resilience of the system since those storms.

My master's research concentrated on nekton, the finfish, and other animals in the water column. Carmen worked on benthic or bottom-dwelling worms, clams and related organisms.

In addition to our research, we both were teaching assistants for our advisers. Boredom and too much spare time wasn't an issue with me. Dr. Pointer, my adviser, made sure that I had plenty to do.

I FIRST MET Carmen Maria Angelina de Ramieres, my best friend for four years, at an estuarine conference at Old Dominion University in Richmond, Virginia, in 1962. At that time, she attended the University of Miami. I was an undergraduate at Washington College in the colonial village of Chestertown, Maryland.

By fact and temperament, Carmen's Cuban-American roots shone through. Her family fled Cuba early in the Revolution, becoming refugees from Fidel Castro's tyranny in the now Communist country.

We both ended up as graduate students at the lab because of the men in our lives. She wanted to be near Ramon, her boyfriend, attending the Duke Medical School in Durham. I had chosen Beaufort because Seymour

Johnson offered F-105 replacement unit training and I could be near Gary.

Although opposites in some ways, Carmen and I became friends on the first day we met. Her jet-black hair was starkly different from my strawberry-blond. Reserved and more formal, I contrasted with her hot-blooded, passionate and challenging approach to life. I hid among the crowd while she danced in front of the room. She spoke English and fluent Spanish and French. I spoke English and high school German. Through her repeated exclamations, I gradually took up *Espanol*, especially the curse words.

We routinely wore each other's clothes. I had fought to retain my weight and size 6 after my marriage to Gary. With all of her dancing and singing, she easily maintained her size, a bit bustier than me. We ran to wear the pounds off. When jogging through the streets and alleys of Beaufort, a beautiful old coastal village, we waved at the locals as they went about their business of fishing and running shops.

Carmen loved to dance and sing and used every opportunity to perform. She entertained her fellow graduate students at our weekly pizza nights in Atlantic Beach on the Crystal Coast, a resort area on the Bogue Banks barrier island off Morehead City. Her naughty rendition of "These Boots Are Made For Walkin'," drove us into hysterics, each one doubling over with laughter.

Depending upon the weather, we took a boat or drove to Atlantic Beach. Beaufort, a dry town, wouldn't do for pizza nights. What good is pizza if you can't have beer?

I loved her dearly and thought the gods had brought us together. In more ways than one, Carmen ended up being the friend who saved me from myself.

TOSSING NUKES
13

Gary Bishop Deale, First Lieutenant, USAF
Nellis AFB, Nevada
22 December 1966

GARY'S F-105 IDLED at the very end of the runway waiting for the control tower to issue clearances to the bomb range. Major Hooper's plane sat to his right. The sun peeked over the eastern horizon casting long sideways shadows of their fighters across runway 210.

A green light flashed from the tower. Gary pointed his right arm forward and looked at the major, sitting fifty feet away. Major Hooper saluted.

The two F-105s blasted down the runway side-by-side, in a tactical takeoff. The roar from the J75 engines vibrated through the cockpit. Gary felt his bones quivering. As his plane accelerated, he was pushed back in the seat. The distance markers to the end of the runway wound down, 6,000, 5,000, to 4,000. His airspeed tape edged past 190 knots. He eased back on the stick, slightly raising the nose. Passing through 210 knots, Gary pulled back further and his plane lifted from the ground, with Major Hooper's fighter tucked in nice and tight on his right wing. Gary led this mission. Major Hooper followed, evaluating each step along the way.

Gary looked south at the sprawl of Las Vegas, city of sin, and then turned his fighter northward toward the bombing range. Once clear of the developed area around the base, he descended to their pre-briefed minimum altitude, where they would remain until very near their target.

He had already qualified for several types of special weapon deliveries over the previous days. This mission, assuming all went well, finished his course requirements for F-105 operations, including dropping conventional and nuclear weapons.

His airplane's Doppler system, designed specifically for delivery of nuclear weapons, controlled navigation by providing their current position, course, and distance to the target. To a degree, Gary went along for the ride, bird-dogging the systems, checking to make sure everything went as planned. Of course, he had to set-up the flight profile and load it into the plane's computer in the first place.

Gary had flown over and through the range during the past week and spent hours studying the aerial photographs of the target, a large bull's-eye scraped in the desert. It was much easier for him to think about this simulated target than to consider dropping a nuclear bomb on an enemy airfield.

He swiveled his head checking the airspace around the aircraft. Gary's usual flight position as number four conditioned him to always look around—better safe than sorry. Clearance onto the bomb range in no way guaranteed that other fighters had departed the area. Hotshot pilots always lurked in the clouds, waiting to jump some poor unobservant soul, trying to obtain bragging rights at the Officers' Club.

He visually checked waypoints as the flight progressed, making sure in his mind that the Doppler navigation system worked properly. Major Hooper's plane anchored itself to Gary's right wing. Every time Gary looked his way, the major held up his left thumb.

As his plane flew over the initial point, rapidly approaching the target, he engaged the afterburner and ascended. The airspeed greatly increased to near supersonic velocity. Below, the stark brown desert zipped by in a blur, making it impossible to focus on any one object on the ground. Thus far, the plane's systems worked perfectly. Gary watched the target approach, directly in his flight path.

Nearing the bull's-eye, the fire control system opened the bomb bay doors and the inert nuclear-shape, as they called it, plunged from the plane.

Gary thought he achieved the desired Circular Error Probable of 550 feet, but he wasn't about to hang around in the area to find out. Folks on the ground took care of scoring each pilot.

Pushing his throttle and control stick ahead, he descended to ground level. Trying to get behind a ridge, he headed for nearby hills. His F-105 bumped as it went supersonic.

At 750 knots, they traveled about six miles away from the target before the simulated time of detonation. If it ever came to this in a real-life situation, he planned to find a hill or mountain to hide behind to avoid the blast wave.

Gary often wondered about the wisdom of flying directly over the target, even at extremely low altitude. He mistrusted the eye patch provided to pilots to shield one of his eyes from the nuclear flash. He didn't know if he could fly back to his base with only one eye, or even if home would still exist.

In his own mind, he questioned all of it: the eye patch, surviving the shock wave, and the belief that the pilots could directly over fly a target and not get hammered by enemy gunners on the ground or by a MIG lurking in the clouds. But, he knew making decisions about Air Force doctrine exceeded his pay grade.

The two planes roared down a valley, trying to get far away from the target as fast as possible.

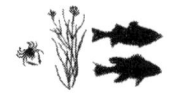

NEWPORT RIVER ESTUARY

_____ 14

Allison Faith Deale
Marine Lab, Pivers Island, Beaufort, North Carolina
January 11, 1967

GARY PUSHED THE boat away from the dock while Carmen and I fussed with the sputtering outboard motor, which refused to cooperate in the early morning cold. Though we hoped the sun's rays would warm us later in the day, it simply wasn't cutting through the marine layer of fog just yet.
  We tested the water monthly in the Newport River Estuarine System during winter months, trying to do it on the first day of the month, if it were a weekday and weather permitting. This month, a New Year's Eve snow and ice storm had blanketed the area and other bad weather delayed our day on the water.
  Gary had finished his F-105 course in late December, just before Christmas. Since then, he flew training missions with Major Tracey or Captain Mims once a week to qualify for flight pay and remain proficient. Flying now for fun rather than syllabus qualifications pleased Gary and the other pilots. Following graduation, he had more free time because he didn't have to study flight manuals. He had decided to spend this day on the boat with us.
  Our first Christmas together in our own home proved to be a joyous occasion. We decorated the house and tree after he returned from Nevada on December 23. I had purchased decorations beforehand and waited for him to come home before actually putting everything up. Even

now, the house looked fantastic, decked out in wreaths and garlands with bright red bows.

We splashed along in the skiff, waves slamming into the side throwing salt spray into our faces. Our Nor-Easter rain suits protected us from getting soaked.

"Kind of choppy," Gary said.

"Really, it's not bad," I said. "You ought to be out here when the wind is really blowing. This is just a gentle breeze."

I loved this place. Even though each trip on a boat generated mountains of work, being here kept me happy. Searching the estuary for fish and crabs excited me. Finding a new fish I hadn't seen before made my day. My graduate adviser kept telling us that our research was very important and that our grant sponsors, the National Science Foundation and the U. S. Navy, were happy with our work. That pleased me.

To study the recovery and resilience of the estuary, Carmen and I had divided the research area into four zones, depending on water salinity. About eight miles long and two miles across at its widest, the system looked like a cornucopia on aerial photographs.

Carmen captained the boat while Gary and I sat on the bench just beside her. Tall pine trees with a mixture of oaks, American holly and sweet bay magnolia lined the shore. Just to our west, the Newport River, a black stream saturated with tannin, flowed through the Croatan National Forest and into the estuary. A series of rusted and dilapidated menhaden plants spaced here and there along the shoreline processed the small fish into oil, fertilizer and a variety of products.

Few houses and farm buildings existed here. We rarely saw any people, especially at this time of year.

Near the ocean, Morehead City and Beaufort provided a different scene. The boats of commercial fishermen and weekend recreational craft filled Bogue and Back Sounds and the ocean inlet during the summer season. Now, however, we saw only the occasional waterman.

Carmen piloted the skiff following the Newport River Channel to a point known as The Narrows where she slowed the boat to a crawl. Even though we followed a natural channel, sandbars, which shifted with the wind and tide, made navigation here treacherous. Wind whipped the water, stirring up sediment, making it impossible to see the bottom.

I pulled my watch cap down over my ears and tightened my scarf around my neck. I tried to warm my hands and fingers, shaking them and stuffing them into my pockets.

Gary and I moved to the front of the boat to keep the prop higher in the water. As we neared The Fishing Camp, an old structure used as a private retreat, Carmen cut the motor and I threw out the anchor.

We sat for a time looking at the tall trees lining this part of the river. This peaceful serene place had become my favorite spot. Pouring coffee from my thermos, I filled three tin cups.

"Get the pastries out of the lunch bag," I said to Gary. "We eat before we work."

For a few moments, we sat there eating and drinking our coffee, bouncing with the waves, enjoying the scenery. I looked at Gary. He appeared calm and relaxed, not as tense as he had been during flight training. He caught me looking at him and smiled.

Gathering the instruments and collection bottles from our kit, Carmen began labeling the jars.

A red-shouldered hawk called in the nearby woods, breaking the silence, and then soared across the water, directly over top of us. "Look," I said, pointing. The bird glided into the forest in search of a squirrel or rabbit. These raptors migrated from the north and remained here during the winter. No matter how many times I heard or saw them, I paused to watch. They were free to come and go as they pleased, not tuned into any schedule. Their only worry was the source of their next meal.

"How's Ramon?" Gary asked.

"He's working his butt off, eighteen or twenty hours a day," Carmen said. "I go once a fortnight for a conjugal visit."

"A what?" I said, blushing.

"I know we're not married, but that's what we call it anyway, conjugal."

"A what?"

Gary laughed.

"What about you guys?" Carmen asked.

"Once a fortnight, whether we need it or not," Gary exclaimed.

With that, I caught on. "Jesus, Carmen Maria Angelina de Ramieres," I sputtered.

Carmen gave me The Look.

"Why do we always end up talking about sex?" I asked.

"Because it is truly one of the finest pleasures in life," Gary said. "When I was growing up, one of my greatest memories was worrying about Santa Claus, who he was, would he find my house and would he fill my wish list. When I found out that Santa didn't exist, I became bitterly disappointed in life, having been told a big story for all those years.

"But, miracle of miracles, a few years later I found out about sex, and that has more than compensated for the big Santa lie." He took a sip of coffee. "Conjugal, yeah that's a good word."

"¡Merde!" Carmen said, convulsing and laughing. Her long dark hair fell across her eyes.

"Shit," I said. "I don't know half the curse words in Spanish and now you're starting with French ones."

We laughed until we cried. It was a moment in time I will always remember, the three of us filled with mirth, joy and love.

GARY'S OFFICE

_____ 15

Gary Bishop Deale, First Lieutenant, USAF
Seymour Johnson AFB, North Carolina
18 January 1967

GARY FOLLOWED BEHIND the group, brushing aside a red REMOVE BEFORE FLIGHT streamer hanging from the fuselage. Allison, Carmen and Ramon listened attentively as Sergeant Cavett, the maintenance crew chief of the plane, and Airman Guercio, his assistant, explained the intricacies of the F-105D Thunderchief, Number 62-4353.

"These are the speed brakes," Airman Guercio said, pointing to the petal-shaped devices located above, below and on both sides of the engine exhaust. "The pilot uses these while in flight to slow the aircraft."

When Gary had cleared this visit with Colonel Mather, Operations Officer of the 335th Tactical Fighter Squadron, he hoped the maintenance troops would step up and describe the fighter in detail. He wanted them to know their work mattered, and that the pilots greatly appreciated everything they did. The men worked long hard hours to ensure the planes operated safely. This tour offered a brief chance for Gary to show his respect. Exposure to his wife and friends helped remind the mechanics that the pilot's families loved them and wanted them to come home in one piece.

Sergeant Cavett and Airman Guercio seized on the opportunity and provided more details and information than his guests could possibly absorb. Gary smiled at their performance.

"Here we have the business side of the J75," Sergeant Cavett said, pointing toward the rear of the engine. "This is the afterburner area where raw fuel is injected into the engine exhaust to increase power."

"The burner also eats fuel like crazy," Gary said, "so, we have to use it with caution."

"When do you use the burner?" Ramon asked.

"During takeoffs, while climbing and when we're maneuvering," Gary said, "but, you really have to be careful with it. We don't carry that much fuel so conservation really counts."

Gary held Allison's arm and steadied her as she stood on her tiptoes staring into the engine. Her nose twitched as kerosene fumes enveloped them.

A cold wind whipped across the parking apron. While the sun shone brightly, it was ineffective against the January chill.

Sergeant Cavett led the group around the side of the aircraft pointing out the external fuel tanks on pylons underneath the wings and the single bomb mounted on an ejector rack underneath the fuselage.

"We hung one bomb on the rack for you look at," Airman Guercio said. "Don't worry, it's inert, a fake bomb."

Gary led Allison underneath the plane's fuselage. They stooped and duck walked to the bomb. He placed Allison's hands on the green colored casing. "This is what I do," he said. She brought her hands to her mouth and closed her eyes.

"This is so—" said Allison, unable to finish.

Gary placed his arm around Allison's neck. "Shocking, isn't it?" he said. Gary put his hand in Allison's hair to prevent her from bumping her head against the aircraft's belly. They continued to the front of the plane.

"We have here the Vulcan 20 mm cannon," Airman Guercio said, placing his hand on the six muzzles. "It's the modern version of the historic multi-barrel Gatling Gun used in the old west. This thing spews death."

Allison winced at the airman's graphic description.

While the group moved around the front of the F-105 to a maintenance rack, Gary climbed the crew ladder.

Perched there, twelve feet above the tarmac, Gary said, "Welcome to my office."

Sergeant Cavett helped Allison climb over the canopy railing. Gary held her arm as she settled on the ejection seat.

"Don't worry," Gary said. "These red streamers mean that the safety pin is in and locked, so the ejection seat isn't armed. You can touch anything in the cockpit."

Seeing the fear in her eyes, he sensed her unease. "Everything to make the plane go and stop is over here on the left side," Gary said, placing Allison's hand on the throttle.

Allison took the stick in her right hand and rotated it, causing the various control surfaces to move on the wings and tail. Gary proceeded to point out the maze of tapes, dials, switches and levers located to her front and sides.

"I'm so freaked out by this," Allison said. "I had no idea."

Gary touched her shoulder. "Don't be upset," he said, "showing you this will help you understand what I do."

Carmen and Ramon also took turns sitting in the cockpit. Gary checked his watch. "We need to move down to the end of the runway. There's something coming up you may want to see."

Sergeant Cavett drove the maintenance van, while the airman remained behind to button up the aircraft. The sergeant parked on a ramp near the end of the runway.

Six planes sat on the tarmac, their engines running. Maintenance airmen dressed in green utility uniforms swarmed over the aircraft, making final checks. Sitting in the cockpits, the pilots had their hands sticking up, visible through the canopy.

"You see the pilots have their hands up," Gary said, raising his hands and fluttering his fingers. "They do that so the ground crewmen know that the pilot is not messing with switches."

Some of the men surrounding the aircraft began to back away. Others began pulling red streamers from bombs. Engine noise increased as the pilots began final checklist procedures.

"The two planes closest to us are F-4 Phantoms," Gary said. "The other four are F-105s just like the one we just showed you."

"Are those F-4s the same kind of plane that shot down all those North Vietnamese MIGs two weeks ago?" Ramon asked. "I read about that in the paper."

"Yes, the F-4 Phantom," Gary said. "Colonel Robin Olds led a group that shot down seven MIGs on 2 January."

"Colonel Olds," Ramon said, "I remember that name."

"This is the arming area," Gary said pointing, speaking loudly over the screaming engines.

"What do you mean by arming area?" Allison asked, sounding scared. Her hair whipped into her face as the wind whistled through the van.

"Each plane is checked one last time before takeoff. The maintainers look for leaks and pull the safety pins from the plane and whatever weapons they may have on board. That's what you see happening over there."

Two F-105s rolled ahead, taxiing toward the end of the runway. Nestled under the fuselage, each of the planes carried six bombs.

Pointing at the two planes on the runway, Gary said, "We call two planes together like that an element. All four of the F-105s is called a flight."

Aligning themselves side-by-side on the runway, the first two fighters ran up their engines. The pilots sat in the cockpit, leaning forward checking their instruments. A crescendo of roaring noise swept across them. Red, green and white lights flashed from the tail and wingtips of the F-105s.

As the first two planes began rolling, a long tongue of flame erupted from their engine exhaust. "Afterburner," Gary said.

Blast and vibration rocked the van. "Jesus," Ramon said.

As the planes sped down the runway, at first slowly, but gradually much faster, sunlight sparked from the canopies.

Shortly thereafter, the black smoke emitting from the planes thickened. "Water injection," Gary said. The two F-105s thundered down the runway for a long distance and then reluctantly lifted off the ground. Without a pause, the second element taxied onto the runway and repeated the takeoff procedures.

"This is fantastic," Allison said. "I've never seen anything like this."

Allison grabbed Gary's hands, her fingers icy cold. Gary had wondered whether showing this to Allison and her friends was a good idea. But he wanted her to experience what he would soon be doing, far away. He wanted her to touch one of his airplanes, to hear, smell and see what happened when an F-105 loaded with bombs took off. He hoped she understood.

THE CRAVENS

_____ 16

Allison Faith Deale
Seven Springs, North Carolina
January 28, 1967

"WHAT DID YOU barbeque?" I asked. "It smells delicious."

"We call it shoat on the spit," Jacob Craven said, carving a piece from the side of the pig. "This'll melt in your mouth."

"I can't wait," Gary said, holding the platter where Jacob deposited the meat.

"Look at all this food," I said. "There's enough here for an army."

"Are you ready?" Sara, Jacob's wife, yelled from the sunroom door.

"Hurry up lil' bro," Samuel said, carrying away a serving tray heaped full of BBQ chicken and spare ribs.

I followed the brothers and Gary into the Craven's sunroom. A full-fledged North Carolina BBQ lay before us. From my dish of brussels sprouts to Sara's roasted winter root vegetables and finally the meat, the table sagged under the steaming platters.

The room filled with late afternoon sunlight, fighting the late January chill. Sara had decorated the room in bright colors, marking the transition from the dark interior of their farmhouse to the outdoors. The three window walls provided abundant sunshine. Outside, the limbs of a starkly bare deciduous tree danced in the wind.

We had gathered for the Cravens' hail and farewell for Gary. Not goodbye forever, but in the military sense of the term, where airmen went away for a while, with full expectations of a safe return.

Sara and Jacob stood on my right. Samuel and Laverne, his wife, circled to the other side of the table. Laverne, a part time minister in their small rural church, gave a rousing blessing with a special invocation for Gary. Her words of comfort and hope were aimed directly at him. I felt proud of him, of what he had accomplished. But a ripple of fear for him crossed my heart. Now that his day of departure rapidly approached, I was afraid.

"To the Cravens, heroes of our country's prior wars," said Gary, raising his glass in salute.

"To Gary," Jacob said, "with our fervent prayers."

We clinked our glasses and sat, diving into one of North Carolina's grand delights.

"Allison, what do you think about all of this?" Laverne asked, waving her fork in the air. "I mean Gary's assignment. Leaving and going off to war."

"Gary wants to be an Air Force pilot more than anything else," I said, shifting my eyes from Laverne to Gary. "He has trained hard. Gary believes in serving his country." I smiled, trying not to show how scared I was. "My duty is to support him." I said those words because I believed them to be true. But I could not say how anxious and frightened I felt.

Gary wrapped his arm around my waist and nuzzled my ear.

"Well spoken," Jacob clapped and everyone joined in.

"You trained under Major Hooper?" Samuel asked.

"I did," Gary said. "An excellent pilot."

'You'll do fine, having suffered under his leadership," Jacob said.

"He still stealing food?" Samuel asked.

Gary cracked up and the rest of us hooted. We had witnessed or heard stories of the major's stealthy manner when it came to food.

"No way in hell, excuse me Laverne, could I protect my plate around that guy." Gary said, waving a beer in the air as he spoke. Gary looked happy. BBQ sauce smeared his chin. With his soiled bib tucked in the neck of his shirt, he winked at me and smiled.

Those few comments set the tone for the repast.

After becoming fully stuffed with BBQ and the trimmings, I thought I couldn't eat another bite. That's when Laverne carried her three varieties of pies from the kitchen.

From that day and well into the future, the Craven family became my self-appointed guardians and protectors. For the rest of my life, I knew Gary went away worry-free knowing that the Cravens watched over me.

FIRE AND DEBRIS

_____ 17

Gary Bishop Deale, First Lieutenant, USAF
Over Wayne County, North Carolina
2 February 1967

IT COST GARY some good will and political capital to get Major Tracey to agree to a change in the flight plan—not to mention several rounds of beer at the Officers' Club. But the major went along with the diversion after being convinced of the opportunity to build good will and community relations. It didn't hurt that Major Tracey knew the Cravens well or that Allison had charmed the major at squadron parties. This flyby saluted her and the Cravens.

The two F-105D Thunderchief jet fighters, in close formation at 1,000 feet, knifed their way across Wayne County, headed for Seven Springs. The major set his speed at 480 knots, or about 550 miles per hour. Gary tucked his plane nice and tight, close to the major's right wingtip.

Every flight brought new challenges and problems. Gary knew complacency and indifference killed pilots. He had no desire to end up in a hole in the ground surrounded by fire and debris.

Flying his last mission from Seymour Johnson proved to be bittersweet for Gary. He loved to fly and all those training flights over the recent months had greatly sharpened his skills. He looked forward to the challenges and the unknowns involved with flying and fighting. Yet, he knew that he was leaving Allison behind.

"Bear left a bit," Gary radioed.

As they flew over the Route 903 bridge on the Neuse River, the fields of the Craven brothers' farm and his own house appeared straight ahead. And, there at the intersection of Park Road and Park Circle Court he could pick out people, one with a bright yellow sweater.

"There she is!" Gary radioed. His heart ached for Allison. In a few days, he would be leaving her behind. What's going to happen to me? he wondered. What's going to happen with her?

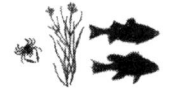

YOU'RE THE BEST THING

_____ 18

Allison Faith Deale
Goldsboro-Wayne County Airport
Goldsboro, North Carolina
February 8, 1967

AFTER TWO WEEKS of total immersion in each other, the time came for Gary to depart for that nameless place. Gary called it SEA, but I knew it as Thailand. Further, I strongly suspected that Takhli was the specific base where he would be stationed.

We had done everything possible to and with each other physically. I felt fulfilled and alive.

Gary held me in his arms kissing me and whispering, "I love you, Allison."

"I love you, Gary."

"You're the best thing— —"

The fear of the unknown, that's what pushed us into this awkward position. I was afraid to say "Be careful, Gary," and he could not say anything else. We parted with this great chasm between us—fearful, isolated, and with words unsaid.

He held me at arm's length. His grin turned into a grimace as he swallowed hard, trying not to cry. Gary turned, picked up his kit and B-4 bag and walked toward the waiting airliner.

Incapable of matching his strength, I stood, weeping as the plane taxied away.

PART 4

War is cruel and you cannot refine it.

—General William Tecumseh Sherman, 1864

THE PATRIOTS

Our country,
afraid of dominoes falling,
called men and women to fight.
An idea. A mission.
Freedom. Democracy.

Guerillas and insurgents, an
enemy to vanquish,
a nation to keep free.
A just cause, perhaps,
lost in the quagmire.

Citizens witness
the bloodied path.
Wondering, who is the bigger
fool. The grunts obeying orders,
 or the ones pulling the strings.

Patriots continue
on their march to oblivion,
doing their duty.
Bearing on their backs,
the hypocrisy of others.

From the combat diary of Gary Bishop Deale,
First Lieutenant, USAF, 28 February 1967

TRANS-SIB

Yuri Vaskilev, General Lieutenant
Soviet Troops of National Air Defense
Trans-Siberian Railway, Near Irkutsk, USSR
18 February 1967

YURI'S SOLDIERS GATHERED in the troop railcar as he and Sergeant Komarvsky described the sunlight and warmth of North Vietnam. A great contrast with the scenery outdoors, where the wind blew great clouds of snow across the countryside. Each of the hand-picked officers and enlisted men from the Moscow Air Defense Sector were specialists in radar units, missile systems or tactics.
   The platoon of soldiers had two missions, first to conduct an inspection tour of air defense facilities in the vast area of eastern Siberia. Their ultimate purpose was to ask questions and gather ideas about improving the air defenses in North Vietnam and select equipment and have it transported south.
   Wanting especially to hear about the women, rumored to be a fine looking mixture of French and Asian blood, the soldiers nodded appreciatively as the sergeant described a previous lover in Hanoi.
   "Monique was her name," Sergeant Komarvsky said, raising his glass of vodka, "I salute her. Though not much in the breastworks department, her fine dark long legs were a stark contrast with my stubby white ones."
   An officer slapped the sergeant on the back, and the men loudly voiced their approval of such a description.

They were all four sheets to the wind, with nothing to do except ride on the train, eat, drink and sleep.

While Yuri's rank entitled him to a special car suitable for a senior general, he preferred to ride with his men. He loved them all as much as he loved his son.

At each Air Defense District that the men passed along the way, they conducted an Operational Readiness Inspection. Yuri's soldiers were well trained and knew precisely where to look for deficiencies or shoddy procedures. Issuing commendations and recommendations to each sector commander, they made their way across Siberia. At one surface-to-air missile support facility near Krasnoyarsk, Yuri found conditions so deplorable that he sacked the commander on the spot and replaced him with an officer from his own staff.

Asking questions proved to be the most important benefit of the trip. Many of the enlisted men and officers knew shortcuts or had devised tactics that Yuri planned on using to destroy American aircraft in North Vietnam.

Each travel day began the same. Yuri and Sergeant Komarvsky described what they had learned from their three previous trips to North Vietnam. Other veterans of the war also pitched in with their experiences. Then the men brainstormed, searching for new tactics to counter the American bombers.

After a light lunch of bread and cheese, Yuri had each man describe his boyhood, parents, neighborhood, wife or lover and children if there were any. He tried to build a sense of teamwork and collaboration. The men at first hesitated, but then joined in after Yuri and his sergeant had described their lives together, going back to the great tank battle with the Germans at Kursk. It had taken them several days to describe their struggles during the Great Patriotic War.

Of course, the Political Commissar accompanying the men also had to make a daily presentation, reminding them of the true Soviet path. Then, the card or chess games began. And the drinking.

One day, when they were well east of Irkutsk, the sun shone brightly on the vast plain of barren trees covered with snow and ice. As the train rounded a long curve, Yuri clearly saw the engine ahead, chugging along, emitting a long cloud of dark smoke and white steam. It was as grand a sight as he had ever seen. "I want a picture of that," Yuri said, motioning to one of the professional military photographers accompanying him.

With more than three weeks remaining on their rail journey to Vladivostok, located on the Sea of Japan, the great white void of Siberia spread before them.

BOLO

_____ 20

Gary Bishop Deale, First Lieutenant, USAF
Clark AFB, Philippine Islands
18 February 1967

GARY SAT AT the Clark Officers' Club Stag Bar, gulping his second double Doctor Jack Black, a time-honored recipe for bruises and pain. Captain Jim Redy, whom he had shared a cell with in the simulated prisoner of war camp, sat next to him.

Sitting by themselves at the bar after the lunch crowd had departed, the two men finished their sandwiches and sat smoking and drinking. Soon, Gary had to leave to go find his scheduled cargo plane. He stared at the Pacific Air Forces and 13th Air Force decals posted on the mirror behind the bar. My chain of command, Gary thought.

The two pilots had just completed snake eater school, their name for the jungle survival, evasion, and escape class. After two days of presentations, one day of wandering around in the jungle eventually failing to evade capture and two days of confinement in a stinking rotting bamboo cage, Gary celebrated graduation with his prison cellmate.

As the class culminating activity, the instructors had the students run five miles out a dirt road in the middle of the night and pushed them individually into the bush with a simple instruction: try to survive while sneaking ten miles through the jungle to safety.

One of the men lasted twenty minutes before he began screaming. A venomous snake had nailed him, although obviously not a Bamboo Krait, a three-stepper. He yelled until the rangers found him and carried him out. Gary found out later that the man had to redo the course after a week in the hospital.

After rounding up nine additional pilots in one hour, it took a platoon of Filipino Rangers six hours to hunt down four more. Gary lasted a total of seven hours. After the Filipino scouts jumped him, they gave him a beating and tied a noose around his neck. He joined two others in the same sorry state. Gary realized that it didn't matter one whit that he and the other men were officers. The rangers proceeded to give each American a beating for making life difficult for them. The rough treatment continued at the simulated prisoner-of-war camp for two days.

"Do you think the course was realistic?" Captain Jim Redy asked. He tried to twist and turn his stiff neck, then took a gulp of JW Red.

"I don't have a clue," Gary said, rubbing the bruises on his arm. "Those Filipino guards thumped me around quite a bit."

"From what I've heard, compared to the camps in North Vietnam, this was a cake walk," Captain Redy said. "At McConnell, I heard all kinds of rumors about beatings, torture and even prisoners being killed." Captain Redy had done his F-105 transition training at McConnell AFB, Kansas.

"I heard the same scuttlebutt at Seymour," Gary said, taking another gulp of his DJB, waiting for the soreness to go away. He rubbed the rope burns around his neck. As he lifted his glass for another slug, his elbow cracked, sending a jolt of pain up his arm. He had fallen over a log in the jungle while running from the scouts, slamming his right side into a tree stump. Then they had caught him. He was still discovering bruises from the beating. Now his right elbow had turned dodgy.

"How soon do you leave?" Captain Redy asked, exhaling a puff of smoke.

"In two hours. I got a hop on a cargo flight going directly to Takhli. What about you?"

Gary dreaded his upcoming flight, seven or eight hours spent in a cramped cargo plane. He had never been able to sleep while riding in an airplane and doubted if he would on the way to Thailand. He had bought magazines and a book to read, but didn't think that would work either.

"Tomorrow morning, on a charter flight going first to Bangkok and then on to Korat."

"I forgot. What squadron did you say?" Gary asked, taking the final slug from his drink.

"The 34th Tactical Fighter Squadron. Yours?"

"The 333rd. The squadron is called the Red Lancers."

Captain Redy hesitated, "You heard anything about Operation BOLO?"

"Only bits and pieces back in the states. I did find out it happened on 2 January. But facts are hard to come by. Rumors are, Colonel Olds designed a trap for the MIGs, and they fell for it." As he said these words, Gary wondered how he would react when he encountered a MIG. He knew such a moment was coming. He hoped he didn't panic.

"Maybe we'll get the straight story in Thailand," Captain Redy said.

RIDING IN A jump seat just behind the pilots of the C-133 turboprop cargo plane, Gary pondered his experiences in the survival class. After hearing the rumors as well as the truth about pilots shot down over Laos and North Vietnam, he hoped he never had to use any of the techniques learned over the five day course. But he knew better than to hope for anything.

Behind him, a red crash rescue truck and pallets loaded with crates crammed the cavernous cargo hold. The plane rattled and shook. Gary's wax ear plugs cancelled out some of the engine noise, but a steady drone filled the air.

He thought about Colonel Olds and the fighter sweep over North Vietnam in early January. Back in North Carolina, the TV news had carried small parts of the story. Seven MIGS had been shot down. Soon he would be flying missions in MIG country. Gary wondered about what the MIGs looked like in flight. Were they easy to see? Major Hooper had said that the enemy fighters didn't leave a smoke exhaust as the American planes did. Would that make them more difficult to spot?

As he traveled closer to Takhli, the Officers' Clubs buzzed about the American victory in an epic air battle, probably the largest since the Korean War. Facts and rumors of the operation not released to the press passed by word of mouth.

Gary knew that Colonel Robin Olds, an Air Force pilot, had designed BOLO using deception and trickery to lure the North Vietnamese into a trap. The colonel decided to disguise a formation of F-4 Phantoms to appear to the enemy as F-105 Thunderchiefs by using the same tactics, jamming pods and flight procedures that the Thuds used. He intended to clear every MIG found from the sky.

Up until the MIG sweep, North Vietnamese pilots used hit-and-run raids against strike missions. Enemy fighters appeared out of nowhere, swooped in behind the American formations, fired their air-to-air missiles and fled. These tactics caused a slow but steady attrition of American aircraft.

Gary heard at Clark that Colonel Olds and his pilots dodged through heavy clouds, circling the mission of twenty-four Phantoms over Phuc Yen Airfield northwest of Hanoi. Enemy fighters rose to challenge them. After a fifteen-minute air battle, the American fighters shot down seven MIG-21 Fishbed planes, the most advanced fighter in the North Vietnamese inventory. By eliminating half of the enemy's advanced aircraft, Operation BOLO proved to be a great triumph for the Americans.

One of the most interesting rumors Gary heard reported that a Russian pilot had flown one of the MIGs shot down. No one knew if the Russian served as an instructor or whether he intentionally got caught up in the fray.

American pilots had suffered atrocious losses over North Vietnam. Gary had heard the stories and read news accounts of the men killed or missing. This one mission led by Colonel Olds offered a bit of good news for a change.

RED LANCERS

_____ 21

Gary Bishop Deale, First Lieutenant, USAF
Takhli Royal Thai Air Force Base, Thailand
19 February 1967

AS GARY WALKED down the cargo ramp of the C-133 at the Takhli Base in Thailand, he was greeted by one hundred degree heat and soaking humidity. While partially adapted by his time in the Philippines, the conditions here seemed to be worse. After the stifling weather, the next thing he noticed was the strong odor, which seemed to pervade the base. Smelling just like but more intense than the outhouse Gary used to visit on his Grandpap Bishop's farm, he sniffed the air and decided it could only be one thing. Gary carried his B-4 bag to the waiting pickup and asked to be taken to wing headquarters.

While riding across the ramp, a line of sixteen F-105s loaded with fuel tanks and bombs taxied from the parking apron, heading toward the end of the runway. A mission going out, Gary thought. Carts loaded with bombs passed by, pulled by small tractors. All of the men, dressed in green utility uniforms, moved with a sense of urgency.

After checking in at the 355th Tactical Fighter Wing, he began clearing onto the base. The personnel sergeant told Gary that he would be living in a hooch, the local word for a wooden barrack-type building. Gary asked for a ride to his quarters to unpack before beginning to tread all over the base getting ticks on his clearance forms. Airman

Upton drove the pickup, taking Gary on an orientation tour of the base. They drove by the flight line where about thirty-five F-105s, in addition to the sixteen which had just taken off, were parked. A line of KC-135 tankers and RB-66 electronic reconnaissance planes sat farther down the ramp. Maintenance men swarmed over the aircraft. The airman explained that about 1,000 Air Force officers and enlisted men served at Takhli.

The American portion of the base consisted of squadron buildings, the Officers' Club, Flight Surgeon's office, chapel and other essential facilities. Some of the buildings were constructed of concrete blocks while others were made entirely out of wood. It appeared to Gary that permanent buildings were being built to replace the wooden ones as there were many active work sites.

Riding with the windows open, sweat began soaking Gary's uniform. Even with sun glasses, he had to squint in the sun's penetrating glare. In the drainage ditches, which Airman Upton had referred to as *Klongs*, lush green plants grew in profusion. Each building was surrounded by a neatly trimmed lawn.

As Airman Upton carried Gary's B-4 bag and duffle bag into the hooch, he pointed out the building in back used as the shower and latrine.

The hooch looked like a pole barn, Gary thought. There were no windows in the structure. Screening made up the top half of the external wall. A metal roof covered the building, with a wide overhang on all sides to prevent rain from blowing into the structure.

"The hooch girl runs the whole show around here, laundry, shining shoes, making your bed and cleaning," Airman Upton said. "The girls are usually the daughter or niece of a local Thai officer. They're hands off."

"No problem," Gary said. "I'm married."

"Good to go. I think I know where there's an empty cube, unless someone has claimed it."

Leading Gary down the center aisle formed by the backs of wooden wall lockers, Airman Upton called off pilot's names as they passed each cubicle. "This hooch is home for sixteen pilots," the airman said. Painted in basic government green, the lockers divided the room into personal spaces for the pilots. Each cube had an opening for access with no door. The first thing Gary noted was that the arrangement offered little privacy. Ceiling fans barely stirred the hot humid air.

"The hooches are constructed of teak or mahogany. Seems like a waste of good hardwood, but that's all that grows locally. Here we go. I helped the First Sergeant and the Court Officer clear this yesterday."

The airman must have noticed Gary's puzzled expression.

"Whenever a pilot goes missing, we clear and pack their personal effects. Seems to happen quite a bit around here."

"I see," Gary said. He thought that bluntly describing a pilot as being missing and then moving quickly on was a cold indifferent approach. But then he realized that according to everything he had heard so far, missing pilots were a common thing around Takhli.

This was the first time Gary had encountered the process for missing pilots. He had thought that there must be a procedure, and now he knew.

"I think you'll like this corner space. It will catch the breeze very nicely. I'm surprised no one else has claimed it."

The cubicle was simply equipped: A cot rested in the corner, next to a small desk and chair. A mosquito net draped over the cot. Fastened to the corner beam over the desk, a reading light provided some illumination. A lamp sat on the desk. He had access to two wall lockers in the cubicle and a footlocker rested by his cot.

"I bought three new locks for you at the Base Exchange. You owe me two bucks."

Gary handed the airman two dollars. While he began unpacking his clothes, Airman Upton briefed him on things Gary needed to do or avoid. Buying a bicycle from the local dealer would be a priority, but bikes were problematic. The bikes came and went. Some thought the dealer stole the bikes and resold them.

Gary should check with his roommates as to how much to pay and tip the hooch girl and other Thai workers. Eating at Takhli Tan's Noodle Shop on the Thai side of the base would be OK, while it was best to avoid Thai Mary's.

The most excellent number-one full-body massages, emphasizing full-body, were readily available in Takhli Town, a few miles from base. If the lieutenant wanted, a full range of female companionship services were offered in the village.

Bangkok, about an hour away by bus or cab, was the greatest leave city in the world. You can get anything you want there, just like at Alice's Restaurant.

Assume any snake seen was a cobra, don't even go near snakes.

Airman Upton continued. "If you have anything valuable or a lot of cash, it can be locked up at the squadron. You can trust folks around here only so far."

"OK. What's the strange odor?"

"Night soil. Human waste the Thais use to fertilize their rice paddies. I don't even notice it anymore. You'll see the locals peddling around the base with their honey pots on carts which they use to clean out the latrines. We call them honey wagons."

"It kind of hit me in the face."

"You'll get used to it."

By the time Gary finished unpacking thirty minutes later, his uniform was soaked through. Using locks provided by the airman who had returned to headquarters, he secured his clothing and valuables. Carrying clean underwear and a flight suit, he walked to the shower on a wooden walkway, which connected the two buildings. On the way, he passed by a beautiful Thai young lady doing laundry.

"Do you work there?" Gary pointed at his hooch.

"Yes. I Helene."

"I'm new. I'm Lieutenant Gary Deale."

"*Sa Wa Dee*," Helene said, bowing her head and pressing her hands together under her chin.

Or at least, that's what Gary thought she said. He bowed his head in return and also pressed his hands together.

After his shower, Gary walked to the headquarters of the 333rd Tactical Fighter Squadron. The intense afternoon sunlight caused him to sweat profusely. He wiped his brow with a hanky. Two red crash trucks roared past, lights flashing, headed toward the flight line. His uniform soaked through, again. As he entered the building, a master sergeant approached. "May I help you, sir?"

"Yes. I'm Lieutenant Gary Deale, newly assigned."

"Yes, sir," the sergeant said, offering his hand. "I'm Sergeant Heydt, Squadron Operations. We've been waiting for you. Wing called down and said you had arrived. Pleased to meet you."

"Thank you, sergeant. I'm happy to meet you. That means I'm finally here."

"Yes, sir. You are. Come along with me. I have something for you. Then I'll take you to the Orderly Room. The commander is out on a mission, but someone should be around to get you checked in."

"This is a squadron decal for the 333rd," Sergeant Heydt said, handing Gary a cloth patch. "Welcome to the Red Lancers."

"Thank you."

Taking the patch, about the size of a coffee saucer, in his hands, Gary studied the artwork. Across the top, 333rd FTR SQDR appeared in dark blue letters on a tan background, while on the bottom, LANCERS. The middle of the patch was a red circle. Embossed on the circle were two lances held by iron fists, imposed over a blue globe.

"I'll send this one to Allison, my wife. She's starting a collection."

"Very good, sir. You can buy more at the Base Exchange and get that Seymour Johnson stuff off your flight suit."

Gary patted his patch from Seymour. "Ah, yes. Good old Seymour."

"Been there myself. Let's get you checked in. Come see me when you're ready to begin flying."

IN WHAT SEEMED to be the middle of the night, movement in the hooch woke Gary. After looking at his watch, he saw that it was 0300. He thought for a moment and decided that some of his hoochmates were preparing for an early morning mission. Men cursed and stumbled as they went to the latrine, trying not to let the screen door slam, but failing. Rain pounded against the metal roof, sounding like a hundred drummers drumming. No wonder the pilots are cursing, Gary thought.

Gary turned the lamp on to make movement easier for his fellow pilots and checked out his cube. As the alarm clock hands moved, the rain intensified; a moving waterfall of rain. More rain than Gary had ever seen before. Cascades of water filled the *Klongs*, the canals which wandered across Thailand, to overflowing. Gary now realized why raised wooden walkways extended from the hooch to the latrine. But even they began flooding as the deluge continued.

The earthly aroma of night soil from the neighboring fields pervaded the air. Rain and fog spread the rank smell over everything. The cube where Gary lived, his clothing, even he himself, Gary supposed, carried the lingering scent of the rice paddies.

Even with the rain, humidity and heat invaded his room. It really wouldn't be correct to call it a room but this is where he lived. Gary thought that he could cut the thick air with a knife. His bed sheets and underwear were damp. He couldn't tell if that was from sweat or from the fog drifting through the screens.

For color, Gary had taped two posters from his favorite movies, *Thunder Road* and *South Pacific*, to the back of his neighbor's wall lockers. While on his way to Thailand, he had purchased the posters in a second hand book shop in San Francisco.

He hung three pictures on the corner post. One showed Gary kneeling in front of an F-105. Allison had done a self-portrait in watercolor just before he departed for Thailand, and that hung in the middle. The other was of Allison and him sitting together on a commercial aircraft, both smiling at the camera. Allison described the photograph as showing the two of them on their first date. "This is where we really first met," Allison had said, even though they had known each other as remote acquaintances during high school.

On his desk Gary had placed a framed photograph of Allison and him on the Shackleford Banks near Beaufort. He picked up the picture. The first thing he noticed was Allison's smile. Then her skimpy two-piece red swim suit. He sighed and placed the photo back on his desk.

Gary sat on his bunk listening to the pounding rain. Soft music played on his newly purchased Sony short wave. He was dressed in his skivvies trying to catch a breeze from the ceiling fan that weakly stirred the air. As he scanned the radio frequencies, he discovered that Radio Australia played "Habanera," from Bizet's *Carmen* early each morning as their signature sign-off piece. Gary would come to count on this music as a serene beginning to each day when he had to get up early for a mission.

The other pilots made their way out of the hooch, headed for breakfast at the Officers' Club and then on to briefings. Realizing that in a few days he would be joining them in this early morning ritual, Gary turned off his lamp, lay back on his cot and drifted off to sleep.

IN THE VALLEY OF THE SHADOW OF DEATH

_____ 22

Gary Bishop Deale, First Lieutenant, USAF
Takhli Royal Thai Air Force Base, Thailand
20 February 1967

SWEAT DRIPPED FROM every pore. Even with the gradual transition to tropical conditions, first in the Philippines and now in Thailand, Gary had not yet adjusted. The oppressive heat and humidity caused him to think about the performance characteristics of F-105s in such extreme conditions.

While checking in at the 355th Tactical Fighter Wing Headquarters, flight surgeon, chaplain, finance, supply and a dozen other offices, Gary wandered the base on his newly purchased bicycle in a sweat-soaked daze. When finished getting ticks in all the little boxes, he returned to his unit, the 333rd Tactical Fighter Squadron. After finding Sergeant Heydt, he asked about the flight schedule.

"How about early tomorrow?" asked Sergeant Heydt. "We have a bird ready for a maintenance check flight."

"The sooner the better," Gary said.

"You'll be going up with Major Foxe, who's waiting for you down the hall," the sergeant said, pointing to the squadron planning room.

"Have a chair," Major Foxe said, as he glanced through a stack of forms. The major, built like an offensive lineman, had closely cropped hair. An ugly red scar ran from his left ear to the corner of his mouth.

Major Foxe must have noticed Gary staring. "Got hit by shrapnel before a recent ejection," he said, matter-of-factly, running his fingers along the scar.

Jesus, Gary thought. Explosion. Shrapnel. Ejection. What happened? he wondered, not daring to ask. Another pilot had told Gary that Major Foxe had been shot down, injured, rescued by helicopter, and just returned to duty. The major volunteered no additional information.

"We're very proud of our squadron's legend and heritage going back to the Pacific in World War II," Major Foxe said, pointing at a mural of a fighter plane firing its guns at another aircraft. "Those guys were real fighter pilots and racked up forty-five kills against the Japanese, flying out of Saipan. All we are is bomb droppers."

"P-47s?" Gary asked, having noticed the fighter in the wall painting.

"The Jug. You know that term?"

"Yes, sir."

"I have about an hour's work to do, getting checked back into the squadron," Major Foxe said. He pointed to a stack of forms he'd been completing. "In the meantime, have you studied the Rules of Engagement folder?"

"No, sir, I haven't."

Major Foxe placed a thick folder bearing red TOP SECRET stamps in front of Gary. "Read this and weep. Then you have to pass the ROE quiz before you fly any combat missions."

"ROE Quiz?"

"Don't look so awestruck." The major scowled. "That isn't the half of it. After each mission, you'll have to sign a BOT form."

"BOT?"

"Bombs on Target. You have to certify that all your bombs were dropped on the briefed aim point."

"I never heard anything about this," Gary said, using his hand to cover the consternation in his face. Why did pilots have to sign such a form? Gary wondered. We were trained to drop our bombs on the target. We are called professional fighter pilots. Why would anybody drop bombs on anything but the target? Do I really need to be worried about this?

"I never did either until this fucked—excuse me—this sorry assed war. Just sign the damned thing. We're only allowed to bomb what the chain of command selects, not what really needs to be destroyed. It's the way we fight this war, with one arm tied behind our back. Fighting a war, with rules and restrictions, we call it."

"That's what my instructor, Major Hooper, said."

"Nick Hooper? He's at Seymour?"

"Yes, sir. He's now transitioning into F-4s."

"I'll be! Nick Hooper, getting ahead of me into Phantoms. He still stealing food?"

"He's very sneaky about it, but yes, sir, he is."

Major Foxe laughed and Gary joined in.

The major paused, taking a sip of coffee and a long drag on his cigarette. "We're here to prove that the United States is not a paper tiger, afraid of its own shadow." He sighed. "Whether that means that we actually have the endurance and *cojones* to win this war remains to be seen.

"One more thing for you to think about," Major Foxe said. "There are twenty-five pilots in this squadron eager to fly in combat. They will scheme against each other for the opportunity to fly the really tough missions. We came here to fight. That's what we do and that's why we are here."

Pointing at the thick Rules of Engagement folder, Major Foxe said, "Read those ROEs and weep."

Gary began to study the pages of rules.

Do not fly within 30 nautical miles of Hanoi.

Do not fly within 10 miles of Haiphong.

Absolute prohibition on flying within 10 miles of Hanoi and 4 miles of Haiphong.

Do not fly within 30 miles of Communist China.

Do not attack enemy airplanes while they are on the ground.

Enemy airplanes must be airborne before being attacked.

SAM sites may not be engaged until after missiles have been launched.

Do not attack merchant ships anywhere.

Only targets authorized by the chain of command may be attacked in the Hanoi/Haiphong area.

A Bombs on Target form must be signed after each mission.

He read the words, wondering if all wars had been fought like this. He couldn't recall any such restrictions like this in previous conflicts, except for Korea, with its so-called buffer zone near the Chinese border. What are we really doing here? he wondered. What is our strategic objective?

Later, Gary and the major sat in the flight planning room. "Study these maps as though your life depends on it, because it does," Major Foxe said, pointing to the tactical pilotage charts spread under Plexiglas on the briefing table. "We use grease pencils to map our ingress and egress routes so that everyone can see what's going on. Tomorrow we're going to do this."

Drawing a line from Takhli north into Laos, the major offered commentary as he drew. "We'll hook up with the tankers here, and you'll have to cycle on and off several times because your bird took a hit and suffered some damage in the receiver area." He glanced at Gary. "You ever been shot at?"

"No, sir."

"We'll fix that tomorrow."

Ah shit, Gary thought. In his mind, he had pictured receiving a gradual transition into combat. He fully anticipated being shot at, just not on his first flight. A chill ran up his back. He coughed, and drummed his fingers on the table.

"We're going up early," Major Foxe said. "I want to get ahead of the strike mission leaving at dawn."

As the briefing continued, Gary discovered that his aircraft had suffered battle damage, disabling the air-refueling system. Somehow, the wounded pilot on that mission had coaxed the F-105 back to the base and landed. Major Foxe's F-105 had received a replacement engine after its old one malfunctioned.

"We're going to do a very quick takeoff, then go hit the tanker, take a supersonic tour of Laos and then come home," Major Foxe said. "Just do as I do! You got any problems with any of that?"

Gary looked the major in the eyes. "No, sir. I've done it all before."

"One more thing to remember," Foxe said. "You're going to see some terrible, painful things while flying in combat. It's going to happen! You have to, repeat have to, compartmentalize these unfortunate events and lock them in a box in your mind."

"Yes, sir," Gary said. Major Hooper had told him the same thing back at Seymour.

That night, after Gary had drunk two beers at the club and had taken a hot shower to relax, he found that sleep was elusive. His anxiety level had increased after Major Foxe told him to expect enemy gunfire. Am I really ready for this? he wondered. When he last looked at his alarm clock, it was 1 A.M.

IN THE PREDAWN grayness, Gary climbed the crew ladder. Settling his butt on the survival kit, he twisted his body trying to make himself comfortable. He put his arms through the parachute straps, while the airplane crew chief cinched him tight and fastened buckles. It had been several weeks since he had flown an F-105. He quickly checked the controls. Flipping the pages in his flight manual strapped to his right thigh, he began reading the Engine Pre-start Checklist. Throwing switches and turning dials, he proceeded to get the plane running and ready to fly. He noted carefully where his plane was parked because he would have to return the plane to the same spot.

Major Foxe's aircraft taxied in front of Gary. He saluted the crew chief and followed. The major wasted no time as they sped along the taxiway toward the end of the runway.

Gary's plane thumped over the expansion joints in the concrete taxiway. He carefully noted the location of the control tower, fire station and maintenance buildings. Learning mission procedures and protocol one small step at a time, Gary followed the major's fighter. Early morning mist swirled across the taxiway. An older Thai man with a goatee, wearing a colorful sarong, stood in the grass and raised his walking stick in greeting. Gary saluted.

He lined up next to the major's F-105 and braked his aircraft to a halt on the arming check ramp at the end of the runway. Mechanics gathered on the tarmac waiting to service twenty F-105s scheduled for the early morning mission to North Vietnam.

The major planned to have their two planes checked and in the air before the North Vietnam bound strike force arrived on the ramp. Airmen swarmed the two aircraft looking for leaks and loose external fuel tanks. Their two airplanes carried no bombs.

The whistling sound of their idling jet engines filled the air. Gary's flight helmet shut out some of the noise, but he still heard the swirling whizzing sound. He sat in the cockpit sweating as heat and humidity shimmered from the ramp.

Gary raised his hands over the cockpit railing for the mechanics and armament airmen. If the pilot's hands disappeared from sight, then the maintainers on the ground fled. Their worst fear, of a pilot suddenly throwing switches or pushing buttons, caused an overabundance of caution.

The chaplain standing on the ramp raised his hands in blessing for the two pilots. Major Foxe had briefed him that one of the chaplains always showed up for combat mission takeoffs.

Gary believed in God, probably as much as any of the fighter pilots. He said a short prayer for protection and guidance.

Aside from the drinking and the typical fighter pilot's cursing, he led an upright life. The question lurked in his mind about the sufficiency of his meager efforts. He hoped that a loving God cut him some slack if worse came to worse. There he was, hoping for something again—Bad Karma!

The priest looked down the ramp towards Gary's plane and started walking. Gary had talked with him at the chapel while waiting for the Protestant services to begin. He believed that it was an ironic juxtaposition, a padre offering his blessing to planes and pilots on their way on a combat mission to kill people. On the other hand, that act might very well be the very last religious rite for some unfortunate pilot.

Gary talked with the maintainer directing the inspection on his F-105 over the intercom line. The mechanics working on his plane found no problems.

He checked the cockpit one last time and began stowing maps, checklists and other papers out of his way. Taking a long drink from the water line, which snaked over his shoulder, Gary watched the mechanics swarm over his airplane from nose to tail.

Major Foxe obtained clearance over the radio to taxi. Gary didn't understand what the major's crew chief's gestures meant as he pointed his index fingers straight up followed by a thumbs up. A strange foreboding suddenly overtook him.

The canopy, a transparent Plexiglas bubble enclosing the cockpit, of the other F-105 began to drop. Pilots kept the canopy open because the air conditioning system did not work on the ground. Gary closed his and strapped on his oxygen mask.

Sweat soaked through his flight suit. He released his brakes, tweaked the throttle and followed the other plane toward the end of the runway. Nervously scanning the tapes and dials, Gary checked and rechecked the instruments, searching for anything amiss. He wanted his first takeoff in Thailand to be perfect.

Members of the ground crew gathered at the edge of the ramp nearest the runway, which surprised Gary. Normally, they would be busy preparing for the outgoing strike mission. He looked down the taxiway and saw a collection of vans and crash trucks. Why were they all there, parked facing the runway, he wondered. Very unusual. Then it hit him. Oh, Shit! Oh, Shit, he thought. What is the major going to do? And, then he remembered the words, "Just do as I do!"

Gary mirrored everything Major Foxe did. So far, he anticipated every move the other F-105 made. A few minor details remained open such as exactly what a very quick takeoff meant. But, Major Foxe had asked him if he had any problems with anything planned. "Just do as I do," left a lot open. Now, Gary wished he had asked a few more questions.

He followed Major Foxe's F-105 off the arming ramp and taxied his plane to the right side of the runway centerline. Using the right side of the runway provided a clear path for Gary to complete his takeoff if some problem developed with the major's plane on the left side.

"Texas 2, lanyard check, follow in 10 seconds," Major Foxe transmitted.

Gary raised both hands with thumbs extended, signaling that he understood. He was good to go.

"Texas Flight of two, requesting permission for max," he stopped to cough, and then continued. "Maximum performance takeoff." He was slurring his words as he continued to cough

"Roger, Texas Flight, you are cleared."

Major Foxe ran the engine of his aircraft up to full power, the plane shuddering trying to break free. The F-105 sat there vibrating and straining against the brakes. Then, the engine noise decreased. Maybe we aren't going to do this, Gary thought. We can all go back to the club and relax. Maybe the other plane was broken. The major looked his way, pointing down the runway. Gary knew something unusual was about to happen. He had no idea what it might be. He thought that the shit was about to hit the fan.

Maybe God will watch over me, he thought as the other pilot increased power. Major Foxe's plane began rolling, and the exhaust flared as the afterburner lit. The aircraft rapidly picked up speed, and the engine smoke thickened and darkened as water sprayed into the exhaust. Even with a 9,000-foot runway, takeoff required the use of both the afterburner and water injection, especially when combat-loaded with bombs in ninety degree heat and high humidity.

Major Foxe's plane blasted down the runway. The new engine appeared to be working.

Quicker than Gary thought possible, the airplane lifted off the runway. Major Foxe cleared the ground and then steeply raised the nose so that the angle of attack increased to the most dangerous stage. A very thin edge existed between one hell of a show and a complete disaster. Gary had seen and done maximum performance takeoffs before, but never with Takhli's heat.

Just as he prepared to push the throttle, the rim of the sun poked through the haze over his right shoulder, marking the beginning of a new day on his first flight from Takhli.

Now it's my turn, Gary thought. As he released his brakes, the F-105 began rolling. Gary pushed the throttle forward. Bad things happened very quickly, and Gary fully understood that he must stay ahead of the aircraft. If the plane got ahead of him, a strong possibility of death ensued. He strained, using all of his senses to listen to what the airplane told him. Every plane behaved differently. Each one had its own quirks and idiosyncrasies. The slightest shudder in the control stick or vibration in the plane sent a message, which Gary had to heed. As his F-105 cleared the ground, Gary eased back the control stick, pointing the nose more or less straight up.

Gary imagined what the takeoff looked like to the men standing on the ground—the F-105 climbing, balancing on the tongue of fire blasting from the afterburner. Pilots killed themselves doing this. It provided one hell of a show for all of those guys on the ground who worked their butts off to keep the planes flying.

Once he got back on the ground, there would be hell to pay for the dangerous takeoffs. But then, he had followed the major's orders. "Do as I do" offered not much of an explanation, Gary thought. The Nuremburg Defense offered no justification for following the major. But Gary quickly decided he needed to show he could handle the airplane and master the situation. Sierra Alpha, Sierra Alpha, Major Hooper's words, bounced around in Gary's memory.

Looking over his shoulder, Gary saw that he was more or less straight up over the end of the runway. Glancing at the altimeter, he blinked in disbelief upon seeing 10,000 feet. When unencumbered by 5,000 pounds of bombs and bomb racks, the F-105 climbed like a rocket. Gary looked back at his smoke trail and realized he had just burned up 3,000 pounds of Uncle Sam's jet fuel.

Squinting in the sun's glare and haze, he saw the dark exhaust trail from Major Foxe's plane. The nose of the lead plane dropped, and then the exhaust decreased as the major disengaged the afterburner. Gary left his own throttle in the afterburner détente but eased off the stick to decrease the climb rate. The distance between the two fighters slowly decreased. He gradually reduced power and eased into position just off the right wingtip of the other F-105.

Flying north, he watched the landscape of Thailand roll past. Green rice paddies and small villages passed under his wing. A system of canals, which the locals called *Klongs*, interconnected the populated areas. Every now and then, a colorful white and gold-gilded Buddhist temple appeared below, poking out from among the trees.

"The Mekong River and Vientiane. We're in Laos," Major Foxe radioed.

Gary wobbled his wings, showing he understood.

Just after passing over the river, their tanker appeared.

"I'm going in first, and then I'll watch you as you refuel to see if you have any leaks," Major Foxe radioed.

Gary placed his F-105 behind the right wingtip of the KC-135 jet refueling tanker and stabilized his fighter as the major's plane approached from below. Major Foxe lined up his plane slightly behind and below the tail of the tanker. The refueling operator nestled in the belly of the tanker lowered and extended the boom, making the connection with the F-105.

Major Foxe's plane took on fuel at a rate of 2,000 pounds per minute. The plane quickly reached its capacity of 14,000 pounds including the auxiliary tank in the bomb bay and the two tanks carried on pylons under the wings. Fuel vapor flew back by the major's plane as the operator disconnected the boom.

Fortunately, in spite of the weather forecast, only a few clouds appeared near the tankers. Gary had executed air-to-air refueling only a few precious times. He wanted to connect with the tanker with no difficulties.

"2, Lead. I'm off the tanker. You're in next."

"2," Gary radioed.

The major's F-105 dropped back and moved under the tanker's left wingtip making room for Gary's plane to approach. He rolled his plane to the left and lined up just below and behind the tanker's tail. The refueling operator nestled in the belly of the tanker just above Gary extended the boom. The boom swiveled and then stabilized, connecting with the fuel receiver located just in front of Gary's cockpit.

To test the fuel transfer system, the operator disconnected and then reconnected the boom several times. Everything appeared to be working as his fuel gauges crept towards full. Gary ran his hand across his throat signaling that he was nearing capacity.

"Texas 2, cutting you off now," the operator said. "Good luck."

"Roger that. Thanks," Gary said, raising his left thumb.

The boom operator replied with a crisp salute.

Gary followed the major's plane to the west. He checked to make sure he had set the switches so that the fuel from the two external tanks emptied first.

"Look back at the tankers," Major Foxe radioed.

A formation of twenty F-105s in flights of four fighters each had approached the tanker stream. Gary had never seen this many in the air at one time.

Major Foxe flew northwest in Laotian airspace. As Gary checked his pilotage chart, he concluded they were near the town of Louangphrabang. He easily recognized it because of the big hook turn in the Mekong River.

He followed as the major's plane banked to the east. They began a gradual descent. Slowly, the landscape changed from the flat river valley of the Mekong to steep rock escarpments known as karst.

Haze and smoke drifted through the abrupt valleys. Small villages appeared randomly scattered in the lush verdant jungle below.

Major Foxe radioed. "The next checkpoint is very important. Study it carefully. Notice the little air strip and the village of Sam Neua."

Bomb craters covered most of the landscape around the village. The airfield and a road intersection offered several easily recognizable landmarks.

"We're in gomer land now," Major Foxe radioed. "Home of the Pathet Lao."

Suddenly, a series of black clouds blossomed in front of their aircraft.

Gary automatically rolled his F-105 to the right, jinking by rapidly turning and weaving the plane. Pilots used this standard evasive maneuver to throw off the aim of the enemy gunners. The major's plane began a steep descent. Gary followed.

Shells snapped by his plane with a supersonic crack. Orange-red puffs appeared on all sides, each one throwing a storm of shrapnel. Gary hadn't expected this. Yes, he knew that the enemy would be shooting at him. But not so soon. For an instant, he was highly pissed at Major Foxe for exposing him to enemy fire on his first flight. Reason soon took over from emotion, however, because he realized that this was his new normal.

Major Foxe had given him the lowdown on Antiaircraft Artillery (Triple-A) fire in the briefing. "Hell, we all thought that Triple-A was obsolete until we arrived in Thailand back in '64," Major Foxe had said. "Rumor had it that Triple-A went out with World War II and Korea. Turns out those little bastards are shooting us poor saps down on a regular basis with obsolete weapons."

Gary saw the fuel tanks drop off Major Foxe's plane. He punched the jettison button and his now empty external tanks fell behind, tumbling toward the ground. Punching the tanks off the F-105 resulted in clean airflow, which enabled higher airspeed and increased maneuverability.

Pushing his throttle ahead to maximum afterburner, he continued jinking his plane. Major Foxe began a wide left turn. Their airspeed continued increasing. Gary felt the bump as his aircraft went supersonic. They skimmed over the tops of the karst escarpments and turned back toward the valley, in the direction of the Antiaircraft Artillery sites.

Why are we going back into that hellfire? Gary wondered. This was crazy. It violated every rule he had learned about repeatedly flying over enemy Triple-A positions. He felt a building resentment against the major and his actions, violating one edict after another. Rational men did not do such things, Gary thought. Then he realized that war wasn't rational or logical.

"I bet these are the same motherfuckers who shot me down," Major Foxe radioed.

"Say what?"

"I call this place the valley of death."

Then what in the hell are we doing here? Gary wondered, growing more and more bewildered at the major's decisions.

"Just one little pass to tell them I'm back," the major said. "Keep your spread and kick it up."

The bursts of exploding Triple-A shells divided and began tracking the two aircraft. Major Foxe's F-105 thundered down the left side of the narrow valley and Gary's down the right. They both hugged the karst escarpment on opposite sides of the valley, very low and fast.

A chain of white puffs from 37 mm Triple-A tracked Gary's plane. These guys are good, Gary thought. He had heard of the pucker factor, the tightening of the rectum in tough spots. Now, he experienced that feeling first-hand.

Then the major's words came back to him, "---the same motherfuckers who shot me down."

Gary breathed fast, taking in gulps of musty smelling oxygen through his mask. His flight suit, which had thoroughly dried due to the plane's air conditioning, was now soaked through with sweat. His pulse pounded in his ears as the exploding shells crept closer to his plane. Gary knew they had no weapons to fight back with, only a 20 mm cannon. That would be like a cowboy in the old west using a pile of rocks against some other dude armed with a Colt 45.

He glanced at his airspeed tape registering over 650 knots—750 miles per hour. The bursts still tracked him. Humidity contrails boiled off Major Foxe's wings as he rolled the plane and climbed slightly to the crest of the karst ridge and then disappeared over the other side.

If the major has had enough of this, then so have I, Gary thought, as he rolled the plane and then flipped up over the ridge on his side of the valley.

He kept the plane low and fast for a few seconds and then gradually crept up to see if he could see Major Foxe's plane.

"Check your six."

Gary looked over his left shoulder to see an F-105 in back of his left wingtip. How in the fuck did he do that? Gary thought. There was no way in hell that Major Foxe could have found him that fast. If it were a MIG instead of an F-105, he would have been dead.

"OK, enough of this shit for one day," Major Foxe radioed. "Let's go find those tankers." Major Foxe took the lead as the two aircraft turned south.

Gary was surprised. He thought sure that the major would lead him over the flak site again. That would prove to him that the major was in fact crazy. But Gary would take whatever small gifts the major offered.

Later, he floated the F-105 toward the runway and touched down just as Major Foxe pulled his plane onto the taxiway. After shutting his plane down and discussing the flight with the crew chief, they walked around it looking for holes and leaks. Gary then leaned against a maintenance rack by the jet exhaust deflection wall, catching his breath and waiting for whatever was to come.

"Could I bum a cigarette?" Gary asked the sergeant, hoping to calm his nerves.

"Sure," Sergeant Ford said, offering his pack. After seeing Gary's shaking hands, the sergeant fired up his Zippo.

Major Foxe walked down the line of aircraft, carrying his flight kit, smiling and waving at the various maintainers working on the planes.

"How did it feel to get shot at?" the major asked, bumming a cigarette from the sergeant.

"The most exciting fear-provoking thing I've ever done," Gary said. "Those first red bursts scared the shit out of me."

"Radar controlled 85 millimeter Triple-A. Accurate as hell. Damned dangerous stuff."

"I figured the white bursts to be 37 mm."

"Fast firing, nasty mothers. Someday soon I'm going up there and lay a world of hurt on those little fuckers."

"Please take me with you," Gary said, bravado overcoming fear.

"Payback time is coming on those little gomers' heads. Any dings in the bird?"

"We didn't see any at first look."

"Here comes trouble."

Colonel Batts drove his ragtop Jeep down the line looking behind each plane. He passed by where the major and Gary stood and then circled back, stopping in front of them.

Major Foxe motioned Gary into the rear seat so he gathered up his flight gear and hopped aboard. Major Foxe rode shotgun. *This is where I get taken to the woodshed,* Gary thought.

Colonel Batts drove to a small parking pad near the north end of the runway and parked where they faced incoming traffic. Major Foxe turned and gave Gary the look, which sent a very clear message. Do not say one fucking word! Gary followed his instincts and did just that. Heat shimmered off the concrete taxiway. A C-47 Gooney Bird cargo plane approached and bounced off the runway several times before finally settling to the ground. No one said anything for what seemed like hours.

Gary heard a muffled exchange over the radio and then heard the sound of approaching jets.

"Lieutenant, you count the airplanes," the colonel said, handing Gary binoculars and a clipboard filled with call signs and aircraft data.

"Yes, sir," Gary said.

"So major, looks as though you fucked up again, didn't you," Colonel Batts said. "Not only that, but you also took this young lieutenant astray with you."

"Yes, sir, I did," Major Foxe said. After most of the base had witnessed the takeoff, uttering words in support of the act proved pointless.

Gary remained silent as the two officers in the front of the Jeep glared at each other. Wondering how he fit into the conversation, he felt relieved when the first planes began appearing.

Checking off the flights of F-105s as they began landing gave him something to do with his hands and kept his brain occupied with a task. He dreaded thinking about what Colonel Batts planned for him as punishment for the dangerous takeoff and journey into the land of big guns.

The first three flights each had four F-105s, but the last two flights showed gaps. Gary saw that one had three planes and the other flight only had two. Twenty planes took off on the mission and only seventeen came back. Three missing, Gary thought, experiencing for the first time one of the results of flying combat missions. As much as the thought of three missing men upset him, he realized that he would very soon be doing what these pilots landing just did, facing daily peril.

Gary wondered what had happened to the missing three planes. They could have landed at another base. Maybe they had been shot down. It was the colonel's responsibility to figure out the fate of the missing pilots.

"Bad news, Colonel Batts, only seventeen birds," Gary said.

"Goddamnit, three missing," the colonel said.

Gary resumed his vow of silence.

"Where are the fuel drop tanks you two had when you took off?" Colonel Batts asked.

"We didn't have any drop tanks when we took off, did we, lieutenant?" Major Foxe asked.

Gary was afraid to say anything, so he simply shook his head.

"You know you're a piss poor pilot and a piss poor liar," Colonel Batts said.

"Yes, sir."

"You're a sorry assed excuse for a pilot, Major Foxe."

"Yes, sir, I know, in spades," Foxe replied. "But you sure didn't think that when I smoked those MIG-15s that were on your ass over the Yalu River in Korea."

So that's the story on Colonel Batts and Major Foxe, Gary thought.

"Yeah, well, wasn't that a real clusterfuck?" the colonel asked.

Batts reached into a cooler in the back of the Jeep and lifted out three Buds handing one to the major and Gary and keeping one for himself. Passing a church key, the colonel smiled for the first time.

Major Foxe reached over, patted the colonel on the arm and took a long swig of beer.

"What about the LT back there?" Colonel Batts asked, pointing toward Gary. "Is he any good?"

ROLLING THUNDER

_____ 23

Gary Bishop Deale, First Lieutenant, USAF
333rd Tactical Fighter Squadron Planning Room
Takhli RTAFB, Thailand
22 February 1967

"I GOT A note from your old pal back at Seymour, Major Hooper," Major Foxe said, twirling his coffee mug in his hands.
 The two men sat in the squadron planning room, preparing for a combat mission. Other pilots stood around them, studying charts and completing their mission cards.
 "How's the major doing?" Gary asked.
 "He's well along in transition to the F-4. He sends his regards, says you're a good stick man."
 "I liked him a lot," Gary said.
 "He's a fine man, as long as he can keep his hands off other people's lunch plates."
 Gary laughed.
 "He talk to you about what's going on over here?"
 "He told stories. He hated the futility."
 "No one likes this operation, but we're here and— —" said Foxe, raising his hands in frustration.
 "Duty calls, that old song," Gary said.
 "You're right there. What do you know about North Vietnam?"
 "An undeveloped county trying to dig its way into the future," Gary said, sweeping his hand over the chart on the table. The major's question had surprised him. Gary hadn't

thought of North Vietnam being anything other than a bull's-eye.

"As of 1964, you are dead on. But lately, Uncle Ho and his peasants have acquired very lethal weapons and they're kicking our butts. You know how we got to this lovely spot?"

"No, sir."

"Time and politics. People being polite to each other, negotiating and compromising. Everybody calls this a war, but we are sent out with one arm tied behind our backs. It's like swatting flies. Welcome to Rolling Thunder, our great bombing campaign to force the North Vietnamese to negotiate. Not to end the war or to win, mind you. But to negotiate."

The major paused, wrinkling his face in disgust, taking a drink of coffee and then wiping his face with his hands.

While the room was air conditioned, sweat dripped off Gary's face. His flight suit was soaked. As the tension in his gut increased, he concentrated on the major's thoughts. Taking a puff on his cigarette, he noticed the major's scar had turned from pink to vivid red.

"Phased escalation, the chain of command calls it, trying to get the North Vietnamese to stop sending men and materiel down south. I call it pissing into the wind. All we're doing is getting ourselves wet and losing a lot of good men in the process. But, that's what happens when politicians in the White House choose our targets and tell us how to fight this war. I've never heard of such bullshit."

The major looked at his watch. "Almost time to go play," he said. "You get shot down up there, everybody will do all they can do to get you out. There are a lot of pissed off peasants in the rice paddies. They don't treat Americans too well. They've been known to hack pilots to death very slowly with hoes. Believe me. I've seen it with my own eyes. Don't let them get you."

Gary shuddered, at first not fully comprehending what the major had just said. Then it came to him. He now fully understood why one piece of his personal equipment was a .38 caliber revolver.

"Let's go flying," Major Foxe said, gathering his flight kit. "Welcome to Rolling Thunder, the war that isn't a war."

ROUTE PACKAGE ONE

_____ 24

Gary Bishop Deale, First Lieutenant, USAF
Takhli RTAFB, Thailand
22 February 1967, Counter Mission Number 1

A FEW MOMENTS later, Gary stood in the small Personal Equipment shop crowded in with the other pilots. On this, his first mission to North Vietnam, Gary double checked every piece of gear.
 Wrapping the G-suit around his legs, he first ran the zipper from the right ankle to his crotch and then did the same thing for the left leg. He fastened the waist snaps. Reaching for his survival vest, he pulled it over his right and then left arms, then zipped it shut. He took the survival radio out of his vest, extended the antenna and began talking nonsense, joining the crowd testing their transmissions. Patting the .38 caliber revolver just below his left shoulder blade, he then checked his survival knife. Finally, he draped his parachute over his right arm, picked up his kit and followed the men outside.
 Gary climbed onto the back of the blue pickup and sat on the bench facing Major Foxe and another pilot. Major Eton rode shotgun. An airman hopped into the driver's seat and slowly drove to the parking apron.
 Gary attempted to swallow, but his mouth was too dry. His knees bounced in anticipation. The tension and anxiety coiled like a wound-up spring in his gut.

After takeoff, the planes turned northeast, headed for southern North Vietnam. Once crossing the border, Gary rolled his fighter to the right and rotated his head, scanning the sky behind the formation for MIGs. The three F-105 Thunderchiefs to his left jinked left and right, up and down, trying to dodge the intermittent flashes from exploding Antiaircraft Artillery fire. White flashes from exploding 37 mm Triple-A shells tracked the planes as they turned, searching for their forward air controller, the F-100 Super Sabre which would lead them to their target. Large puffy clouds and ground haze limited visibility. Finding the controller's aircraft challenged the four pilots.

Through the clouds and off to the east, Gary could see the Gulf of Tonkin. Their target wasn't far from the coast.

Gary's third encounter with Triple-A fire didn't scare him as much as his first flight with Major Foxe. Not that he was a seasoned veteran, but taking fire on that first flight and the one after that had taken the edge off.

According to the briefing, Gary's flight was to join up with a forward air controller southwest of Dong Hoi to bomb a newly constructed suspect truck park. Once they arrived at the coordinates, clouds and haze made the connection difficult.

This flight duplicated his first combat sortie. The previous day, Gary had dodged Triple-A fire and then dropped bombs on a suspect truck park in Laos near the Mu Gia Pass.

This mission, however, counted as his number one against the required one hundred to complete a combat tour. Regulations stated that a pilot had to expend ordnance, bombs or gunfire, over North Vietnam to count.

Gary looked ahead to his left and saw Major Foxe scanning the terrain ahead of them, hunting for the controller. Beyond that, Major Eton, the mission commander known as Pinto Lead, raised his right hand, as if saying "Where in the hell is that plane?"

From all he had seen thus far, this appeared to be another dog shit mission as the pilots called the air strikes against any kind of *suspect* targets—truck parks, storage depots, fuel dumps, or ferry crossings. The northern part of North Vietnam, around Hanoi, contained *hard* targets such as army barracks, large bridges, thermal power plants, railroad facilities or airfields.

As the North Vietnamese logistical network, known as the Ho Chi Minh Trail, neared South Vietnam, the enemy camouflaged and hid the storage depots, making them more difficult to find and attack. Hence, the word *suspect*, because confirmation proved to be the bane of the forward air controllers.

Route Package 1 covered the southernmost area of North Vietnam, just above the Demilitarized Zone (DMZ). Originating in Pack 1, the Ho Chi Minh trail branched into Laos and South Vietnam. Many guns and a few surface-to-air missiles defended Pack 1, though not as many as farther north.

Squadron operating procedures sent new pilots to Pack 1 or Laos for their first ten missions. These familiarization flights eased the pilots into flying combat missions in Pack 6, the heavily defended area around Hanoi.

Dog shit mission or not, Gary had spent years preparing for combat. After all those days in training, he had finally reached the payoff.

One of the debates he overheard in the Officers' Club concerned the fairness of flying one hundred combat missions over North Vietnam while the bomber pilots in the World War II European Theater only flew twenty-five.

Each battlefield proved lethal, no doubt about that. Most of the men surmised that the number of trained pilots available to fly in combat weighed against the task at hand factored out to be one hundred missions. Relishing their lot, the pilots in Gary's squadron eagerly flew against an enemy of the United States in the only war at hand.

"Pinto Lead, Misty 5."

"Pinto."

"I have you passing high to my west at nine o'clock. Turn to 90 degrees."

Gary looked right and spotted the elusive camouflage painted F-100 Hun orbiting low off to his right.

"Pinto Lead, 4. Tallyho on Misty," Gary radioed, informing Major Eton that he had a visual on the controller. "At our three o'clock low, in the weeds."

"4, keep Misty in sight," Major Eton, the flight leader radioed. "4's leading us in. Right descending turn, execute."

"4," Gary transmitted.

"Good eyes!" Major Foxe, Gary's element leader radioed.

Gary turned hard right in a descending turn keeping his eyes glued on the Hun, with the other three planes falling in line to his left.

Major Eton radioed the Misty controller informing him that the flight had a visual. The pilot of the F-100 asked for the weapon load, which the major quickly provided. After briefing the strike aircraft on the target and nearby defenses, the flight turned eastward.

"Coming up," Misty radioed.

The Hun abruptly climbed and then dropped like a rock, firing a barrage of rockets. White phosphorous exploded with orange flashes in trees near a dirt road.

Gary pushed his throttle ahead and out into afterburner. The flight climbed in a turn, arced over the top just entering clouds, and then dived toward the target.

Following Major Eton's plan, the flight spread out, widening the coverage of their bombs. The major had briefed the flight to remain in one formation during the climb and dive, rather than having each pilot drop bombs in sequence, to ensure less time over the target.

Major Eton punched his bombs off just above 7,000 feet. Gary centered his pipper on the south side of the smoke from the Hun's rockets and pushed the red button on his flight stick. He pulled the stick back, lifting the nose of his F-105 out of the dive and jinked, trying to throw off the aim of the enemy below.

White puffs from Triple-A exploded around Gary's plane as he searched for the other members of the flight. With his brain on automatic, he set switches and dials to GUN-AIR.

Gary spotted the three Thuds just ahead, going fast, heading west. As he joined the formation, the four fighters crossed into Laos. He looked back over his shoulder. Several columns of black smoke rose from the target area.

Major Eton radioed the controller for the Bomb Damage Assessment from the mission. "Continuous secondary explosions and several trucks on fire. Looks like we caught them for once," the controller responded.

Gary smiled. He jotted notes on his lineup card. His first counter mission had caused a suspect target to blow up. Gary hoped this auspicious beginning boded well.

A sense of dread quickly replaced his exhilaration. He thought that he may have just killed fellow human beings, albeit North Vietnamese soldiers. The pilots rarely saw at first-hand the lethal results of their strikes. It was like shooting a rifle at a target ten miles away.

He wondered how other pilots from World War II, Korea and, now Vietnam, felt about their duty to bomb and destroy targets. In his experience, pilots were a boisterous crowd, loudly boasting of their achievements. Mastering the Thud, that thundering beast, required aggressiveness, stamina and intelligence. Only Type-A hard charging individuals need apply. Gary wondered how much of the male machismo he observed was real and how much was an act for others.

His internal conflict and duality of emotions, churned in his head. He was proud of his accomplishments. Still, inner doubts persisted. All of his life he had been taught that killing was wrong. Killers were punished. Now, he had helped destroy an enemy storage depot and probably killed enemy soldiers.

Gary wondered if his fellow pilots thought about killing when they went to bed at night.

"Sierra Hotel!" Major Eton radioed the air controller. "That was a shit hot job!"

After landing, Gary stood at the edge of the parking apron next to the maintenance crew chief talking over the plane's condition. All around them, mechanics labored, loading fuel and preparing for the afternoon set of missions. A tractor towing a cart full of bombs, stopped by the plane Gary had just flown.

As the junior officer in the squadron, Gary flew a different F-105 on each mission. Flying a new fighter each time broadened his skill set as he learned to cope with a variety of aircraft idiosyncrasies.

"It's a swell bird," Gary said. "No complaints, no faults."

"That's good, sir," the crew chief said. "She goes back North this afternoon."

"You have any extra?" Gary asked, pointing to the crew chief's cigarette.

"Didn't know you were a smoker."

"I quit, several times, but I need something to steady my nerves."

"You'll be sorry, sir," the crew chief said, offering his pack of Marlboros and a lighter.

Gary lit one and felt the jolt of nicotine and tar hitting his system. What a nasty habit, he thought, as he stood, puffing away.

The flight crew paddy wagon screeched to a halt in front of Gary with Major Foxe at the wheel. The other two men from Gary's just completed mission sat on benches in the back. The pilots walked over to Gary and accepted cigarettes from the crew chief.

"Congratulations," Major Eton said, handing Gary an Aussie bush hat and red and black felt tip ink pens.

"Thank you, sir."

Gary took the hat and the pens, making his first tick mark in black ink on the front band of his newly acquired Go To Hell hat. The pilots wore these hats even though official uniform regulations forbid them. No one hassled the pilots about it because the wing commander wore one.

"First counter mission in Pack 1," Major Foxe said. "You're not a virgin anymore."

"No, sir," Gary said.

"You're doing great," Major Foxe said. "Soon you'll be going with us to Pack 6, up there with the big guns."

"Let me borrow that black pen," Major Eton said. "Number ninety-nine, one more to go."

As the men rode to wing headquarters for debriefing in the back of the pickup, Gary thought about what he just heard. Major Eton had flown ninety-nine missions including eighty-five in Pack 6, the most dangerous part of North Vietnam, near Hanoi. The major had bested the impossible mission completion statistics.

In contrast, Gary had flown one mission in Pack 1. He hoped, in about seven months, to be standing in Major Eton's shoes with one hundred missions behind him. Then he cursed himself for invoking the Bad Karma of hoping for anything while flying in combat over North Vietnam.

WHISKEY TANGO FOXTROT?

_____ 25

Gary Bishop Deale, First Lieutenant, USAF
Southwest of Vinh, North Vietnam
24 February 1967, Counter Mission 3

"THAT FUCKER'S GOT to be down there, close to the river bank," Major Eton radioed. "Keep your eyes open."
　The four planes thundered over the Song Lam River passing over bombed-out road and railroad bridges. Trolling along, the pilots searched for a camouflaged barge used to ferry vehicles, bypassing a bridge resting in the water. Officially, the U.S. Navy operated in this area, known as Pack 2. Air controllers had diverted Gary's flight after Navy pilots reported this hot target.
　"BUGLE CALL WEST OF VINH!" blasted through the static on the Guard radio channel, which the pilots monitored during flight. "FAN SONG UP! SAM LAUNCH!" Emissions from a Fan Song Radar, the guidance system for SA-2 Guideline Surface-to-Air Missiles had been detected by a reconnaissance aircraft.
　"Whiskey Tango Foxtrot?" Major Eton radioed. There had been no reports of SAM sites in this area.
　"SAM LAUNCH! Close! Eight o'clock!" Captain Fromm called out from the left side of Gary's formation.
　"Take it down! Kick it up!" Major Eton said, ordering the flight to descend and increase speed.

Following Major Foxe's plane, Gary pushed his throttle forward and dropped his nose. The shadows on the river from the planes merged into the F-105s.

The fighters skimmed the river, throwing up a spray of water behind them.

Sweat poured from his body. He huffed oxygen from his mask and tensed waiting for an explosion.

A white missile, like a flying telephone pole trailing fire, blasted over Gary's head and exploded into a hill to his right. My first SAM, Gary thought. Too damned close!

"We're going after that SAM," Major Eton radioed, his plane dropping even closer to the river. "Keep it down! Keep it down!"

Gary's pulse hammered in his ears. He inhaled deeply, forcing oxygen into his body. Sweat ran into his eyes.

"Climbing right turn. Burner. Execute!" Major Eton said.

Gary pushed his throttle forward into afterburner and gently pulled back on the stick.

As the fighters climbed toward 10,000 feet, Gary rolled his F-105 upside down. He observed the missile's contrail leading back to a dust cloud hovering over the ground.

Orange and red flashes from large caliber Triple-A fire, spreading a storm of shrapnel, enveloped the planes.

Major Eton and Captain Fromm's planes arced over the top of their climb and dropped.

Gary held his plane tight on Major Foxe's right wingtip.

Major Foxe dived toward the target, rolling his plane upright. He turned slightly to the right, spreading out the formation to provide wider bomb coverage. Gary mirrored his element leader's moves.

As his plane dropped through 8,000 feet in altitude, Gary saw a series of brown trailers covered by camouflage netting. Dish antennas lined the top of one van. The radar, he thought. He rolled slightly right, centered his pipper on the radar van and punched off his bombs. Pulling back on his stick, he felt the G-forces push him down.

Coming off the target at 550 knots, he jinked by dodging and weaving. White puffs from 37 mm Triple-A fire chased him to the west, where he joined with the other three fighters, heading home.

Gary had no doubt. He knew he had just killed twenty or thirty men. On his previous missions, the bombs exploded in the jungle. He had no way of knowing what he had hit. This time, he'd seen the vans and the radar antennas. As he bottomed out of his dive, he'd seen men running. Then the bombs hit. This time, he knew. Seeing soldiers disappearing in orange blasts jarred him. He had become a killer of men.

No matter how much Gary had prepared for this moment over his years of training, his emotions churned. He felt rattled, unglued. The reality of killing someone was much different from bullshitting about it.

After refueling, the planes turned south for home. "Takhli Tower. Cougar Flight of four, request one hundred mission show," Major Eton radioed, asking permission to put on an air show celebrating his last combat mission.

This was the first time Gary had heard about conducting an air show after completing an assignment. He had wondered what happened when a pilot reached the end of his combat tour. He was about to find out.

"Tighten it up," Major Eton radioed.

Gary inched his plane even closer to Major Foxe's right wingtip.

"Burners. Down we go," Major Eton said, lowering his nose.

Gary hung tight to Major Foxe's wing as the four planes made a Foreign Object Damage pass the length of the runway. Exhaust from the four planes blew dust and anything else from the concrete. As the F-105s blasted along, Gary looked up at the glass canopy of the control tower. The men there looked down at him. After completing a series of looping turns over the base, they made one final low pass, noses high with landing gear and flaps extended.

Major Eton ordered the other three planes to land. Once by himself, the major made a series of high speed, low altitude passes combined with acrobatic maneuvers, saving the most dangerous parts for his individual show.

Gary had done many of the maneuvers under Major Hooper's tutelage at Seymour Johnson. But he was impressed with Major Eton's precision and artistry.

Upon landing, Major Eton led a parade of crash trucks, Jeeps and pickup trucks to the parking ramp. It was common practice for a one hundred mission pilot to extend the refueling probe from the F-105. The pilots thought that image of an F-105 sporting an erection sent a specific message—fuck everyone.

After shutting his plane down, Major Eton stood by his F-105 on the ramp, stripped to his skivvies, soaked in champagne. He presented a case of beer to his crew chief. The wing commander gave the major a cigar and said a few words of thanks. Major Eton reached into his flight bag and pulled out his red 333rd Squadron party suit. "Let the games begin," he shouted.

Later, viewing the strike film, Major Eton said, "I don't know why they didn't launch another missile at us. That would've been fun."

Jesus Christ, Gary thought. One SAM proved to be enough for him. He signed his Bombs on Target form and handed it to the debriefer.

"Obviously, they had three more," Major Foxe said, pointing to the screen. The missiles sat on their launchers, poised, ready to go.

"We got 'em," Major Eton said, watching as bombs exploded on one of the launchers. "Captain Fromm's bombs got this one."

"Now for the lieutenant," the sergeant operating the projector said.

The men watched as Gary's bombs dropped and obliterated the trailers.

"Good show," Major Foxe said. "This proves it. You're ready for Pack 6."

Ah shit, Gary thought. Here it comes.

After the films, the pilots sat around the planning table talking about what they had accomplished and how they might have reacted differently to the SAM. "That thing launched too close to us to do anything about it," Major

Eton said, all the while gesturing with his hands simulating their maneuvers. "Climbing meant flying right into that missile's path, so I took us down. Our luck held."

"Enough of this shit for me," Major Eton said, lifting his Go To Hell hat from the floor. The major took a black pen and made a crosshatch over the four tick marks making an even one hundred. "In twelve hours I leave for Bangkok. I'm going home to my wife and kids."

Gary used the same pen to make tick mark number three. It can be done, Gary thought. He was sitting there with a man who had just flown one hundred missions over North Vietnam.

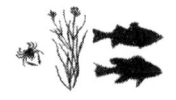

96273

_____ 26

Allison Faith Deale
Seven Springs, North Carolina
February 24, 1967

DURING THE WINTER months, my research work at the lab slowed. While we had stacks of data to keypunch, I spent more time as a teaching assistant than a researcher. I usually returned to our house in Seven Springs on Thursday evening for long weekends. The Cravens collected my mail during the week.

 Each Friday as I approached our mailbox at the end of our driveway, my heart filled with anticipation. I wasn't quite exactly sure where Gary was at this point. But, thought he surely must be in Thailand by now.

 I had received letters and one package from Gary, but they all had been mailed in the Philippines. The package had contained a big surprise, an early gift for my March birthday. Not being able to wait, I opened it to discover a brand new Canon 35 mm camera. The enclosed letter said that he knew I wanted a new camera and he had found a real bargain at the Clark Air Force Base Exchange in the Philippines.

 I tried to be brave, seeing the TV news day after day about the bombing of North Vietnam and the pilots being shot down. Gary's assignment to Takhli, or at least I had convinced myself that it was Takhli, took him into the thick of the action. Very simply, I worried about him and found myself filled with apprehension. Realizing that his assignment was for seven months didn't help my anxiety.

Nervous energy had filled my days since Gary departed. I went to the local hardware store and purchased paint for the inside of our house. On weekends, Carmen helped me with the painting, taking one room at a time. I thought that Gary would really like the pastel blue we used to paint our bedroom, and the pale yellow in the bathroom. I had planned a small garden and the Craven brothers covered it with humus and manure and spaded the ground. "You can plant early crops now," Samuel said. "Potatoes, lettuce and spinach will be okay."

All this and Gary had only been gone three weeks. What am I going to do over the next six months? I thought. I missed Gary helping me prepare dinner, eating at a relaxed pace and talking through our day's activities. Most of all I missed our romantic moments as we made love. I missed the sex: the endearments, the rhythm, the exclamations, the caresses, and the warmth and comfort of his body.

Fortunately, in another month, Carmen and I planned to be out on the Newport River on a daily basis. Once we resumed our research, time would surely move faster.

In the meantime, I walked the neighborhood with my camera, hunting for scenes to paint. I dug through storage boxes and found my watercolor and painting supplies. I had spotted a lovely old church nestled in the trees a short distance away, which offered itself as a subject. Several older Victorian buildings in Seven Springs that in an earlier time were used as inns were very picturesque. While they were past their prime, their survival through the years even though their original intent was lost in time appealed to me. I wanted to paint them also.

Not sure about how often to write Gary, I compromised and began writing letters to him whenever the mood struck. I described the paint job in our house, the Cravens preparing my garden and walking the nearby community searching for subjects to paint. What I really wanted to write was, "God I miss you. I'm so worried about you that I can't stand it." I withheld my true feelings, deciding instead to deal only with the daily grind of keeping house and doing chores.

Please, please, I whispered as I approached the mailbox.

Inside rested three letters and a larger manila mailing envelope, all postmarked APO, San Francisco, CA 96273, the Army Air Force Postal Service code for Takhli. At last, I knew he had arrived at a permanent base.

My heart hammered as I sat in our driveway, opening his first letter by date.

Each of them read the same. The weather and humidity were unbearable already in February. He had flown several maintenance check hops and a mission up North. I had to think for a minute, Laos. Nothing dangerous for him so far.

Gary described the hut he lived in, called a hooch, and the men and women who looked after their living spaces called hooch boys and girls. His hooch girl's name was Helene. He enjoyed being around his fellow pilots and had met one senior officer he really liked, a Major Foxe. That major had taken Gary under his wing, so to speak, introducing him to the life of a combat pilot in wartime.

Inside the manila envelope, I found a cloth patch from the 333rd Tactical Fighter Squadron. A short note from Gary instructed me to add it to his collection.

I read each of his letters several times, cherishing every word. I loved his small precise handwriting. The first word of each paragraph was written in a broad script, setting it off. He signed each letter,

With Love Always

Gary

I'll remember those ZIP code numbers for the rest of my life—96273.

PART 5

War is hell.

—General William Tecumseh Sherman, 1864

IRON BOMBS

Resting in their cradles
on the little carts
they didn't look all that bad,
a dull green color offensive to none.
Sitting inert. Made of iron
and a putty of Tritonal.
Safe up to a point,
a good place to meet for lunch.

Bearing splattered messages
in yellow, red, or white.
EAT THIS!
TO UNCLE HO! YOU LITTLE TURD!
ADIOS! MOTHERFUCKER!
KILROY WAS HERE!
WITH LOVE! L. B. J.!
And,
DON'T FUCK WITH US!

Waiting to be mated with the bird.
A real stud.
And then carried yonder
never to return
from the objective
circled on a map.

Erupting in red and yellow flame,
sending bridges, homes, guns, factories,
kids, soldiers, trucks, men, missiles, pigs,
Communist trees, fine young ladies,
and all their various pieces
helter-skelter into the smoky sky.

Iron Bombs used in some wars
helped carry the day,
pointing to victory as they
laid waste to the land.

Iron Bombs used here,
stacked to the sky,
send messages
which are left unopened or misread.

But Iron Bombs can't see
what the other side sees
other than more of the same.

From the combat diary of Gary Bishop
Deale, First Lieutenant, USAF, 2 June 1967

MIG

27

Gary Bishop Deale, First Lieutenant, USAF
Over the Gulf of Tonkin
9 March 1967, Counter Mission 9

TOPEKA AND WABASH flights, each with four F-105s, departed the tanker orbit, steeply descending to wave level to get under North Vietnamese radar beams. Major Foxe led Wabash flight with Gary as Number 4.

On Gary's previous missions, the fighters had flown over land, first Thailand, then Laos and finally to the target in North Vietnam. Now, the planes flew as low as possible over the Gulf of Tonkin, rapidly approaching the North Vietnamese coast, a new mission profile for him.

As the formation approached land, he saw for the first time several cargo ships anchored offshore, awaiting dock space in Haiphong harbor. According to his pilot friends, these very ships were carrying missiles and shells which would soon be aimed at Gary. Why don't we mine the harbor? Gary wondered. Previously, he had thought the United States was at war, but the ships waiting to unload told him a different story. Maybe that's why Major Hooper back at Seymour called this a half-assed war.

Normally, pilots flew ten learning missions in Pack 1 or Laos before being committed "Downtown," but Major Foxe agreed that Gary was ready after Counter Mission 8, so he found himself nearing Pack 6, ready or not.

Once over land near Cam Pha, a series of open pit coalmines dotted the landscape. The flight turned sharply west toward Kep, one hundred miles inland, and almost immediately ran into clouds and ground fog. A few bursts from enemy Triple-A appeared, but passed quickly behind as the planes neared 540 knots. Gary looked at his pilotage chart and checked the timing lines drawn leading to the target—ten minutes.

The four planes of Gary's flight followed the land contours, porpoising along, climbing and descending while staying as close to the ground as possible. Wisps of ground fog whipped past, at times obscuring the plane just off Gary's left wing.

He rolled his plane a little to the right providing a bit more separation from the Thud to his left flown by Major Strong. His flight weaved and turned, trying to set up an approach to the Kep Rail Yard, their assigned target. He wanted more air between his F-105 and the major's.

Intermittently flying through ground fog and low lying clouds, the pilots looked in vain for anything on the ground resembling a rail line.

Since this mission took the F-105s near Kep Airfield, Major Foxe had warned Gary during mission briefings to be extra vigilant. "Keep your eyes open," Major Foxe said. "Those fucking MIGs from Kep are sneaky bastards."

Gary scanned the sky, doing his job, looking for MIGs.

Just to his right rear, Gary caught a flash of reflected sunlight through the fog. He squinted through the sweat as a plane zoomed by, about a mile to his right, running in and out of clouds. Shaking his head, he felt adrenaline surge through his body. No, it can't be one. He ran through the mental checklist. Sleek delta wing. Smaller than an F-4 Phantom. Silver in color. Not much smoke from the engine. A MIG-21. His first sighting. Shit!

He radioed a warning message to Major Foxe, Wabash Lead.

"Topeka flight, MIG closing on your six o'clock!" Major Foxe said, warning the four planes ahead of him. After lighting his afterburner, the major dropped his nose and turned, leading the flight toward the MIG. The formation ended up just behind and below the enemy plane.

"Rattler in the air!" Major Foxe radioed, transmitting the codename for launching a heat-seeking missile.

Gary didn't understand how Major Foxe reset his switches so fast from BOMBS-DIVE to MISSILE-AAM. Two of the planes in the flight, Major Foxe's and Major Strong's, carried Sidewinder air-to-air heat-seeking missiles, while Gary's and Captain Fromm's, on opposite sides of the formation, carried radar jamming pods.

The missile dropped from the major's outer wing pylon and whooshed away leaving a spiraling smoke trail as the infrared missile homed in on the MIG. The enemy plane disappeared in an orange flash as its fuel exploded.

"Splash one," Major Foxe radioed.

"Sierra Hotel," Colonel Batts, the mission commander, transmitted. "Follow us, we've got the rail line."

After the first flight cleared the target, Major Foxe led his flight directly in and the pilots dropped their bombs. Descending to near ground level, the planes turned southeast toward the coast and the tankers waiting offshore.

According to custom, whenever a pilot achieved one hundred missions North or when a fortunate one shot down a MIG, Major Foxe led his flight of four in a celebratory air show upon reaching Takhli. The F-105s first pass in button-tight formation took them down the runway at ground level. After making several loops and passes over the field, Major Foxe instructed the three pilots of Wabash flight to land.

As Gary touched down on the runway, he saw the major's plane approaching from the opposite end at about 5,000 feet altitude. He knew the plane was moving very fast as he could see the shock wave. As the plane passed overhead, a sonic boom jolted him. Oh, No, Gary thought.

The major just stepped into the shit. Breaking the sound barrier near Takhli was forbidden.

After landing, Major Foxe stood by his F-105 drenched in champagne, a celebration of his fifth enemy plane shot down. On that day, he became an ace, a rare feat. When coupled with the four MIGs he had shot down over Korea and the newest one over Kep, he had accomplished something few pilots did.

Major Foxe pointed his finger at Gary. "You're the one!" the major shouted, spraying champagne Gary's way. "You gave me that fucker to eat alive. I smoked his ass!"

"I never saw that bird until you called it," Major Strong said.

"The son-of-a-bitch went by me like a bat-out-of-hell," Gary said, making a quick motion with his right arm.

"That was fast work with the missile," Major Strong said. "Sierra Hotel!"

"Luck, just luck," Major Foxe said.

"Luck, my ass," Major Strong said.

"Here's the man," Major Foxe said, patting Gary on the back. "This LT's got good eyes. He's good to go!"

"Just doing my job," Gary said, trying not to sound boastful. True he was proud of himself for seeing and calling out the MIG, but he didn't want to get carried away.

Later, Gary sat in his hooch holding his Aussie Go To Hell hat. He took his red felt pen and made a tick by the existing marks, signifying his first mission Downtown and his ninth overall.

The bodies are starting to pile up, Gary thought. He had just seen a man, albeit the enemy, killed. The bombs he had dropped exploded in a rail yard. Surely there were people there. He didn't know how he would ever tell Allison about this. What do I tell her? he wondered. Would she understand?

ASSTHUMPIN'

_____ 28

Gary Bishop Deale, First Lieutenant, USAF
Takhli RTAFB, Thailand
10 March 1967

"YOU HAVE TO understand, I'm just giving you the gist of a royal ass-chewing that went on for twenty minutes," Lieutenant Colonel Foxe said, pacing the floor in Gary's cubicle.

Gary sat at his desk, cigarette dangling from his lips, following with his eyes, his newly promoted friend. There had been a night of debauchery at the club following the great victory. Gary's head hurt and his stomach felt queasy.

"I got called over the wing headquarters way too damned early this morning for what I thought was going to be a minor chewing out. Turns out, Colonel Batts made me turn around to report to a two-star general from Saigon sitting in the shadows. Well, I knew the guy with the stars on his shoulder from way back. He stood me at attention, braced me up stiff and straight."

Lieutenant Colonel Foxe paced excitedly, waving his arms in the air and puffing on his cigarette. "General Swift gave me a real assthumpin', throwing papers into the air, swearing like a drunken sailor and tearing me a new one. Broken china, shattered glass, the Thais are pissed off, hell, I'm pissed off also, the general said. Here's what I'm going to do, he said. He read me a letter of instruction. Then he read me a letter of admonishment. He sat there chewing on me for another ten minutes. I thought a court-martial was next."

The colonel sat on Gary's cot, itching the scar on his left cheek. He tried to keep a straight face, but his mouth twisted into a smile. "You know what the general did next?"

"No, sir," Gary said.

"He tore up the letters. Then he said, I don't have the authority to give you a medal, which you will no doubt get. You're an ace, so I can promote you right here and now, which is what I'm going to do. Lieutenant Colonel Foxe, you have a way of stepping in shit and coming out like a rose. I've known you for what? Eighteen years. You're as good a friend as I ever had. We've lost many a buddy together. I've always thought that if any of our peers shot down five planes, it would be you. Well, the general pins the silver leaves on my shoulder and takes me to the club for a drink. How about that?"

"Amazing," Gary said. "Congratulations, sir."

"Good to go. Let's go get a drink and celebrate."

As the two men walked toward the O Club, Gary felt amazed that he had helped score a great victory. He felt proud and honored to have been a part of the major's, now lieutenant colonel's, achievement. I'm lucky to be here with this great pilot, and to be learning from him, Gary thought.

In the Stag Bar, Gary bought the colonel and himself a double Doctor Jack Black. After a few words in honor of the occasion, the two men tapped glasses and took a sip. God, it's not even noon yet, Gary thought.

The small room was empty except for the Thai barkeep, the colonel and Gary. It was too early for the pilots from the morning mission to have returned and the afternoon briefings were underway. The two men sat at the bar on high stools while the Thai busied himself emptying new glasses from boxes, no doubt replacements for the ones thrown against the wall the previous night. The jukebox whined away in the background, with Tony Bennett wailing about leaving his heart in San Francisco.

Now entering his second month at Takhli and having flown his first mission Downtown, Gary came to realize that fighter pilots had two faces. During his time at the Academy and flight training, he had believed that fighter pilots were tall, lean, smart, respectful, devout, clean-cut and above all, willing to follow orders.

Since Gary had arrived, two F-105s had turned into junk piles in North Vietnam. He had lived the life of a warrior in combat and now had a slightly different perspective. He thought that fighter pilots were coarse drunkards, heavy smokers, foul-mouthed, and borderline contemptuous of the chain of command and the orders they received, which his friends thought originated in a third grade classroom in an elementary school in D.C.

As bad as it was, these same pilots were more than eager to fly combat missions into the heart of North Vietnam.

Worst of all, he had fallen in among them.

IT'S EASY TO GET BURNED

———————————————— 29

Gary Bishop Deale, First Lieutenant, USAF
Red River Valley, North Vietnam
12 March 1967, Counter Number 10

AS THE TWENTY plane strike force crossed the Red River, Gary looked for the landmarks that Major Strong had pointed out on the planning maps. He found "The Bra," where switchbacks in the river formed an unusual shape. To his right at Viet Tri, three rivers flowed together to form the larger Red River. And to his left, the sprawling Yen Bai airbase, home of MIG fighters.

This was his first time using the land approach through Laos to Downtown. Gary scanned looking for distinct geographic features to help him with future navigation in the area. Large puffy white clouds cast shadows on the land. Smoke from cooking fires spiraled upward merging with the perpetual haze lurking over North Vietnam. Orange and red bursts from enemy flak erupted ahead of them. Gary no longer flinched at these distant Triple-A blasts. The close ones, however, still jarred him.

After crossing the river, the formation flew around the northwest side of a towering mountain chain and turned southeast. This was Gary's first view of Thud Ridge, by legend the burial place of many F-105s. According to his fellow pilots, the mountain seemed to draw damaged fighters to it like a magnet.

Using the ridge to hide from SAM radar beams, known to the pilots as terrain masking, the planes rapidly closed on their target, twenty miles or two minutes ahead. Flying at 1,000 feet, the ridgeline towered high above. Just off his right wing, tall rainforest trees swept by. Flak bursts from enemy Triple-A exploded near the planes. Even though they flew low next to the mountain, North Vietnamese gunners fired at them from the valley below.

The lead planes far ahead turned directly toward the target. Partially obscured by smoke, steam and dust, the Thai Nguyen Iron and Steel Plant loomed before them. Large buildings and smokestacks filled a rectangular area, which must have covered hundreds of acres. From a distance, the factory looked like the sprawling Bethlehem Steel complex south of Baltimore, which Gary had flown over on commercial flights. The first air strikes against Thai Nguyen had occurred two days before.

In the past few months, the Americans had begun bombing cement plants, thermal power plants and fertilizer plants located in the Hanoi and Haiphong area. These attacks were designed to increase pressure on the North Vietnamese to stop assisting the guerilla war in South Vietnam.

The American campaign of phased escalation against industrial targets had gradually worked its way north to the area the pilots called Downtown. This priority target, known as Joint Chiefs of Staff Number 76, had finally moved its way to the top of the bombing list.

Built by the North Vietnamese, with technical assistance from the Chinese and Eastern European countries, the steel plant was to be a great leap into the future. With the intention of switching the country away from an agrarian economy, the North Vietnamese in recent years had constructed several industrial projects. These facilities became priority American targets.

Among other products, the steel plant manufactured barges, oil tanks and bridge trusses. The North Vietnamese used these items for military or logistical purposes, making the plant a valuable target.

Ahead of Gary, four formations of F-105s dive bombed the target and then flew away. Major Strong led Gary's flight into the pop-up climb. After arcing over the top, Gary rolled his F-105 upright and selected his aim point at the southwest corner of the industrial complex.

Captain Nick Jeners, his element leader, flew through a large red burst from an antiaircraft shell and continued diving toward their target.

Having been bombed on the previous day, the Thai Nguyen plant appeared to be operating as Gary saw smoke and steam from the various buildings before the bombs from the planes in front of him began exploding.

"DRUM ROLL OVER THAI NGUYEN," the alert call for a SAM launch, blasted from Gary's earphones. Out of the corner of his eye, Gary saw a SAM emerge out of a dust cloud. The missile had an orange tongue of flame trailing behind as it lifted from the ground. Tracking in their direction, Gary couldn't decide if the SAM was aimed at him or Captain Jeners. A second SAM blasted from the ground, also aimed at the two planes.

At this point, Gary and his leader were committed to their bomb run. They could not abort. Chills ran down Gary's spine. He shook his head, trying to steady his nerves. His hands vibrated with stress and tension.

Within seconds, the first missile struck Captain Jeners' F-105 directly in the cockpit canopy, and the plane disappeared in a red flash. Gary felt his stomach roll over. He swallowed, fighting nausea.

Turning his plane slightly to the west to avoid the flaming debris, Gary tried to determine if Captain Jeners had ejected. He rolled back on to the target and centered his pipper on the blast furnace area. The second missile roared by Gary's plane like an express train. He felt the heat from the missile's flaming tail through his canopy.

After punching his bombs off, Gary pulled back on his stick, fighting to pull out of the dive. While dangerous, he rolled the plane into a turn back toward the plant, trying to see if he could detect a parachute. All he could see were flaming pieces of wreckage tumbling from the sky, and no chute.

Rolling his F-105 toward Thud Ridge, Gary scanned for the remaining two planes from his flight, then radioed to Major Strong, his flight leader. "Buick 3 got hit by a SAM over the plant and went down."

"Any chute?"

"Negative. No beeper either."

"Fuck!"

We fly alone, Gary thought. We fight alone. And, most scary of all, sometimes we— —

He couldn't bring himself to think the words. But they slipped out anyway. Die alone, he whispered to himself.

The previous two minutes were totally crazy. Now he fully realized the individuality, randomness and finality of death. Why didn't that second missile hit me? Gary wondered. Why am I still alive?

Gary blinked back tears. He had never seen anyone die like that before. After a moment, tears of futility, frustration and rage streamed down his cheeks.

Later that night, Gary sat at his desk thinking about what he had seen over the Thai Nguyen plant. Up until that moment he had enjoyed preparing and executing the assigned missions. The socializing and comradeship with his fellow pilots had been so much fun. Now that he had seen a pilot blown out of the sky, all was different.

Hearing about it and actually seeing it happen were two different worlds. Gary had seen the darkness at first hand and it scared him.

THE FIVE Fs

_____ 30

Gary Bishop Deale, First Lieutenant, USAF
Takhli RTAFB, Thailand
13 March 1967

EARLY THE FOLLOWING morning, Gary sat at his desk listening to Radio Australia sign off with the traditional "Habanera" from Bizet's *Carmen.* Rain pounded on the metal roof. Jotting notes in his diary, he thought of the new words and phrases he had learned since arriving at Takhli. Somehow, he hoped to fit them into a poem he had been working on for a few days.

Aside from alcohol, smoking and running, Gary found that writing poetry helped him best cope with the stress and anxiety of flying combat missions. He had been writing poetry since taking a creative writing class in high school. Now I understand, he thought, what that writing teacher was talking about. "Writing poetry helps soothe the soul," she had extolled.

The screen door at the other end of the hooch opened. Quiet footsteps echoed down the hallway set off by the vertical lockers. The person paused outside his little cubicle.

"Gary, have you had breakfast?" Lieutenant Colonel Foxe asked.

"No, sir," Gary said.

Foxe stood with water dripping off his rain coat. He was soaked up to his knees, though getting wet in rainstorms made little difference. With the oppressive humidity, everything was always damp anyway.

"I guess you know there are no early missions." the colonel said, taking off his raincoat and hanging it on a hook.

"Sergeant Heydt stopped by to tell us a while ago. I was just listening to some music and doing some writing. I'll go with you."

"What are you writing?"

"A poem. The title is THE FIVE Fs."

"May I read it?"

Gary hesitated. He wrote his notes in a small loose-leaf notebook, which according to regulations, he should not be doing.

"I can see what you have there. I know, and you know, that pilots aren't supposed to keep combat diaries. But everyone does. I won't rat you out."

"I'm still tweaking it," Gary said, handing the small notebook to the colonel.

He sat on Gary's cot and began reading.

"This is really good," Lieutenant Colonel Foxe said, rubbing the scar on his left cheek. "You have talent. You should read this at the club." He handed the book back to Gary.

"I don't know about that," Gary said, closing the book and locking it into his footlocker. "Some of those words are blasphemous."

"True. But we all say them." The colonel paused. "What happened up North yesterday? I hear your element leader got hammered. Nick Jeners, was that the guy?"

"Yes, sir. He got picked off by a SAM while going down the chute. I was right behind him. I watched the whole thing."

"Did he know it was coming?"

"Yes, he was evading and jinking but couldn't shake the damned thing off. I don't understand it. He turned sharply into the missile just as you are supposed to do and it still nailed him."

"That's your first one, isn't it?"

"Yes, sir." Gary swallowed hard. "I still haven't processed it. I've heard about it. But this is the first time that someone got shot down while flying right next to me." Gary sighed. "Just like that, gone."

"Believe me, it's not easy to deal with. I can't even count the number of times I've seen someone get nailed."

"How do you cope?" His words sounded quiet against the noise of the rain on the roof.

For a moment the colonel didn't answer. And then solemnly he said, "Like your poem says there, with frustration and finality. Even if he's alive, he's not coming back soon. You have to shake it off. Moving on, we call it. No matter how much you lament the poor soul, you can't change anything."

Foxe paused and lit a cigarette. "Remember what I told you a while back. You have to isolate things like this. Take these bad memories, seal them in a box in your mind, and continue with your mission. Otherwise, you won't cope."

"I can't clear that scene out of my mind." Gary shook his head. "His F-105 simply disappeared in an orange flash. The second missile went by me like a bat out of hell."

"You say he turned into the SAM and it still hit him."

"I don't understand. He did everything he was supposed to do."

"Those little gomers up north must have something new up their sleeve, unless it was pure luck. We'll have to really watch for this in the future. Did you know that was the 213th F-105 we've lost over North Vietnam and Laos?"

"I didn't know the exact number." The magnitude surprised Gary. He knew it had to be a lot, but 213?

The colonel stood and reached for his coat. "Let's go see what No Hab has cooked up for breakfast."

No Hab was the generic name for the waiters and waitresses at the Officers' Club where the pilots ate their meals and drank various liquid refreshments. They asked for a variety of items for breakfast and the stock reply was No Hab for anything other than scrambled eggs and bacon. Sometimes it was No Hab for even that.

Gary and Lieutenant Colonel Foxe made their way to the club walking through the downpour. The clouds were beginning to thin and the rain was gradually decreasing.

"You think it's going to rain?" asked Foxe.

"This sunshine is great," Gary said. "I'm working on my tan."

"That's all this world needs, another Troy Donahue."

"It does look as though we'll be flying this afternoon though," Gary said as the sun rays poked through the rain clouds.

As they walked into the dining room, Lieutenant Colonel Foxe asked if Gary truly felt prepared for flying over North Vietnam. Had his training been sufficient to execute the task at hand?

"I think that the flight training at Seymour did prepare me for flying combat missions," Gary said. "The four years at the Academy certainly gave me the discipline I need."

The colonel, an ROTC man, snorted at that.

Gary smiled at the colonel's demonstration of contempt.

"Today, sunny side possible," No Hab proudly proclaimed as he announced a special treat for the day. This was one of the few times Gary could remember when you could actually order real eggs rather than something out of a can.

It didn't take them long to vote for the sunny side proposition. No Hab walked away smiling, proud at having accomplished his task of getting rid of more of the fresh eggs before they spoiled.

They were halfway through breakfast when Gary looked up and said, "There's a personal favor I have to ask of you."

The colonel nodded, showing his understanding of what Gary was going to say.

Gary maintained a positive attitude and avoided becoming obsessed about the possibility of death or getting shot down and captured. But the events he witnessed the day before had shaken him to his core.

He had filled all of the forms required by the Air Force in case of mishap. Believing that he had to go beyond the official notification process, he had decided to ask someone to tell Allison in person what had occurred in the event the worst did happen.

Pilots believed that nothing bad would ever happen to them. They thought they were too good a pilot to crash or get shot down. Bad things only happened to the other poor slob. They had to believe that down deep down in their very soul. Otherwise, it would be too difficult to climb into the cockpit of an airplane loaded with fuel and bombs.

Gary rationalized his mission as being honorable in support of his country. He couldn't let his friends, his fellow pilots down. How else could he strap on an airplane loaded with fuel and bombs and fly 600 miles to get shot at? But the events of the previous day had emphatically shown how random it was for pilots to get shot down. Now, he fully understood the statements made at Seymour that it was statistically impossible to complete one hundred missions over North Vietnam.

"I saw something yesterday which really spoke to me," Gary said. "I saw a very good pilot die. I hope that doesn't happen to me. If something bad were to occur, I want you to promise me that you will find out happened. I want you to go tell Allison. She will go out of her mind if she doesn't know the truth."

"You're smart to think about what you will want done," Lieutenant Colonel Foxe said. "Colonel Batts will look after my affairs. I will look after him if the crap hits the fan. Yes, I promise I will go tell her face to face, if I'm able to."

Gary walked to his hooch alone after breakfast. Sounds of mission preparation carried over from the flight line. Trucks and carts rushed up and down the ramp carrying fuel tanks and bombs. Just another day in paradise, Gary thought.

The humidity dampened his flight suit and body. Fear disquieted his soul. Before he had departed North Carolina, Gary had told Allison that he wasn't afraid. Now he knew that he was.

Sorting through his mail, Gary found two letters from Allison. He had attempted writing earlier in the morning, but could not put into words what he had seen the previous day. Sitting at his desk, he stared at the photograph of Allison and himself on the beach. She's so beautiful, he thought. I hope I live long enough to see her again. He wondered if invoking Bad Karma by wishing for anything would bite him in the ass.

He had seldom written any details of missions, keeping his letters to benign subjects. Gary described the base, the people of the local Thai village of Takhli Town and the kinds of plants, birds and snakes he had observed. Somehow, he would have to relate the death of another pilot without making it too specific. He didn't want to scare her.

Having danced around the truth in his previous letters, he thought that in the end Allison would see through his deception and realize that he was scared.

While her letters had always been positive, he began to sense an undertone in the writing. He thought that she really missed him and was worried about him. But maybe the separation bothered her more than she had revealed.

He picked up his pen and began to write.

13 March
Dearest Allison
There's something I have to tell you. I saw one of the pilots killed in action yesterday.

CAPTAIN JAMES REDY

_____ 31

Gary Bishop Deale, First Lieutenant, USAF
355th Tactical Fighter Wing Planning Room
Takhli RTAFB, Thailand
15 March 1967

TWO DAYS LATER, Gary sat at a planning table at wing headquarters, with the Frag TWX (mission order) and pilotage charts before him as he plotted attack profiles. Lieutenant Colonel Foxe had suggested that Gary "volunteer" to do this job. Since he happened to be a lowly lieutenant, a suggestion carried the weight of an order.

The large table dominated the room. A detailed map of North Vietnam filled the table, covered by a Plexiglas sheet. Enlarged aerial photographs of targets, past, present and future, were taped to the walls. The pilots studied the map and photographs as they prepared for missions.

"Some jock from Korat got hammered today near Phuc Yen Airbase," Major Strong said, flipping through a bundle of mission summary messages. "388th Tactical Fighter Wing, 34th TFS, one Captain Redy."

"Sir, Captain James Redy?" Gary asked, a quiver in his voice.

"Roger!" Major Strong looked at Gary.

"Jesus, I knew him," Gary said, rising to look at the casualty TWX. "The Philippine rangers roped us together over at Clark E and E a month ago. We shared a bamboo cage for two days."

"Knocked down by Triple-A. The Thud exploded. No chute. No beeper. No nothing."

"Fuck!"

Gary finished his task and retired to the Officers' Club for a quick beer or two, his limit because he had to get up at 0300 to prepare for his mission the next day. Having just plotted everything, he already knew the target. Joining Lieutenant Colonel Foxe and a couple other pilots at a table, Gary related the story of his now lost friend.

He raised his third beer in salute. "To Captain James Redy," he said. Those near him had heard his story, so they also raised their glasses to another good man now gone, blown to bits by a SAM. Well over his limit prior to flying the next day, Gary begged off the fun and games yet to come at the club and headed for his hooch.

After showering, he sat in his cubicle at the desk. A ceiling fan emitted a slight thump as it stirred the air. Down the hall, a vet was whispering lessons learned to a new guy. No one made much noise at this time of day because some pilots flying the early missions were already asleep.

At quiet times like this, he thought of Allison. He felt very close to her, even though she was twelve time zones away. After rereading her recent letters, he thought that while she sounded positive, there was something in the tone, the way that she expressed herself, that made him believe she wasn't coping too well.

Opening his footlocker, he removed his diary, found the poetry section and wrote the word, ONCE.

A few beers sometimes opened his mind. Self-medication added clarity and vision. The rough outline of a poem wandered in and out of his brain. Gary began chasing words.

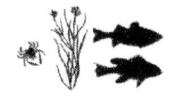

READING BETWEEN THE LINES

_____ 32

Allison Faith Deale
Beaufort, North Carolina
March 20, 1967

AFTER RETURNING TO my apartment from the lab, I ate a takeout sub sandwich and drank a beer while skimming a base newspaper from Seymour Johnson. A short article caught my attention. The American State Department and the Thai Government had jointly announced that bases in Thailand, including Takhli with its F-105s, were being used in the bombing campaign against North Vietnam. Before, this had been a big secret. I pumped my fist in the air, celebrating the fact that I had previously figured out exactly where Gary was. Despite his repeated assertions that he was stationed somewhere in SEA, I had decided that he was at Takhli. This article confirmed my belief.

I went outside to my small balcony carrying a cold Bud. While the remainder of my apartment was basic and plain, the balcony offered a lovely scene, the town of Beaufort, with its historic houses and churches. In the distance, I had a view of the Beaufort inlet and beyond that, the Atlantic.

Taking a sip of beer, I removed a letter from my pocket that Gary had written a week before. I had already read it, but wanted to read it again.

In his opening lines, he said that he had seen one of the pilots die on March 12.

Reading the letter several times, I found scant facts. While I realized that he couldn't write anything specific because a censor looked over every letter, I wanted more details. What happened, what was the target, how did it happen, and who was the pilot? Disclosing only the date of the incident provided little to work with.

After deciding that I wouldn't find any more information in the letter, I looked through the stack of base newspapers and local papers I brought with me from Seven Springs to see if there were any articles which may apply.

Several news stories reported large bombing raids on the Thai Nguyen Iron and Steel Plant on March 10, 11 and 12. A report stated that one unnamed F-105 pilot had been shot down on March 12 and declared missing.

I read Gary's letter again trying to correlate the few facts. I realized that I had to read between the lines of his letter. I knew Gary very well, how he reasoned and what he believed.

What I sensed were feelings of frustration, futility and the finality of death. And, for the first time since our marriage, fear.

I took a long drink of the beer. At that moment, I feared for Gary's life. I wanted to be with him, to hold him, to comfort him and to make love with him. What must it be like, I thought, to see a friend blown to pieces right in front of you?

STEEL TIGER

_____ 33

Gary Bishop Deale, First Lieutenant, USAF
In flight over central Laos
12 April 1967

GARY HAD COMPLETED eighteen missions over North Vietnam during the previous month. Now, nearly in mid-April and two days after Easter, he flew over central Laos beside Major Strong, his element leader.

Reconnaissance aircraft sent ahead of the bomb-laden fighters reported storms with no bottom to the clouds over their primary target in North Vietnam. And so, the strike force of sixteen planes headed for their secondary target in North Vietnam near the Ban Karai Pass.

Trying to protect the Ho Chi Minh Trail, the transportation network leading to South Vietnam, the North Vietnamese had placed large numbers of antiaircraft weapons in southern Laos. Knowing that the Americans repeatedly bombed the trail network, the enemy placed their guns along the roads and bridges. Using trucks, bicycles, elephants, carts and coolies on foot, the North Vietnamese transported munitions and supplies to the south. The American chain of command separated Laos into different operating areas, each with its own particular rules of engagement.

Gary followed the gaggle of airplanes. Being the most junior officer, he became tail-end-Charlie, the last plane in the formation. The F-105s flew through towering clouds as they crossed southern Laos. As the planes approached the North Vietnamese border, the clouds thickened. Flying through continuous clouds gave Gary a mild case of the creeps, because the risk of mid-air collisions increased. Major Strong's plane, just beyond his left wing, appeared and disappeared into the swirling mist.

The cloud bank turned into a white wall. No way in hell are we going to fly into that mess, Gary thought, just as Colonel Broughton, the mission commander, changed the plan of the day.

"Eagle Mission, Lead. Chain Saw's scrubbed. No joy here. Divert to Fat City."

Flipping the pages of the notebook strapped to his right thigh, Gary located the reference to Fat City, the codename used to switch to their tertiary target. The mission briefing had set up the target, call signs and code words. As the briefing officer laid out the plan, pilots took notes on lineup cards, which they then placed in plastic sleeves in the small notebook. The notebook also contained necessary information including tanker rendezvous, emergency procedures, aircraft checklists and airfield approach charts.

Fat City called for the larger group to separate into two units of eight F-105s each. Breaking away, the other eight fighters led by Colonel Broughton headed farther south in Laos to lay waste to a ferry landing. Gary's group reversed course and headed west to the tankers to fill up again. After air-to-air refueling, the plan called for them to head north to the Steel Tiger Operating Area in east-central Laos near the North Vietnamese border.

The American interdiction campaign of bombing logistical facilities in Laos consisted of three separate geographic operations: Barrel Roll, Steel Tiger and Tiger Hound. These bombing programs aimed at stopping, or as the pilots more realistically thought, reducing, the flow of men and munitions from North Vietnam through Laos to South Vietnam.

Each of the men Gary flew with made a mockery of the interdiction campaign. To them it was a big joke, albeit a deadly one. Many pilots had been shot down over the Ho Chi Minh Trail.

His friends all had a clear vision of what it was like using a high performance jet fighter against men wearing flip-flops walking through the jungle, or individual trucks winding down some God-forsaken mud-rutted road. Moving along at 500 knots, even the best pilot had little hope of doing anything except stirring up the mud or knocking down Communist trees. Gary took at least some pleasure knowing that every tree in this part of Laos was Communist.

True, every now and then a dumb iron bomb did hit something, which blew up. But for the most part, they just rearranged dirt. From all that he had seen, Gary thought perhaps one bomb out of one hundred dropped in interdiction strikes hit a worthwhile target.

Still, the enemy on the ground shot at them the whole time, turning the mission handed to them, albeit a stinking Dog Shit one, into a sometimes deadly encounter. It seemed to Gary that the "gomers" had better results than the pilots did. More days than not, he summed the score as LITTLE BASTARDS ON THE GROUND 1; USAF 0.

Colonel Batts led his group of eight planes to the tankers for their second AAR. The new target required flying north. They had already burned half their fuel load since leaving the tankers, having gone north, then south, and now northwest again.

The planes maneuvered around and through the towering clouds. At times, the ground appeared through gaps in the white mass. Having no other way to do it, the pilots charged straight ahead. Flying formation through cloud banks tested them, though they flew through such weather every day and were used to it.

Much of the flying in Thailand, Laos, and sometimes North Vietnam ended up with the wingtip ten feet away disappearing. Gary tried to keep a stable hand and prayed that his wingman held a steady course. They flew too close together to make mistakes.

After refueling, the planes headed for the part of Laos offering the best hope for getting rid of their bombs. If storms obscured the alternate target, a radar controller located on a secret snake-infested hilltop in Laos would direct them. A free-fire zone on the Ho Chi Minh Trail near Mu Gia Pass would be used to dump their bombs, no doubt killing more Communist trees.

At the preflight briefing, Lieutenant Colonel Foxe prepared the pilots in his flight for the alternatives. Changing the ground location where the bombs struck didn't matter much to Gary. He followed the leader and put his bombs in the same spot on the ground as the man in charge.

The tertiary target that day found its place on the mission Frag Order after being identified on film from an earlier photo reconnaissance mission. Because of various peace treaties, the UN had ironically identified Laos as a neutral nation. For that reason, all missions over Laos were secret.

Gary and the rest of the pilots didn't buy Laotian neutrality for one minute. Somebody shot at them on every flight. "Those bastards on the ground shooting at us sure aren't neutral," Lieutenant Colonel Foxe had said after Gary's first flight over Laos. "I'm not neutral when I'm dropping bombs on their heads. What about all those goddamned trucks driving down the trail? I just don't buy all that neutral shit."

As part of his preparation for the mission, Gary had read the message describing the target known as Fat City and also looked at the reconnaissance photographs. The flimsy TWX message stated that several structures and fuel tanks had been identified in a wooded area with extensive vehicle tracks. A set of tracks led to a cave entrance in a karst escarpment. At least two Antiaircraft Artillery (Triple-A) sites were located near the facility, increasing the odds that it was a legitimate target.

Gary had decided that the photo interpreters who had found the target nailed it on the head. The area believed to be a cave looked very interesting. He hoped to be the one who nailed it.

On the way to their target, the fighters swooped from one cloudbank to the next. Gary watched the tip of his element leader's wing and kept his eyes on the instruments.

Colonel Batts checked in with Hillsboro, the code name for the command aircraft orbiting over Laos. After relating their status, the colonel asked for link up information for the Forward Air Controller (FAC), known as Invader 6. The F-105 formation turned east toward the Laotian town of Mahaxay.

One of the planes in the lead flight spotted their controller who was flying an A-26, a twin engine propeller driven bomber. "Falcon Lead, 3. Tallyho on Invader 6 at two o'clock low."

The conversation turned serious.

"Invader 6, Falcon Lead," Colonel Batts radioed. "Visual on a black A-26."

"Falcon Lead, Invader 6," the FAC replied. "You have me."

The FAC pilot radioed his rundown on the target giving weather and terrain information. "Smoke and haze in the valleys. Winds light. Valley runs east–west with valley ground floor elevation 1,200 feet. Steep karst ridges both north and south of target going up to 2,500 feet. NKP barometer is 29.95. Do me a favor; don't push too low today."

Gary checked his altimeter setting to make sure that it was correct. The ground information and barometric pressure relayed to pilots enabled them to determine bomb release altitude to avoid antiaircraft fire. The altimeter recorded altitude in feet above sea level, referred to as indicated altitude. In the heat of battle, pilots at times forgot to factor in ground elevations, thus exposing themselves to intense flak. Sometimes, pilots fixated on the target and dropped their bombs so low they had no hope of pulling out. His friends referred to this major *faux pas* as controlled flight into terrain, or airplane meets ground and ground wins.

The FAC pilot had flown over the target earlier and seen activity. He told the F-105 pilots to expect Triple-A fire.

"Mu Gia Pass is just to the north so don't venture up there too far. Suggest bomb runs from east to west. There are SAMs just over the border so watch it. Best bail out area is thirty miles west or across the Mekong."

A dirt road emerged from the clouds to Gary's north, snaking through the Mu Gia Pass from North Vietnam into Laos. Talk about hell on earth, he thought. The Mu Gia Pass had a bad rep. North Vietnamese gunners shot down enough airplanes there to scare the shit out of any pilot. This is not a nice place, Gary thought. Too many pilots had been shot down near Mu Gia, putting the fear of God into the ones who came after them.

Trying to use the steep mountain terrain as a natural barrier, the Americans regularly bombed the Mu Gia, Nape and Ban Karai Passes to create chokepoints.

Mu Gia Pass looked like the face of the moon, pock-marked with bomb craters. Strikes by B-52 strategic bombers, which carried one-hundred bombs each, had left behind strings of bomb craters. Their bombing chewed up the mud and knocked down trees. North Vietnamese peasants used picks and shovels to fill the holes in the road. What a waste of bombs, Gary thought, although he had recently dropped a few there himself.

On every mission like this, Gary thought of his favorite movie *Thunder Road*. That film portrayed the interdiction program against moonshine (devil's dew) in Appalachia. Robert Mitchum starred in the movie and sang the title song. Gary liked the parts of the song about thunder being his engine and how his engine roared. He didn't care much for the line in the chorus where the devil got the hero first.

The federal officers portrayed in the film had about as much success stopping the devil's dew as American efforts had accomplished thus far to stop the flow of men and supplies down the Ho Chi Minh Trail. Those *Thunder Road* good old boys with their fast cars and hot babes created quite a stir among Gary's friends in the late 50's.

"Falcon, Lead. Arm up."

Gary's reverie came to a quick end. It was time to face the flak. Flipping the switches on the panel controlling bomb release, he set up for BOMBS—DIVE and checked the instrument lights.

Colonel Batts directed Gary's flight to attack first with two of the planes doing flak suppression.

"Hawk Flight, Lead," Lieutenant Colonel Foxe, Gary's flight commander said. "Hawk 3 and 4 go in first and hit those flak sites going east to west. Hawk 2, we're taking the woods right by the road. Our run will be south to north for a change in attack direction. Watch those fucking hilltops."

Gary hated flak suppression. But that was what he had just been ordered to do. Going nose to nose with Triple-A spooked him.

"Invader 6. We're ready."

Lieutenant Colonel Foxe turned his flight away from Colonel Batts' formation and took a sweeping turn to the south. Hawk 1 and 2 turned more to the south while Major Strong and Gary headed east.

The A-26 suddenly banked to the left and dived straight for the ground. Triple-A shells began exploding around the A-26. The pilot fired two White Phosphorous rockets and pulled up trailing smoke.

"Invader 6 is hit. Fuck! They got my navigator."

Gary trailed behind Major Strong, his element leader. The two planes turned north and then west, approaching the target marked by the two Willie Peter rockets fired by the A-26.

The major's afterburner lit, and he began climbing. Gary pushed his throttle to the burner détente and eased back on the control stick to begin a pop-up climb. Gary rolled the plane upside down so he could keep his eyes on the other F-105 lining up on the leftmost flak site and watch the ground at the same time. He pulled back on the stick to put the nose down and began his dive.

Rolling his plane right-side up as the F-105 began to drop, Gary lined up his pipper sight on the right Triple-A position. Six bombs dropped off Major Strong's plane. His leader then began to bottom out of his dive well above the karst. Gary ignored the white and gray puffs from exploding shells outside his canopy and kept the pipper squarely in the middle of the circle of guns. Flak bursts on his first few missions scared the hell out of him. After being shot at on every mission, he no longer blinked. Except for the close ones, which caused his stomach to roll.

With one slight rudder correction, Gary punched the red button on the stick. While too late to do anything about it, he wished he had carried a load of cluster bombs, which contained hundreds of small bomblets, to drop on the little bastards. But the load for their primary target had been iron bombs. That was what he had.

After pulling back on the stick and rolling the plane to the right, he sharply jinked to the left, and then back to the right to throw off the aim of the gunners on the ground who had suddenly gotten a good taste of Tritonal and hot iron as his bombs exploded.

Finding himself pinned back in the seat from the G-Forces, Gary's plane turned and bottomed out from the dive. He was sweating profusely. One quick breath followed another as he sucked oxygen through his mask. His heartbeat raced. He felt the slight sensation of blackness and light-headedness from the excessive G-forces exerted upon his body.

As he climbed, Gary looked over his shoulder to see both flak sites enveloped in smoke, fire and dust. Tough shit on you guys, he thought. He picked out his leader's exhaust trail and pointed his aircraft in that direction.

Gary looked back to see Lieutenant Colonel Foxe and Captain Fromm drop their bombs on the truck park and climb away.

Colonel Batts' flight of four F-105s dived on the truck park in echelon formation, the planes arranged in a diagonal. Twenty-four bombs dropped into the target area, some of them centered on the cave entrance. The explosions threw trees and dirt into the air. After that, a series of secondary explosions flashed, including one large blast, which appeared to blow away part of the side of the escarpment.

Major Strong radioed Lieutenant Colonel Foxe and told him that the FAC plane had taken a hit from flak.

Lieutenant Colonel Foxe said. "Didn't hear it with all the yelling. We'd better find him. Did he crash? Do you see him?"

"Negative," Major Strong said. "I have a blip on the radar about ten miles southwest."

Lieutenant Colonel Foxe passed the information on to Colonel Batts.

Gary spotted a smoke trail and called it out to Lieutenant Colonel Foxe. The A-26 appeared ahead of Gary. While he didn't see any fire, the right propeller of the A-26 hung motionless and smoke streamed from the engine. Pointing to his leader and at the damaged plane, Gary tapped his helmet, meaning no radio transmission from the twin-engine bomber

Just then, Gary faintly heard something on the Guard Channel. A static buzz covered up most of the transmission.

"Mayday. ---US ---craft thi--- Bron---3."

Oh shit, Gary thought, what else can happen? He realized that he had overheard someone on the Guard radio channel yelling for help. He flipped through his notebook looking for the call sign Bronco 3.

There it was, written at the early morning briefing. Colonel Broughton had announced that a photographic reconnaissance pilot flying a RF-101, call sign Bronco 3, had disappeared on a mission over Tchepone, Laos, southeast of his current location. Gary put the story together and decided that this guy needed help.

Immediately, he punched the Guard channel button on his radio and slowly transmitted his message.

"Bronco 3, Hawk 4. I hear you."

"Ha—4. Mayday! Help m----."

"Bronco 3, Hawk 4. Keep talking."

Setting up his radio directional finder to trace the source of Bronco 3's transmission, Gary concentrated on what the other pilot said.

"----4. Bronco 3. ---down ----day. ----miles north of ---Crotch. I've ---- running all night."

"Bronco 3, Hawk 4. Got you! Hang on. I'll be right back."

Tracking a bearing from the transmission, Gary figured the pilot on the ground at about 120 degrees or southeast of his present location. Plus, the guy informed him that he was north of Tchepone, known by pilots as the Crotch. The North Vietnamese had placed many Triple-A sites around the town, making it a deadly place for American pilots.

Flipping back to the strike frequency, he called his boss. "Hawk Lead, 4. Did you catch that on Guard?"

"Hawk Lead," Lieutenant Colonel Foxe responded. "Only part of it. What's up?"

"I picked up a Mayday from Bronco 3, that photo jock they briefed us on this morning. He's down on the ground southeast of us."

"Hawk 4, Lead. You've been talking to the guy so you and Hawk 3 head down that way. I'll stay with the FAC."

"Falcon Lead, Hawk Lead," Lieutenant Colonel Foxe said. "Did you hear this?"

"Hawk Lead, Falcon Lead," Colonel Batts said. "Affirmative. Hawk 4, keep talking to that guy. Ask him questions. What's his story?"

"Hawk 4," Gary said. "Will do."

Colonel Batts radioed Hillsboro, the command aircraft informing them that Bronco 3 had been heard from. "I'm calling a RESCAP," Colonel Batts said.

A pilot on the ground needed help. A RESCAP, the code name for a Rescue Combat Air Patrol, meant that all air assets available suddenly had a new mission.

Every pilot had a hand written card on file at his home base for authentication purposes. This piece of paper recorded several miscellaneous facts about the pilot's life: his favorite dog, his mother's maiden name, his favorite baseball team, his favorite movie, his favorite teacher, or the color of his wife's hair. Interrogation of the pilot on the ground using those questions and the proper answers made sure everything was kosher and ensured he was not under duress—or to put it bluntly, to ascertain whether the rescue forces were being led into a trap.

Gary knew one thing for sure. According to his friends, very few pilots shot down and on the ground in this part of Laos were recovered unless they were picked up within the first twenty-four hours. There was a strong belief that the unfortunate ones simply ended up dead.

Less than five minutes after the A-26 had fired its spotting rockets, the target ceased to exist with many secondary explosions as ammunition and fuel tanks blew up. Fire and smoke climbed into the sky. Forty-eight bombs had dropped on the target. One American plane suffered damage. The navigator in the A-26 took some hits.

Gary thought this mission was a tossup. Now they had a chance to save Bronco 3, so maybe there was still hope for the day. Somewhere on the ground just to the south of his position, an American pilot needed help.

RESCAP

_____ 34

Gary Bishop Deale, First Lieutenant, USAF
Twenty miles southeast of Mahaxay, Laos
12 April 1967

GARY DID WHAT the colonel said. Punching the Guard button on his radio, he called for the pilot on the ground. While Gary didn't know the specific information on Bronco 3, he decided to ask the man general questions.
 "Bronco 3, Hawk 4. I'm back. I have questions."
 "Hawk 4, Bronco 3. Roger. Mayday!"
 "Where are you from?"
 "Louisiana. Cajun country!"
 Call signs went by the wayside. Gary knew the voice by now, so he wanted to keep it short and get information.
 "Roger that. What do they call that big city by the river?"
 "New Orleans, man. The Crescent City. The Big Easy!"
 "What's the name of the river?"
 "The Mississippi. The big muddy."
 "Roger. What's the name of their big party?"
 "Mardi Gras, man. Lots of beads and shit there. Women, too."
 "Roger. Got all that. We're coming your way. Yell if you hear us fly by."

The six F-105s from Falcon and Hawk flights formed up and headed southeast. Colonel Batts led the formation while Gary continued talking with the man, trying to keep his hopes alive.

"Hawk 4, Bronco 3. I just heard you go by to the east."

Colonel Batts began a sweeping 180 degree turn to the right pointing his plane toward the northwest. Holding formation, the flight followed the colonel, paralleling the track they had just flown down, but five miles farther west.

"Here you come. Here you come. You just went over me," Gary heard over his radio. He looked down at the ground and marked the location in his memory. Oh man, Gary thought. I hope we get this pilot before the enemy gets there.

"Falcon Lead, Hawk 4. Did you get that? We just went by that switchback in that stream."

Colonel Batts stated that he had fixed the location and was calling the rescue force, giving them directions. He began a large circling orbit about five miles west of the pilot on the ground, keeping some distance away from where the downed man was hiding.

"Bronco 3, Hawk 4," Gary radioed. "Where are you? Are you alone? Any bad guys there?"

"I'm on top of a karst ridge. I'm alone. There are some people yelling down over the hill."

"Roger. Sit tight."

Gary turned with the formation, trying to maintain a visual sighting of the position on the ground where the pilot waited, while talking with the man. His pulse raced, and he was so excited that he almost forgot to breathe.

"Bronco 3, Hawk 4. Hold on. The Sandies are close. Just a few more minutes."

"Copy. I don't hear anyone right now."

"Falcon Lead, Sandy Lead," the commander of the rescue force radioed. "Visual. I've got you."

"Sandy Lead, Falcon Lead. Roger. We got a fix on this guy as we flew past. Down that valley, there's a big switchback in the stream. He's right near that on top of some karst. He says there are troops in the area."

"Falcon Lead, Sandy Lead. Copy. I assume command of this RESCAP." At that point, Sandy took control. They were going in, wasting no time.

Sandy Flight, with four heavy single-engine propeller-driven A-1 fighters flew past Gary's F-105. He cheered. The Sandy pilots used their massive ordnance load to clear the way for the rescue helicopters.

Sandy Lead began talking with the downed pilot on Guard. The rescue unfolded. Flying along the karst ridge, the four A-1s dropped to tree top level. Two Jolly Green HH-3 rescue helicopters arrived and began a low orbit below where the F-105s circled.

"Fire a pencil flare now," Sandy Lead radioed.

A red streak emerged from the trees.

"I got you on top of the karst escarpment," Sandy 1 said.

"Roger that."

"Okay. I have questions," Sandy Lead said. "What was your favorite cat's name?"

"I never had a cat."

"Copy. What is your favorite car?"

"My 64 Corvette."

"What was your favorite dog's name?"

"Nipper."

"Copy. Is your favorite dog alive?"

Gary suspected they had arrived at the payoff question. If the pilot said yes, then he was under duress. If he said yes, even though it may be a little white lie, then the whole scene was probably a trap. That meant the enemy had the pilot, using him as bait. If he said no, even though that may be a lie in real life, then he was free and clear. Every pilot had a question like this on their little card. Gary looked at his own card every day to make sure he knew the right questions and the right answers.

"No!"

Gary breathed a sigh of relief and thanked God that he had not led all of these people into a trap.

"What is your mother's maiden name?"

"Ressou."

"Copy. Is your mother still alive?"

"Yes!"

"Copy. Yell when we come over top. Fire another flare."

The four A-1s had circled around and headed from west to east. Their first pass had been roughly north to south, so this flight past the downed pilot should give a precise location.

"Now!" the pilot on the ground screamed. "Shots! They're shooting at you! The southernmost plane went right over me."

Tracers arced up from the valley towards the A-1s. Someone on the ground had panicked and started shooting, thus giving away their position. This fire could be deadly to a helicopter.

"Break!"

The four A-1s maneuvered to evade the gunfire.

"Bronco 3, Sandy Lead. We have your location. You get under cover and put your head down."

"Falcon Lead, Sandy Lead," the rescue pilot radioed to Colonel Batts' flight. "Falcon Flight, stand by."

"Sandy Lead, Falcon Lead. Roger. Six Thuds with guns."

"Falcon Lead, Hawk Lead," Lieutenant Colonel Foxe radioed. "Make that eight Thuds with guns. We're on your six. We turned that A-26 over to a Sandy. The navigator's really messed up."

"Falcon Lead. I'm going to mark a spot with White Phosphorous on the side of the karst. Do not shoot at the top. I want eight Thuds in trail shooting at my mark."

The eight F-105s moved into trail formation, one plane behind the other and began descending toward the A-1s.

The lead A-1 turned left and dropped toward the ground firing a Willie Peter marking rocket. A white cloud rose from the jungle.

Colonel Batts dived first. He fired his 20 mm Vulcan cannon, concentrating on the mark at the base of the karst escarpment. His cannon shells slammed into the trees near the spot designated by the A-1 pilot. One after another, the remaining F-105s in front of Gary made a long firing pass, shooting at the Willie Peter smoke. When Gary's turn came up, he pushed the stick forward and placed his pipper on the mark. He squeezed the trigger on the stick and the cannon fired one hundred rounds. Gary released the trigger and pulled back on the stick, climbing out of the valley.

Colonel Batts led the formation back to a safe orbit formation well above the helicopters. At that point, four F-4 Phantoms flew past and checked in with Sandy Lead. Reinforcements, Gary thought. He breathed a sigh of relief. What Sandy needed was bombs, not guns.

"Sandy Lead, Kestrel Lead, checking in."

"Kestrel, Sandy. We need your bombs."

The enemy soldiers who had fired at the planes from the valley were about to get a taste of their own medicine.

Sandy Lead marked a target in the valley with rockets. The Phantoms made one pass aiming at the smoke, dropping sixteen thousand-pound bombs. Fire, smoke, trees and dirt flew into the air as the bombs dropped by the F-4s exploded.

"Kestrel flight clear and done." The Phantoms wagged their wings at Gary's formation as they flew west.

Continuing with suppression of enemy gunfire, Sandy Lead and the other three A-1s dived toward the escarpment firing pods of rockets into the steep ridge. After the bombs and rockets had exploded, no ground fire came from the valley.

"Bronco 3, Sandy lead. Are you okay? Do you hear anything from the valley?"

"I'm okay. You were close, but missed. Negative on the noise, but I can't hear too well after all the blasts."

The four A-1s dropped and flew down the valley at tree top level. No ground fire rose up to greet them.

"Bronco 3. I'm calling the choppers in for a pass. I want you to fire a pencil flare when they approach. Do you copy?"

"Copy all that."

"Jolly Lead, Sandy Lead. Suppression complete. The guy on the ground is going to fire a flare when you get close to mark his position. He's on the ridge just above that switchback in the stream. Maybe a little south."

"Sandy, Jolly. Copy all that. I'm going to go right down the top of the ridge."

One HH-3 Jolly Green rescue helicopter approached the karst escarpment from the north and slowly flew down the crest of the ridge hugging the trees, while the other orbited higher off to the west. A red flare shot into the air. The low chopper began to hover as a rescue sling descended into the forest. Seconds later, it began rising toward the hovering Jolly Green with a man in the harness.

After four hours in flight, the hard steel machete in the back of the parachute wore into Gary's spine. His thighs and butt burned from riding on the padded survival kit. No matter how much this hurt, Gary believed the man hanging on the sling was probably in worse shape than he was, after running through the jungle all night.

Pounding his left knee with his fist in celebration, he shouted, "Yes!" Gary felt a sense of pride. He had helped save a fellow pilot in a desperate situation. He smiled to himself, thinking, what else could one hope for?

"RESCAP, Jolly Lead. Rescue complete. We got our guy."

SAM SLAYER

_____ 35

Gary Bishop Deale, First Lieutenant, USAF
Takhli RTAFB, Thailand
28 April 1967, Counter Number 35

AS APRIL NEARED its end, Gary pulled on his gloves and walked around his F-105 doing a preflight check before another mission over North Vietnam, counter thirty-five. Sergeant Crawford, the maintenance crew chief followed him, pointing out mechanical issues just resolved. Gary stood by the belly of his fighter placing his boot on the tail fin of a CBU-24 cluster bomb and pushing against it, shaking the weapon. After checking the ejector rack connections and fuze wires on each of the six bombs, he duck-walked to the front of the plane. Walking around the aircraft, he scanned the wings and fuselage for loose panels or bullet holes, ending up at the crew ladder.

Gary looked for puddles of fuel or hydraulic fluid on the tarmac. He didn't see anything dripping from the plane. Pulling the maintenance log from the slot in the crew ladder, he skimmed through it, searching for discrepancies. Everything seemed to be fixed and checked. His fighter looked ready to fly.

His rank as a junior pilot meant that he flew a different F-105 on each mission. Senior officers had their own plane, reserved for them whenever they flew. Rarely would Gary fly the same aircraft in a month's time. He learned to trust the crew chiefs of the various planes, putting his life in their hands each time he flew. That was the way the system worked.

Sergeant Crawford, the crew chief, carried Gary's helmet up the ladder and placed it on the top of the canopy rail above the instrument panel. After the sergeant returned to the ground, Gary put his arms through the parachute straps and climbed twelve feet to the cockpit. He lifted himself over the rail and settled onto the ejection seat. Sergeant Crawford followed carrying Gary's flight kit. With the sergeant's assistance, he fastened the chest strap and the two leg straps, cinching them tight.

Gary put on his camouflage helmet and connected his oxygen mask. Hoping to clear the remnants of the previous night's excesses, he took deep breaths of pure oxygen. After stowing his gear and maps, he began reading the preflight list in the notebook strapped to his right thigh. Checking the various switches and dials, he made adjustments as necessary.

The mechanic removed the safety pins with their red streamers from the ejection seat and stowed them in the cockpit. Gary attached the seat lanyard, which separated him from the ejection seat in case of a problem and low altitude ejection at takeoff. The crew chief shook his hand and gave him a thumbs up. He saluted Gary and backed down the ladder, lifting it off the rail as he reached the ground.

Gary checked the engine start checklist and began throwing switches. When large numbers of planes started at the same time, a black powder cartridge in each plane was fired to spin up the turbine and provide ignition. Soon, his plane was engulfed in a black cloud of swirling smoke, which was another reason for the oxygen mask. The engine rumbled to life. Once everything stabilized, Gary saluted the crew chief and signaled to pull the chocks. He was good to go.

Taking his place as the number four plane in line, the SAM suppression flight taxied towards the south end of the field. He wished he were bombing the Thai Nguyen Steel

Plant rather than destroying SAMs, but that was his mission for the day.

Assigned to attack the Thai Nguyen Plant, thirty miles north of Hanoi, twenty F-105s were preparing for a re-strike mission. Despite having been bombed several times, the iron and steel facility still partially functioned. Designated by the Joint Chiefs of Staff at the Pentagon as a priority target and officially known as JCS Target 76, the pilots had bombed the plant weekly since March. The strikes gradually carved away at the facility, reducing parts of it to rubble.

Likewise, the North Vietnamese also whittled away, knocking down American planes on almost every mission.

Gary had previously flown two strike missions to Thai Nguyen. One F-105 had been shot down both times.

He had heard other pilots talking about Secretary of Defense McNamara and his obsession with statistics and numbers. The pilots in his squadron thought that the secretary ignored the increasing number of American pilots lost over North Vietnam.

Gary pondered the appalling loss of aircraft and pilots over North Vietnam with little to show for it. The war in South Vietnam continued with no sign of slowing. That was one of the bombing campaign's objectives, to convince the North Vietnamese to stop supporting the war in the south. The futility of the Rolling Thunder operation appalled him. Alarm bells must be ringing someplace, but he didn't know where.

The pilots often speculated about who would retreat first and who would hold fast. Americans had never cut and run before when it came to a war, but this enemy was different.

"This is a bad war," Lieutenant Colonel Foxe had said, during one long night at the club. "Lots of people are dying for nothing." He was drunk, but right, Gary thought.

"Stop thinking about it," Gary whispered to himself, as he turned his attention to his mission. The decisions about winning or losing the war were far out of his realm. He flew his F-105 and fought the enemy. That's what he always wanted to do, so that's what he did.

Gary taxied onto the hot arming apron and positioned his F-105 in line with the three others. He continued taking deep breaths. Pure oxygen began clearing cobwebs from his brain.

Two of the airplanes carried a crew of two men, a pilot and an electronic warfare officer, commonly referred to as the "Bear." Gary and Captain Fromm, the other pilot in the formation flew single seat fighters. The two-seated aircraft were specially equipped F-105s known as Wild Weasels, used for SAM suppression missions. Each Wild Weasel carried Shrike anti-radar missiles.

The first two planes cleared the arming area and took off, followed by the second Wild Weasel F-105 and then Gary.

After refueling over southern Laos, the Wild Weasel flight turned toward North Vietnam. Arriving at the target area before the strike force, the flight split into two elements. First-in, Last-out was their motto. Captain Heaps and Gary circled south of the plant, while the other two planes were on the north side.

About five minutes later, the leader of the strike force assigned to bomb the plant radioed that they were inbound. Two seconds later, things went crazy.

The Bear in Captain Heaps' plane radioed a warning. "SAM at six o'clock is hot."

"Turning left. Get ready," Captain Heaps, the element leader said, banking his airplane into a sharp 180 degree turn. Gary slammed the control stick to the left and stomped the left rudder pedal while sweeping his head around looking for MIGs and SAMs. The twenty-plane strike force approached from the west.

The abrupt turn meant that the Wild Weasel crew believed that the SAM site previously at their six o'clock position, but now directly in front of them, posed the greatest threat to the strike force. Gary leveled his aircraft when he saw the leader's aircraft lift its nose, preparing to loft a Shrike anti-SAM radar missile. Here we go, Gary thought as he sucked oxygen and said a prayer.

A missile dropped off Captain Heap's plane, with immediate ignition. Gary turned his F-105 to the right. He rolled the left wing down while dropping to the right of the missile smoke trail. The missile climbed and then arced downward.

"SAM launch! SAM launch! Take it down!" the Bear screamed as a missile blasted off the ground ahead of Gary.

The Shrike descended pointing directly at the area where the SAM just lifted off. Moving incredibly fast, the SAM remained at the same relative position on Gary's canopy, meaning the missile had locked onto him. He was the target.

Pushing the throttle forward and outboard, he engaged the afterburner and steeply descended, waiting for the precise second to climb. As the SAM came closer, Gary decided enough was enough, and he slammed the stick back into his belly to climb and rolled the plane upside down, keeping the SAM in view.

Gary climbed. The missile tracked him. His airspeed dropped off. He knew that he offered a fat inviting target to the missile. Oh Shit, Gary thought. Here it comes! Sweat ran down his face and he sucked oxygen into his body.

"Take it down," Captain Heaps yelled.

Gary pulled the stick back to his belly and the nose began to drop. "Dive, you whore," he yelled, trying to build airspeed and get away from the missile. Having done his best to execute the standard SAM evasion maneuver, he had dived and then climbed, waiting for the last second to put the plane into a steep dive, turning behind the SAM. Gary had done this maneuver before. The timing of the climb and dive were critical, and if he miscalculated, the missile would hit him.

"Good hit. Shrike rode the beam," the Bear yelled.

The Shrike destroyed the Fan Song guidance radar or the North Vietnamese turned the unit off to avoid being hit by the missile.

Just then, the SAM answered Gary's prayers. It went stupid, steered away from him and exploded well above his plane.

Gary turned his fighter and glanced at the SAM radar site, now covered by smoke and dust.

"You should've taken it down sooner. Take out that SAM," Captain Heaps said.

"I'm on it," Gary said.

He turned to the east, huffing and puffing oxygen. Sweat ran into his eyes. His helmet visor blocked any attempt to wipe his face. Gary blinked and concentrated on leveling the SAM site. Too stressed to lift the visor and wipe the sweat, he let it run.

Gary turned back towards the site and began a pop-up climb. He didn't remember engaging the afterburner, but realized he must have done it before climbing away from the SAM. Leaving the plane in burner that long drastically cut down on his fuel. Not good, he thought. Only enough fuel remained to make one pass on the target and haul ass. His remaining fuel dropped at an alarming rate, nearing Bingo fuel level, the bare minimum amount to make it back to the tanker.

He rolled the plane upside down and waited for the altimeter to nudge past 10,000 feet. He disengaged the burner and pulled the stick back flattening the climb while watching the SAM site. Once the airplane began to descend, he rolled the plane right-side up and centered the aiming pipper on the burning radar van. He shook his head and took a deep breath, centering the pipper on the fire and punched the cluster bombs off.

Red balls zipping by and flak bursts all around him reminded Gary to jink like crazy. He whipped the control stick to the left, then to the right and then back to the left again as the F-105 bottomed out of the dive and began ascending.

Gary spotted his element leader's plane headed west so he turned toward Thud Ridge and looked over his shoulder at the SAM site. Hundreds of sparkling balls of fire enveloped the site as the cluster bomblets exploded, spreading shrapnel over the radar vans, missiles and enemy soldiers.

"Bingo fuel. Bingo fuel," Gary said, informing Captain Heaps that he was low on fuel.

The two planes joined together and began hunting for the other two Wild Weasels. Captain Heaps radioed for a link-up point.

"Lead was shot down. Triple-A got him," the other pilot said.

"Fuck!" Captain Heaps said. "Any traffic from Lead?"

"Negative! No traffic. No beeper. Nothing. The thing blew up. Period. I already called it in. Negative SAR."

"Negative. They're gone," Captain Heaps said.

"I have visual on you just crossing the river," Captain Fromm said.

"Roger. Visual."

Gary realized that he was the lucky one. With the help of the Shrike missile, which worked to perfection, he had been saved. Major Wertz, the lead, and his Bear had been shot down, and two more friends disappeared into the void of North Vietnam. No RESCAP for those guys, Gary thought. The Sandies and Jolly Green helicopters never came this far north. It was too dangerous. If the two survived, the North Vietnamese had them.

WAKE

_____ 36

Gary Bishop Deale, First Lieutenant, USAF
Takhli RTAFB, Thailand
28 April 1967

LATER THAT NIGHT, the pilots held a wake for their three friends who had not returned from the day's mission. Major Wertz and Captain Lindy, the two Wild Weasel crewmen from Gary's flight, plus one pilot from the strike force had been shot down. Gary didn't know the third pilot all that well. He had talked with him at the club but that was it.

Wakes were always somber affairs, at least until the alcohol took hold. On this night, three friends would be remembered and spoken of kindly. No one knew what happened to them. There had been no communication from any of the three from the ground. They were gone.

Pilots jammed into the larger party room, filling the space. Standing in line at the bar, Gary waited to order his first double Doctor Jack Black. His name wasn't on the list for flying a mission the next day, so he had no worries about limiting alcohol. The jukebox had been turned up. Acker Bilk wailed away on his Saxophone, or whatever, offering his rendition of *Stranger on the Shore*.

Gary's emotions felt like a rollercoaster ride. At one moment, euphoria overtook him. He had dodged a SAM and lived to tell about it. But the next moment, grief, sorrow and anger took him to a dark place. Three more Americans would not be going home to their families. At least not anytime soon.

A close friend of each of the missing men said a few words about them. This was a fighter pilot's wake, a drunken memorial event for the missing man. Or, in this case, for three. This was not a celebration. The gathering was more of a lament for the missing.

Then the action began. Each of the four squadrons had their own colors. The 333rd Tactical Fighter Squadron Red Lancers wore red flight suits. A local Thai seamstress custom made the party uniforms.

The liquor and beer were cheap at the Officers' Club; fifteen cents for a beer or liquor, except for dime specials. San Magoo, the pilot's name for the Philippine beer San Miguel, was often only five cents. Gin or vodka was the favorite, after Dr. Jack Black, of course. Drinks flowed freely. It didn't take long to get the pilots into a dark mood, when almost anything could and did happen.

The Party Master selected Dodge the SAM as the wake game of the day. How poignant, Gary thought. One of several party activities enjoyed by the pilots, this one was in the moderate scale of potential damage to the club, its contents and the men. Whatever damage did occur was billed to all pilots' accounts on an equal basis.

Gary helped move tables and chairs aside, making a clear path through the center of the room from wall to wall. Pilots ran the gauntlet, jinking and dodging full bottles of beer thrown at them by their friends; Dodge the SAM.

When it came to be his turn, Gary placed his back hard against the wall and pushed off, gaining momentum. Some pilots relied on speed, some on stealth, evading the missiles thrown at them. Gary used speed and limited maneuvering. Bottles flew by, sloshing beer over him. Bottles crashed into the wall and also the pilots waiting their turn. One bottle hit his forehead, flooding his eyes with beer and as it turned out later, blood. Cheers at his being shot down echoed in his ears. Blinded, he ran smack into the wall face first, which rang his bell.

Gary floundered on the floor, shaking his head trying to clear his vision. Someone handed him a towel, which came away with a red splotch. Another person bandaged his forehead and offered an ice pack. Several men lifted him from the floor and plopped him onto a waiting chair. Gary shook his head, trying to slow down his spinning brain. Such a nice party, he thought. He decided to retire from play for the night.

The various games were just a crazy way for the pilots to reckon with the futility of their mission, blow off steam, deal with frustration and accept the finality of seeing good men disappear. First the men were there. Then they were not.

Gary staggered to his hooch, exhausted after flying more than three hours, debriefing and then partying. He felt tired, frustrated and pissed off. Mad at the world and baffled by what seemed to be aimless policy, he shook his head. Whiskey Tango Foxtrot, he thought, what the fuck? What the fuck are we doing here?

He struggled along the passageway between wall lockers in his hooch, bouncing along the center aisle, feeling the effects of San Magoo and Tennessee sippin' whiskey. Smiling at the ridiculousness of the game as he shucked off his beer-soaked red party flight suit, Gary thought he had just participated in one of the better wakes. Better in that now he could have an open discussion with himself about the futility of this war. He made his way to the latrine and took a quick shower, keeping his head and the bandage out of the spray.

After drying himself, he staggered back to his room. Turning on his desk lamp, he stared at the letter he had started writing to Allison before his early morning briefings. He knew he had to finish it soon. The squadron commander had just given final approval for his mid-tour leave dates in May. He had to let Allison know soon. But he was drunk and exhausted. Finishing the letter would have to wait.

Gary had planned a trip to Hawaii to meet Allison with the assistance of Sergeant Heydt in squadron operations.

After previously informing Allison of his tentative plans, he had been waiting on the final approval. He wished he were leaving the next day. He turned to his cot and saw a cloth patch and a note lying on his pillow. A Bald Eagle in flight with a SAM grasped in its talons, SAM SLAYER embroidered across the top in red. A short note read, "*You earned this! MF*"

Flying that day's mission and killing that SAM site had given Gary a profound case of the shakes. Death had ventured too close to him. But drinking and participating in the wake had eased his sorrow and grief. This patch, earned by destroying the SAM site, made Gary smile.

I'll be damned, Gary thought. The patch was a really cool gesture from Lieutenant Colonel Foxe. Gary hadn't received much recognition from anyone else other than a few kind words from Colonel Batts. This patch meant a great deal.

He stumbled to his cot and fixed his mosquito net. Darkness wrapped itself around him. The ceiling fan whirled, laboring to send a breeze wafting over him. A band of drunken pilots cursed as they walked to their hooch. He held a picture of Allison dressed in a swim suit on her boat, which he had just received in the mail. Wondering what she was doing right at that instant, he wished he could hold her. His last conscious thoughts before sleep overtook him were of his three buddies who were shot down. If alive, they were lost and scared shitless somewhere near Hanoi, North Vietnam.

MY PLAN

_____ 37

Allison Faith Deale
Pivers Island, Beaufort, North Carolina
April 29, 1967

"YOU HAVE TO concentrate on this summer's work," Dr. Pointer, my adviser, said. Sitting in his cluttered office at the marine lab, he pointed at my revised research plan. He looked at the outline of my research and teaching responsibilities for the upcoming year. "We should be able to finish your research this summer, if the weather cooperates."

The late afternoon sun peeked through venetian blinds covering his office window. Dust mites floated in the sun's rays.

"I hope so," I said, taking a sip of coffee.

"Just to be on the safe side, don't make any plans for the summer of 1968."

"Why?"

"Our research sponsors always seem to find something else for us to look at," he said, pointing at the pile of documents stacked on the floor.

"I plan on being here. I'm beginning to think about my doctorate, where I want to go, what I want to do."

"Allison, we hope you will remain here with us," Dr. Pointer said, taking a drag on his cigarette.

"I hope so. It all depends on where Gary is assigned next."

"Don't you know yet? He's almost half-way through his tour, isn't he?"

"Not quite. He wrote and told me he eventually wants to go to graduate school and teach at the Air Force Academy."

He did teach there after graduation, and one of his professors has kept in contact with him and opened up that possibility. But, he has to fly for several more years before they'll approve such a plan."

"Will he come back to Seymour?" Dr. Pointer asked, moving my papers aside, preparing for his next appointment.

"He hopes so, probably for transition training into the F-4 Phantom."

"Soon you'll be off to Hawaii."

"Yes," I said. "I can't wait to see him."

We continued talking for a short time. Dr. Pointer was my adviser and friend. His knowledge and depth of experience in research on the Newport River Estuary had helped me push ahead with my master's degree.

After our meeting, I returned to my apartment to begin revisions on my plan. After dropping carrying bags filled with research charts and documents to the floor, the only thing I had on my mind was salsa and chips and a cold beer.

I stripped and put on a bikini to catch some rays. Grabbing a beer and salsa from the fridge and picking up a bag of chips, I walked out on my balcony to catch the ocean breeze. Slowly sinking to the west, the sun's warmth lifted my spirits. I sat and propped my feet up on the railing, popping open a beer.

While Dr. Pointer had praised my research and the sponsors were well pleased with the results thus far, I felt frustrated by the possibility of having to spend another full year repeating what we had done the previous season and what we planned for this year. I didn't know where Gary would be in the summer of 1968. I planned on being wherever he ended up.

I was very lonely. Carmen tried her best to keep me engaged and active. But I missed Gary very much. We had eight wonderful months together. Then he departed. After these three months of being apart and not seeing each other, I began to ache for his presence. While I knew it wasn't possible, I wished that there were a way for me to see him now.

But I knew I had to finish my degree. This is what I want to do, I thought. This is my plan. I have to live with what I started.

PART 6

Oh, East is East, and West is West and never the twain shall meet.

—Rudyard Kipling, *The Ballad of East and West*, 1889

ON TO THE CLUB

We return
trying not to stare
at the empty nest
where a Thud
once proudly stood.

The debrief short,
blunt to the point.
A flaming spear leapt
from the ground,
a flash of light
then flying trash.

Thousands of pounds of
Tritonal and jet fuel
erupted in the air
creating a big hole
in the sky
swallowing all.

On to the club.
Guzzling tall cold ones
stacking dead soldiers
until the pile is higher
than us.

He is gone.
Honor his memory,
swear loyalty
to those who remain.

But
shedding a tear is
not
in the cards.

From the combat diary of Gary Bishop Deale,
First Lieutenant, USAF, 12 March 1967

THE RUSSIANS ARE COMING!

_____ 38

Yuri Vaskilev, General Lieutenant
GRU, Soviet Military Intelligence
Aboard the Cargo Ship, *Admiral Gorshkov*
100 Kilometers East of Taiwan
11 May 1967

YURI SMILED AS the captain indicated that the cargo ship had crossed the Tropic of Cancer. From this point south, water temperature increased. After passing by Taiwan, the captain's proposed course paralleled the coast of Communist China going south of Hainan Island and then straight to the port of Haiphong, North Vietnam.

Yuri and his sergeant eagerly anticipated the tropics after another tough Russian winter. He was a bear of a man, hardened by war. By his calculation, this was his third major conflict, The Great Patriotic War, which the Americans called World War II, then Korea and more recently, Vietnam. He entered the Soviet Army in the 1930's as an artillery officer. Posing no threats to anyone as a new junior officer, Yuri survived Stalin's purges. Many of his superiors had been taken away to Lubyanka Prison, where a bullet to the back of the head awaited them. Either that, or a long one-way train ride to the white void of Siberia.

In this, Yuri's twenty-ninth year in the military, his wife constantly reminded him that he was too old to be playing young men's games. He thought this would be his last fight. It was time for him to retire to his *dacha* and raise vegetables.

Gripping the deck railing, he watched the bow of the ship cut into waves. His toned body soaked up the sun.

Having just finished the daily routine of weight lifting, his muscles ached. He and his aide, Sergeant Komarvsky, had a long-term lifting competition, trying to outdo each other. Sweat ran down his chest. He craved sunshine. His shorts provided all the cover he needed. The old slow cargo ship barely stirred the humid air, but Yuri relished each hot breath.

One method he and Sergeant Komarvsky used to cool off after exercising was to ride their ancient Harley motorcycles around the deck. The crew of the large hatch cargo ship thought that strange.

The Americans had sent thousands of Harleys to Russia as part of Lend-Lease during The Great Patriotic War. Yuri and the sergeant laid claim to their machines after the war. They had cannibalized other bikes over the years to obtain parts, keeping the motorcycles on the road. Sergeant Komarvsky crafted whatever parts he couldn't find elsewhere in the machine shop at the airfield near Moscow.

He tapped his hands on the railing, wishing for time to move faster. On this, his fourth trip to North Vietnam, Yuri eagerly anticipated his arrival. He brought with him new counter-measures to thwart evolving American tactics. He was anxious to test them in combat.

While nominally a general officer in Soviet Troops of Air Defense Forces, Yuri often found himself seconded to Soviet Military Intelligence. Such was the case, whenever he was in North Vietnam.

Yuri had a long history with Soviet air-defense operations, from artillery to missiles. He had engineered the *Dvina* S-75 Surface-to-Air Missile system and stood by its accomplishments.

Beginning in 1956, the Americans had flown secret U-2 reconnaissance flights over the Soviet Union with impunity. Desperate attempts by MIGs and missiles failed to shoot down any of the high-flying aircraft, causing extreme embarrassment for the Soviet leadership. It cost millions of rubles to design and perfect the system to shoot down the U-2s, which his motherland could ill afford.

Finally, on 1 May 1960, one of Yuri's missiles, a *Dvina*, shot down a U-2 piloted by Francis Gary Powers over Sverdvlovsk in central Russia. Following that success, the Communist Chinese used his system to shoot down Nationalist Chinese U-2s and unmanned aerial vehicles or drones, which had taken off from Taiwan.

During the so-called Cuban Missile Crisis in October 1962, an S-75 had shot down another U-2 flown by Major Rudolf Anderson over the island. The crash killed the pilot, nearly touching off a full-blown retaliation by the Americans. An American attack against Cuba would have touched off a nuclear Armageddon.

In 1965, the Soviet Union supplied the first surface-to-air missiles to North Vietnam. Yuri had delivered the *Dvina* S-75 system, which the Americans called the SA-2 Guideline SAM.

Yuri proudly stood by his missile system. Each refinement led to additional successes. With each journey, Yuri delivered increasingly sophisticated radars, missiles and guidance equipment. This ship carried a few surprises for the Americans under tarps on-deck and in the cargo holds.

For the Soviets and for Yuri, Vietnam's War of Liberation was a proxy war. His country provided weapons and materiel to the North Vietnamese. He actually used the war to test new air defense systems. The North Vietnamese carried the brunt of the fighting and dying, although some of Yuri's men had been killed.

Americans viewed the war much differently. While the Americans provided training, equipment and supplies to the South Vietnamese, their soldiers, airmen and marines were being killed in large numbers. For the Americans, Vietnam was much more than a proxy war. They were heavily involved, getting maimed and killed.

On this day, Sergeant Komarvsky and several other technicians labored on the deck under a canvas tarp, calibrating the new system. The four 23 mm antiaircraft cannons and small dish radar mounted on a tank chassis, prototyped a new defensive weapon. Yuri and his sergeant had designed the rapid-firing system to combat low flying aircraft. He had successfully pleaded with his ministry to bring the deadly weapon along on this trip to field test in a combat setting. He called it the **дракон,** The Dragon From Hell, because it spewed fire.

As a special favor to Yuri, the sergeant and his crew had carefully painted the image of a fire-breathing dragon on the chassis of their new toy.

Haiphong harbor lurked several sailing days away. Then he and Sergeant Komarvsky planned to turn this **дракон** loose on the Americans and watch it devour its prey.

GUIDING STAR

_____ 39

Gary Bishop Deale, First Lieutenant, USAF
Takhli RTAFB, Thailand
11 May 1967

GARY TURNED THE corner at the hot arming area at the south end of the taxiway and ran north. Just ahead, Lieutenant Colonel Foxe squeaked along on his rusty bicycle, setting a languid pace. As the bike passed over the concrete expansion joints, the tires thumped.

On this May morning, the temperature had already crested at one hundred degrees at 0700 hours. No one set speed records. The early mission North, consisting of sixteen F-105s, had just taken off adding one more noxious thing to the air, jet exhaust fumes.

"There's no way in hell that I'll run those taxiways, but if you buy me a beer, I'll ride my bicycle," the colonel had said, establishing conditions for his participation. "They tell me to get plenty of exercise. The only things I'll go along with are riding my bike and lifting my elbow."

Gary was grateful that he'd finally convinced someone to go with him, even if he did have to pay bribes. He alternated between running and riding his bike. Lieutenant Colonel Foxe always rode.

"You know the flight surgeon wants you to do this," Gary said as they proceeded north on the taxiway.

The flight surgeon lectured the pilots about getting exercise. "Run, ride your bikes, and lift weights," Captain Raines had said. "You guys are fighting high G-forces all of the time and the exercise will help prevent blackouts. A tighter turn may save your ass someday."

Gary was all for that so he ran or rode his bike on his days off the flight schedule. When he flew a morning mission, he lifted weights and went for a swim at the club's pool in the afternoon. If flying an afternoon flight, the routine was reversed. Gary helped plan missions in his off hours and spent the remaining time writing letters or taking a nap. Boredom was never an issue.

Now, as he followed the colonel, he remembered running the country roads in Wayne County with Allison, her pony tail swinging in the wind, breathing in tandem with him, as she matched his pace, running full-out on the dirt lane. As his tour in Thailand progressed, he thought of her more often, wondering where she was and what she was doing. Scheduled to depart the following day to meet her in Hawaii, his sense of anticipation increased with each passing hour.

"Know where I'm soon going to be?" Gary asked, panting and wiping sweat from his face with his shirt, as they neared the halfway point with 4,500 feet to go on this leg of the circuit.

"Where the hell's that?" Lieutenant Colonel Foxe asked.

"Running barefoot on the beach with Allison," Gary said.

"Why do you always bring up women?" the colonel asked, wiping sweat from his face.

"Okay, sir," Gary said, respectfully, "what are we doing here?"

The roar of a jet engine filled the air as mechanics tested an F-105 at the end of the runway, drowning out conversation. Humming with activity, airmen bustled about the parking apron loading planes with bombs, preparing for the afternoon mission. In the distance, farmers from the nearby village worked in their rice paddies setting plants. As always, the strong odor of night soil wafted from the adjoining fields.

Thudding down on the runway, a C-130 cargo plane on the daily Milk Run from Bangkok to American bases farther north reversed pitch and slowed. The plane lumbered to a crossover and turned onto the taxiway in front of them. Standing in the grass verge, the men turned their backs to the swirling exhaust from the C-130 as it taxied by. "Maybe they're carrying fresh eggs and milk," the colonel said.

Turning south with one more circuit of the 9,000 foot taxiway ahead, Gary took a swig of water from his plastic baby bottle. He cheated and counted the distance as two miles. Running twelve miles each time to meet his goal, he made three circuits of the taxiway.

Continuing with the threads of a conversation the men had just started when the F-105 silenced them, the colonel said, "The thing everybody has to decide is whether this a war or not. Are we here in this Charlie Foxtrot to win? Or is this going to be another clusterfuck like Korea? If we're here to lose, we might as well get the hell out of Dodge right now. This SNAFU is going to hurt a lot of people before it's over, from the top right down to the bottom."

How did I happen to meet this man? Gary asked himself. The colonel had taught him how to survive while flying in combat. His leadership had saved Gary's life more than once. Gary had come to think of Lieutenant Colonel Matt Foxe as more like a guiding star rather than just a colleague.

PART 7

A fool lies here who tried to hustle the East.

—Rudyard Kipling and Wolcott Balestier,
The Naulahka, 1892

THE SEPARATION

A wide ocean
separates
love and life
from evil and death.

One in the West
dances
freely and wildly,
flowers in her windswept hair.

Another in the East
despairs,
honoring but cursing
his fate and chance.

From the combat diary of Gary Bishop Deale,
First Lieutenant, USAF, 12 May 1967

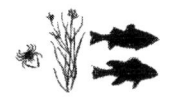

PARADISE

_____ 40

Allison Faith Deale
Camp Bellows Air Force Station
East Coast of Oahu, Hawaii
May 14, 1967

THE SERGEANT AT the camp's reception center checked me in. "Welcome to Paradise," Master Sergeant Decker said. He rode with me in my rental car to our cabin on Wavecrest Lane, perched near a magnificent beach. Shaded by ironwood trees and isolated from the other cabins, it lived up to Gary's description. Sergeant Decker helped with my luggage and shopping bags.

After entering the concrete block cabin, I looked around and checked out the amenities. It was your basic government furnished efficiency, functional and utilitarian. But you couldn't beat the location.

Placing my perishable food, desserts, wine and beer I had purchased at a small market into the refrigerator, I popped the cap off a Bud. Sitting on the front stoop, I took a sip, trying to calm my nerves. Gary's almost here, I thought. I hadn't seen him in three long months. I couldn't wait to hold him and make love with him.

One hundred feet away, waves pounded against the sandy beach. My first and lasting impression of the Pacific was the turquoise ocean, which had such intensity that the sky appeared darker. The vivid aquamarine shades of blue and green amazed me. Several small islands shimmered in brilliant sunlight. Surfers rode the waves. A booby flew by skimming the ocean's surface. The scene before me, ironwood and palm trees dancing in the wind and with the ocean in the background, set my heart racing.

The sergeant who had checked me in stopped by to see if I needed help. "Just got a phone call from your husband at Hickam. I told him you were here. He said to tell you it'll be a couple hours. He's checking on a hop back to Takhli."

I smiled at the mention of Gary's base. Months before, that information had been a secret. "Thank you, sergeant."

After the sergeant departed, I sat on the stoop, drumming my fingers on the concrete. Each minute seemed to take hours to pass. How can time slide by so slowly? Gary was so close and yet so far away.

Rather than simply sitting there and waiting, I decided that the ocean looked too inviting. I put on my bikini and beach top and walked along the sand until I found a quiet spot, away from the other families. Testing the water with my foot, I decided it was warm enough. I dived in and swam a short circuit along the beach. Multi-colored tropical fish swam unhurried in front of me. Tiny gray and white fish kissed my face, tickling my skin. Having spent a full day on airliners, the water felt refreshing and invigorating. I rode a wave ashore and stood. Goose bumps covered my body. As I wrapped myself in a large beach towel, I watched small children splashing and playing at the water's edge.

I coated myself in sun tan lotion, stretched out and watched the waves crashing ashore. How peaceful, I thought. Gary will love this.

BEACH BUMS

Gary Bishop Deale, First Lieutenant, USAF
Camp Bellows, Oahu, Hawaii
14 May 1967

AFTER TAKING A shuttle from Hickam, Gary checked in at the camp's office and got directions. He walked the short distance to their assigned cottage and saw the note taped to the cabin door, which read simply, *ON THE BEACH! LOVE YA! ALLISON.* Gary looked at the note and thought, my God. Allison wrote that! She's actually here. His heart raced and his body hummed in anticipation of seeing her again. But at the same time he felt nervous. He wasn't sure how much he should tell her about what he had seen and done over the past few months. How can I possibly tell her about killing people and watching my friends die? he wondered. How much would she want to know?

Plopping his B-4 bag, the standard canvas luggage used by most pilots, on the small porch, he unlocked the door with the key the sergeant gave him, carried his bag inside and quickly changed into a swimsuit.

Walking toward the crashing surf, he stopped to breathe in the refreshing ocean air.

The setting matched the photographs Sergeant Heydt had shown him back at Takhli. The pictures depicted tiny tan cottages nestled in a grove of trees within a stone's throw of the beach. Located northeast of Honolulu, with the Koolau mountain range lying in between the two, Camp Bellows had been an active airbase. Japanese aircraft had bombed Bellows Airfield during the Pearl Harbor attack. After the war, the Air Force converted part of the base into a recreation facility for military personnel and their families.

Although Gary had flown over the Pacific twice, this was the first time he had seen its waters up close. Sun rays sparkled in the turquoise breakers. A small crowd stood by the surf yelling at a couple snorkeling. Families scattered about, lying on towels and blankets. Nowhere did he see an unaccompanied young lady. He continued strolling up the beach. Then, he saw her.

Allison lay belly down on the largest beach towel he had ever seen, her sunglasses resting in her neck-length strawberry-blond hair. He had almost forgotten about the reddish tinge, but there it was. Gary's chest felt tight and his hands trembled. His chin quivered. He stood there with his hand covering his eyes, holding back his emotions.

Her green bikini blended with the palm tree design on the towel. Quietly Gary walked around the towel and stopped. He looked at her face. Her tanned skin glistened with oil. Gary lifted his camera and began framing the scene. He wanted to get all of Allison with the two islands in the background.

Gary took a series of photographs of Allison, both close-ups and distant settings. He stood there looking at her. She's beautiful, he thought. How did I end up being so lucky to have married her? He wanted to touch her and hold her and make love to her, but did not want to wake her up.

As he sat down on the towel, Allison startled and looked at him. "Gary," she said, "finally, you're here."

He hugged and kissed her, running his hands through her hair. Both of his hands ended up on her breasts. "I love you. You're beautiful!"

"No touchy feely randy stuff allowed on the beach."

"I'm just trying to figure out if I'm really here."

"You're here! I love you!" Allison said, blushing, as she sensed a growing hardness between them. "Oh my, something else is alive too."

Gary thought that it must have been one of the quickest erections he had ever experienced. "Well, we'll just have to beat that thing into submission, very soon."

"Good things come to those who wait, no pun intended."

Gary thought he had better wait until things cooled off a bit before standing. He raised himself on his elbows and said, "What's the water like?"

"Very different from the Atlantic. I went for a swim and the visibility underwater is fantastic. The fish have the most incredible colors."

He watched Allison watching him. Neither one spoke. They sat staring at each other. This is surreal, Gary thought. Two days ago I was in a war. Now I'm sitting on this spectacular beach with the most beautiful woman in the world. Something very wonderful is going to happen very soon.

"I've got to wash this oil off," Allison said, standing. "Let's jump in." They walked down to the surf and dived into the ocean bobbing through the waves. Swimming along the beach, they turned and paddled back.

Gary splashed around, watching Allison laugh at him. He swam to her and held her head with both hands, kissing her repeatedly. Holding hands, they quietly stood in the surf facing the ocean, watching the waves curl in from the vast Pacific.

Shortly after, back at the cabin, laughing and out of breath from running in their hurry to be alone together, Gary peeled her beach note off the door, bumped the door closed and locked it. He didn't resist as she slid off his swim trunks. Easily removing her bikini, he wrapped both of their bodies in the beach towel. They stood there locked in an embrace.

He complied as Alison gently nudged him backward onto the bed. He lay there waiting as Allison straddled him, arranged things, and gently, slowly lowered herself, sliding into home.

Gary stared into her eyes as Allison rocked gently forward and placed her hands behind his head. She lifted herself then lowered, thrusting him deep inside her, again and again. Allison stopped moving and then Gary felt her squeeze and then relax her inner muscles, surrounding him. He placed both hands on her butt and began pushing down, ramming her even tighter against his groin. Feeling the muscles in her back tighten and her body stiffening, he pushed her even tighter. She began to moan, as heat radiated off her body, sweat pooling between them. He felt her begin to quiver, and the moans changed into whimpers. Gary sensed her massaging him into bliss as she convulsed. He shuddered, and Allison followed him, lost in passion.

He had looked directly into her eyes the entire time. "I love you so much," he said. As he spoke those words, Gary felt the tension seep out of his body even though he knew that the fear and frustration of the war lurked over his shoulder. He grasped her head in both hands and pulled her lips down to his.

They snuggled together caressing and exploring each other's bodies as the cool ocean breezes stirred the window curtains. The sound of the crashing surf and children's voices drifted into the room, blending with the sounds of pleasure Allison made as Gary touched her.

After a pause, Allison rose from the bed, gathering her robe, walked to the refrigerator, grabbed two beers, flipped off the caps and handed one to Gary. "Here's to us," she said, tapping her beer against his.

Allison sat on the bed as he chugged his beer. And then wordlessly, she got up and retrieved letters from their parents that she'd brought for him. By the time she returned from taking a quick shower, Gary was asleep, the letters still in his hands.

Later after a dinner of perfectly grilled steaks and a tropical fruit tart for dessert, Gary and Allison sat on the front stoop sipping from water tumblers filled with wine. Stars sparkled above them in the clear black sky. A brisk sea breeze rustled through the trees around them. Waves crashed ashore.

During dinner, Allison had begun asking him questions about what he had seen and what he had done over the past three months. As they sat on the porch and her wine consumption increased, Allison's questions became more direct.

"Tell me about your missions, beginning with the first," Allison said.

"A major and I took up two birds for a test hop. We ended up over Laos and flew through this valley. Enemy soldiers on the ground shot at us, but missed."

"You got shot at?" The tone of her voice changed. She sounded incredulous and surprised.

"Yes."

"Does that happen often?"

"Every mission." Gary could see a change in her face, suddenly filled with tension. Her jaw quivered. He could actually see the fear in her eyes.

"What do they fire at you?"

"Flak—antiaircraft guns, and SAMs—surface-to-air missiles."

"Are you afraid?" she asked, her voice breaking.

"I can't allow myself to be afraid while I'm flying," Gary said. "It's when I'm not flying that I begin thinking about the pilots who are hit and shot down. That's when I feel the fear closing in."

"Jesus, Gary, how do you continue doing this?" she asked, tears streaming down her cheeks.

"It's what I've been trained to do. I can't let my fellow pilots down. No way in hell am I going to walk away from what I'm doing. While I've been at Takhli several pilots handed in their wings and quit flying combat. It's a big blot on their records."

"Can you do that?"

"I couldn't face myself if I did something like that. This friend of mine, Lieutenant Colonel Foxe, says that we don't want pilots flying missions who are afraid to fight. He says it's better to let the cowards go than to get someone killed. That's what I would hear if I walked away—coward. I simply can't do it."

GARY AND ALLISON used the rental car to take side trips each day. One day they drove across northern Oahu, stopping at beaches to swim and watch the surfers ride the monstrous waves on what the locals called The Pipeline.

On another drive, they went to a Polynesian Cultural Center located near Laie on the north coast. Early LDS missionary work in the area led to the development of a Temple, university and later the cultural center at Laie. As part of the attraction, they toured recreations of villages of the Maori, Tongan, Tahitian and Hawaiian people.

A special journey for Gary was to the USS Arizona Monument at Pearl Harbor, where they rode a tour boat to the remains of the ship. Surprisingly, oil smears continued to float to the surface twenty-five years after the catastrophe. On their way back to Camp Bellows, they stopped at Waikiki Beach so that Allison could window shop the high-end stores.

OVER THE FOLLOWING days, they talked about his experiences. He told her as much as he thought she could bear. He didn't discuss the blinding explosions from Triple-A shells or feeling the heat from a SAM as it blasted by his cockpit. Nor did he describe the F-105 and his buddy disappearing in a ball of fire as a missile hit the plane. He avoided the fifty-two combat missions he had yet to fly.

"I have found one true friend, Lieutenant Colonel Matt Foxe," Gary said. "He, more than anyone else, taught me how to survive."

Foxe had also provided another lesson to Gary; how to compartmentalize his fear and rage. The colonel had told Gary that his true feelings about flying into combat and the bad things he had witnessed had to be set aside and sealed into a box in his mind. Otherwise, he would be crippled.

AFTER DINNER ON their final night, Allison sat on Gary's lap telling him how much she loved him. She ran her fingers through his buzz-cut, saying that her preference was for his hair to be longer. "But this is much cooler," he said.

Wrapping his arms around her, he kissed her and nestled his face in her hair, smelling her and casting into memory Allison's scent—of wine, roses and lavender.

"I have a small gift for you," Gary said, taking a chain containing dog tags from his neck and draping it around hers.

"What's this?" Allison held up a small metal device.

"It's a P-38, the can opener I use with C-Rations and K-Rations. Sometimes, when I'm sitting in the plane waiting for a mission to go, I eat a canned pound cake. It's really good, especially with raspberry jam."

"I'll wear this always." Allison kissed him for the thousandth time. "But aren't you supposed to wear it?"

"That's a spare set. I'm never without my good luck charm." Gary showed her another set around his neck. These are old, those are new."

"I see."

"Just so you know where they've been, I wore those on missions."

"I'll cherish them," Allison said.

Gary put his forehead against hers, closing his eyes and holding her as tightly as possible. All his hopes, which had built up over the past few months had been fulfilled. He made love to Allison, ate her special meals and simply lived each day, free from fear. He wished their stay at this place would last forever.

Allison had surprised him. Sometimes, when he had read her letters before the leave, she seemed to be having difficulties dealing with the separation. Maybe he was reading too much between the written lines. He hoped she was doing okay, but knew they had only been married eight months before he departed for Thailand. They hadn't had much time to really learn about each other, as training had been hectic and he also spent intervals of time away on Temporary Duty (TDY).

Over these few days, she had been abundant with love, affection and sex. What more could he ask for? He hoped those sweet memories lasted forever. But there he was, hoping again and knowing he only had a short time before the demands of combat pushed any thought of Allison into the background.

Nothing this good can last, he thought. Mentally he had already begun making the transition from this peaceful place to Takhli.

THE FOLLOWING DAY, as they stood on the tarmac near the waiting KC-135 tanker and four F-105s at Hickam Airbase, Gary and Allison draped Orchid Ti Leaf Leis, the leis given for good luck, around each other's necks.

"Goodbye, Gary," Allison said, "I love you."

"You're the best thing that ever happened to me," he said, kissing her one last time.

"I hope this works," he said, patting the lei and then, turning away. Gary waved as he walked toward the planes, not daring to turn around and face her.

As he climbed the crew ladder into the tanker, he waved one last time. Leaving her standing there crying on the Hickam parking apron with her red dress flowing and rippling in the wind was the most difficult thing he had ever done.

P-38

Allison Faith Deale
Hickam AFB, Hawaii
May 23, 1967

NERVOUSLY TWISTING THE P-38 and dog tags Gary had given me, I watched the tanker taxi from the parking apron followed by the four F-105s.
 The fighters lined up on the runway, revving their engines. At intervals, each plane shot down the runway with its afterburner blasting, lifting off the ground and turning west. The tanker quickly followed. Gray swirls of engine exhaust streaked across the sky behind the disappearing planes.
 The tanker gradually faded from view as I wept.
 "Maybe this will help." A bird colonel was offering his handkerchief.
 "Thank you," I said, wiping away the tears.
 "Colonel Marks," the officer said, "PACAF Operations."
 "Pleased to meet you. Allison Deale," I said, returning his hanky.
 He waved it away. "No, you keep it. I have plenty."
 "Thank you."
 "Your husband on one of those planes?" Colonel Marks pointed at the smoke trails.
 "Yes, sir."
 "Going to the war?"
 "Yes."
 "Pray for him. Each and every day."
 "I do, sir. I do."
 "Good for you. Well, back to the grind for me. Take care of yourself."

"Thank you."

When I turned back to the runway, the wind had dispersed the smoke trails, leaving behind no evidence of the planes or men.

PART 8

War is part of God's Creation.

—Helmuth von Moltke, 1914

CRASH

Those watching the show
critiqued his performance.
Lift off and eject now!
Ride it down the line!
Decide, dumb shit!

Pondering whether
to get out
or ride the beast
to the end,
the young pilot froze.

Red crash trucks
and blue ambos followed
skid marks to the
plane upside down in a ditch,
flames haloing the pyre.

Cursing airmen collected
smoking bolts, turbine blades,
a wheel wrapped by a tire
and parts, engine,
miscellaneous,
littering the runway.

Bearing aluminum suits
the crash crew killed time smoking
their brands and scratching their asses
waiting for the junk to cool
to dig out what remained.

A smiling face, a lover
and a friend,
now a lifeless body.
No longer responding,
it waits.

From the combat diary of Gary Bishop
Deale, First Lieutenant, USAF, 19 June
1967

COAST IN

_____ 43

Gary Bishop Deale, First Lieutenant, USAF
Over the Gulf of Tonkin near South Vietnam
25 May 1967

THE COAST OF South Vietnam became visible through haze and clouds. After seven days with Allison in Hawaii, Gary headed back to war. He sat behind Major Freer in the cockpit of the KC-135 jet tanker. The major reminded Gary of Lieutenant Colonel Foxe, very gruff and all business. Wearing a faded and shabby leather flight jacket bedecked with cloth patches, the major sank back into the pilot's seat. In the right seat, the copilot flew the plane. "Giving the youngster some experience," the major said.

The air-to-air refueling tanker and four F-105 fighters had taken off from Anderson Air Force Base on Guam hours before on the second day of their journey from Hawaii.

Major Freer had told Gary that this was his first time seeing action. He was just beginning a three-month deployment to Don Muang Airbase near Bangkok, on temporary duty (TDY), from Wurtsmith Air Force Base in Michigan. Up until this time, the major had flown tankers refueling strategic bombers as they prowled the northern skies, waiting for the Soviet Union to go crazy and do something stupid.

"I don't know what the ground war is like," Gary said, continuing their conversation interrupted by radio traffic from Danang Airbase. "It's got to be hell for those soldiers and marines down there. We keep putting in more troops and more grunts are getting killed."

"I hear that the military calls the ground war down there a counterinsurgency," Major Freer said, pointing down at the ground.

"Yes, that's it," Gary said, leaning forward to get a look at Danang as they passed over. "The grunts assault areas in the bush. Later the troops abandon the ground they fought over. The chain of command calls that Search and Destroy."

"From all I hear back home, a lot of searching and destroying has gone on, with not much to show for it, except for a lot of dead Americans," Major Freer said.

"Doesn't the bombing up North work?" the copilot asked.

"No. We bomb the shit out of North Vietnam and Laos. They just keep coming," Gary said.

"What's it like, flying up there?" Major Freer asked.

"It's Delta Sierra, some deep shit you don't ever want to have to deal with," Gary said, thinking of all the gunfire and missiles directed at him on previous missions over Laos and North Vietnam.

Gary amazed himself. He had said words never spoken by fighter pilots in their testosterone-filled world. No one expressed feelings of fear or reluctance to fly their fighters into combat. It was bad form, not to mention bad luck.

Maybe the week with Allison softened me, he thought. Now that he had spent seven days with her, loving her and being loved in return, Gary felt the turmoil in his gut. Going back to war, to what he had done, over the past three months troubled him. *Will I be okay?* he wondered. *Can I do the mission expected of me?*

"Air Force 793, Monkey Control. Execute immediate left turn to 230 degrees. Traffic coming behind you from the east. Confirm visual."

Gary leaned over the copilot's shoulder to check on the aircraft approaching his flight on the starboard side. Six giant B-52 eight-engine bombers came into view. Each bomber carried multiple bombs on wing pylons. The planes were in two formations, one behind the other, each with three planes in a V-shape.

"There they are. Arc Light B-52s coming in from the east," Gary said, pointing to his right. "Six of them."

The major radioed visual contact.

Operation Arc Light missions used B-52 strategic bombers to drop bombs on South Vietnam, southern North Vietnam and Laos. The Laotian missions were highly classified, but Gary saw the resulting evidence every time he flew over the country.

As Gary watched, the bomb bay doors of the six distant B-52s swung open, as the two widely separated flights of aircraft flew parallel headings. "Somebody's going to get it," the copilot said, just as a cascade of bombs began dropping from the bombers. At first the dark specks seemed to hang there. But then they fell away, rapidly gaining speed and falling behind the bombers. He knew each B-52 carried 110 five hundred pound bombs. A total of 660 bombs exploded in the jungle, shaking the tanker even at their distance from the strike. Strings of flashes and fire erupted from the mountainous terrain below. Anyone down there had gotten a glimpse of hell on earth.

"Jeez," the commander said, standing up from his seat. "Could you imagine being on the receiving end of that?"

"It does churn up the landscape," Gary said. "Too bad they don't use them up North."

"They don't go into North Vietnam?" the copilot asked.

"Only in the extreme southern part. B-52s have hit the Mu Gia Pass many times. It's a major infiltration route, part of the Ho Chi Minh Trail. The area up there in the pass looks just like that," Gary said, pointing to a wide swath of bomb craters, from a previous strike, cutting through the jungle to their left.

After the tanker landed at Don Muang near Bangkok, Gary walked to flight operations. Trying to hitch a ride to

Takhli, he discovered that he had to wait four hours until the Milk Run cargo plane departed.

As he waited, he thought constantly of Allison and smiled. Warmth crept up his thighs. Those intense feelings of lust and passion hadn't diminished. Even now, he could smell and taste and remember her. All of her.

He closed his eyes and thought of her standing on the tarmac. Saying goodbye to her had never been easy, but this farewell unsettled him. He had looked back at her while climbing the ladder into the KC-135 tanker. That last sight of Allison burned an image into his brain, standing there with her red dress rippling and shimmering in the sunlight and wind.

While hoping that he and Allison had a long future, he realized that he had again broken one of his basic rules. It was Bad Karma for a fighter pilot to hope for anything.

AS THE C-130 cargo plane climbed away from Don Muang, Gary unbuckled his seat belt and walked toward the rear of the plane. Even with wax earplugs, the roar of the engines vibrated through his head. Sunlight streamed through the small windows. His fellow passengers glanced at his flight suit patches. One patch for the 333rd Tactical Fighter Squadron, one for the F-105 Thunderchief, and one for the Red River Valley. This patch caught the most attention.

He looked out one of the small windows and watched the rice paddies and *Klongs* pass by underneath. The plane flew over a magnificent Buddhist temple far below. Painted stark white, with gold gilded spires sparkling in the sunshine, the temple marked a stark difference with the surrounding rice paddies and *Klongs*.

Gary wove around straps securing pallets and crates to the cargo deck. He blinked and looked twice at the crates stacked on one of the pallets. The cold military nomenclature sent shivers up his spine: POUCHES,

REMAINS, HUMAN, QUANTITY, 100 EACH. A whole stack of the things. Another stack of crates carried only the words HIGH EXPLOSIVES. He thought that was a crazy juxtaposition, ordnance and the results.

Reading the *Stars and Stripes,* the airman who sat next to him looked up. "Sir, I see your patches. What's it like, flying up North?"

"We spend most of our time in Delta Sierra," Gary said, taking his seat.

The airman scrunched up his brow. "I get it, Deep Shit."

"What's going on?" Gary asked, pointing to the paper.

"The lead article is about a marine action in northern South Vietnam near the Demilitarized Zone called Operation Prairie IV," the airman replied. "They say that 337 Americans were killed in action last week. That's the most killed in one week since the war started."

"Sometimes I think it's really hard to figure out whether we're making any progress," Gary said.

"I know for sure they send plane loads of American bodies home from Tan Son Nhut," the airman said. "I see the transfer cases covered with flags on the tarmac every day. I guess that's one way to measure our progress."

Gary read the labeling again on the crates stacked in front of him. He couldn't imagine what Allison would think if she saw the stack of Pouches, Remains, Human, with their heartless labels. Would she look at those crates like specimens in her science lab? What in the world have we gotten ourselves into? The conflict between his memories of Allison in Hawaii and the empty feeling of going back to war unnerved him.

TURKESTAN

_____ 44

Gary Bishop Deale, First Lieutenant, USAF
Takhli RTAFB, Thailand
6 June 1967

GARY HAD FLOWN several maintenance test hops and three missions Downtown after his return from Hawaii. He settled back into the now familiar routine of flying, then killing time, waiting to fly again.

Several days previously, a major "Charlie Foxtrot," Lieutenant Colonel Foxe's words for a clusterfuck, occurred. There was no official version, but lots of scuttlebutt about the incident.

Gary knew few facts aside from what he had read in the *International Herald Tribune* and *Stars and Stripes*. Over the past few days, both papers had carried stories about the Soviets going apoplectic over an alleged F-105 attack on one of their so-called civilian cargo ships. According to the articles, American fighter jets allegedly strafed the *Turkestan*, docked in the Cam Pha Harbor in North Vietnam.

While Washington authorities discounted such claims by the Soviets, an icy chill descended on Takhli. According to scuttlebutt, Colonel Jack Broughton, vice wing commander, stood up for and protected two pilots after a mission on 2 June, with facts to follow. But rumors have a way of swatting facts aside. When truth is not readily available, stories fill the vacuum. Everyone knew something had happened. No one knew what. Those who knew remained silent.

Gary had checked his diary and discovered that he had flown a mission on 2 June bombing the Kep Rail Yard. Lieutenant Colonel Foxe had led the attack. Their planes had flown close to Cam Pha on the way in to the target at Kep. They didn't strafe anything, period.

SEVERAL DAYS AFTER the rumor-plagued incident, Gary sat in the wing briefing room, waiting for pilots to assemble. He squashed his cigarette in the ash tray and began flipping through his notebook, hunting for a blank lineup card. He jotted down the date and time. Another early morning briefing covering a target to bomb, Gary thought. Will this ever end? Settling back to wait, he waved at Lieutenant Colonel Foxe as his friend took a seat in the row ahead of Gary.

"What's going on with Colonel Broughton?" he asked, leaning forward to whisper in the colonel's ear.

"Lay low is my best advice," the colonel said. "You don't know nothing."

"Nothing?"

"Yes. The shit's gonna' hit the fan and you don't want to be anywhere near it."

WHAT'S GOING ON?

_____ 45

Gary Bishop Deale, First Lieutenant, USAF
Takhli RTAFB, Thailand
18 June 1967

AFTER FLYING TEN missions over North Vietnam since returning to Takhli three weeks before, Gary prepared for another airstrike. He gathered his gear and walked to the briefing room.

Lieutenant Smith, the Wing Intelligence Officer began the briefing with a new twist. As he usually did, the lieutenant began with a serious voice, giving the date, time and classification level. His mouth twisted in a slight smile, then he paused. Gary looked around wondering what was up.

"My first item is a trophy and certificate," the lieutenant said, trying to keep a straight face, but failing. He reached behind a curtain to retrieve a bent and mangled Jeep bumper. "This trophy, given by the Worker's Committee at the GAZ Truck Assembly Plant Number 43 in Kuybyschev, USSR, and awarded to the 355th Tactical Fighter Wing upon the destruction of the one thousandth GAZ truck this year on the Ho Chi Minh Trail thereby guaranteeing the comrades in said plant plenty of overtime. This, they hope, will give them many more rubles to buy borsch for their babushkas."

The pilots went crazy, jumping up and down and slapping each other on the back, fully appreciating this meager bit of comic relief. Gary joined the other pilots in a standing ovation with lots of foot stomping. Lieutenant Colonel Foxe had been in on the joke as he proceeded to pass around cigars.

Then the briefing took a serious turn. "I don't want to presume that I know what's going on, but there's a lot of strange stuff happening in southern North Vietnam," Lieutenant Smith said, with no hint of a smile on his face. He paused, looking through a stack of TWXs in his hand. "All these messages report greatly increased activity, trucks, coolies, and bicycles hauling materiel south. The folks at 7th Air Force want you to do armed reconnaissance along the roads there whenever your fuel and the weather allows. Specifically, they want you to make a gun-run whenever you're coming back from a mission in the southern Route Packages and shoot at any logistical activity."

Lieutenant Smith paused, changing flip charts and maps on the easel. Pointing at a series of poster-sized aerial photographs, he continued. "We're collecting photography and intelligence reports on troop and supply movements from the north to the south. The North Vietnamese Army's moving tons of supplies south. There's a lot of truck activity and something is going to blow in the future. The problem is that we don't know when, where, or what. Oh, by the way, I can also add that more SAMs and Triple-A sites are showing up down south. We have definite intelligence on that. You can expect more launches and more flak from Thanh Hoa south. But don't worry because those little fuckers can't shoot straight anyway."

The intelligence officer's concluding remark ended the briefing and brought a volley of cat calls and raspberry sounds.

"That's more stuff to shoot at," Lieutenant Colonel Foxe called out.

"What do you think that was all about?" Gary asked as he and Lieutenant Colonel Foxe walked toward the squadron.

"I'll be damned if I know. The chain of command only tells us so much. We guess or make up the rest."

The two men paused, lighting cigarettes. "All I know is that he brought more bad news," he said, turning toward the squadron building. For the first time, Gary detected concern in the colonel's voice. He looked worried. A tractor pulling a chain of loaded bomb carts rattled by heading toward the parking apron.

"What's going on?" Gary asked.

"Something is blowing in the wind. The brass at 7th Air Force wouldn't be crapping in their pants about the movement of supplies toward the south, unless they had something to crow about."

"This doesn't feel right. I'm getting bad vibes about this whole interdiction thing." Gary didn't know how to express his feelings to the colonel. His doubts had increased after each mission over the Ho Chi Minh Trail, bombs dropping into endless rain forest, with Communist trees flying through the air and countless craters appearing in the muck. What the fuck are we doing here? Gary wondered. But he knew he could never say those words to the colonel.

"We can't stop the North Vietnamese, so we're screwed, and the war in the south has gone south. We can drop bombs forever and not stop the infiltration," the colonel said, taking a long drag on his cigarette and blowing away the smoke. He squashed the butt with the sole of his boot, and lit another.

The colonel stood there for a moment, shaking his head. "Uncle Ho and General Giap don't care how many people die on their side. The North Vietnamese just keep sending men and materiel south on the Ho Chi Minh Trail, never to return. The cost doesn't matter to their leaders. Eventually the U.S. will get bored and tired of the killing and pack its bag and screw out of town. Just like we did in Korea."

Foxe paused a beat and looked around to ensure that they were alone. He pointed North. "This Rolling Thunder operation, what we are trying to do, is FUBAR. Keep that to yourself."

"Then, what we're doing doesn't really matter," Gary said, a sinking feeling enveloping him, like settling into quicksand.

"We have a mission to do. Period! They tell us what to do and when. Our job is to put the bombs on the target and to get back home alive. Let the brass worry about the big picture."

"We end up being a little cog in a big wheel," Gary said, realizing that their role in the war was of little concern to the chain of command. The men and planes lost were just numbers. But Gary knew the men as individuals, not ticks on a whiteboard, and that is what bothered him.

"Yes! All we're doing is putting up statistics. The number of bombs dropped, the number of sorties, the number of trucks destroyed and the number of SAMs launched. Numbers and statistics, my ass. I thought this was a war! So, there you have it. We're screwed!" Lieutenant Colonel Foxe sneered and threw his cigarette into the *Klong*. "Fuck!" he said, shaking his head.

Gary's head swirled. He couldn't let himself think about his insignificance. Somehow he suspected that he had become almost trivial, lost in the big picture of the war. Whether he lived or died seemed to bear no consequence.

Several official staff cars loaded with men in dress blues passed by. Lieutenant Colonel Foxe and Gary both saluted when they noticed that one of the cars had a blue flag with stars fluttering in the breeze.

"Oh, oh, the blue suits have arrived," Foxe said.

"What?" Gary asked.

"Brass from Hawaii and the Philippines. Looking for someone's scalp."

"Whose?"

"Colonel Broughton's. I hear that there are generals and colonels who want to hang him from the flagpole. At least that's the scuttlebutt. A plane load of generals, colonels,

Inspector Generals and Office of Special Investigations people is making the rounds in Thailand hunting for whoever was near Cam Pha on 2 June."

"Ah, the *Turkestan.*"

"How did you know that?"

"I read it in the paper. Do you remember that we flew near Cam Pha on that day?"

"Christ, yes. Don't tell that to anyone and keep quiet about it, or you'll get your nuts crushed."

"Yes, sir," Gary said as they walked toward the 333rd Squadron building for flight and element briefings and to suit up.

The sky had turned from black to gray. On the flight ramp, airmen loaded fuel and bombs on the F-105s. The first sunrays beat their way through the clouds and mist.

EASY RIDER

_____ 46

Yuri Vaskilev, General Lieutenant
GRU, Soviet Military Intelligence
Hanoi, North Vietnam
18 June 1967

YURI STOMPED ON the starting lever of his Harley. The engine roared to life as he rotated the throttle and then settled into the usual Harley grumble. He turned to see Sergeant Komarvsky ready on his machine. Yuri motioned for Colonel Thon to climb on behind him as he adjusted his goggles.

Colonel Thon served as Yuri's liaison with the Peoples' Army of North Vietnam (PAVN) and smoothed entrance to military or restricted areas. The three men freely traveled about the countryside. The colonel's clout provided access to missile sites and antiaircraft artillery positions. After studying each site, Yuri and Sergeant Komarvsky made suggestions for the best way to use the weapons against the Americans.

Yuri, the sergeant, and Colonel Thon scouted the area around Hanoi on motorcycles, looking for sites to place missiles and antiaircraft weapons. They sought to counter the American tactics, defeating their systems. Yuri played the game of cat and mouse, tit-for-tat, or measures and counter-measures with the American pilots. As he devised new schemes, the Americans developed new tactics. Then the North Vietnamese, with Russian guidance, developed counter-tactics. One new move by either side resulted in a counter-move by the other. And the deadly game continued.

This day the trio headed west from Hanoi toward a mountain chain, which the American warplanes used as a navigation aid and for terrain masking. The pilots flew low along the ridge to hide from the North Vietnamese radar. The ridgeline pointed directly to Thai Nguyen and to Hanoi.

The American pilots referred to the mountain chain as The Thud Ridge. Yuri had acquired this information from the War Criminals, as the North Vietnamese called the captured pilots. Yuri had witnessed the harsh tactics used by the North Vietnamese on the prisoners and wanted no part in torture. On the other hand, the pilots harbored information that he needed. He had to have a method of obtaining it.

His days of riding about since arriving in North Vietnam had been partially successful. Yuri observed one raid from a great distance away. He wanted to get closer. Maybe this time they would get lucky.

Yuri didn't hate Americans. His job was to kill them. He had loved his time in Washington in 1961, when he was stationed there as a military attaché. Now with this war, his behavior towards Americans changed from adversary to deadly foe. Yuri knew it was a contradiction—killing airmen from a country that he liked. He assumed they didn't take it personally. One thing he knew for sure; he loved American motorcycles.

This morning, the North Vietnamese officer selected the Thai Nguyen Iron and Steel Mill for their observation point. He led Yuri and the sergeant to a hillock overlooking the plant where they proceeded to eat their breakfast of bread and cheese. Americans bombed the plant once or twice per week like clockwork.

Yuri heard the planes first and spotted them coming from the northwest, flying along the ridge.

Four fighters passed overhead at low altitude, splitting into two groups of two planes each. One group flew toward the north and the second set headed south, where they began maneuvering. This is good, Yuri thought. We can't get much closer than this.

The Americans called these first planes on the target Wild Weasels. Yuri had learned this from captured pilots.

While he didn't want to participate in an inquisition of one of these pilots, he had questions. He needed information. No matter how much brutality it took, he would get his answers.

WE'LL NEED THE SPARE

_____ 47

Gary Bishop Deale, First Lieutenant, USAF
Takhli RTAFB, Thailand
19 June 1967, Counter Number 60

GARY HAD WATCHED the crash while waiting to pull onto the runway. The last F-105 taking off in the first flight blew an engine at the most critical part of the takeoff, just before liftoff. First, a large puff of black smoke came from the back of the plane, followed by a blast of flame. The plane shuddered and then veered off the runway into a field. Suddenly, it flipped over onto its back and exploded.
   "Fuck," Gary said, shocked and stunned as the fireball climbed into the sky near the north end of the runway.
   Lieutenant Colonel Foxe, the mission leader turned his plane back toward the airfield followed by the two other F-105s in the flight. "Did he get out?"
   "Negative, no chute. Nothing," Major O'Shane said.
   The fire blazed and smoke drifted over the airfield. Drivers of the crash trucks warily approached the wreckage, spraying the pyre with foam. Six bombs were mixed in the wreckage. A man had just died. Gary had seen pilots die in plane crashes before but this stunned him nonetheless.
   He had sat next to the new pilot, a fellow lieutenant, during the morning briefing. Gary had told him that this, his fifth mission and his first over North Vietnam, would

be a piece of cake. After all, the target was a suspect truck park. Now he was dead. In an instant, dead.

The tower informed the pilots waiting to takeoff that the runway would be cleared of debris and reopened in about fifteen minutes. The mission would proceed.

Gary sat in his plane waiting. He wondered why this had to happen. He understood that pilots were shot down and perhaps killed in combat. Being killed by mechanical failure seemed to be such a waste, especially when the strike target was a suspect truck park in southern North Vietnam. He shook his head, cursing this fiery congruence of fate and chance.

Twenty minutes later, Gary pushed his throttle ahead and followed his element leader down the runway. Their mission resumed. Waiting until his airspeed passed 200 knots, he eased back on the stick lifting the plane off the runway well before the skid marks began. As his plane climbed, Gary rolled slightly to his left so that he could see the flaming wreck surrounded by crash trucks. The pilot had done everything possible to save himself short of ejecting. The F-105 had plowed through the field just fine right up to the second the plane went into the ditch and flipped over. The pilot must not have seen it coming until it was too late.

A bulldozer piled dirt around the unexploded bombs, which the pilot had jettisoned. Charred areas began at the edge of the runway, showing that the external fuel tanks burned when they popped off.

Gary forced the fireball out of his mind. He thought about the young pilot's wife waiting back home just like Allison. Just for a second, he thought of Allison lying on the beach in Hawaii. Then the image faded away replaced by the climbing ball of fire from the crash.

SUPPORT YOUR LOCAL SAM SITE

_____ 48

Yuri Vaskilev, General Lieutentant
GRU, Soviet Military Intelligence
Over Hoang Tien, North Vietnam
20 June 1967

WIND FROM THE helicopter rotors swirled in the open doors and roared through the passenger compartment. Yuri leaned over and peered out, cursing mightily. Pointing to the buildings and exposed vehicles below him, he shook his head. Sergeant Komarvsky leaned over his shoulder and scrunched his face. "Fuck your mother," the sergeant yelled in his ear. Colonel Thon, Yuri's North Vietnamese liaison officer, looked out the other side of the helicopter. A disaster loomed if he didn't get the situation on the ground corrected.

The Hoang Tien SAM Support and storage facility, located forty kilometers north of Hanoi, had a reputation for carelessness. The helicopter pilot looked about anxiously, eager to return to his home base at Hanoi/Gia Lam Airfield. The enemy would be coming soon. He had no intention of being caught in the air in a helicopter with American fighters circling about.

Nonetheless, Yuri ordered the helicopter to land so he could read the riot act to the commander and comrades at the installation. The facility had been a railroad equipment repair yard, but Yuri expropriated it to assemble SAMs because it already had high bay buildings, which contained cranes to lift the canisters and missiles.

In open view, Yuri spotted SAM canisters and missile transporters. No camouflage netting covered any of the missile equipment. Destruction of these facilities ranked high in the Americans targeting scheme.

Maybe we'll get lucky, he thought. But the feeling of a looming catastrophe enveloped him.

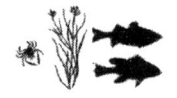

LITTLE WHITE LIES

_____ 49

Allison Faith Deale
Seven Springs, North Carolina
June 24, 1967

I STOOD AT our kitchen window looking at the cardinals at the bird feeder. My day was mixed with happiness and sadness, joy at the news I had received. Sadness at the fact that Gary wasn't here to share it with me.

My sin of omission committed while in Hawaii added to my unease. Everyone tells lies, little white lies, bold-faced lies, innocent lies, or harmful lies. While thinking about our time in Hawaii, the only thing that came to mind is that Gary didn't tell me the whole truth.

As I had listened to him describe bursting antiaircraft shells, MIGs flying by shooting at him, surface-to-air missiles zooming through the air and bombs exploding on the ground, his portrayals scared me half to death. It was clear that he coyly avoided telling me his full story. After reading newspapers back home, I knew that Gary and his friends were flying missions into danger. Many had been shot down. How could anyone help but not be afraid under such circumstances. I wondered how much of the truth he concealed from me.

Sitting in our house with the doctor's report in my hand, it became very evident to me that I had also lied. Committing a sin of omission would be more correct, because I didn't tell Gary that I had stopped taking the pill before traveling to Hawaii. In my heart, I wanted it to be my decision. I didn't want to create any more anxiety for him.

I sat at the table composing a short letter to Gary telling him that he would be a father in February.

PART 9

You have a row of dominoes set up; you knock over the first one, and what will happen to the last one is that it will go over very quickly.

—President Dwight David Eisenhower, 1954

UNCLE HO

There is an uncle named Ho
who eats his grub from a bowl.
He wears a conical hat
and squats as he shits
through a little round hole in the floor.

Caring not, sending his people
south along his trail
on a one-way trip.
Glaring at our lines in the muck
and our bombs with contempt and defiance.

That fucker is mine.
I'll knock him supine.
If Tex and Mac give us the go.

From the combat diary of Gary Bishop Deale,
First Lieutenant, USAF, 1 July 1967

A 100 MISSION PASS AND A WAKE

_____ 50

Gary Bishop Deale, First Lieutenant, USAF
Takhli RTAFB, Thailand
29 June 1967

"DID YOU SEE the good captain's swan song?" Lieutenant Colonel Foxe asked, using his hands to mimic the upside down pass Captain Heaps had made over the airfield while down in the weeds.

The two men sat in the Officers' Club Stag Bar having their last drink before retiring for the night. They were both on the mission board for the following day.

Every pilot put on a show upon returning from their 100th combat mission over North Vietnam. Nobody talked beforehand about what they planned to do to celebrate liberation from flying up North because that was a jinx. In fact, nobody talked about what they were going to do when they came back from any mission.

"Yes indeed, very original," Gary said. The final pass made by Captain Heaps had greatly impressed Gary. He had never seen F-105s perform an aerobatic maneuver like that, upside down with the tail almost touching the weeds.

Gary dreamed of the day when he got the chance to put on a show because then he would get to see Allison again. He would just have to let the creative juices flow and push the envelope when his time came, if it did. Then he realized that he had double jinxed himself by using the word *if.* But at least he had only thought it and not said it.

Though Gary remained outwardly optimistic, fatalistic visions had been creeping into his dreams. Too many planes got shot down on missions Downtown. Scuttlebutt about North Vietnamese treatment of prisoners weaved through the stories told on base. Torture, the pilots said. That was what you could expect. One pilot said, "Reminds me of Korea. We heard rumors. But no one knew how bad it was until the war was over."

Somebody had to know the truth, but they weren't talking. News pictures of welcoming parades in Hanoi had appeared, with the peasants beating the POWs as they staggered past. The guests of honor looked defeated, like walking dead men. Gary had seen news photographs of prisoners, bowing stiffly, looking shriveled, emaciated, mere specks of what they once must have been. Sitting at attention on hard wooden chairs, speaking like robots.

War Criminals is what the North Vietnamese called the American prisoners. On his darkest days, thoughts of becoming a forgotten prisoner in the North scared the shit out of Gary.

A group of pilots dressed in their red, yellow, blue and green party flight suits crashed into the room. The men began moving tables, scraping them across the floor.

"Looks as though the party is about to begin, Lieutenant Colonel Foxe said. "These guys want us to move."

Gary and the colonel moved to the bar to watch the festivities. First there would be a celebration for the captain and his one hundred missions North. Then, after everyone had enough to drink, a wake with testimonials for the pilot from the 354th Squadron who didn't come back from that day's mission. Triple-A had knocked him down over Kep.

As the group of pilots drank, the noise level went up. Loud conversation filled with braggadocio flooded the room. Glasses clanked together as the men offered toast after toast to Captain Heaps, the one who survived flying one hundred missions North. Every now and then, someone threw a drink against the wall. Shattered glass and whiskey flew through the air.

The bar game of the night appeared to be full contact football, without pads, another way for the stressed-out pilots to blow off steam and frustration. Alcohol consumption played a large role in their lives, helping them cope with the five hundred pound gorilla lurking in each man's mind—FEAR! Arranging chairs to mark the end zones for this game, the pilots busied themselves with party details.

"Enough of this," Lieutenant Colonel Foxe said. "I'll see you at 0315 for breakfast."

"Yes, sir, thanks."

Gary shook Captain Heap's hand. Fully decked out in his red party suit, his friend smiled, well on the way to getting shit-faced.

He departed the club, walked toward his hooch and looked at the clouds overhead. Red, pink, purple and magenta clouds swirling above him made it one of the most spectacular sunsets he'd seen in Thailand. What was the saying? Red sky at night, sailor's delight. That was it.

Though he was sorry that he couldn't remain for the entire party, Gary knew he couldn't remain at the club. He had to get up at 0300, now six hours away.

Sorting through his mail, he noticed two letters from Allison. That's nice, two letters in one day, he thought. Opening the thin envelope, he received the biggest surprise of his life.

June 24, 1967
Dearest Gary
This will be a very short letter as I have to go to bed soon. I have to make a very early morning drive to Beaufort to meet Carmen to go out on a boat.
I want you to know that I have good news for you. I'm pregnant.
The clinic confirmed today.
The biologist in me tells me that you will be a father in February and the woman in me believes it's true.
I miss you and love you so much.
Allison

Gary couldn't hold back the tears running down his cheeks dripping onto the letter. He wondered how it had happened. Allison was taking the pill. But then he remembered that he never thought about the pill or pregnancy or anything like that in Hawaii. He had only thought of devouring Allison's body and loving her to death.

He pushed the other letters aside and began a note to her.

My dearest Allison
Thank You! Thank you! Thank you!
You have made me the happiest man in the world.

CHINA EXPRESS

_____ 51

Gary Bishop Deale, First Lieutenant, USAF
Kep, North Vietnam
30 June 1967, Counter Number 66

"SAM LAUNCH! BREAK! Break!" The words thundered over Gary's earphones. Immediately, he pushed the throttle and slapped his control stick to the right while stomping the right rudder pedal rolling the plane downward, following Captain Klepperson's plane.
   Surface-to-air missiles flashed upward in front of him. One, two, and then three flaming spears erupted from the ground and streaked toward the strike aircraft. Gary tracked the missiles using a spot on his canopy. If the missiles appeared to change relative location, then he would be okay. If the missiles remained in the same relative spot, that meant they were aimed at him.
   A large flash at the front of the attack stream engulfed one of the F-105s. A second later, the plane disintegrated in a massive detonation.
   "Who's down?" Lieutenant Colonel Foxe radioed.
   "Gold Lead. He's gone!"
   Reorganizing the planes, Lieutenant Colonel Foxe took command of the mission, replacing the pilot in the lead. According to radio traffic, the mission commander was now riding his parachute toward the ground. Foxe ordered

Gary's flight to attack the SAM site, while the other planes bombed the primary target.

Aside from a parachute beeper blasting over Guard Channel, silence ruled. The plane was down far in the North. Even if the pilot survived, there was no hope for rescue.

The seven F-105s of the newly reconstituted Silver Flight broke away toward the Kep Rail Yard, about one mile north. Gary's flight circled back to the south toward the SAM site.

Smoke and dust from the launches drifted over the site. SAM launchers and radars intermingled with buildings and hooches in a small valley. A road and a rail line cut through part of the missile installation.

The pilots engaged their afterburners and the planes in front of Gary began a pop-up climb. He checked his six position and eased the control stick back to begin his climb.

Gary breathed deeply several times sucking oxygen to clear his head. He arced over the top and centered the bombing pipper on the target.

The bombs from Bronze 1 hit the site at that instant, throwing fire, smoke and dust over the area, followed almost immediately by the bombs from the second plane. Gary concentrated on a cluster of structures, which looked like the Fan Song missile guidance radar, only to see the area erupt in orange flashes as Captain Klepperson's bombs struck.

"4, there's a missile on a launcher where the road and railroad cross," Captain Klepperson, just ahead of Gary, called out as his aircraft bottomed out from the dive and turned north away from the site.

Gary locked his eyes on the crossing and found the SAM. People were covering the missile and launcher with netting. Gary centered the missile in his pipper sight and punched off six bombs. Pulling on the stick with all his might, he pushed the throttle forward, fighting the dive, while trying to gain airspeed.

Coming off the target at 550 knots, he flinched at the WHACK as antiaircraft shells zoomed by his cockpit at supersonic speeds. White blossoms from 37 mm Triple-A surrounded his plane. He huffed and puffed oxygen, fighting the G-forces. Jerking as the concussion from the exploding bombs jarred the F-105, he turned his head to see the road and railroad crossing and the missile obliterated by fire and smoke.

The four F-105s joined up in spread formation and turned east, racing to link up with the other planes. Gary continued jinking and looking behind, checking for other flying objects.

Small specks in the air, well to the south of Gary's formation, emerged from the haze, coming toward him. He recognized the planes immediately, small dart-like delta-winged planes, no smoke trails, silver in color: MIG-21s. He took a deep breath. His heart raced. We're going to get cut off, he thought

Gary called out a warning, "MIG-21s at five o'clock high."

Lieutenant Colonel Foxe radioed to increase speed and to descend. "We're going down. Kick it up," The nose of his aircraft dropped and he engaged his afterburner.

Gary pushed his throttle forward to the afterburner détente and followed the other planes to near the ground as the formation turned to the northeast. Now that he was down low, the MIGs faded from view. He knew two things. There was no possibility of engaging the MIGs. His plane was critically low on fuel, as were the others. They could not get involved in a dogfight, whereas the enemy fighters had just taken off with a full load of fuel. Secondly, they had to go low and fast to run away from the MIGS. After dropping as low as they could go, the pilots disengaged their afterburners.

Lieutenant Colonel Foxe radioed, "Turn IFF off!"

A second later, Gary realized that the colonel meant for the pilots to turn off their Identification Friend or Foe transponders so that they couldn't be monitored. Gary figured out that their leader didn't want reconnaissance planes to track the flight and hit the IFF transponder switch.

"Shoot anything in front of us," Foxe said as he led the planes skimming the hilltops and dropping down into the valleys to get below radar coverage.

Just below on the hills, giant trees whipped by Gary in a green blur. In the valleys, flooded rice paddies glinted in the sunlight.

Far northeast of Kep by this time and headed at about 45 degrees, he checked his chart. They had entered the prohibited area near the Communist Chinese border.

The F-105s cruised along at over 550 knots, putting eleven miles per minute behind them. Nothing could outrun the F-105 in level flight at low altitude.

Porpoising over the hilltops, just skimming over the trees, the F-105s raced to the northeast. True, with afterburners they could go faster, but that burned fuel at a prodigious rate.

Gary realized what the colonel was doing. Jesus Christ! There's nothing where we're headed except Communist China, he thought.

One of the Rules of Engagement required that American aircraft never penetrate the thirty nautical mile buffer zone along the China border. The planes had already done that. Gary figured they must be inside China. Rules didn't stop pilots from doing what they had to do to save their own lives. If surviving meant breaking rules in times of great danger—so be it. No one talked about such things later.

Following the gaggle of airplanes as they turned south, Gary checked out the trees as they blasted over the hilltops and settled down into the valleys. Green treetops flashed by, just below his wingtip.

The formation made a series of turns, following a wide river toward the coast. Once over open water, they climbed slowly, hunting the tankers.

Gary didn't say a word during the debriefing. Lieutenant Colonel Foxe did all of the talking for his pilots, explaining about the shoot down and evading the MIGs by going very low and sweeping southeast from Kep.

After his shower, Gary returned to his hooch to take an afternoon nap. As he moved his pillow, he saw an envelope stuck underneath. He opened it, finding an embroidered cloth patch and a note, *"Don't ever wear this and don't talk about it. MF."*

The colorful patch bore the words *"CHINA EXPRESS"* at the top. Below that, an F-105 streaked in front of a Red Star. "Very cool," Gary whispered to himself, stashing the patch with the collection in his footlocker.

ON SPITTING: WHY DOESN'T ANYONE STAND UP FOR US?

_____ 52

Gary Bishop Deale, First Lieutenant, USAF
Takhli RTAFB, Thailand
1 July 1967

AT DAWN, THEY stood at the edge of the runway looking at the charred and churned up ground. An odor of jet fuel and smoke lingered in the air from the two week old crash. Green shoots pushed their way through burned grass. Gary and Lieutenant Colonel Foxe rested, catching their breath after their last lap. The colonel, as usual, rode his bike.

Most of the debris from the crash had been hauled away. The lieutenant's remains, dispatched with full military honors, were already buried back in his hometown.

Gary held his hands over his ears as the last of the sixteen F-105s on the early morning mission lifted off the runway and roared overhead, riding a wall of thundering sound.

"Isn't that a beautiful sight?" Lieutenant Colonel Foxe exclaimed as the planes climbed away.

The strike force pilots had sounded excited to Gary as he'd passed the parking ramp earlier because they knew they were going near Hanoi. Every pilot wanted to go Downtown, because they sensed they were destroying a significant target. Otherwise, the pilots swore they spent their time killing nothing but Communist trees.

Gary wished he had been on the morning mission. He would get his chance later in the afternoon during a strike on the Viet Tri Thermal Power Plant.

"I salute them," the colonel said, lifting his Go To Hell bush hat off his head. He wiped his face with a hanky and then held it over the scar on his left cheek.

Gary doffed his hat and the two men stood there watching the smoke trails from the F-105s drift away.

"What did you hear about Colonel Broughton?" Gary asked, knowing that the rumor mill had churned out fifty variations of the vice wing commander's fate.

"Court-martialed and found guilty of destroying government property is the official result," Foxe said. "With a fifty dollar fine. You can't convict a commander of doing what's right and standing up for his men, so they dropped some chicken shit charge on him."

Colonel Broughton had recently been relieved from his duties and hauled away to the Philippines along with two pilots who had allegedly committed the offense. Word had gradually leaked out over the previous month that the two officers had fired their cannons at an antiaircraft gun site near Cam Pha, North Vietnam, on 2 June. The Soviets alleged that some of the cannon shells hit the *Turkestan*, a Soviet cargo ship, an action that violated the Rules of Engagement. After the Soviets vigorously complained, the chain of command reacted.

Gary heard that the two pilots had told Colonel Broughton what they thought happened upon landing, so the colonel or a mechanic had destroyed the gun camera film. The destruction of government property became the only charge that would stick.

"The people based here who have looked at this think the ship was hit by Vietnamese Triple-A," Foxe said. "The Russians showed some 20 mm casings collected from the *Turkestan*, but we here know that the F-105 cannon doesn't eject anything from the aircraft. The witch hunt continued and the investigators tagged the colonel."

"Is Colonel Broughton finished?" Gary asked.

"Finished, gone, done, career over. Never would've happened before. People used to stand up for each other. Commanders up the chain used to put their careers on the line and stand up for their men. Now all the brass wants to do is bust your nuts, even if you're doing the right thing by protecting your people. I don't know how far up the line all this chicken shit goes. I think it probably starts with LBJ, then proceeds to McNamara and finally to Pacific Air Forces in Hawaii. I can't imagine someone in Saigon sacking an excellent combat commander."

The men paused, smoking cigarettes, studying the crash site. The colonel sighed and peddled away.

Gary stood alone, remembering the lieutenant who had died on this spot. He recalled the sight of the ascending fireball and the horror he felt as he watched his buddy die. His opinions about the chain of command no longer corresponded with the way he was supposed to feel. He felt frustrated, tired and depressed.

While fear lurked in his mind, Gary had also become upset. He felt anger at the choice of targets made by the chain of command. Each time another pilot was shot down while bombing a worthless target, he seethed. The young pilot who had died on this spot had been assigned to attack a suspect truck park in the jungle.

Gary did the only thing he could think of doing when in a funk. Taking a pencil and notepad out of his pocket, he began to write a little ditty, which just popped into his brain.

ON SPITTING
Things do go round
in this deadly game.
But I spit on the ground
upon hearing
Tex and Mac's names.

GARY'S DREAM SHEET

_____ 53

Gary Bishop Deale, First Lieutenant, USAF
Takhli RTAFB, Thailand
1 July 1967

GARY ASKED THE personnel sergeant at wing headquarters to place the documents into an envelope and seal it because he didn't want to peek. He did not want to know what the papers said until he reached the privacy of his own room.

He had filled out his wish list, or dream sheet as the pilots called it, a month previously. He had been in Thailand since February and had flown sixty-eight combat missions over North Vietnam. Another two months in Thailand and then he would move on to other grand adventures.

Now he would find out whether he had received his requested assignment. Or, he would find out that the Air Force, working in its own mysterious ways, had sent him someplace else.

His first choice had been to return to Seymour Johnson and transition into F-4 Phantom jets. Gary knew F-105 attrition limited the aircraft's days remaining in combat. Seymour had already switched to Phantoms. A North Carolina assignment meant that Allison could continue with her studies at the marine lab.

Secondly, he wanted to be assigned to the Air Force Academy as an instructor. One of his former professors maintained contact and thought that he would be an excellent teacher. Gary thought such an assignment would be great, even though he would have to give up flying fighters.

Gary walked back to his hooch watching two F-105s circling the field. Burning up fuel, he thought. Must be a problem with one of the planes.

After saying hello to Helene, his hooch girl, and inquiring about his laundry, he took a shower and organized his gear for an afternoon mission.

Sitting at his desk, he contemplated his unopened envelope. There was also a package from Allison, probably one of her cassette tapes.

Opening the envelope and scanning the documents, he found a set of orders assigning him to the 4th Tactical Fighter Wing at Seymour Johnson. A two month temporary duty assignment to MacDill near Tampa preceded that for transition to F-4 Phantoms.

Allison will be pleased, he thought. Now she will be able to remain at the marine lab and continue with her doctorate. He didn't know for sure, but maybe the baby would change her plans.

He continued reading the papers. For long term planning, there was a preliminary notification of his assignment to the graduate program in astrophysics at MIT or Stanford beginning in September 1970, which would lead to a faculty position at the academy. I really want to be a good instructor, he thought. We will love Colorado Springs with all of its skiing and outdoor activities.

As he predicted, the small box from Allison contained a cassette tape. Listening to her sweet voice on the machine nearly led him to tears.

"Hello Gary," Allison said. "I love you very much. I have more news from the base clinic about the baby. I'll read you the report."

Gary heard the joy in Allison's voice. Just two more months and I can hold her again, he thought.

It pleased Gary to know that he would be returning to their house in Seven Springs. He looked forward to the birth of his child. It will be a wonderfully happy time.

BUMPY ACTION Mission 67-58
Gulf of Tonkin
50 Miles East of Nam Dinh, North Vietnam
1 July 1967

THE RYAN AIRCRAFT Firebee Remotely Piloted Vehicle (RPV or drone) dropped off the wing pylon of the DC-130 mothership and began processing instructions from the inertial navigation system. Following a preprogrammed command module, the small aircraft self-checked its systems and communicated the fact that everything appeared normal.
    Descending to low altitude, the RPV turned northwest toward the area between Haiphong and Hanoi. At about two hundred feet above the ground, the drone crossed over the coast and headed inland. Changing course every ten seconds and flying at four hundred knots, the drone gave enemy air defense gunners about two seconds to react and fire before it disappeared over the horizon.
    Except for the brief time over each target, the aircraft otherwise flew a preprogrammed erratic flight profile, which appeared to be designed by a drunken sailor.
    While the enemy fired at the RPV, no shells hit it. Following the designated course, the drone circled Hanoi counter-clockwise and turned southeast toward the Gulf of Tonkin. After reaching the coast, the RPV slowly climbed. It continued flying over the gulf for a distance. Once the engine cut-off, a large parachute deployed.
    A CH-3 cargo helicopter used large grappling hooks to snag the smaller plane's parachute. The chopper carried

the drone westward to Danang Airbase, where the film was removed and sent on to Tan Son Nhut near Saigon.

This RPV had survived its fourth mission over North Vietnam. Tradition dictated that five successful missions over North Vietnam must be flown before the aircraft received a name and appropriate nose art.

Pussy Galore, the record holder, had flown thirty-seven successful missions. Her nose art paid homage to Honor Blackman's portrayal in *Goldfinger,* the James Bond movie. An airman at the base paint shop served as the resident artist. Planning ahead, he had started his painting for the next drone to be christened—Honey Ryder. Featuring a scantily clad Ursula Andress astride a human dung cart, known locally as a honey wagon, the artist honored Honey Ryder from *Dr. No.*

THE AIR FORCE Strategic Air Command Special Air Relocatable Photographic Facility (SAC SARPF) at Tan Son Nhut Airbase near Saigon handled film processing and analysis for drone missions flown over North Vietnam. Within the photographic facility, bedlam reigned. Film cans were stacked to eye-level. A swarm of photo interpreters bent over light tables with magnifying lenses and stereoscopes.

A combination of luck and serendipity happened to coincide on just two negatives. A photo interpreter, per chance, took a second look at the film on the light table. The drone had tipped its wing to make a turn extending photographic coverage. In the far distance, the airman spotted strange equipment.

He recognized it for what it was. The image sent his blood pressure soaring and pulse racing. He immediately requested film from a 30 June high altitude mission covering the same area. The facility hadn't been detected by the photo interpreters who had looked at the 30 June photography. Using nets and screens, the North

Vietnamese had well camouflaged the facility. The images from the two missions created a stir, resulting in a classified FLASH Photo Intelligence TWX message.

SECRET
FLASH Photo Intell Report
DTG: 020767:0300 Zulu
FROM: SAC SARPF, TSN
TO: 7th AF
  COMMUSMACV
  HQ, SAC
  CINCPAC
  JCS
  SECDEF
  CIA
  NPIC
  DIA
  WHITEHOUSE
Bumpy Action Mission 67-58 of 1 July reveals a SAM Support Facility at Phuc Ve, North Vietnam, 1.5 NM west of Phuc Ve (18 NM SW of Hanoi) at 205430N 1053220E. Facility consists of three high-bay buildings and several other structures. One SA-2 missile on transporter evident covered with camouflage netting. This facility confirmed by imagery from Bumpy Action Mission 67-54 (30 June 67) (High Alt) with two missile transporters and SA-2 missile canisters covered by camouflage netting evident. Negation: 20 June: Bumpy Action 67-45. Agricultural machinery present on 67-45 but no SAM related equipment.
END
SECRET

IN RESPONSE TO the FLASH message, another TWX was issued from the headquarters of 7th Air Force at Tan Son

Nhut Airbase near Saigon. American operational plans specified that no high-threat target in this area of North Vietnam could be bombed without giving the chain of command forty-eight hours to veto the strike. Once the imminent threat strike TWX was sent, the chain of command had the option of cancelling the mission. Otherwise, the strike would fly on 5 July.

TOP SECRET
OPERATIONAL FLASH
FROM: 7TH AF, TSN
DTG: 020767:0745Z
TO: COMMUSMACV
  CINCPAC
  JCS
  SECDEF
  WHITEHOUSE
SUBJECT: IMMINENT THREAT STRIKE AUTHORIZATION
RE: BUMPY ACTION MISSION 67-58 FPIR
DTG 020767:0300Z and BA 67-54

In accordance with OPLAN, 7th AF will conduct strike upon Phuc Ve SAM Support Facility at 205430N 1053220E on 5 July. Forty-eight hour strike hold expires 040767:0745 Zulu.
END
TOP SECRET

THE BIG HURT

_____ 55

Gary Bishop Deale, First Lieutenant, USAF
Takhli RTAFB, Thailand
4 July 1967

GARY STOOD BY his F-105 as Sergeant Weinert from the base paint shop made the final brush strokes of yellow paint. Finally, after months of waiting, Gary had been assigned to his very own fighter. Other men would also fly the jet. But each time he flew, this one was his. Having just arrived from the United States, the plane had been newly painted in tan on green camouflage.

Gary had told Sergeant Cash, the crew chief, to find an artist and have the 'nose art' he had designed painted on the fuselage just below the cockpit.

The following day, Sergeant Weinert arrived with his paint and brushes.

"You know someone will bitch at you and have the painting removed, don't you, sir?" Sergeant Weinert asked.

"Yes, I do. Just another sorry-assed regulation we have to follow. But I may get a couple days before someone jumps on me." He patted Sergeant Weinert on the back. "You do beautiful artwork."

"Thank you, sir."

"I'll have to give you a chit for a case of beer."

"I'd appreciate that."

The design Gary chose came to his mind because of a hit song by Toni Fisher. The title was "The Big Hurt." He had also envisioned the damage soon to be done by the bombs dropped from this, his plane. The words, THE BIG, arced over the top of a bomb silhouette, while below, the artist finished painting, HURT.

Gary popped the cork off a bottle of champagne he had brought along for the occasion and splashed a small amount on the nose of his very own F-105. "Here's to THE BIG HURT," Gary said, taking a swig and passing the bottle.

SOME DAYS YOU EAT THE BEAR

_____ 56

Gary Bishop Deale, First Lieutenant, USAF
Takhli RTAFB, Thailand
5 July 1967, Counter Number 71

STANDING AT THE edge of the parking ramp before dawn with Sergeant Cash, the crew chief, Gary lit a cigarette. Taking a couple long drags, Gary looked at the tail end of the plane, scanning for leaks. "The bird's ready."
"Very good, sir," the sergeant said.
After finishing his cigarette, he walked to the crew ladder. Pausing, he looked at the "nose art" painted on the fuselage. As a sign of respect to his F-105, he reached out and patted the painting. THE BIG HURT stood ready. He smiled approvingly. It was a creative work of art.
He climbed the ladder and slipped onto the ejection seat. Sergeant Cash helped buckle him in. Checking his watch, Gary began working through the engine start checklist. This was another cartridge start, so Gary fastened his mask and began breathing pure oxygen. Soon a cloud of black smoke engulfed the aircraft and the J75 engine rumbled to life. After signaling for the wheel chocks to be removed and saluting Sergeant Cash, he extended his thumbs. He was good to go.
Leading the mission exactly as he briefed it, Colonel Jacobs descended to tree level after crossing into North Vietnam. The formation of F-105s flew even faster than Gary remembered from previous missions. This guy isn't

screwing around, Gary thought, as the strike force thundered over the land.

The target, a SAM Support Facility at Phuc Ve, was about twenty miles southwest of Hanoi and the fighters arrived there six minutes after entering North Vietnam. Just as the sun cleared the horizon, the jets struck, diving out of the eastern sky with the sun behind them.

The eleven fighters ahead of Gary dropped their bombs and headed out. He flew his fighter down the chute aiming his pipper on the center of the smoke and fire. The valley filled with dust and smoke from previous bombs. He aimed and punched his bombs off.

Gary began jinking as the plane bottomed out from the dive. Orange light flashed through the smoke as his bombs exploded. Concussions rattled his fighter. Heading west, he joined with the three planes from his flight.

Later at the debriefing, the pilots watched the strike films. As the bombs struck, transporters, canisters, missiles and buildings were blown apart, blasted and burned.

"Victory is sweet," Gary said, raising his fist. "Once in a while, we win."

YURI'S PLAN

_____ 57

Yuri Vaskilev, General Lieutenant
GRU, Soviet Military Intelligence
Phuc Ve SAM Support Facility, North Vietnam
5 July 1967

YURI STOOD ASTRIDE the Harley taking in the smoking ruin. He really needed to check on his men, but delayed taking action. Worst of all, three Soviet and several North Vietnamese soldiers had turned up missing. Yuri feared the Americans had caught them by surprise at first light and killed them. He doubted their remains would be found.

Yuri's recent surprise inspection had found no problems at this facility. Somehow, the Americans had discovered the site.

The commander of the local air defense regiment had reported that one high altitude and a very low altitude aircraft passed nearby several days before. Yuri checked the radar plots for the previous five days and found the tracks for the drones, as the Americans called them. That's it, he thought. They sneaked them by us!

The plan against the Americans began to coalesce in his brain. He called for shovels to dig through the wreckage. He wanted to find his men. What remained, waited there in the charred ruins.

Yuri asked Colonel Thon to order up a helicopter for the next day and to have his men assemble damaged missile equipment. He also told Sergeant Komarvsky to prepare the **дракон** with its four 23 mm cannons.

SETTING THE STAGE

_____ 58

Yuri Vaskilev, General Lieutenant
GRU, Soviet Military Intelligence
Van La SAM Support Facility, North Vietnam
8 July 1967

YURI HAD TOURED the countryside by helicopter on 6 July looking for the right setting. He selected a dilapidated bus and truck repair complex. Since that day, he had worked tirelessly, gathering props to set the stage. His soldiers and those under Colonel Thon's command diligently gathered damaged or inoperable SAM transporters, canisters and missiles.

Each succeeding day he changed the location of the props within the facility, trying to deceive the Americans. When notified of a high-flying reconnaissance drone passing nearby on the previous day, Yuri thought the Americans had possibly caught the scent.

Surely, they will spot the props he had carefully set, Yuri thought. He then requested Colonel Thon to begin deploying the antiaircraft guns and SAMs. He issued precise orders that the guns and missiles be well camouflaged.

Yuri, Colonel Thon and Sergeant Komarvsky supervised the preparation of six hidden SAM sites, each with four missiles. In addition, fifty antiaircraft guns had been dispersed in the area. The **Дракон** remained hidden away in a warehouse most of the time, but Yuri decided this scene in his play required a new actor. So he had it moved to Van La, dug in and camouflaged southwest of the target. He hoped some of the American planes would head that way en route to Laos and then Thailand.

The two Russians and Colonel Thon spent all day each day at the site. They rode their motorcycles, ate their cheese and bread, smoked their cigarettes, kicked the dirt and cursed. Surely, they have to come soon, Yuri thought.

SHEEP DIPPED

_____ 59

BLACK SHIELD Mission 6707
100 Nautical Miles South of Hainan Island
Communist China
10 July 1967

AFTER TAKEOFF FROM Kadena Airbase, Okinawa, and refueling from a tanker south of the Philippines, the pilot had pushed the throttles and gently eased back on the control stick, climbing toward 80,000 feet. He set a course south of Hainan Island, located just off the southern coast of Communist China.

A short time later, the pilot applied pressure on the stick and depressed the right rudder. Gently, very gently, he thought, as abrupt maneuvers with this airplane caused things to go drastically wrong. The thin air at 84,000 feet provided little friction in the turn. He shivered when remembering his flight speed of 2,300 miles per hour, aware of what friction did to objects traveling at such speed.

The curving turn around the south and west of Hainan Island avoided violating Communist Chinese airspace and hopefully prevented them from raising the alarm about his reconnaissance flight.

As a contract employee of the Central Intelligence Agency, the pilot loved to fly the A-12 Blackbird. Technically, he still belonged to the Air Force, but the CIA had "sheep dipped" him, as they called it, placing him under cover and transforming him into a civilian.

Resembling a martial arts throwing knife, the A-12 answered a pilot's dreams for speed. No one could touch him, up there in the thin air, where he could look out and see the curvature of the earth.

Nearing the North Vietnamese coast, the pilot turned on the camera and data recorders, and nudged the throttle up to give the highest airspeed. Likewise, he gently eased back on the stick to provide maximum altitude. Cruising this high, the cameras provided photographic coverage thirty miles on each side of the aircraft track.

He noted coast-in over Hon Gay. The A-12 ground speed neared 2,500 miles per hour and the plane stabilized at 85,000 feet. Steering northwest, he ticked off the cities and towns as they passed by far below—Uong Bi, Kep, Thai Nguyen and Yen Bai. The pilot looked at his stopwatch and logged the elapsed time at 5.5 minutes. The inertial system showed 230 nautical miles covered on the first pass. He flew far above the altitude which produced contrails. But if he were leaving one behind, that would be his business card. Alone with his thoughts, he passed over the ground at forty-two miles per minute.

He kept the camera and data recorders on as the airplane crossed the Laotian border. After another minute of flight, he turned off the reconnaissance equipment and began nudging back on the throttle. Descending gradually to 20,000 feet, he linked up with a KC-135 jet tanker over Udon, Thailand.

According to his mission plan, he had made a photo egress pass over North Vietnam parallel to, but fifty miles south of his initial path. Once over the Gulf of Tonkin, he turned southeast, headed for refueling south of the Philippines, and then on to his home base at Kadena, Okinawa.

The pilot had declared a fuel emergency as he neared the base. He didn't want anyone in his way so he could land straight in with no other traffic to worry about.

The plane landed sweetly. He pulled off the runway onto the first convenient crossover and stopped the mission clock at 4.75 hours elapsed time. The inertial navigation system display showed 4,545 nautical miles distance. Not bad for a trip to Vietnam and back, including slowing down for refueling. He set the engines to low idle and took a long drink from his water line.

Glowing with heat, the A-12 shimmered in the Okinawa sunshine. No one approached without wearing special clothing. One of the maintenance crew reluctantly summoned the courage to hook up the ground power unit for air conditioning. The pilot shut the plane down.

TWO DAYS LATER, photo interpreters at the National Photographic Interpretation Center (NPIC) in Washington, D.C. labored over their light tables peering at the film positives with small hand-held magnifiers. An alert PI identified a new SAM Support Facility on the film from the second run, which sparked much excitement. The photographs revealed SAMs, missile transporters and canisters clustered around six buildings.

The team leader picked up the secure phone, which encrypted voice traffic, and called her good friend at the Committee on Overhead Reconnaissance. The associate at COMOR had direct contacts at the Secretary of Defense, the Joint Chiefs of Staff, the Director of the Central Intelligence Agency, and the White House National Security Council. A written flash TWX was also drafted and transmitted.

This time the strike authorization TWX originated at the top and went down the chain of command.

TOP SECRET
OPERATIONAL FLASH
DTG:120767:2043Z
FROM: JCS
TO: SECDEF
    WHITE HOUSE
    CINCPAC
    CINCPACAF

7th *AF*
SUBJECT: *IMMINENT THREAT STRIKE AUTHORIZATION*
RE: *NPIC FPIR 67-23: BLACK SHIELD 6707*
Immediate strike authorized on Van La SAM Support Facility located 2.0 NM north of Van La (12 NM SSW of Hanoi) at 205130N 1054600E.
End
TOP SECRET

SOME DAYS THE BEAR EATS YOU

_____ 60

Gary Bishop Deale, First Lieutenant, USAF
Takhli RTAFB, Thailand
14 July 1967, Counter Number 76

SITTING IN HIS cubicle in the hooch, Gary placed a newly written poem and letter into the envelope and addressed it to Allison. He sat at his desk listening to the radio. "Habanera" played softly as Radio Australia signed off on the short wave for the night. A gecko perched on the corner post by his desk was looking at him. His lamp, provided a small cone of light in the darkness. Gary lowered the zipper on his flight suit, hoping the ceiling fan provided a bit of relief from the early morning heat. Looking at his watch, he saw it was 0310, nearly time for breakfast.

He heard the door open and familiar footsteps.

"Are you ready, Gary?" Lieutenant Colonel Foxe asked.

"Yes, sir, I am," Gary said.

""Let's get breakfast. We have 45 minutes 'til the briefing."

At 0400, Gary sat in the wing briefing room with two pilots from his flight, Major O'Shane and Captain Klepperson. Lieutenant Colonel Foxe slouched in his chair. Gary lit a cigarette and blew a mouthful of smoke into the air. Captain Klepperson yawned and rubbed his face with his hands.

A total of sixteen F-105s, divided into four flights of four planes each, was scheduled for the mission. The strike package consisted of twelve F-105Ds. In addition, four Wild Weasels would precede the flight.

Gary glanced at the colonel. Lieutenant Colonel Foxe winked. Gary smiled, knowing he was assigned to the last flight led by Foxe. He liked to fly with the colonel because the man knew what he was doing and knew how to convey vital information to his men. Gary believed deep down in his heart the colonel would do all he could to make sure his flight of four fighters made it back home safely. Sitting with his friends, he experienced a profound sense of belonging.

Yet, the truth was that ultimately, each pilot flew alone, enclosed in his cockpit and strapped to the ejection seat. They were on their own to fight and perhaps die alone.

Lieutenant Colonel Foxe walked to the front of the room, talking with Colonel Jacobs, the mission leader.

"Are you ready with the lineup, Gary?" Foxe asked as he ambled back to his seat.

"Yes, sir," Gary said, distributing the maps and documents. "All checked and double checked."

"Colonel Jacobs doesn't understand the big push with this target," Lieutenant Colonel Foxe said. "It seems to have appeared out of a black hole and now the powers up above want it wiped off the face of the earth, like last month. Jacobs thinks the politicians are stirring the pot and the chain of command is reacting. These rush jobs sometimes turn into Charley Foxtrots. Watch yourselves up there!"

"Yes, sir," Gary said. "I'll be following your lead."

Two hours later, the strike package of twelve F-105 jet fighters and four Wild Weasels thundered over a karst ridge and dipped down into the flatland south of Hanoi. Ahead, flak bursts from antiaircraft guns blossomed in red and orange flashes. Blasting along at 540 knots, the verdant rice paddies passed below in a green blur. Workers in the fields gawked at the planes as they thundered by just overhead.

Lieutenant Colonel Foxe pointed Gary's way and offered a thumbs-up. The wings on the colonel's plane did a little dance telling the other three pilots to fall back into trail formation.

Each of the three flights took a different track to confuse the gunners on the ground. The flight leader of the fighters just ahead of Gary broke away and headed to the south. Gary realized that when those planes pulled off their target, they would be over downtown Hanoi. They were headed straight into hell, not to mention prohibited air space. No American planes were allowed to fly over the capitol city of North Vietnam, one of the crazy Rules of Engagement pilots were forced to comply with.

Lieutenant Colonel Foxe turned his plane to the west and north, trailed by the three remaining F-105s. Then, he turned southeast toward their target. The flight path assured them of being far south of Hanoi when the planes came off the target bomb run.

The three F-105s in front of Gary lit their afterburners and began to climb. He rolled his fighter to the right to spread out his flight track from the other fighters and then turned back to the southeast. Pushing the throttle ahead with his left hand to engage the afterburner, he eased the stick back.

At the top of his pop-up climb, he rolled his plane upside down, watching Lieutenant Colonel Foxe's plane arcing over. Fire and smoke from the bombs of the earlier planes obscured the target.

Suddenly, nasty red and orange flashes from enemy shell bursts surrounded the planes. Gary looped over the top of his climb and began to dive.

Multiple SAMs blasted from the ground aiming at Lieutenant Colonel Foxe's formation.

We're screwed, Gary thought. He had never seen this many SAMs in the air at one time. The missiles leapt from the ground, trailing a tongue of fire.

Lieutenant Colonel Foxe figured it out first. "Take it down! It's a SAM trap!"

Ahead of Gary, a missile struck an F-105 which exploded in an orange flash. A missile, that he hadn't seen, flashed from behind and roared by. The sky filled with red flak bursts and missile contrails.

Gary pushed the control stick forward. His F-105 bucked and rattled from the violent maneuvers. Maps, papers and dust flew about the cockpit, sweat poured from his body, fogging his eyesight. His heart raced, blood pounding in his ears.

He weaved between SAMs thundering by, slamming his control stick to the left and then to the right. Missiles exploded ahead of him. His plane shook with the concussions.

Two SAMs were aimed directly at him. His eyes widened, tracking the missiles. He gulped oxygen through his mask. The missiles kept coming straight and true.

"Take it down! Turn! Turn!" Lieutenant Colonel Foxe screamed.

Gary slapped the stick against his left thigh trying to turn into and behind the SAMs. He steepened his dive, pushing the left descending turn.

Two thunderous blasts bounced him from one side of the cockpit to the other. A fusillade of shrapnel struck the F-105, like a softball-sized hailstorm. His plane yawed and slid out of control.

"Buick 4's hit hard," Gary shouted. Smoke filled the cockpit, blocking his sight. Sucking oxygen, he fought to save his plane. His nose and throat burned from the acrid fumes.

The F-105 rolled into an uncontrolled dive. Trying to level his plane, he punched the button to drop his bombs and then jettisoned the external fuel tanks. The fighter dropped lower as the speed increased.

Finally the plane stabilized. The controls and throttle seemed to work. He breathed a sigh of relief. One second later, another SAM blast struck his plane. *I'm truly fucked*, he thought. In his gut, he knew it was the end.

Flames flashed into the cockpit. His flight suit began to burn. Searing pain hit him like a shock wave.

"4's on fire," Gary screamed as the plane started to fall apart.

Fire swirled under his helmet visor. Reaching for the left handle to fire the ejection seat, Gary realized that arm wasn't working. Piercing pain. Fire. Burning. "Fuck!" Gary screamed, convulsing in terror.

"4's done!" Gary shouted, grabbing the right ejection handle and pulling.

"Allison," Gary screamed as the canopy blew off and the ejection seat fired. A torrent of 23 mm cannon fire tore the plane to pieces.

THE STAGE, THE SCENE, AND THE SCORE

Yuri Vaskilev, General Lieutenant
GRU, Soviet Military Intelligence
Van La SAM Support Facility
14 July 1967

YURI AND SERGEANT Komarvsky had driven their motorcycles to the site of their trap early each day. Pacing the ground, fussing, kicking dirt clods and cursing, the two Russians and Colonel Thon passed the time. Yuri's patience ran thin. Soon, he hoped, soon.

At dawn, Sergeant Komarvsky cupped his hands over his ears and heard it first. "Fuck your mother," he yelled, pointing. The thunder of approaching jets elated Yuri. He counted them—sixteen planes. The Americans split apart and began lining up on his trap. Circling away from the target, four of the aircraft remained at low altitude. Wild Weasels, Yuri thought. He walked to his motorcycle, opened the carrying case and grabbed an unopened bottle of vodka. It was time for a toast.

Yuri had given specific orders to the soldiers: limited numbers of antiaircraft artillery should fire as soon as the planes appeared. Don't begin the real attack until the last flight of planes started their climb. He desperately wanted to destroy all of the planes in the final bombing wave.

The target had no significance. It consisted of broken down buildings, ruined buses and junk SAM equipment. He wanted all four planes from the last flight as trophies. An eye for an eye, and a tooth for a tooth, Yuri thought, remembering the three dead Soviet soldiers he helped scoop up nine days before.

Eight American aircraft flew away unscathed after their bomb runs. When the last flight of four fighters began their climbs, Yuri signaled Colonel Thon to begin the attack.

Sergeant Komarvsky radioed two soldiers equipped with 35 mm movie cameras to begin filming.

Yuri and Sergeant Komarvsky stood there mesmerized. They had never seen twenty-four *Dvina* missiles launched in short order. True, the radars couldn't guide all of the SAMS to a target at the same time, but the missiles did their job. Their real purpose was to drive the American bombers down to lower altitude. That is where the antiaircraft guns and the **Дракон** took over.

The first American plane twisted and turned, evading the explosions. At that point, Yuri realized that he had sprung his trap about ten seconds too late. Missiles obliterated the second plane and damaged the other two, forcing the bombers lower where the guns destroyed them. The **Дракон** caught one bomber, which was already on fire, and chewed it into flaming pieces. Yuri was impressed.

Within hours, Yuri stood at the improvised grave and watched as the soldiers piled dirt over an American pilot. His movie crew filmed the burial. They had not bothered to dig, but placed the burned dismembered pieces into a hole blown into the ground by aircraft wreckage. A portion of the torso strapped to what was left of the ejection seat had yielded a set of dog tags, as the Americans called identification discs. After taking photographs and drawing a rough map of the gravesite, Yuri turned and walked toward his motorcycle. He wanted to look at the other two pilots.

Yuri had written the names and other information from the dog tags of the three pilots into his notebook. Studying the names—Deale, O'Shane and Klepperson—he stood by the village where the other two pilots lay. Standing there by the two men stripped to their underwear, blindfolded, bound and gagged, he glared at them. One appeared badly injured and burned, the other less so.

He wasn't sure which pilot was from which plane. It really didn't matter, he thought, wondering if they would someday wish they had been killed outright, rather than going through the hell awaiting them.

Yuri had seen some of the interrogations. There was critical information he wanted to get from the Americans. Knowing what these two Americans faced, he had requested that certain questions be asked, but had no stomach for it. It wasn't certain that one would survive his wounds, let alone the inquisition. By the time the North Vietnamese, North Koreans and Cubans had finished with them, the pilots might wish they had died.

Looking up, Yuri thanked his God. He had avenged the death of his three soldiers with the same number of American planes. The trap evened Yuri's score.

The generals back home would be pleased with the film taken today. He had done all he could do on this trip. Now, it was time to pack up his toys and go home. Sergeant Komarvsky and he would soon return with even newer weapons.

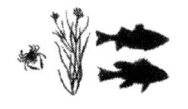

ON BEHALF OF THE SECRETARY OF DEFENSE

_____ 62

Allison Faith Deale
Newport River Estuary, Beaufort, North Carolina
Eighteen Hours Later, July 14, 1967

THE THREE BOATS, tied together, rocked gently with the waves. Time melted away. The men sat waiting while Carmen held her arms around me whispering words I could not hear.

I desperately wanted to jump into the water and swim away from these men dressed in blue.

Finally, she broke through my seizure of fear and dread. "These men came a long distance to talk to you."

"No!" I screamed.

"¡Mi hermana! You must listen to them!"

I knew I had to let the men do their job. Please don't tell me this, I thought. I nodded my assent.

Carmen held me tight. "Okay," she said.

The colonel rose from his seat and said, "I am Colonel Asher, Vice Commander of the 4th Tactical Fighter Wing at Seymour Johnson. Are you Allison Faith Deale, the wife of First Lieutenant Gary Bishop Deale?"

"Yes," I sobbed, my body shaking. I looked the colonel in his eyes, reading what he had known for hours.

Colonel Asher spoke in a rehearsed, matter of fact tone, "Allison, on behalf of the Secretary of Defense, I regret to inform you that your husband, Lieutenant Gary Bishop Deale, is missing in action over North Vietnam. His F-105 did not return from a mission. There was no possibility of a search for him. We have no further information at this time. An officer will be appointed to contact you as more information becomes available."

It was the standard message and he had delivered it verbatim, professionally, coldly—in a voice empty of emotion.

I stopped listening. If he said anything else, I didn't remember it.

Everyone held their breath, fearful of my reaction.

I sat there shaking uncontrollably. Carmen held me and whispered my name, "Allison, Allison, Allison, I'm so sorry!"

The sad procession of boats got underway and we made our way back to the marine lab dock. The colonel and the chaplain from Seymour both hugged me and informed me that they were available at any time. Jacob and Samuel Craven helped Carmen secure our boat as I sat on the dock, bewildered.

Several other graduate students, my good friends, gathered around, offering tears and sympathy.

This is my new life, I thought.

PART 10

In the final analysis, it is their war. They are the ones who have to win it or lose it. But they have to win it, the people of Vietnam, against the Communists.

>—President John Fitzgerald Kennedy, September 2, 1963

COWBOYS AND WAR

The cowboy waited
straddling the beast
holding tight with illusions of victory
knowing his time had come.

Unleashing the snorting
bucking demon
from its pen
consumed him.

Reality
doomed the cowboy.
War: 1.
Cowboy: 0.

From the combat diary of Gary Bishop Deale, First Lieutenant, USAF, 4 July 1967

SOMEONE TO LIVE FOR

_____ 63

Allison Faith Deale
Seven Springs, North Carolina
July 21, 1967

I DON"T REMEMBER much about the day the officers came in the boat. Carmen took control. She shepherded me from the marine lab to my apartment where we collected clothes and paperwork and proceeded directly to the Seymour Johnson hospital. Once there, she strongly explained that I was pregnant and that my husband had been declared missing. Dr. Naylor admitted me for rest and observation. "I'm very concerned about shock," the doctor said. I presented no argument to his plan of safely treating me and keeping me overnight for tests and recovery from the psychological trauma I had just endured.

Carmen remained at the hospital. My parents arrived after she summoned them. The Cravens came to check on me and reassure me that they wanted to help in any way they could.

The Casualty Assistance Officer came to the hospital and informed me that the Air Force had no further information concerning Gary, other than the fact that he was missing in action. No later messages or radio transmissions were received from him. He said that a Lieutenant Colonel Matt Foxe would be returning from Southeast Asia and that he would have more detailed personal information.

An overnight stay turned into two nights as Dr. Naylor refused to allow me to go home while I wept constantly. "We'll get you calmed down, then you can go home," he said, holding my hand.

"I don't know how I'm going to do that."

"I know it's difficult, but you must not end up in a dark place. You have someone to live for right here," he said, patting my belly.

UPON RETURNING TO Seven Springs, I discovered that Mom and Dad had cleaned the entire house and prepared mountains of food. I began taking long walks with my dad. From that day, many years before, when my father first took me out in a boat and began teaching me about creatures in the water, I had known what I wanted to become. He had always been my closest and truest adviser and, yes—friend. Now, talking with him proved difficult.

My anxiety about Gary's situation seemed to be shutting me off from other people, including my closest friends. Before, my life had been so cool. After discovering that I was pregnant, everything seemed to have lined up for Gary and me. Even though I knew that Gary could get shot down, it never occurred to me that he would, for real.

My father and I took our time, meandering along paths through fields and forest in the late afternoon, avoiding the heat of the day. "What's next?" he asked.

"I don't know. Finishing graduate school was the most important thing in the world for me at one time, but— —" I raised my hands, showing my doubt.

"Take one day at a time. I think the Air Force will tell you if they find out anything about Gary. You have to take care of yourself and your baby."

"Maybe I'll move to Beaufort. There's no reason to remain here, except for access to the hospital."

"There you go. You're thinking ahead already."

I hugged my mom and dad as they departed, sad to see them go. I knew they wanted to help me but the best way for me to move on was for them to actually leave. After a few days, Carmen returned to Beaufort, leaving me alone in our home with my thoughts.

Now what? I wondered. I had a house with a mortgage and bills and an apartment in Beaufort. A graduate student without much income, I found myself pregnant and alone.

OVER THE NEXT few days, I wandered through the house, trying to restore order to my life. I spent hours sitting in the study, studying photographs of Gary and me together. I carried his dog tags in my hand. Touching his model airplanes, I remembered how happy he had been while flying. Sitting on the floor in our closet, I held his uniform shirt to my face, hoping to fill my nose with the scent of him.

Surely, Gary has to be alive, I prayed. Maybe he's hiding in the woods. Maybe he's floating around in the Gulf of Tonkin in a raft. Later, nobody heard anything from him on the radio; maybe it malfunctioned.

Being a prisoner in North Vietnam would be very bad, I thought. But that would be much better than being dead.

Please, God, I prayed, please let him be alive.

SITTING AT OUR picnic table on the screened porch, I scanned papers just left behind by the Casualty Assistance Officer and the representative from the base legal affairs office. They had provided copies of Gary's will, Power of Attorney, pay allocation forms, and written legal opinions about what could and could not be done with his pay.

Among the papers the officers provided were copies of the orders promoting Gary to captain. Further, they told me, Gary would continue receiving promotions in step with his academy classmates so long as he remained missing in action.

What hurt the most was what the officers related about our finances. It was mandatory that Gary's base pay be placed into an escrow account. I would still receive my allowances. My income had taken an immediate and sharp decline. This situation created extreme anxiety. Now I also had financial difficulties in addition to the stress and worry over Gary's status. Was he dead or alive? I wondered. Was he a prisoner, or did he get killed on that day one week previous? I didn't know. Nor did those men, or anyone else.

Deep in my heart, I believed in one truth. I must never give up hope.

WHY?

_____ 64

Allison Faith Deale
Seven Springs, North Carolina
July 31, 1967

I SAT AT the picnic table on our screened porch, unable to repress the thought that someone is thinking of me. I wondered if that person were Gary. Candles flickered in the breeze. A sweet vanilla and citronella scent filled the air.

After taking a sip of red wine, I put my head down on the unopened envelopes piled in front of me. These were his last few letters, Gary's last messages to me. Also in the pile, notes I had written to him just before he disappeared, returned and marked "UNDELIVERABLE." I hadn't the courage to read any of them. Nor did I want to desecrate them by opening the envelopes.

The letters could be my last contact with Gary, containing his last thoughts, his last words. In my heart, I wanted to delay that final touch as long as possible. My body began shaking. I'm not going to let myself cry, I thought. But tears came anyway.

Gary knew he was going to be a father. I had received letters from him acknowledging the good news. He looked forward to having a child and sharing his life with us. It will be so cool, he had written.

The few letters in front of me would have been written after that. The baby's still here, I thought, clutching my belly. Where are you?

Taking a blank envelope from a manila folder, I began addressing it to Gary in care of the North Vietnamese Embassy in Paris. I had just finished writing a letter to him. Several of the wives of missing pilots had advised me to do this. They thought it was the only way we could communicate with our husbands.

Carmen had issued orders, no more being alone. In the morning, I had to pack my car, drive to Beaufort and go back to work. I closed my eyes and for the first time in two weeks, let myself float away.

Hours later, disoriented, I awakened to the crash of thunder. A lightning bolt, zipping across the sky startled me. Gusts of wind snuffed out the large candle on the table. Was someone sending me a message, I wondered.

A wall of rain hit the house, spraying the porch. I jumped up, grabbing the envelopes and ran inside placing them on the counter. Standing by the porch door, I strained, listening. Then for no reason, I walked out into the downpour.

I raised my face to the deluge of water. Tears mingled with raindrops. "Where are you?" I cried. "Why?"

MATT FOXE

_____ 65

Allison Faith Deale
Seven Springs, North Carolina
September 15, 1967

USING A DOCTOR'S appointment at Seymour Johnson as an excuse to return to Seven Springs, I decided to remain at our house over the weekend and catch up on chores. Carmen kept a close watch on me in Beaufort. The Cravens looked after our house in Seven Springs. I used this opportunity to get away by myself.

After lunch, I knelt in my flowerbed in the back yard, weeding and cutting perennials. Sweat ran down my face.

Gary and I had planted the flowers, shoulder to shoulder. It felt good to be kneeling in the garden, pruning plants that we had both touched. I cut Purple Cone and Black-eyed Susan flowers for a dried plant arrangement. Weeds had gone wild over the past two months. With fall in the air, as much as I didn't want to, I knew I had to clean the flower bed.

A car entered the driveway, followed by a loud knocking on the front door and then, "Miss Allison, Miss Allison."

Ah, the Craven brothers, I thought.

"I'm out back," I yelled.

"You have visitors," Samuel Craven said, turning the corner by the screened porch. Jacob followed with a man and woman I didn't know.

Holding out his hand, the man smiled as he approached. "Hello, Allison. Matt Foxe. And this is Shannon Hastings, a very good friend of mine."

The first thing I noticed about Matt was a pink scar extending from the corner of his mouth to his left ear. My immediate emotions tore my heart in two directions. First, a sense of grief. This man was one of the last men to have seen Gary. Then, gratitude. Finally I might know what happened to him.

I have seen beautiful women before, but Shannon was stunning. Long blond hair cascaded over her shoulders. A short black sheath accentuated Shannon's body, transforming her into a Scandinavian goddess. A sharp contrast with my flowing peasant blouse and jeans, I thought.

Hugging Lieutenant Colonel Foxe, I said, "I've been aching to meet you." This man had been in my dreams for the past two months. I had been anxious for him to visit me.

"This is my first opportunity to get here. I reported to MacDill as soon as I returned from Thailand. Now I'm at Seymour."

"Lieutenant Colonel Foxe, thank you for coming to see me," I said.

"Matt is my name. That's all you need to remember."

"Sara and Laverne are cooking supper," Samuel Craven said.

"I'm so rude," I said. "Would anyone like something to drink? Iced tea, soda or a beer?"

"Iced tea for me," Shannon said. Everyone else nodded.

"I'll get it for you. Let's sit on the screened porch."

After washing my hands in the kitchen, I lifted the pitcher out of the fridge. Shannon filled the glasses with ice. Sara Craven had delivered a peach cobbler earlier that day so I unwrapped that and turned to cut lemons.

Just then, Shannon surprised me. She put her arms around me, giving the softest sweetest hug I had had in months. "I'm pleased to meet you."

"Likewise," I said.

"Tell me, when are you due?" Shannon asked.

"February 15, more or less."

"Good grief," Matt said, "I didn't notice that."

"Men are like that," Shannon said, patting Matt on the shoulder.

"She's a doctor in Memphis," Matt said. "She notices stuff."

"A doctor, as in physician?"

"Yes. I try to blend in, so I don't overplay it. I don't like to intimidate my friends."

Talk about intimidation, I thought. There she stands, this stunningly beautiful woman dressed to kill. Then I find out she's a physician.

Shannon's accent was British, but with a rough edge. "Where are you from?" I asked. "Obviously, not Carolina."

"I'm from Australia, Brisbane actually," Shannon said.

"You're a long way from home."

"This country is my home, at least for the time being," she said. "I'm so sorry about Gary."

Shannon stepped back and put both of her hands on my face so that we were looking eye to eye. "I understand your suffering. My husband was killed in a plane crash one year ago."

"I'm sorry to hear that. We do have something in common, one grieving widow and one woman in limbo."

Shannon hugged me and held on as though we would never part. The tears ran down my cheeks and we stood there, silently remembering the good days in the past and consoling each other's pain.

We moved to the porch and sat at the picnic table. I passed the peach cobbler.

Matt took a pack of cigarettes out of his shirt pocket and held it up, a question mark on his face. I nodded.

"How did you end up in Memphis?" I asked. "That's a long way from Brisbane."

"It's another story with a sad ending," Shannon said.

"In the beginning, Shannon married a pilot friend of mine," Matt said, lighting his cigarette and blowing the smoke away from the table.

"I did do that," Shannon said. "I met Aaron in Australia when he was there on R and R, as you Yanks say. We met in a club in Sydney and danced the night away. After that, we never looked back. I know it's a cliché, but it really was love at first sight."

"Did you get married right away?" I asked.

"No, not until after his tour in Vietnam was over. He was flying F-100 Super Sabres in South Vietnam when we met, and still had six months to serve at Danang when he went back. After Aaron completed his assignment, we were married in Brisbane."

"When was that?" I asked.

"14 June, last year," Shannon said. She related that after their marriage, they had honeymooned in Australia, then had traveled to MacDill Air Force Base, near Tampa. But on a routine training flight the previous September, another plane collided with Aaron's F-4 Phantom over the Gulf of Mexico. He had tried to eject but the canopy failed to separate properly and broke his neck.

"That's so sad," I said.

"It's been difficult. There are times when I think he's alive. It took me a long time to deal with his death. But, at least I know what happened to him. It's not at all like your situation."

"How did you cope with Aaron's death?' I asked.

"Not very well at first, I was a wreck," she said, running her hands through her hair and sweeping it behind her ears. "I'm now doing a fellowship in Memphis and a friend recommended a psychologist. Therapy has helped."

"Do you really think the psychologist was necessary?" I asked, wondering if a therapist would help me. Gary had been gone for two months, and the shock hadn't worn off for me yet. But I wondered about what would happen in the long term.

"It's made all the difference. Then another thing helped. This past winter, a guy showed up at my door in Memphis." Shannon looked at Matt, smiling and placing her hand on his shoulder.

"That was me," Matt said. "I heard about Aaron's crash while I was in Thailand. The next thing I knew, I was shot down in Laos and got banged up a bit. I was sent to the states on recuperation leave and didn't really have anyplace to go, so I tracked Shannon down in Memphis."

"Matt was Aaron's best man at our wedding," Shannon said, pushing hair out of her eyes.

"Aaron and I were very close friends," Matt said, cigarette dangling from his lips. He took a puff and scratched the scar on his cheek.

"Matt stayed with me in Memphis while on leave. Then he volunteered to go back to Thailand to complete his one hundred missions."

"That's when I met Gary at Takhli," Matt said, staring at me.

I flinched at his mention of Gary's name. For the first time, Matt had acknowledged what he was here for. I took a sip of iced tea and looked down at the table.

"Isn't it strange how things seem to go in a cycle?" Jacob asked. "People just randomly seem to run into each other over and over again. Samuel and I met Aaron back before we retired."

"I can't tell you how many times I have been in situations like that," Matt said.

Sara and Laverne Craven walked around the corner of the house carrying platters filled with food. "There's more in the back of the truck," Sara said, placing a dish of her southern fried chicken on the table.

The scent of cooking oil and chicken filled the air. Sara touched my arm and smiled. "Thank you," I said. "It smells delicious."

Samuel, Matt and Jacob left to get the remaining food, while Shannon and I went into the kitchen to prepare drinks. Fortunately, I had a good supply of beer and wine on hand.

"Is anyone helping you cope?" Shannon asked, popping the cork off a wine bottle.

"My friend, Carmen. She's a fellow graduate student in Beaufort."

"Great. With a baby coming, you'll need someone."

"Carmen was there the day the officers came. I would have died if she hadn't been there." I described that day and how Carmen had held me and carried me through the trauma.

We returned to the table to find it loaded with platters of chicken, roasted red potatoes in their skin, green beans and corn on the cob. Shannon poured wine, while the men preferred beer.

As we ate, the conversation centered on living in the South during recent years, with its racial tension and violence. Shannon was particularly interested in the Craven family's perception of the civil rights movement. "Australia is one hundred years behind you when it comes to dealing with our aboriginal people," she said.

Sara dished peach cobbler and Laverne topped off each piece with a scoop of vanilla ice cream. Shannon and I poured coffee. We settled to finish an excellent southern supper.

Shadows filled the porch as the sun sank lower. I lit several candles. We cleared dishes from the table. Even with three couples present, I felt alone, adrift. While I had participated in the conversation during dinner, I felt detached. I seemed to shrink into a cold shell of my former self.

The fifty ton elephant, which I had avoided until now, sat on the porch with us, taking in our conversation as we skirted the topic lurking in each other's minds. True, we had hinted about Gary and danced around the topic, but never approached mentioning him directly. I've often heard people mention whistling past the graveyard, and I was witnessing that old cliché at work.

Matt's sudden appearance presented the chance I'd been waiting for. I decided to speak, not really wanting to hear what was coming. Looking Matt directly in his eyes, I asked, "Is there anything you can tell me about Gary's disappearance?" My voice cracked. I sat there trembling.

Shannon grimaced. Matt wiped his face and eyes with both his hands and breathed deeply. The Cravens lowered their heads, as if in prayer. Silence hung over the porch.

"Before I answer, I'd like to know what you have been told thus far. Has anyone provided any details?"

"I spoke with the squadron commander, the Casualty Assistance Officer, the Chaplain, Judge Advocate Officer and a couple pilots from Seymour. I've been told that Gary was on a bombing mission over North Vietnam and disappeared." I paused and swallowed hard. It was difficult for me to think these words, let alone say them. "He was never heard from or seen again."

Matt looked solemn. He blinked and squashed his cigarette in the ash tray. "I need to get some things out of my car."

"More wine for anyone?" Shannon lifted the bottle. "We're going to need it."

"*In vino veritas*," Samuel said.

Candles sparkled in the breeze. The scent of lavender filled the air. A subtle fall chill settled around us. The rumble of passing jet planes from Seymour Johnson shook the house.

"Four F-4s just went over," Matt said, returning to the table and sitting directly across from me.

Matt paused. He lit a cigarette, took a long deep drag and blew the smoke away from the table. Then he began.

"Six months ago, I made a promise to Gary. I swore that I would tell you in person if anything bad happened. Here I am.

"This is the chart I used when Gary went down. You may recognize his handwriting. He drew these lines and made the notations. You can have it."

"Oh!" I exclaimed, coughing and taking a deep breath. This map was probably one of the last things remaining that Gary had touched. I stared at the map, recognizing his small printing, the way he made 7's and 0's with a slash.

He reached into his flight kit. "I have more." Matt handed me one large bulging manila envelope. "I took papers and letters from Gary's room right after I returned from that mission. Not supposed to do that, but— —"

Now I have another sealed envelope to open, I thought.

"The target's right here," Matt said, pointing to a spot on the chart, "about twelve miles southwest of Hanoi. It was a Surface-to-Air Missile, or SAM Support Facility identified on aerial photography." He turned the map around so that we could see where he was pointing.

It was deadly quiet. Shannon held my arm. I sat there trembling. Candles flickered, casting shadows across our faces.

Matt continued. "Russia and China provide the missiles. The missile components are delivered in parts and reassembled at places like this. The parts come in canisters, which helped the intelligence people identify this facility. There were canisters all over the place on the photographs. That should have provided a clue to us that something wasn't kosher, because normally that stuff would be well hidden."

Matt paused, took a swig of beer, and turned the map around to look at it from a different angle. His voice was quiet, almost a whisper. "Orders came down to bomb the facility on 14 July."

"Where were you during the mission?" I asked.

"Two flights of four F-105s hit the target ahead of us," Matt said, using his hands to simulate the two formations diving at the spot on the map. "I led the last flight of four planes. My wingman, Major O'Shane, flew immediately behind me. Then Captain Klepperson, followed by Gary. Okay so far?"

Matt looked at me and then glanced at Shannon. He wet his lips and reached for another cigarette.

"Why was Gary last?" I asked.

"He was the junior pilot. They are at the end of the formation, last in line," Matt said.

"Each pilot is alone when you drop your bombs?" Shannon asked.

"Yes, that's right. There are planes in front of you or behind you, each taking their turn. That way you don't get in each other's way and hit one of your own planes."

"How far apart are you?" I asked, trying to form a mental picture of where Gary was in relation to the other men.

"About five hundred to a thousand feet."

"What do you do next?"

"We do a pop-up climb before reaching the target," he said, using his hands as fighter pilots will, to simulate the climb and dive. "You then dive the plane and 'pickle the load,' as we call it. We punch the bombs off at about 6,000 feet while we're in a dive. Then we pull out of the dive and blast out of there. Understand?"

"Yes. It's got to be really spooky being alone," I said, shivering at the idea of Gary being there by himself, cut off from everyone else.

"After you do it a hundred times, you get used to it. We fly as a unit and sometimes fight as a unit. But there are times when you are there all by yourself. When you're dropping bombs, each pilot makes his own run. It's just you enclosed in the cockpit."

"Gary was alone, then," I said, trying to form a clear picture in my mind. While I knew each plane had only one pilot, I had thought that the other men were closer, like all four in one formation. That's the way I had always pictured it in my brain. I didn't know that Gary was absolutely alone.

"The four of us were in the bomb run. The eight planes in front of us had already hit the target. There was smoke and dust everywhere. My flight followed. I had just arced over the top of my climb and started down when all hell broke loose. The North Vietnamese started firing flak and SAMs at us like crazy. I've never seen that many missiles or such concentrated shooting from the ground. It was like a wall of fire."

Matt paused. "That's when I realized it was a trap."

He showed us news photographs of a SAM and the canisters. "Missile canisters like these were left out in the open on purpose, as bait."

I looked at the SAM pictures and shuddered. The missiles looked menacing, deadly. Passing them on to Shannon, I shook my head.

"The enemy set a trap?" Samuel asked.

"They sure did. They outfoxed us on that one."

"What happened then?"

"Each of us jinked, weaving, trying to avoid the SAMs and flak. Somehow, I got through. The other three guys didn't make it. I turned, looking over my shoulder to see what was going on. I didn't know for sure which F-105 was which but saw two of them get hit and go down. I never saw what happened to the other plane. It just disappeared."

"Oh, God," I said, shaking. "So, Gary was in one of those planes." Shannon grabbed my arm with both of her hands and held on.

"No doubt about that," Matt said. "I flew to our assembly point and none of the planes appeared. I circled there for a good while. My fuel ran really low, and I had to go find a tanker and refuel. Then on to Takhli."

"There's no way he could have gotten away then without you knowing?" I asked.

"The planes never came off the target. Any one of the three pilots could have ejected and gotten out of their 105, but they couldn't have flown away without me seeing them or else being detected by the radar reconnaissance plane located offshore whenever there's a strike underway."

"You didn't hear anything on the radio?" Jacob asked.

"Yes, I did," Matt said. "I'll get to that in a minute. Do you understand what happened so far, Allison?"

"I think so," I said, twisting and squeezing crumpled tissues with my hands. "Three airplanes were shot down. One of them was Gary's." I felt numb, cold, like an arctic blast of air had just hit me. I had heard those words. Now it was real. I looked at the faces of the others, shocked into silence.

"That's right," Matt said. "Each pilot carries one or more hand held survival radios and uses them to communicate if they have to eject. Plus, there's a beeper on the parachute rig which goes off after ejection."

"You can talk to the pilots on the ground?"

"Yes, we can, on a radio channel known as Guard. The problem is the beeper's on the same frequency. It blows away any other communication. The usual procedure is to turn off the beeper as soon as you can after you eject so you can talk to the people in the air."

Matt reached into his flight bag and pulled out a hand-held radio. He extended the antenna and showed us the controls. "This switch is used for the beeper, to listen only or talk. As I departed the target, I heard one or more beepers blasting everything off the air and an intermittent voice calling out, but I don't know who it was or what they were saying."

Pausing and looking me straight in the eyes, Matt said, "Allison, I will tell you that was one lonely flight back to Takhli. All I could think about was my three friends. There have been many missions when I lost one man. But never three at one time. It was the saddest hour of my life."

"Couldn't you save them or rescue them in some way?"

"Sometimes we can use helicopters to pick a pilot up, but not this time," Matt said, pointing out the target on the map. "This was too close to Hanoi. There were too many defenses there. It would have been suicide for a helicopter. The simple truth is that pilots shot down this far north can't be rescued."

"What happens to them?"

"They become Prisoners Of War held by the North Vietnamese, who refer to them as War Criminals. After a pilot has been captured, the North Vietnamese are supposed to report the name of the POW to the Red Cross. When someone is shot down and we don't know what happened to them, they're called Missing In Action. Gary is MIA because we don't know if he's a prisoner or if he was killed. Anyway, the North Vietnamese are supposed to turn over the names."

"But they aren't doing that, are they?" I asked. I had never heard anything about Gary from the government or the Red Cross. "Some of the wives of other missing pilots told me to write to Gary in care of the North Vietnamese Embassy in Paris. I've done that, but the letters come back unopened, marked refused. All we have is this group of wives with missing husbands. We don't know how to help them."

"You know as much about this as I do," Matt said. "The North Vietnamese have released several POWs and turned them over to various peace groups. I've seen movies of groups of POWs in parades in Hanoi. The North

Vietnamese have never released an official list of prisoners, so far as I know."

"Are they being mistreated?" I asked, trying to confirm rumors I had been hearing from the wives of other MIAs. Officially, the American government was very low key about the ill treatment of American POWs held by the North Vietnamese. There were early efforts underway to organize the wives of the POWs and MIAs to present a united front and to push for action to help the men.

"I don't know," Matt said, looking away, avoiding my eyes. "I'm going to make a trip up to D.C. to talk to some intelligence guys that I know. Maybe I'll learn more up there. After I do that, I'll talk with you again."

I felt empty. Now I knew more. But the information made me feel helpless and disoriented.

"I was their leader," Matt said, holding his head in his hands. "They were my men. All three of them—gone!"

Trying to hold together but failing, I found myself sobbing. I shuddered and couldn't stop myself from shaking. Shannon put her arms around me and held me. "Time will pass. You have a baby to look after. It will be alright," she whispered, calming me.

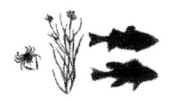

GIVE PEACE A CHANCE

──────────────────────── 66

Allison Faith Deale
Seven Springs, North Carolina
October 20, 1967

I TRIED TO avoid any newspapers or TV shows concerned with the Vietnam War. But on the same day, October 17, two events in direct contrast with each other had occurred. Stories about the war and also demonstrations by peace groups to end it leapt from the pages of newspapers across the nation.

In South Vietnam, an American search-and-destroy operation known as Shenandoah II occurred in the jungle thirty miles northwest of Saigon, which resulted in sixty soldiers being killed.

Before Gary had left for Thailand, he told me that the Army frequently moved large units of soldiers into the jungle in search of enemy forces to destroy. He explained the ill-conceived nature of such missions. Known as search-and-destroy, the American forces deployed in the jungle looking for the enemy. Rather than providing security and safety for the South Vietnamese peasants in the villages, the Americans chased a mobile elusive enemy in the swamps.

Shenandoah II proved him right. The soldiers fought an enemy regiment, which stood its ground rather than melting away into the jungle. Even with the fight still raging, news reports stated that the Americans were going to abandon the battlefield and move on to other operations.

"Those missions may kill enemy soldiers, but Americans are dying in large numbers," Gary had said in Hawaii. "Our troops don't hold onto the land or secure it after these operations, we just leave and move someplace else. And, the civilians in the hamlets and villages still aren't safe."

What are we accomplishing? I wondered. Why are American soldiers and marines thrashing around in the countryside, when the peasants are unprotected? Why do the troops fight in one area and then simply walk away to go to another battle someplace else?

I remembered reading one of Gary's books written by Bernard B. Fall. He wrote that securing the civilian population was the key to winning insurgencies, the kind of war we were supposed to be fighting. Hadn't anyone in authority ever read his writing? I wondered.

Meantime in contrast, at the University of Wisconsin, a peace demonstration turned violent. A representative from Dow Chemical, one of the manufacturers of napalm, had been detained by a student sit-in in an administration building. Police forcefully evicted the protestors and arrested them. Graphic pictures of police beating students and of those with blood flowing from head wounds dominated news reports.

The two juxtaposed events created even more confusion about Vietnam for me. While our young men fought and died in Vietnam to preserve freedom for that nation's people, students in the United States ended up being beaten in a peaceful protest. Wasn't the point of a democracy to hear the voices of all the people? I wondered. Was it right for us to fight in Vietnam to protect their democracy, if that's what it was, when students in this county were beaten and arrested for exercising their freedom to question our government's policies?

Seeing no end to the war, I only envisioned more fighting and dying. Senator John Stennis had conducted hearings in Congress in late August. His view and that of some of his colleagues was that President Johnson and Secretary of Defense McNamara were not aggressively fighting to win in Vietnam. The senator stated that the Johnson Administration deliberately withheld strategic North Vietnamese targets from the American bombing campaign. Hawks in Congress and the media demanded unlimited bombing of North Vietnam and also blockading the country by dropping mines in harbors. These men thought America wasn't doing enough to win.

I knew about the war and the bombing of North Vietnam, at great personal cost. To me, any mention of widening the war was reprehensible, especially when the leaders talked about expanding the bombing. I questioned what more bombing would accomplish, other than having more pilots end up like Gary.

After three years of intensive fighting and over 20,000 Americans dead, our troops were sinking into a quagmire, with no hope of resolution or peace. Over and over, the cries of the beaten students ran through my head.

"All we are saying, is give peace a chance!"

TET

_____ 67

Allison Faith Deale
Seven Springs, North Carolina
February 2, 1968

MY FATHER SAT with me in the kitchen, drinking morning coffee. He put several spoons of sugar into his cup and winked at me, knowing that my mother would have a fit if she saw him do that. Gary's disappearance had hit my father hard. Dad had known him for years, in his part-time position as an assistant high school football coach. Now he smiled often and told jokes, trying to help lift the fog which seemed to surround me. A pair of knitting needles clicked together as Mom sat in the living room, making an afghan for my baby.

Having them in our house for extended visits several times over these past months brought about a transition in my thinking. It seemed somewhat unusual to have my primary role shift from being a wife back to being a daughter, but that is what happened.

Since Gary's disappearance months before, I had come to rely on my parents more than ever. I knew they were doing their best to see me through the rough times, and hoped my love and appreciation for them showed through my dark moods.

In a figurative sense, my parents had wrapped their arms around me and taken me back into their loving embrace. Now that I no longer had any prospect of Gary returning soon, if ever, I welcomed it.

Gary's parents had visited me, once in Beaufort and several times here at Seven Springs. I told them everything I knew about Gary, including what I had heard from Matt

Foxe. They were very hopeful that Gary had survived and was alive and in prison. Sharing their hope and confidence provided the boost I needed to continue.

Feeling the baby squirm, I placed my hands on my belly. Dad watched and smiled. He knew what was happening.

Filling time, my father told the story of how he and my Uncle Bill bought our farm. I had heard it dozens of times before, but always enjoyed listening to how they took a great financial risk after World War II and went deeply in debt to purchase the property on St. Martin's Neck in Maryland.

Mom's call startled us. "Fred, Alli, come look at this about Vietnam."

Dad and I hurried to the living room to find Mother leaning over a chair. "Look at this mess," she said in a strained voice. She sounded on the verge of tears. Her hand rose to cover her mouth. Looking into her eyes, I saw anguish, uncertainty, and fear.

The TV reporter was saying, "... typically a time of cease fire due to the Lunar New Year's holiday known in Vietnam as Tet, but that is not the case this year." On the screen thick black smoke engulfed the streets of what the reporter informed us was Saigon. Debris from blown up houses and shops littered the streets. Flames and smoke erupted from structures. "Over the last thirty-six hours," the reporter continued, "nearly every large city, including the capitol, Saigon itself, has come under attack by Communist forces." Images of American and Vietnamese soldiers crouched behind buildings firing down the street filled the screen. "Dozens of American troops have been killed. No one knows how many Communists are dead."

My gut reaction was to vomit. I shuddered, thinking about those dead American soldiers and their wives and mothers.

Dad said, "This can't be happening! I thought we were making progress in Vietnam!" He stood behind Mother with one arm draped over her shoulder, his hands clenched tightly and his jaw sternly set. Frown lines crossed his forehead.

Then I saw the bodies. The reporter continued, his tone flat, "The bodies of two American soldiers can't be recovered because of the intense enemy fire."

We kept hearing that Vietnam was the first TV war, but nothing came close to this. The news showed fighting in the jungles almost every day. Now the battles raged right in the middle of Saigon. We were seeing the war happening right before our eyes.

As we stood in silent fascination, photographs appeared showing the execution of a Viet Cong guerilla by a South Vietnamese police official. Still pictures taken during a shooting, showed a Vietnamese holding a revolver at a man's head and the execution itself. I flinched, having never seen anything like this.

The reporter continued. "The officer said the man he executed had killed a South Vietnamese police officer and his entire family. There is no official reaction from the White House or Pentagon on these developments. President Johnson is meeting with his advisers."

"What in the hell is happening over there?" my father muttered to himself.

I wanted to shout or scream, but couldn't do it while they were watching me so carefully, their eyes dark with concern.

Pictures of the chaos in the cities of South Vietnam flashed on the screen. I walked across the room, took hold of Mom and Dad's hands and started crying.

Later, I sat holding a picture. It seemed to have appeared from nowhere. I didn't remember taking it off the shelf. The teardrops on the frame and glass must have been mine, but it was all a big blur. In the picture, I am wearing a bright yellow sweater, and my two neighbors, Jacob and Samuel Craven, are both pointing into the air. Two jet fighters were visible in the background. My husband, Gary, was piloting the left-most plane.

I had used the picture as a touchstone since July, something to take me back to earlier times when I was happy and when laughter and joy filled our home.

BE STRONG MY LITTLE ONE

_____ 68

Allison Faith Deale
Seven Springs, North Carolina
February 2, 1968

IN JULY, A black cloud descended over my life. I lost my way. Focusing on research and writing my thesis helped me get through each day. There was no sense of direction or purpose in my life other than the baby and science. Using my work as a crutch, I stumbled through one day and then the next. Beyond that, I did not have a life.

My friends from the marine lab helped me, but they had lives of their own to live. Some of the pilots Gary had known transferred to other bases. In fact, most of his friends were now in Thailand.

Everything I had believed in changed: my goals and my life. I used my work and remnants of faith to point me in the right direction. I must admit that the small quantities of wine I drank helped cast a certain haze on my difficulties. After I told him about the wine, Dr. Naylor at Seymour convinced me that this was an unsatisfactory solution. He lectured me sternly, "Look, Allison, there are professionals here who can help you cope with this. You have someone else to consider other than just yourself."

From that day on, I had a renewed purpose in life which helped provide stability and direction. That fact along with desperate soul searching and long solo walks transformed my life.

Each day I prayed that Gary was alive and would return to me. This provided a measure of comfort and increased my hopes that he would. I tried to deal with the horrible truth of his disappearance. Like Sisyphus, I continued to roll the rock up the mountain. And, for the most part, I emerged from the dark pit.

Then all at once this Tet Offensive storm hit. I found myself wallowing in tears and misery.

After watching the news on Tet from Vietnam, my dad and I decided to go ahead with our daily walk to the state park. I put on multiple layers, hoping to remain warm in the cold wind blowing from the north.

We ventured along the dirt road pausing at the top of each rolling hill to catch our breath. Everyone told me to walk and keep busy. Our ritual of trekking down Park Road to the Cliffs of the Neuse State Park fulfilled the doctor's orders.

I smelled the strong aroma of pine. There was still a lot of devastation from the previous week's surprise freezing rain and sleet storm. The sounds of limbs crashing down in the forest had wakened me. The day after the storm, sunshine created a winter wonderland, sparkling off ice-covered utility lines, pine and hardwood trees. Some of the trees were untouched, but the storm sheared off the tops of others and stripped the branches, leaving the trunks naked. Power lines were knocked down, cutting off electricity for three days. Debris littered the roadside.

Now, my father and I stopped to look at a squadron of turkey vultures soaring over the fields. Several swooped down and landed far away from the road. "Probably a dead deer or something back there," my father said. "They say those guys can smell something dead from miles away."

The pine woods on the right side offset the Cravens' fields to the north. Though the fields lay dormant preparing for the spring and summer planting, the adjacent trees had been brutally beaten by the storm.

Walking next to my father with my hands touching and lingering on my belly, I felt kicking and movement; life and hope.

My dad asked, "What's going on with money? Do you need anything right now?"

"I get Gary's Dependent's and Quarter's Allowance. That continues as long as Gary's declared missing in action. They place his base pay into escrow."

"Does that mean you have to get along without any of his money?" Dad turned to face me, an incredulous look on his face.

"If there's an emergency, I can ask for access to his account, but they must see documentation of the reason and receipts for the spending. I'm on my own with day-to-day stuff."

I thought the system was unfair. Missing husbands were in one part of the world, while their wives and children were in another. There was no provision for increased expenses due to travel, childcare and the thousand other things a single wife or mother had to do. The open indifference to the financial plight of women I had met over the past six months with missing husbands hurt deeply. Gary's parents and my dad had given me money to pay housing and college expenses. Otherwise, I wouldn't have made it.

We continued walking, stopping now and then to look at birds. A doe and a fawn loped out of the woods ahead of us and ran across the Cravens' field.

"Look, Alli, if you need help, call us," he said, his hand on my shoulder. "Do you need money now?"

"You already helped with the mortgage." I hung my head, tears welling with the simple truth of my admission. "But right now the house insurance is due and I don't have the money to pay it."

"Give me the bill. I want any other bills you have. Your mother would have a fit if she knew you were worried about money." He mumbled a few words about bureaucracy and the government.

"This is some mess." Putting his hands on my shoulder, he gently turned me towards him, as he had done when I was a child. "I know you have the inner strength to help you through this. Be strong my little one."

I thought my crying was over for the day, but the tears started again. Dad had tears on his cheeks too. This was not how I liked to spend a day with my dad.

My father decided to visit with Jacob and Samuel Craven to talk about farming. I continued down the road a short distance to my driveway. Our brick rancher had escaped damage but the storm had pruned the trees.

I smelled lasagna baking as soon as I entered the house. Mom was cooking provisions for future use. I poured myself a cup of coffee and walked to the guest room where I found her packing their suitcases.

"You're heading home soon?" I asked.

"Probably tomorrow or the next day. Your dad has work to do on the farm, and I have to check the motel."

"I just had a conversation with Dad about paying my bills."

"Allison, you know very well—"

"Mom, I'm worried about this whole mess. I don't know if Gary is alive or dead. I don't know what I'm going to do."

"Honey, we're here to help you," she said, placing her hand on my shoulder. "All you have to do is tell us what you want. Your father and I both love you dearly."

"I know. But not knowing anything about Gary is the worst thing that could happen to me."

"You must never give up. You've always been a strong person and you'll make it through this."

"I feel lost."

Mom reached out her hand and lifted up my chin looking me straight in the eyes. "Alli, you'll find your way out of this. Sooner or later, you'll find out what happened. You've someone else who needs you now. You have to be strong."

STARRY STARRY NIGHTS

_____ 69
Allison Faith Deale
Seven Springs, North Carolina
February 7, 1968

ANOTHER SLEEPLESS NIGHT, I thought, opening the drapes. The stars shimmered. With two weeks remaining, I was getting heavier, unable to sleep. Night after night, I stood by the bedroom window. Exhaustion dulled my senses, but finding a comfortable position in bed and sleep evaded me, one more reason why I wanted this baby to be born soon.

The baby's movements, which seemed to increase at nighttime, caused some of my insomnia. At times, when I was napping, Braxton-Hicks contractions snapped me awake. Dr. Naylor had told me to expect the false-labor or near-term contractions. "Don't be fooled," the doctor had said. "These will be minor compared with the real thing."

I moved through the room as quietly as possible, not wanting to awaken Sara Craven, who slept in the guest room. Since I was getting close to my due date, the Craven ladies had taken turns watching over me since my parents had returned home. Uncle Bill had called from Colorado confirming his airline reservation and said that he would be arriving in two days.

The moon cast its beams on the pictures on the alcove wall above the small window seat. I touched the one of Gary with his plane. He rested on one knee in front of the F-105, his flight gear spread around him on the tarmac. Gary smiled and looked straight into the camera's eye, just as though he were looking straight into mine. He grasped his helmet in his hands, the same hands, which had held and caressed me. I will never forget his holding me tightly. I stood there thinking of those last times we made love in that little cabin in Hawaii and shuddered.

Staring at the stars, I wondered where he was and what had happened to him. Are you up there Gary? What have the North Vietnamese done to you? Are you alive? Your baby is going to be born soon!

GARY'S B-4 BAG

Allison Faith Deale
Seven Springs, North Carolina
February 12, 1968

I GENTLY CLOSED my bedroom drapes to shut out the moon shining through the window. Uncle Bill, who had arrived several days before, slept in the guestroom. The large wooden rocking chair, which I borrowed from my mom and dad's house, beckoned. It provided the only place for me to take short naps. The bed didn't work, nor the sofa. I wished I could have a stiff drink. Relaxing back into the chair, I closed my eyes and waited for sleep.
"Allison, are you awake?" Bill asked, sticking his head into my room.
For a moment, I thought I was dreaming. It seemed so strange hearing a man's voice in our house.
"Yes, I'm alive," I said, stretching, trying to make sense out of where I was.
"I didn't ask if you were alive, although that's nice to know," Bill said, entering the room and replacing the afghan over my shoulders. "I'd been standing there for a while. You're totally zonked out."
"I haven't been sleeping well. All I do is nap."
"Do you want any breakfast?"
"Hot tea and toast would be wonderful," I said as Bill held out his hands and pulled me from the chair. He headed off to the kitchen while I waddled into the bathroom.
Bill had taken time off from his civil engineer job in Colorado to come help me while I waited for the big event. "I'm weary of snow and skiing for this year and hope to do

some fishing and hiking along the coast," Bill had said when I phoned him the week before.

THE NEXT DAY, Matt Foxe called to say he had returned to Seymour from F-4 Phantom flight instructor training at MacDill. Uncle Bill invited him for dinner because he wanted to hear what had happened to Gary first hand.

Reminding me of my father in his mannerisms and stature, Uncle Bill was more of an extrovert. Always eager to meet new people and be socially active, he contrasted with my father who was more of a "stay at home and mind the fires" farmer. In some ways, I used Uncle Bill as a behavior model.

NOW REMNANTS OF the chicken burrito appetizers Uncle Bill had made littered the coffee table in the living room. He had made me a bland one with no chilies, but Shannon and Matt had snapped up the ones labeled Hot and Hotter.

A green salad, strip steaks, baked potatoes, and glasses of red wine filled the kitchen table to overflowing. The flowers Shannon brought put spring on the table in the middle of winter.

"Time to dig in," Bill said, inviting us to the table with a sweeping gesture of his hand.

I cut a small piece of steak and prepared my small baked potato. My portions had grown smaller over the past month. But I craved chocolate and ice cream.

After answering Uncle Bill's questions about flying over North Vietnam, Matt retold how Gary had been shot down. It was the same information he had given me back in September. He said that he had nothing new.

"Have you heard anything additional about Gary?" Shannon asked, with a low calm voice.

"I don't know anything beyond what Matt just said," I said, looking at her directly. "There's been no hint of him since July 14. Gary's name has definitely not shown up on any lists. But my contact at the Pentagon won't tell me what lists he is talking about."

"I checked with some spooks at the CIA and they told me the same thing about lists," Matt said, cutting a piece from his steak.

"Doesn't anyone know anything about Gary?" Uncle Bill asked, pushing his glasses up his nose.

"No."

"You mean to tell me there's no news at all on any of the missing?" Bill asked, with an incredulous look on his face.

"Nothing factual, only propaganda crap that the North Vietnamese put out."

"Why is this happening?" Bill asked.

"Same damned thing happened in Korea," Matt said. "Pilots disappeared. When the war was over, either they showed up or they didn't."

"The man from the Pentagon has told me not to talk to the press," I said, laying my hand against my belly. "I'm supposed to refer any questions to Seymour Johnson or to the public relations office in the Pentagon. He says that they don't want us to say anything which will make conditions worse for the prisoners."

"Now that we have thousands of troops in Vietnam, is ending the war a political action, rather than a military one?" Bill asked.

"The military has done everything they can do," Matt said. "We bomb whatever the politicians will allow us to bomb in the North. There are lots of targets which should have been bombed years ago, and they haven't been touched so that's a political issue."

Matt thought for a second, looking down at his plate. "In South Vietnam, the American soldiers have done about all they can do with the number of troops on hand. They're trying to train South Vietnamese soldiers, but those guys don't seem to be too willing to fight, and the South Vietnamese government is corrupt and unstable. I don't know how many governments they've had since President Diem and his brother were assassinated during that military coup. The government is inept. That's a political issue for the United States."

While the others attacked their steaks with great gusto, I nibbled at my food. I took in every word said, hunting for something new that I had not heard before.

"I don't understand this Tet Offensive," Bill said, picking at a tooth with his little finger. "I thought the cities were secure and that most of the countryside had been pacified, but apparently that's not the case."

"The American military presented a very rosy picture before Tet, you know, the story line of seeing the light at the end of the tunnel," Matt said.

"What happened?" Bill asked.

Matt paused, taking a swallow of his beer. "Victor Charlie bamboozled us and all our grand schemes. I can't remember the exact words, but Bernard Fall wrote that he had an interview with Ho Chi Minh in 1962. Uncle Ho told Fall that it took eight years to beat the French in the First Indochina War, and that since America was a much stronger country it would take ten years to defeat us."

"They are willing to pay any price whatsoever to join the two countries together?" I asked, wondering about the cost of American lives, thinking about the price Gary had probably paid.

"Absolutely," Matt said, slapping his palm on the table for emphasis. "Here we are, five years down the road since Fall had the interview with Ho and the little buggers are still at it with no sign of backing off. They take every punch we throw at them and then turn around and throw Tet back at us."

"I have some experience with war, and I know Americans," Bill said. "We have a short attention span and absolutely no patience for the long haul. Probably sooner, rather than later, we'll grow tired of this war and get out."

"Precisely my point," Matt said. "We're screwed!"

"There you go, speaking French again," Shannon said.

"I'll just say one more thing while we're talking about the war," Matt said, standing with his glass of beer. He spoke boldly and forthrightly with a commanding voice. "Gary Deale was an outstanding pilot who did his duty even though the cards were stacked against him. I loved him as a brother. Let's raise our glasses to Gary Deale."

We all stood, me more slowly than the others, and raised our glasses. I took one sip of wine. I figured one taste wouldn't hurt anything at this point. This was the first official toast I had drunk in honor of Gary. While I had raised my glass to him many times since July, this was the first time in a group. It felt good to honor him, but I wished that he were here with us.

I finished my food and watched as the others ate their sweet potato pie with ice cream. My mood had changed. I couldn't decide if this was another of the swings I had been experiencing or if it was something different. I knew hormonal changes produced weird side effects but wasn't sure that was causing this sensation of remoteness and isolation. I felt detached and as cold as an iceberg. Maybe things will get better after the baby is born, I thought. Or, maybe not?

TWO DAYS LATER, Uncle Bill and I sat in the living room, talking about Colorado skiing. While I was in no condition to ski, I had greatly missed my trips west over the past few years.

There was one major task that I wanted to accomplish before Uncle Bill departed. While I had considered having my parents assist, or maybe even Carmen, I had decided to ask my uncle. He had been an army officer, and I thought he would be a dispassionate helper and observer. I trusted him.

"Uncle Bill, there is one more thing I want you to do for me."

"What's that?" he said. "I'll do anything you ask."

"There's a B-4 bag and a wooden foot locker that the Air Force sent here from Thailand. I've not had the courage to open them, and I want you to do that for me."
"Are you sure? What about your mom and dad?"
"No, I want you to do it."
"Okay. Where are they?"
"In our bedroom closet."
Gary's clothes he had left behind when he departed for Thailand also remained in the closet. The closet had become one of my refuges, where I felt close to him. Somehow, in that small space, I felt his presence.
"I can't do anything with his clothes," I said, pointing. "I don't know what to do. I don't know if he'll be coming back."
I sat on the bed as Uncle Bill unzipped Gary's B-4 bag. He handed me an Air Force business envelope addressed to Mrs. Allison Deale, Next of Kin of Lieutenant Gary Bishop Deale. Park Court. Seven Springs, North Carolina.
I opened the envelope to find several sheets of paper. The letterhead showed the insignia of the 333rd Tactical Fighter Squadron. The memorandum addressed to me was dated 21 July 1967 and read, *"Please find attached a true and accurate inventory of the belongings and personal effects of Gary Bishop Deale, First Lieutenant, USAF, AO0645382, 333rd Tactical Fighter Squadron. Attested: Bradley Mims, Captain, USAF; Summary Courts Officer; Kennard Wolburn, Master Sergeant, USAF; First Sergeant."*
Brad Mims was a good friend. He had trained with Gary at Seymour. Now, I had something else to thank him for. He had written a personal letter to me after Gary disappeared explaining, as best he could, what had happened. He said that he was Gary's Courts Officer. I never knew that he had to pack up Gary's belongings.
Uncle Bill took items out of the bag and placed them on the bed. He handled them with care. I touched each article. Everything in the bag was wrapped in paper. I read the inventory list one item at a time:
Suits, Flight, Green (4 Ea.);
Jacket, Flight, Green (1 Ea.);

Cap, Flight (2 Ea.);
Hat, Bush, Australian (1 Ea.);
Trouser, Uniform, 1505 (3 Ea.);
Shirt, Uniform, 1505 (3 Ea.);
Trouser, Blue, Dress (1 Ea.);
Shirt, Uniform, Blue, Dress (2 Ea.);
Jacket, Uniform, Blue, Dress (1 Ea.);
Necktie, Blue (1 Ea.);
and so on.

His hands trembled as he lifted each article out of the bag. He had the saddest look, his chin quivering.

I had seen all of these things before. But Gary had been here to wear them. Now they were simply articles of clothing.

While his flight suits were green in color, one strange one appeared. It was well worn, red in color, covered with cloth patches. Then, I remembered that Gary had wrote that his squadron was known as the Red Lancers and that he had had a party flight suit made.

Another item was a bush hat. A series of tick marks in red and black were located on the front band. I counted them, seventy-five in total.

The itemized list of the "belongings and personal effects" coldly reduced Gary's life to three typed sheets of paper.

Gary's uniforms, civilian clothing, underwear and odds and ends lay in little piles, all properly inventoried and recorded. Everything was so neat. An entire life displayed in straight orderly rows.

"Put all of that back in the bag," I said. "Let's do the locker next."

The military was so organized. They had thought to lock the locker and the keys were enclosed in the envelope I had just opened. Someone, someplace had probably designed a form with a checklist of items to be crossed off as they were packed away.

The key opened the lock. Bill began removing stationery, personal toiletries, a large sealed envelope, several wrapped packages and more clothing.

He handed me the envelope. I hesitated, not knowing what to expect. After a few seconds, I opened it. Inside were the letters I had mailed to Gary. In addition, there were letters to him from our families and friends.

Bill cut the packages apart and handed them to me. The first was a framed picture of me in my bathing suit on the beach in Hawaii. Gary had apparently taken the photograph and never told me, as I had not seen it before. Then, there was another photograph of the two of us sitting in an airliner. I remembered that picture as being our very first date when we flew to Denver. Another picture showed Gary kneeling in front of his F-105. The last package was a self-portrait I had painted in watercolor just before Gary left for Thailand.

I had one more package, the large manila envelope that Matt had given me months before.

Uncle Bill handed it to me and sat down on the bed beside me. The baby moved. Holding my belly, I waited for him or her to settle down.

After I opened the envelope, I found several cloth patches and a small black loose-leaf notebook. Opening the book, I read the words, COMBAT DIARY, GARY BISHOP DEALE. Shutting it as quickly as possible, I lay it on the bed. Then, I picked it up.

Flipping through the pages I saw dated diary entries with poetry mixed in. Gary wrote me poems and mailed them on a regular basis. These must be in addition to the other ones he had sent me.

"There's quite a bit of poetry mixed in with a diary of missions," I said, scanning to the last page with writing. "He flew his seventy-fifth mission on 13 July. That must be where the marks on his bush hat came from. Listen to this, Counter Number 76, 14 July 1967, Van La SAM Support Facility, 2051N 10546E, Weather OK. That's the last entry."

"14 July, that's the day he went missing," Uncle Bill said.

"Yes."

It felt odd to see that date in his handwriting, the date he went missing, the day he may have died.

There were four cloth patches. First, one with the silhouette of an F-105 imposed over a map of North Vietnam. The words RED RIVER VALLEY were embroidered across the top of the patch. Another one showed an eagle clutching some kind of missile in its talons with the words SAM SLAYER. I recognized another as being from the Tactical Air Command. Finally, there was a patch with an F-105 silhouette imposed over a red star and the words CHINA EXPRESS.

"There's got to be stories involved with these patches," Bill said.

"I'll have to ask Matt about them."

Bill sat beside me on the bed. "Well, Allison, there it is," Bill said as he wrapped his arm around me.

I looked at him and at the items Gary had cherished. My life with Gary, as I had known it, was spread before me.

Later that day, I sat by myself in my bedroom while Bill prepared dinner. I read each page of Gary's Combat Diary. Touching each page, reading each entry, I savored his words written in his own hand. I wanted him to be alive.

The poems touched my heart. Now, understanding for the first time how intense his war had been, I sobbed. He must have been so scared.

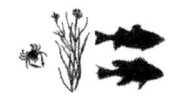

TET, WALTER CRONKITE, AND THE STRAW THAT BROKE THE CAMEL'S BACK

Allison Faith Deale
Seven Springs, North Carolina
February 27, 1968

FOR SEVERAL WEEKS, I'd avoided the news because it was dominated by Tet and the Vietnam War. I wanted to know what was going on but couldn't bear to watch the bloodshed every night.

But Carmen had turned the TV on as she prepared dinner. I sat at the kitchen table watching the set in the living room. Tet dominated the newscast again. Hundreds of marines had been killed in a difficult bloody battle to retake Hue, the ancient imperial capitol and citadel, in the northern part of South Vietnam. Our troops had found mass graves of civilians executed by the Communist forces during that battle.

We watched a CBS News Special Report with Walter Cronkite while eating dinner. Cronkite, the most trusted newscaster in America, had just returned from Vietnam and had seen the devastation of Tet first hand.

At the end of the program, he made a startling comment. He paused for a moment, taking off his glasses, frowning, looking directly at the camera. With preciseness and clarity Cronkite said, "But it is increasingly clear to this reporter that the only rational way out then will be to negotiate, not as victors, but as an honorable people who lived up to their pledge to defend democracy, and did the best they could. This is Walter Cronkite. Good night."

I put down my fork and sat staring at the TV, open mouthed. "Did I hear that right? Did he just say what I think he said?"

Carmen shrugged. "It sounded as though he has seen and heard enough about Vietnam. Tet was the last straw."

A shiver of fear made me shudder. I had always thought winning the war was our government's plan. Gary had believed that. But Cronkite had just said that we had done the best we could, and that negotiation was the only rational way to end it. This made me feel like a ship without a rudder, a person lost in a jungle without a map. I wondered what this meant for me, for Gary, for our child.

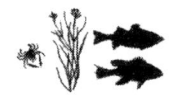

SEVEN POUNDS, EIGHT OUNCES

_____ 72

Allison Faith Deale
Seven Springs, North Carolina
February 28, 1968

I SAT ON the window seat with no hope of sleep as time moved me beyond the starry night and past the dawn. The morning unfolded as blackness faded to gray stillness. A bird called from the swamp behind our house. *Who cooks for you? Who cooks for you all?* That was it. I thought for a minute and then decided; barred owl.

Swarms of blackbirds lifted out of the pine woods headed over to the Cravens' fields to snack. Carmen's slippers scuffed down the hall as she made her way to the bathroom.

Suddenly, a great horned owl called, Who! Who! Then the barred owl went silent. What did that mean? My father told me years ago that great horned owls preyed upon barred owls. My imagination ran wild with possibilities. Did the barred owl hide in his hollow tree? Did the great horned owl kill the barred owl for breakfast? I visualized the slashing talons, and feathers and flesh torn from the bird with the owl's beak. Death of one animal led to life for another. Death gives hope. Perhaps only biologists appreciate the fact that some creatures must die so that others may live.

Is that true for humans as well? I thought. Did Gary die so that some other person could live? Or, is he alive and did the other person die instead? I simply didn't know.

"Breakfast is ready," Carmen called from the kitchen.

I shuffled down the hall. "Speaking of ready, do you think I look ready?" I asked.

"My sister looked just like you right before she went into labor. All puffy and ripe; that's the best way I can put it."
"We'll see, won't we," I said.
"Good grief, first I hauled my sister to the hospital alone. Next, it's going to be you. I have that feeling in my bones."
"This will be a true test of friendship. Will my best friend be able to do the job?"
Carmen grabbed me by the shoulders and gave me the longest hug. "I'm glad it ended up with me being here now. I wouldn't want it any other way."
"I'm glad." I felt a very strange twinge in my belly. Then I felt water running down my thighs. "Oh! Oh! Something just happened."

"YOU KNOW THE old Jonathan Winters bit don't you?" Carmen asked as she coached me. "The crusty marine sergeant says, 'All right you guys, you heard what he said— This ain't gonna' be easy!'"
"That sounds vaguely familiar," I panted. "Sounds just like what I'm going through."
Carmen wiped my face and placed a damp cloth on my forehead as we yet again tried to adjust my body. Sara Craven fed me ice chips, one at a time. I thrashed around trying to find a comfortable position and finally settled on sitting more or less erect.
"Breathe, *hermana*. Please breathe," Carmen said, holding my hand, coaching me along.
Strong contractions began shortly after we arrived at the hospital. Beginning at about every fifteen minutes and then coming closer and closer. This was the real thing, no false-labor here. The cycle repeated: contraction, pain, and then no pain.
Carmen coached. I tried to relax and breathe deeply between contractions. We all had our little jobs to do.
The labor room nurse checked me periodically and assured me. "You are dilated eight centimeters," she said.

"The baby's heart sounds fine, so just keep doing whatever you have been doing. If you keep going like this, it won't be long now. The doctor is here and will be in to see you soon."

All that sounded fine to me, so I went back to my huffing, puffing, panting and relaxing. The pain came in waves. It was bearable so far, and I hoped to get through the birth without having to resort to medication. Once or twice I thought I had reached the breaking point, but then the pain eased.

I concentrated on the fact that pain was a temporary thing. The pain would be here today, but gone tomorrow, or most certainly by next week. I wanted to experience this birth, this beginning of life the natural way.

LATER, IN THE delivery room, Dr. Naylor took another look and said, "Good! Good! This is good. The baby's crowning. Stop pushing. Keep breathing. Stop pushing. Here's a shoulder. Breathe! Breathe! Good. The baby's coming. Here it comes. Good. It's a boy! Congratulations, you did it!"

Dr. Naylor grasped the baby who began to howl and handed him to a nurse who wiped and cleaned him. "Here's your son," the nurse said as she placed the boy wrapped in a small blanket on my belly. "Seven pounds, eight ounces."

He's all I want to see, I thought. How tiny he is. He had Gary's nose, chin and mouth. But those eyes. The eyes were from my dad's Seaford family line, going back generations.

"Looks as though we have a change of baby clothes coming up," Dr. Naylor said. "The girl you talked about turned out to be a boy. Plus, you just missed having a Leap Year baby by a few hours."

The baby squirmed and flung his arms. He made funny baby faces, looking around to be fed. Euphoria rushed through my body. How wonderful, I thought. I actually made this baby. This child was a part of me. Now he is out in the world on his own. We will be excellent parents. Gary will be so happy and proud.

But then I remembered. Gary wasn't here and may never be here. Gary has a son that he may never know. My son may never get to see or know his father. God, I thought. How could this happen? How sad that Gary wasn't here.

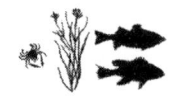

WHERE OR WHEN

_____ 73

Allison Faith Deale
Seven Springs, North Carolina
March 31, 1968

CARMEN STARED AT me from the doorway. "You're lying through your teeth," she snarled, glaring. "I don't believe anything you just said. I get here in late morning and there are no lights on in the house. What do I find? You sitting in a dark room with Gary Junior, looking as though you haven't slept since I left last week." Carmen had stopped by the house to pick up research notes that my adviser wanted to review. She had been in Durham visiting with her boyfriend, Ramon.

I picked up Gary Bishop Deale, Junior and cradled him in my arms. Yes, we had been sitting in a darkened living room. But that suited my mood perfectly. How could I be bright and cheerful when my world had fallen apart.

Carmen followed me into the baby's room, where I checked Gary Junior's diaper. "I decided to call him GJ," I said, fastening his pants.

"I've never seen this house in such disarray. I looked in the kitchen, dirty dishes are everywhere." Carmen threw her hands up in exasperation.

"I'm going to clean today," I said.

"Let me hold him," Carmen said, lifting GJ from the changing table, placing him on her shoulder. "Is he due to be fed?"

"Not yet."

"Allison, you need to get yourself back on track here," she said, sweeping her hand in a circle.

"I'm having a rough time," I whimpered, defensively. When I added up the after-pregnancy blues, the status of my master's thesis, stretching dollars and my worries about Gary, it was a wonder that I didn't feel worse than I did. Some days I felt so miserable I could barely face the world and had even darker thoughts than that. But I did my best trying to put it all behind my smiling façade.

"You don't look good. What's going on with you?" Carmen asked, staring me down. Carmen's passionate Cuban nature showed in her aggressive questioning. Carmen was being Carmen.

GJ squirmed in her arms, not being used to loud excited voices.

"I'm trying to catch up," I said, barely holding back the tears, which had been flowing freely over the past days. "I was just going to get up and make lunch."

Carmen said. "This isn't good for the baby. I'm going to keep checking on the two of you. Things had better be shipshape when I get back from Miami." Handing GJ to me, Carmen went into the kitchen and organized the stack of dirty dishes.

"We'll be fine," I said, following her, gently rocking GJ in my arms.

Carmen looked over her shoulder, glaring at me. I decided to change the subject. "How is Ramon?"

"Ramon is fine. He's too busy."

An uneasy silence followed. Carmen washed the dishes and straightened the kitchen, while I held GJ. He watched with interest as Carmen flew around the kitchen, cleaning.

"At least you managed to keep the bathroom clean," Carmen said, hugging me. After giving GJ lots of hot Cuban kisses, she departed.

"First, I clean. Then you and I will go for a long hike," I said, laying out a plan, adding structure to my life.

I hadn't taken any long walks since before the baby was born and was beginning to feel very sluggish. I was unhappy with the weight I'd put on. These baby pounds have to come off, I thought.

"Okay, I'll do my bedroom and then your room," I stood up purposely.

AFTER DINNER, I gave GJ his bath, put on a new diaper and nightclothes and took him to my bedroom. He threw his arms and looked content as he lay on our bed. I looked through a stack of documents, searching for papers about our house.

Now that he had been born, I began thinking of moving to my apartment in Beaufort. While not ready to sell our house in Seven Springs, renting it to help pay my bills seemed attractive. Moving to Beaufort would save money on gasoline.

Sprawling beside him, I sorted through the folders and envelopes. I searched for the insurance policies and the mortgage agreement, but other papers distracted me. One thin envelope had a note in Gary's writing, *Early Photographs.* I recognized the envelope from Vail Ski Resort. My hands trembled as I opened it.

The two photos in the envelope brought back a flood of pleasant thoughts. One showed Gary and me sitting in adjoining seats on an airliner and the other one was of Gary and me sitting on a chair lift at Vail during the New Year's holiday in 1964. How wonderful those moments were, I thought, remembering our first few days together. They say that love at first sight is rare and never works out in the end. I knew Gary and I would make it from the very beginning. Those were such happy times. I very much hoped those wonderful days would return.

I had been so forward, and was certain Gary must have thought that I was too pushy. Although, he later thanked me for talking with him on that day and for not slamming the door in his face, so to speak. I had never been so direct with any man, but his single tap on my shoulder at Friendship Airport changed my life forever.

Gary had sweet-talked the stewardess into taking our picture. That's the picture I now held. The last thing I did before we parted at Stapleton Airfield was to give him the phone number at Uncle Bill's house in Vail. I wasn't sure he would call and was rather surprised when he did.

Lifting GJ to show him the photographs, I spoke softly. "You know, I told your father when I met him that he seemed so familiar to me. I felt as though we had stood and talked before when I first met him, but I didn't know where or when. Who would've dreamed all of this would happen? Who would've ever imagined that you would come along?"

GJ cooed and threw his hands.

How could anyone believe that your father may be dead? I thought, not willing to say those words out loud.

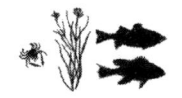

I WILL NOT SEEK, AND I WILL NOT ACCEPT

Allison Faith Deale
Seven Springs, North Carolina
March 31, 1968

LATER THAT EVENING, I sat in the living room, waiting for President Johnson's appearance on TV. What's he going to say? I wondered. I know what I wanted him to say; that the war is ending. Then Gary can come home.

The TV announcer said, "And now ladies and gentlemen, the president of the United States."

LBJ looked haggard and drawn. Heavy creases cut into his face. He looked sad. I liked him as our president. But five years of war had diminished his presidency. All he accomplished by having civil rights and voting rights legislation passed by Congress was torn apart by the quagmire of Vietnam. In my heart, I felt compassion for him.

He looks like a whipped dog, I thought. Thinking about the race riots in many American cities during the previous summer, I knew that LBJ had a wounded spirit. As if he didn't have enough on his plate, the North Koreans decided to hijack the Pueblo, and then along came Tet. I felt that he was lucky not to be dead from a heart attack.

The president spent several minutes summarizing recent peace initiatives he had made to stop the war. Then he dropped his first bombshell. He looked directly at the TV camera and said, "Tonight, I have ordered our aircraft and our naval vessels to make no attacks on North Vietnam, except in the area just north of the demilitarized zone."

"I'm shocked," I said. That meant no more bombing around Hanoi where Gary was shot down.

As LBJ recited facts of the war as he saw them, tidbits of news were revealed. General Westmoreland, commander in Vietnam, had recently asked for an additional 206,000 troops to be joined with the 525,000 already there.

Johnson continued, "The Joint Chiefs of Staff have recommended to me that we should prepare to send—during the next five months—support troops totaling approximately 13,500 men."

No more infantry soldiers? Not the 206,000 requested by Westmoreland? With that announcement, I knew our country had turned a corner in the Vietnam War. The leaders of the United States had decided that the open-ended increases in American combat troops were at the end. Added to the bombing halt that LBJ had described earlier, it was apparent that a fundamental change had just occurred. We were not going to continue expanding this war.

This speech was a fork in the path. One minute it looked as though President Johnson was preparing to take a new direction and in the next, that all changed.

I was stunned when, near the end of this speech, he said, "Accordingly, I shall not seek, and I will not accept, the nomination of my party for another term as your president."

Holy shit! That means that LBJ won't be around to end this war. With a new president, there was no way to know what was going to happen; maybe the war would widen.

I didn't know why I thought that. Something dark gripped my heart. It was difficult to figure out what the speech had to do with Gary's fate, but a feeling of despair descended over me like a black veil.

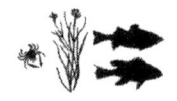

WHAT DOES IT TAKE?

_____ 75

Allison Faith Deale
Seven Springs, North Carolina
April 20, 1968

I SAT ON the window seat in the bedroom of our dark house looking out at the waning moon. More than nine months had passed since Gary disappeared—one full term pregnancy. Strange to think of it that way, but that's what popped into my head. He had been gone the exact amount of time it took to create a new life.

What does it take? I whispered. I wondered if I had the courage and strength to do this—or the cowardice and weakness—depending on how you looked at it. I rolled the prescription bottle between my hands. Twenty-five little yellow pills remained. Valium, described as the drug of the future, had been prescribed to ease my anxiety. A plastic shopping bag lay across my lap.

Yes? No? I took one more look at the moon, now fading from its peak and opened the bottle.

GJ gurgled in his sleep. I looked across the room at him, asleep on my bed. With each passing day he looked more like Gary.

No! I put the cap on the bottle and picked GJ up, preparing for whatever was to come.

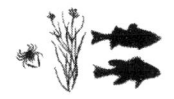

LIGHTNING DOES STRIKE TWICE

──────────────────────── 76

Allison Faith Deale
Beaufort, North Carolina
May 1, 1968

"THIS PLACE IS going to be cramped," I said, carrying the last box from the living room to my bedroom.

"You'll have to make do," Carmen said, "just pretend you're living in a college apartment."

Carmen had watched over me very carefully over these past few months. I knew she was concerned about me, but she appeared satisfied that I had returned to normal. She no longer lectured me about my messy house and dirty dishes when visiting.

By outward appearances, I had improved. Keeping our home neat and in good order became important to me. Planning for the move to Beaufort provided an easy objective for me to accomplish. But inside, all I felt was turmoil.

My apartment in Beaufort seemed much smaller now. All of his baby paraphernalia filled my cramped space.

I had decided to rent our house in Seven Springs. Of several possible tenants who responded to the FOR RENT notice posted at the base housing office, I chose a young married pilot whose wife was a nurse at the hospital in Goldsboro. They asked for first refusal if I decided to sell the house, so that eliminated some of the stress with our move to Beaufort. I couldn't bring myself to sell our first home. Not yet.

As I unpacked the first box, placing my underwear in the dresser drawer, a news bulletin on the radio caught my attention. The words "Kennedy shooting" redirected my thoughts about taking GJ for a walk through town. Why are they talking about the JFK assassination? I wondered.

The newscaster's next words stunned me, "Robert Kennedy was shot in the head early this morning at The Ambassador Hotel in Los Angeles."

I gasped. Another Kennedy killed?

"Did you hear that?" I asked, walking into the living room.

"It can't be true," Carmen said. "How could this happen so soon after Dr. King?" It was only a month since Martin Luther King had been assassinated and race riots engulfed major cities.

She moved closer to the radio. "They wouldn't let that happen to the Kennedy family," Carmen said, her voice flat with disbelief. "He would be protected. Lightning can't strike one family twice. Especially when he's running for president."

Robert Kennedy had just won the Democratic Primary in California. His position on ending the Vietnam War as soon as possible had carried him to victory in several states.

THE TURMOIL WITHIN each of us contrasted with the beautiful sunrise as Carmen started the skiff's motor. Robert Francis Kennedy lingered for one day before dying, and the grief was simply too much to bear.

Seeking a change from the disheartening TV news, we had decided to spend the day collecting research specimens. Carmen and I had been out several times earlier in the week planning our upcoming fieldwork.

Fortunately, the Newport River estuary was flat calm, with no waves in sight. I pushed the skiff away from the pier, with Carmen at the helm. GJ lay in his flotation device, cooing and swatting at the water droplets spraying over the bow as we got underway.

A technician at the marine lab made a life preserver for GJ. He created a Rube Goldberg contraption, which worked beautifully when we tested it. The tech also rigged an umbrella to shelter him from the sun's rays.

I firmly believed he should be out on the water with me. He might as well get used to it because I knew there were years of fieldwork in my future. I had decided to look ahead and apply for a doctoral program. The problem would be in deciding where. Once I determined the university, I could move on with my life.

"Isn't this wonderful, being on a boat after that awful winter?" Carmen asked, guiding the boat toward our first study plot. "Look at the sun's reflection on the water."

I dangled my arm in the water and felt its coolness. "This is the way to live," I said, "without a single care in the world."

Carmen checked her chart and turned south toward Lawton Point, our research area for the day. After she beached the skiff, I carried GJ ashore and lay him in the shade by a big bush. Then Carmen and I undressed down to our swimsuits and walked into the water, stretching out the seine net as we separated.

Finfish, crabs, shrimp, and even a diamondback terrapin floated in our trap. Carmen began identifying and measuring the creatures, while I wrote. We carefully extracted 114 critters out of the net, recording each. Even though I had a great deal of experience, one fish defied identification.

"I can't figure this fish out," I said, placing it into a bucket full of seawater after measuring it.

"I don't know it either," Carmen said. "We'll have to take it back and have Dr. Pointer take a look."

"Someone will know what it is, and embarrass us to death," I said.

As we approached the pier, the larger Research Vessel Eastward turned in ahead of us. The vessel, inbound from a cruise at the edge of the continental shelf, carried several of our friends. They would be eager for a pizza and beer night after their two week voyage collecting specimens.

We tied up at the dock and I carried our bucket with the prize fish toward the R/V Eastward. Carmen carried GJ. Whenever one of the larger ships returned from a cruise, a crowd gathered to discuss and observe newly collected animals. Public humiliation awaited us if our find ended up as a common fish.

To my chagrin, Dr. Caslin, the director of the lab, spotted us with the bucket and ambled over to peer in.

"What is it?" Dr. Caslin asked.

"We don't know," I said.

"Neither of you know?" Dr. Caslin said, prolonging our agony and waiting for the crowd to grow larger.

"Yes, sir. That's correct," I said, after no one else ventured a response to his question.

"It's a Blue Spotted Cornet Fish, *Fistularia tabacaria*," Dr. Caslin said. "You should know that fish!"

That filled the crowd with great mirth and everyone thought it was a real hoot, except for Carmen and me. Dr. Caslin extended our pain and suffering as long as he could by pointing out its long snout, extremely large eye set just back from its snout, and the two sets of triangular shaped fins, well back on the body.

Part of being a graduate student in science is accepting the professional criticism, peer review, good-natured joshing and skepticism associated with research. I stood there, soaking it all in. Our so-called friends really heaped it on.

"You should've known that," and "Where did you go to undergraduate school?" echoed through the small crowd.

"Actually where did you get this?" Dr. Caslin asked, after extending our public humiliation. "I don't think one of these has been seen here in a while. You did a good job bringing it in. This is a good fish. We need photographs."

I must say that brought on a lot of laughter, back slapping and smiling faces, although I heard Carmen mumbling, "*Caramba*," "*Cabrons*" and "*Hijo de putas*," among other things I didn't recognize.

"Guess who gets to buy the beer tomorrow night?" Dr. Caslin asked.

Hours later, I stood alone at the edge of the channel with the bucket containing the cornet fish. Once Dr. Caslin figured out what kind of fish we had caught, I decided to put him back where he belonged. I couldn't bear to see it placed in a tank and held captive.

With Gary missing, the idea of placing any creature into a confined space bothered me. It hit too close to home. After all, Gary may be languishing in a prison cell in North Vietnam. I hoped he was alive, but I didn't know.

"Speak to me, Gary," I said. "Are you out there someplace?"

I didn't expect an answer and none came. Gently lowering the bucket into the water, I watched our prize fish swim away.

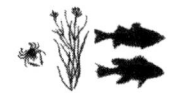

HELP ME IF YOU CAN

Allison Faith Deale
Beaufort, North Carolina
June 25, 1968

"COME IN," I said, responding to a knock on the front door. I sat up in bed very quickly, trying to reach for a book.

"I've seen enough," Carmen said, scanning my bedroom, turning on a lamp and rushing to the crib. "I thought you were improving. I hoped you were okay." She picked GJ up, cradling him in her arms. "That's it. Enough is enough already."

I offered no defense. My apartment was a mess. Cleaning hadn't seemed important to me over these past few weeks. While I took very good care of GJ, housekeeping wasn't a priority.

"What's wrong with you?" she asked, walking to my side and sitting on the bed.

"I'm fine," I said. "It's just that I feel a little sad today."

"Sad, my ass," Carmen said. "I called Ramon's father. He said he can't diagnose from a distance, but if I found you messed up again, to get you to a doctor."

"I'm not going to a doctor about this," I said. True, I wasn't myself. But I wasn't sick or depressed. Not me, I thought.

"Either we go to the clinic or I'm calling your parents," Carmen said. "You are hiding this from them and it isn't right. You're too far down to admit it. You need help from someone who knows what they're doing."

"I'm okay," I kept insisting.

"No, you're not," Carmen said, pacing with GJ. "You don't sleep. You cry too much. You don't talk to me. You sit around in a dark room all the time. You complain about fatigue when we're working. You need help!"

"No, I don't." I tried to dismiss Carmen's statements, even though I knew them to be true.

"Yes, you do. Admit it to yourself. You're going to the doctor. I'm going with you. You have nothing to say in the matter. It's either we go or I call your mom."

"The only thing wrong with me is that I'm worried about Gary," I tried to explain, but she wasn't buying it.

"We're all worried about him. But you're barely functioning. What're you going to do with the baby? You have to think of him. There's more at stake here than just you. Has GJ had his bottle? Have you changed his diaper?"

"I take care of him!" I said, raising my voice in anger.

"Allison, what about yourself?" Carmen yelled, equally upset.

GJ squirmed in Carmen's arms, not being used to loud ranting voices. He began to whimper. That pushed me over the edge.

"All right," I said, crying, knowing full well Carmen was stirred up and would not stop until I relented. For weeks, I had been minimizing her concerns but since we'd moved to Beaufort, things had gotten worse for me.

"I don't know what to do. I don't know anything," I said as the tears streamed down my cheeks. I tried to choke my sobs, unsuccessfully.

"I'll handle it," Carmen said.

THE NEXT DAY, I walked into Captain Naylor's small exam room and sat on the table. I'd been having second thoughts about this visit, but Carmen had practically pushed me into the room.

"I'm going to take your vitals and then we'll talk," Dr. Naylor said.

He took my blood pressure, pulse and temperature and used his stethoscope to check my heart and lungs. I had seen him every three weeks since the delivery. He knew that I had been having some difficulty dealing with Gary's disappearance. He didn't seem at all surprised to see me on an urgent basis at Carmen's insistence.

"Tell me what is going on with you," he said, sitting close to me on the exam table, placing his hand on my shoulder.

I told him that I hadn't been sleeping and that I felt totally stressed out, with fatigue.

He asked if I had any thoughts of hurting GJ or myself and I answered that I would never do anything like that. "Is there anything else you want to talk about?" he asked.

I shook my head, looking into his kind eyes. He smiled, his tanned face breaking into a wide grin.

"I'm going to have Carmen come into the office with Gary Junior and ask her some questions. Is that okay with you?"

"Yes."

After introductions, Carmen passed GJ to me. I lay him on the exam table next to me. Dr. Naylor slid his stool around facing Carmen.

"Having just talked with Allison, I think it was a good decision on your part to insist that she come in to see me," he said with a soft voice, casting a glance at me. "Are there any problems with Gary Junior? Does Allison feed him, bathe him and take care of him?"

"There are absolutely no problems with Allison taking care of GJ," Carmen said. "She's not taking care of herself. That's the problem!"

I sat with my hands on my lap, head down, focusing on my shoes.

"Allison, I have to ask you this again, and I must have an honest answer," Dr. Naylor said, looking straight into my eyes. "Do you ever think about hurting the baby?"

"No! Never!" I said. GJ squirmed and tried to look around, as if following the voices in the room.

"Is there any sign of Allison hurting him?" Dr. Naylor asked, addressing Carmen.

"No," she responded, shaking her head. "I change him and dress him all the time. I've never seen any injuries."

Carmen looked uncomfortable, as if she felt guilty for putting me through this inquisition.

That's how I felt about this appointment, which put me on the spot, trying to force a confession.

"Allison, what about you hurting yourself?"

I paused, unsure of how to answer his probing question. "No. I don't ever think about that," I said, being as honest as I could at that moment in time, not able to confront the full truth.

The truth was that hurting myself had occurred to me. Suicide had been on my mind. I was simply too scared and frightened by the consequences of such an act to do anything about it. Leaving GJ alone in the world was not an option I was ready to act on.

Dr. Naylor pursed his lips and eyed me for a moment. He looked at Carmen. "What do you think about her answer?"

Carmen looked at me for a moment, her dark eyes filled with concern. "She has never said anything about it. I've never seen any sign of her endangering herself." She spoke quickly but I heard doubt in her voice.

"Do you agree with everything Carmen said just now?" Doctor Naylor asked.

"It's difficult for me," I said, wiping the tears away. "Most of the time I think everything is fine and I'm in control of my life. But a lot of the time I find myself upset and crying. I don't want to be that way. I don't want to be sad all the time."

"Most women only have their baby to take care of, Allison," Dr. Naylor said, reaching and placing his hand on my arm. "Your husband is missing and you don't know if he'll be coming back from Vietnam. Some of the wives of missing pilots who come into this hospital can't deal with that issue, let alone having a new child. Plus, I think you may be overworking yourself to compensate for the stress. We have more than a simple case of the baby blues here with you, Allison."

"What can we do for her?" Carmen asked.

"I'm going to figure that out right now. Allison, are you living in Beaufort?"

"Yes."

"I want you to wait here. I need to talk with the hospital commander and then make a phone call. I'll be back in a few minutes."

I sat mired in resentment and relief. My best friend had conspired behind my back, but she did it for my own good. My feelings of comfort came from knowing I couldn't hide anymore. The cards lay on the table for all to see.

I put my hand on GJ's belly and gently vibrated my fingers. He squirmed, looking at me with wide eyes.

Carmen sat by me on the table. "I'm sorry," she said, sighing. "Please don't hate me. I'm so sorry."

I looked at her and smiled. "It's okay."

"We have good news," Captain Naylor said, returning to the room. "The hospital commander has some experience with this and he thinks you should see a therapist. That probably means two sessions a week for a while."

"What kind of therapist?" Carmen asked.

"Technically, a psychotherapist or psychiatrist. The hospital uses several different persons either in Durham or there's one here in Goldsboro."

"Is there any possibility of finding someone around Beaufort?" Carmen asked.

"I was coming to that. A clinical psychologist by the name of Dr. Wendy Semone practices in Morehead City."

"How soon can Allison begin?" Carmen asked.

"I called Dr. Semone," Dr. Naylor said, taking my hand in his. "She's willing to take you on as a patient immediately. Can you cut down on your work hours?"

"I'm working six or seven days a week. The days are very long. It's very important to me that I finish my research this summer. I don't want to be here another year."

"You shouldn't be working more than three days a week. I don't care how important it is, you must take some time off."

"We can spread things out," Carmen said. "It will take longer to do the field work, but it can be done over an extended time period."

"Take Gary Junior to the beach," Dr. Naylor said. "You need to spend time with him. He's only an infant once. Now, let me examine this big boy." He picked Gary Junior up and held him up in the air, singing an old song about an itsy-bitsy spider and a waterspout.

GJ kicked and thrashed his arms, gurgling.

Anxiety and joy mixed together. Someone was taking charge, giving me instructions. I saw a tiny sliver of hope. For the first time in months, I believed there may be a way out.

WHO'LL STOP THE RAIN?

_____ 78

Allison Faith Deale
Beaufort, North Carolina
July 14, 1968

CARMEN AND I decided that it was time to face the demons and revisit a place where we had partied together while swimming, fishing, and cooking the catch. Gary, Carmen, Ramon and I had often camped on the beach when Gary wasn't flying or away on TDY.

July 14, one year to the day after Gary went missing, I walked the beach of Shackleford Banks in my swimsuit, carrying his son in a papoose sling. Carmen and Ramon swam in the surf. The sun sparkled in the waves. A hot wind blew across the sand dunes. Juniper trees and bayberry bushes swayed with the wind.

"This is our own little Shangri La," Gary had often said. He would say that even when we were on the beach in the winter. One time, ice and snow covered the ground outside the tent. We were inside, naked in his sleeping bag and wrapped in each other's arms.

Walking along the surf line, I looked for the familiar spot back in the dunes. A landmark appeared, an old broken off tree snag. Then I knew this was the place where Gary and I had made love. A year of wind and storms had taken its toll on our little hideaway. Some of the grasses and shrubs were no longer there, and the sand mounded in a strange way, but this was the place. We had spent many happy weekends here in our little tent. We were in love, and Gary and I showed each other what that meant here in these dunes. Kneeling, I swept the sand back and forth with my hand as I remembered.

GJ squirmed. I lay him on a blanket I had carried in my backpack and looked around. The green dune grass shoots scratched my arms as I knelt down and placed my hands into the sand. The fresh scent of the sea breeze carried me back to happier times. As our little one lay there gurgling, I sobbed in sadness and frustration.

Wiping my eyes, I picked up GJ, then reached into my backpack, and took a red rose out of it its wrapper. With his hand in mine, we placed the flower on the dune. I took a copy of Gary's poem *The Edge* out of my pocket. I had copied the poem out of his combat diary. I read the words aloud to our son.

THE EDGE

*She loves living at the edge
by the ocean.
Ankles immersed with
that changing line shifting
as waves crashed ashore.*

*Standing there tall and fine
her back to the world.
At the edge
she awaits fulfillment
with the sun's emergence.*

*Beholding a vision as this
at the dune line,
I pause. She smiles.
Loosening a strap,
she beckons, "Come into my world."*

Hearts floating.
Spirits soaring.
Bodies trembling.
Sand attacks
and reality intrudes.

Guiding GJ's hand with mine, we placed the piece of paper by the rose. "This is a special place for your father and me," I said. "I hope someday you will understand what he meant to me." He replied in baby talk, cooing and gurgling. I swallowed hard, but the tears came anyway.

Returning to this place could have been the end of me. Just before I began seeing Dr. Semone, thoughts of ending my life had almost pushed me over the edge. But even on my worst days during that time, I had remembered the good times Gary and I shared, our marriage, living in our first house and Hawaii. Maybe I'm getting better, I thought, because I could think about Gary and come to this beach without wishing I were dead.

I realized then that I had turned a corner since beginning my appointments with Dr. Semone. After seven two-hour sessions of intensive talking with her, I had begun to have hope. Having an impartial person listen to me describe my anxiety, fears and frustrations proved to be a release. I hadn't given up on the dream that Gary was alive and would be returning, but I began to accept the fact that he might never come home to us. Previously, that basic idea had been so repulsive to me that I wouldn't allow myself to even begin thinking it. Now the thought roamed around in my head without making me nauseous. It was almost like a door opening to a new world.

Dr. Semone had talked me through what would have to happen for me to heal. "You're going to have to open and walk through many doors in your future, Allison. The most difficult part is closing the door behind you as you pass through. You are in effect ending a chapter in a book and turning the page. The sad part is that you have closed that chapter in your life. The exciting part is that you get to turn the page and start a new chapter. Your closing of this particular door with Gary behind it is very difficult, but at some point you will have to do it."

"But how will I know when to close that door?" I asked.

"Honestly, I can't tell you that. But when that time comes, you'll know it."

We smoothed the sand as I softly sang the words to "Sweet Dreams of You" by Patsy Cline. *"Sweet dreams of you. Every night I go thru."* Gary and I had loved dancing to this song even though some of the words didn't fit at the time. Maybe now more of them did apply. It was strange for me to be singing those words. Patsy Cline had been killed in a plane crash in Tennessee in 1963. I sang the words to that old song and remembered my husband.

Gathering GJ and my pack, I walked along the beach, watching Carmen and Ramon standing in the surf. As I got closer, Carmen held up her left hand and I saw a ring sparkling in the sun. "Alright," I said as I grasped Carmen's left hand, "tell me."

Carmen looked so happy. She giggled and cried at the same time. Ramon blushed and stood there with his arm around her.

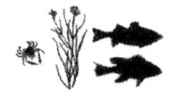

WALKING BACK THE CAT

Allison Faith Deale
Beaufort, North Carolina
August 17, 1968

IN AUGUST, MATT Foxe called. He wanted to see me in person, rather than talking over the phone. Immediately, I thought that he knew something about Gary. I also thought that if it was anything good, he wouldn't wait to tell me. I wasn't wrong. After a delicious Cuban dinner of *Arroz con Pollo, Moros y Cristianos, y plantains*, as Carmen announced the dishes, Matt, Shannon, Carmen—who was holding GJ—and I settled in my small living room.

Matt leaned forward and asked me, "What do you know about Gary?" He didn't look right at me when he asked. Shannon squeezed his hand, as if comforting him.

He's afraid, I thought. Fear pulsed inside me.

"Nothing new. I continue to send letters and packages to the North Vietnamese Embassy in Paris. They all come back marked in red REFUSED. The families of the MIAs and POWs are trying to organize to bring pressure on the government to do something to help the men. The government policy is for us to keep quiet for some reason. I don't understand it."

"That's what I hear also," Matt said. "I don't know how far I should go with this." He glanced at Carmen, then continued. "I've learned a few things. I want Allison to know exactly what I think happened, but if it's too much, too fast, you'll have to stop me."

"I want to know," I said, brushing a tear from my cheek.

"I've talked with friends of mine at the CIA," Matt said. "I helped save some of their people in Laos a while back, and now I'm a good buddy. I call them spooks. My friends did an exercise they call Walking Back the Cat. When an operation goes bad, they walk the whole thing backward in time, trying to determine where events went wrong. They hope to learn and avoid making the same mistakes in the future."

"What does the CIA have to do with this?" Carmen asked.

"I called in a favor," Matt said. "I asked them to take a look at Gary's case to see what happened."

"The Agency has checked on Gary?" I asked. I knew that I had not received anything of substance from the Defense Department. Maybe the CIA knew something, I thought. I was terrified, afraid of knowing, afraid of not knowing.

"The Defense Intelligence Agency is in charge of POW intelligence. The guys at the Agency talked with them and also did some digging on their own," Matt said, sorting through papers he had brought with him.

After looking through his notes, he continued. "Gary's name doesn't come up on any list, but they won't tell me anything about it. I've never seen a list. Major O'Shane's name doesn't come up. Captain Klepperson's name has appeared on a list of captives."

"Do they know what happened to Gary?" Carmen asked.

"No. They did determine that we had been caught in a trap. The pre-strike photography showed that SAM sites and antiaircraft artillery had been moved into the target area and concealed. This reinforcement took place after the target had been first identified by photo interpreters. Apparently, the Soviets or North Vietnamese planned this out pretty well. I say Soviet because there were some spurious radar signals, which had never been detected before, from the area at the time of the strike. Some new weapon was there."

"Is that how they shot down the three planes?" I asked.

"We'll never know the answer to that question," Matt said, pulling a cassette recorder from his flight bag. "I can play you a tape of the strike if you want to hear it. I made a copy for you. This was recorded by the crew on a radar reconnaissance plane over the Gulf of Tonkin. The spooks got a copy from Defense Intelligence."

Matt paused a beat, shrinking into himself. "Quite frankly, this tape creeps me out. Do you want to listen to it?"

"Yes, I have to know."

Matt twirled the tape around in his hands. He looked at Carmen and me, tentatively, not sure if he were doing the right thing. After loading the tape, he sat back and took a deep breath. "You're going to hear different sounds—people breathing, grunting, explosions, and static. We don't say much on a strike unless we have to. Most communication between planes is done by hand signals or by maneuvering the aircraft in a certain way. Anyway, here goes."

I exchanged glances with Carmen. She took my hands in hers and held tight. My heart raced, knowing this was going to be bad.

The first words I could pick out of the static-filled recording were, "Dodge Flight off the target with four."

"That was the flight in front of us," Matt said. "My flight's next. Our call sign was Buick. Gary was number four."

"Fuck! Take it down! It's a SAM trap!"

I recognized Matt's voice. I looked at him, my eyes widening with terror. The sounds coming from the tape haunted me.

A warbling beeper filled the air. "One of my pilots had ejected setting off that beeper," Matt said, pointing at the machine.

"Take it down! Turn! Turn!" Matt's voice on the tape again.

I heard a garbled voice. "Buick 4's hit hard."

Even with all of the noise and static, I recognized his voice. Gary's voice, I thought. What was he doing? What must he have been thinking? I wasn't sure I wanted to hear it.

The beepers continued blaring. I heard a sequence of garbled transmissions. "4's on fire."

"Fuck!"
"4's done."
"Alli…"
All Gary's voice.
After that, the sound of beepers continued for a minute. The tape went silent. Matt turned the machine off. "That's it."
Each person sat at the table, stunned, with tears running down their cheeks.
"¡Madre de Dios!" Carmen whispered.
"I was their leader," Matt said, holding his head in his hands. "They were my men. All of them—gone."
That is the last time I will ever hear Gary's voice, I thought. This was a giant step for me—a time for acknowledging the cold hard facts of Gary's disappearance and uncertain status.
My most fervent prayer was for Gary to walk through my front door, smiling his handsome smile. Right that very second would be fantastic. But— —

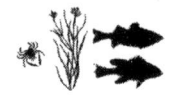

KEEP QUIET

Allison Faith Deale
Seymour Johnson AFB Chapel, North Carolina
November 14, 1968

AFTER RECEIVING A telephone call from Shirley, Major O'Shane's wife, I agreed to attend a meeting of a group of women at the base chapel to discuss the status of our husbands. A representative of a national organization being formed to support families of the missing planned on doing a presentation.

When I arrived at a side meeting room at the chapel, I found about twenty wives drinking coffee, standing around a table. I was surprised at the number present. Pastries and donuts were stacked in the middle of the table.

Naturally GJ caused a great fuss. Each one of the women wanted to hold him. He passed from hand to hand with great delight. After discovering that GJ was a people person, I tried to share him whenever possible.

Of course, I had anticipated the first question always asked—"How old is he?"

"Nine months," I said, monitoring his progress as he was passed around the room.

A delegation of Air Force officers and a middle-aged woman entered the room. Colonel Asher, Vice Commander of the 4th Tactical Fighter Wing, led the group. He made his way around the circle of women introducing himself.

"Hello, Allison," he said, approaching me with a smile and his hand extended.

"Colonel Asher, good morning," I said.

One by one the other officers, the chaplain, Dr. Naylor, and the squadron commanders introduced themselves.

As I shook the middle-aged lady's hand, she said, "Shelby Rice, from San Diego, wife of Navy Commander

David Rice, MIA, shot down over North Vietnam, 15 April 1965."

Shot down in 1965, MIA, I thought. How in the world is this lady still walking? Gary had been missing for sixteen months. I was sick from worry. How had she survived for three years?

"Ladies, if you would take a seat please, we'll begin the meeting," Colonel Asher said.

I found GJ and carried him to a seat along the side. After wrapping him in a blanket, I lay him on a pad on the floor near my seat. I tried holding a bottle of juice for him, but he seemed content and promptly fell asleep.

The officers and Shelby Rice again introduced themselves, then had each of the ladies in the audience do the same.

Our husbands were from the Army, Navy, Marines and Air Force, missing in Laos, North Vietnam and South Vietnam, from 1964 until as recently as October 1968.

"Allison Deale, wife of Gary, First Lieutenant, Air Force, North Vietnam, 14 July 1967," I said, standing and glancing around the room when it was my turn. I blinked, fighting tears and pointed to the bundle at my feet. "This is our son, Gary Junior. I call him GJ, born 28 February."

Colonel Asher again welcomed us, but immediately turned to Shelby Rice.

After again stating the information concerning her husband, Shelby began. "I've just been at McConnell Air Force Base in Kansas, organizing wives there."

She related that recently on the West coast, a group of women had banded together, hoping to find out more information about their husbands. There were no firm numbers as to how many men were being held prisoner or detained, how many had been killed, and in which country.

Continuing with her presentation, relating facts and theories about the MIAs, Shelby told a story that we all knew so well.

"The official policy of the United States Government is known as Quiet Diplomacy," she said, emphasizing the words by forming quote marks with her fingers.

"Government officials absolutely do not want us individually or collectively to do anything to create publicity about our lives or about the status of our husbands. They believe that any such publicity will be turned against our husbands and worsen their conditions. 'Keep Quiet,' they say, 'don't offend or stir up the North Vietnamese.' Furthermore, the White House point-man on POW and MIA matters is W. Avril Harriman. Quiet diplomacy is his policy."

Shelby paused. "Now that Richard Nixon has been elected President, we aren't sure whether there will be a new POW/MIA policy."

While the overall popular vote ended up being very close, Nixon had achieved over three hundred Electoral College votes. Some commentators related that Nixon's so-called "Secret Plan" to end the Vietnam War was the determining factor in the election.

After concluding her remarks, Shelby asked for questions.

"What about mistreatment of our husbands?" asked one wife.

"Maybe y'all saw the movie of the POW parade held in Hanoi in the summer of '66. That was distressing and demoralizing, to say the least. The very few POWs who have been released to peace groups by the North Vietnamese say they were mistreated. Beyond that, again, the official policy is to be quiet and not to raise mistreatment as an issue."

"What about lists?" I asked. "I hear that my husband is not on any list, but no one will talk about what that means."

"I'm in the same spot," Shelby said.

Most of the women in the room nodded.

This is my new life, I thought. I wasn't to ask questions or create issues, because I was supposed to remain quiet about Gary.

MOVING ON

_____ 81

Allison Faith Deale
St. Martin Neck Farm, Bishopville, Maryland
December 24, 1968

IN MID-DECEMBER, after extensive rewriting and defending my thesis before the committee, I finished my master's degree. All that remained was graduation in January. Late in the fall, I sold the house in Seven Springs to the young pilot and his wife who had been renting. Carmen remained at the marine lab to obtain a doctorate. By the time I decided with finality to move back home to Maryland, it was December.

While saddened to leave our house and North Carolina, I realized that there wasn't anything for me there.

After Shelby Rice had said in November that the Johnson Administration had a "Keep Quiet" policy with respect to the treatment of the men in prison in North Vietnam, I began a vigorous letter writing campaign to my senators and congressional representatives. I had been cynical before, but the views of the administration pushed me over the edge. I realized that it really wouldn't make any difference with respect to helping Gary if I returned to Maryland.

Hoping to be moved and settled before the holiday, I packed our belongings in boxes and cleaned the apartment. Carmen and I made two trips back and forth with Gary's pickup and barely managed to finish moving before Christmas arrived. My mom took great delight in caring for GJ while I moved. Now at ten months, he was crawling and trying to stand on his own.

GJ had never seen snow. As I prepared to leave the house to go to Christmas Eve services, the ground turned white. My parents had already departed to prepare St. Martin's Church.

I started the truck to warm it before taking GJ out into the cold. I carried him into the storm, watching his face break into a wide smile as the first flakes hit and melted. He reached out with his gloves and tried to bat the tiny white crystals floating down.

"This is snow," I said, as I carried him to the truck. "I wish your father could see you now."

Snow blanketed the buildings, pines and holly trees creating a Christmas card scene. Our little brick church, where I had married Gary, was covered in white. As I approached, candle light sparkled through ice crystals which coated the windows.

I joined my family in that small church, sliding into a box pew beside them. Red poinsettias lined the aisles. A multitude of candles provided the only light. Shadows danced on the walls.

I gave thanks for GJ, my parents and especially for Carmen, and all the help and support she had given my son and me. I prayed for Gary to come home.

THE LEAGUE

_____ 82

Allison Faith Deale
Seymour Johnson AFB Chapel, North Carolina
May 26, 1969

ONE WEEK AFTER a dramatic news conference by Melvin Laird, the recently appointed Secretary of Defense, Shelby Rice scheduled another meeting at the base chapel to discuss new developments.
 My parents rode along with me to Beaufort. After visiting Carmen, then the Cravens and spending the night at a Goldsboro hotel, we drove to Seymour Johnson and to the meeting.
 "Finally, I can say to you that we have a much different policy," Shelby said, clenching a handful of papers. "Secretary Laird believes that the 'Keep Quiet' policy is not effective and is detrimental. If you watched his press conference last week, you saw how he denounced the torture of our husbands by the North Vietnamese. Now, for the first time, the abuse of POWs is officially in the open."
 Shelby paused, taking a sip of coffee and sweeping her hair out of her eyes. "After the League of Wives of American Prisoners in Southeast Asia was formed in February, we began a national letter writing campaign to bring public awareness to our plight. I know that almost all of you sent cablegrams to your representatives and also to the North Vietnamese Embassy in Paris asking about your husbands. What the League wants to do now is send a delegation of wives to Paris to visit the embassy in person. Will any of you go?"
 I sat in my chair, bouncing GJ on my lap. My parents sat next to me. How can I go to Paris and leave him behind?

Now that I lived with my parents, I had more money, but still didn't have enough extra to pay for a trip like that. I didn't know whether I had the emotional strength for such an ordeal.

Two women raised their hands.

"Good," Shelby said, "see me after the meeting. For those remaining, you can help by continuing to send cablegrams to the Paris Embassy and by contributing money to help our volunteer travelers pay their expenses."

I can do both of those, I thought. Anything to help bring Gary home.

After the meeting concluded, another woman who had been sitting in the back of the room with two other civilian gentlemen approached.

"Allison Deale?"

"Yes."

"I'm Amy West of the Defense Intelligence Agency," she said holding her ID card for me to see. "Most of the other women here have already been interviewed. If you have a few moments, I would like to talk with you in private."

"Okay." I said, stammering, wondering what this was about.

"This will take about a half-hour, and we need to go to wing headquarters. Do you know where that is?"

"Yes."

"Are these people related?" she asked, pointing to my mom and dad.

"This is my son, GJ, and they are my parents."

"I'm sorry, but I can only talk with you. Your parents can wait in the lounge at headquarters."

At the entrance to the wing headquarters building, I handed GJ to my mom and followed Amy West behind a security barrier to the intelligence office. An armed Air Police sergeant stood outside an office door and he opened it for us. Two other wives, each with one of the civilian men I saw at the chapel, followed into the room.

Amy pointed to a chair and sat down across the table from me. "I'm going to be your contact officer at DIA from now on. Here's my card."

"Thank you," I said, staring at the Arlington Hall Station address.

"The reason I asked you to come here is that I have some photographs I want you to look at related to your husband's MIA status. Does this cause any problems for you?"

"No. I can do that."

"First, I have a picture of your husband taken a couple years ago. Is this Gary Deale?"

"Yes," I said, instantly recognizing his picture from his ID card.

"Now I have pictures of men, taken in North Vietnam. I want you to carefully look at these to see if you recognize Gary or anyone else." Amy handed me a stack of 8 by 11 photographs, which she had just taken from her briefcase. "I can't tell you the sources of the photographs."

I slowly began scanning each picture, hoping against hope that I would find Gary. I flipped through them slowly, studying each one.

The men were in different poses. One was sitting on a hard wooden chair. Another stood in front of a room, bowing from the waist. All of the men looked emaciated, ground down to almost nothing. A group of pictures, one after the other, showed men in small groups, walking down a street. Then a photograph shocked me—an injured man lying on the ground, stripped to his underwear.

About half-way through, I found a picture of three men, bound together at the waist by a rope, walking. An enemy soldier followed behind, his rifle aimed at the group. His bayonet prodded one of the men. At the edge of the photograph, a hand held a piece of wood. One of the three held up his arm, warding off the stick. His other arm was in a sling.

Pausing, I set it aside and then continued through the stack. "Gary's not here."

"We thought not."

The other two women in the room had also looked at stacks of photographs. Apparently, they had not identified anyone, as they departed. The men who had talked with the women remained.

After staring at the one picture I had set aside, I decided. "This is Brad Pender," I said, pointing at the man with his arm in a sling. "I met him in Texas in the summer of 1965. He was a flight instructor, a captain, who was being transferred to a McConnell F-105 RTU. I only saw him a couple times, but this is him."

Amy chewed her upper lip, drumming her fingers on the table. Taking a small notebook from her briefcase, she flipped it open and wrote the picture number, Brad's name and the information I had just given her. "Another name for the list."

"May I ask a question about that?" I asked, clenching my arms across my chest.

"Of course. But I can't say anything about the sources."

"Is Gary on your list?"

"I'm sorry. No, he's not."

This time I heard about the list first-hand. There's no hope, I thought. One more nail from the keg.

PART 11

I don't think the people of the country know much about Vietnam and I think they care a hell of a lot less.

—President Lyndon Baines Johnson, May 27, 1964

TIME SWEET TIME

As the minute hand
creeps, the hourglass tips.
Another day slips
away.

Days months years pass
hoping for mention
of a name or
worse.

Despair does not cease
with time
which makes
its sweet merry way
along.

From the combat diary of Gary Bishop Deale,
First Lieutenant, USAF, 13 July 1967

WASTE 'EM

Allison Faith Deale
St. Martin Neck Farm, Bishopville, Maryland
September 14, 1972

DURING THE FIVE years of waiting to discover what had happened to Gary, I had obtained my Doctorate in Estuarine Systems from the University of Delaware in Lewes. After obtaining my degree I taught on the adjunct faculty of Salisbury College in Maryland and also at Lewes, while also obtaining research grants from the EPA, the Chesapeake Bay Commission and other government agencies to study and monitor Maryland's and Delaware's bays and estuaries.

When I first moved back home, my dad remodeled a small cottage that had been used as a guest house. That's where GJ and I lived these past years. Gary's parents had retired and moved to Arizona, so I lost contact with them except for an occasional letter.

Mom and Dad were my baby sitters. She also became my pre-school teacher for GJ.

Early this afternoon, when I returned home after teaching a class, I found Mom and GJ walking along our lane on their way to the mail box. I parked my car and walked with them.

"Where's Dad?" I asked, taking GJ's hand.

"He's over at the Jointer place, getting the combine ready to do corn," she said, pointing over her shoulder. "It's so dry that they may be able to begin harvesting."

We reached the mail box at the end of the lane. Mom placed the contents into her bag and we turned toward home.

"Now that you're home I'm going to head over to the motel," she said. "We're going to begin shutting down some of the rooms now that the season is over."

"Thanks for watching him," I said.

"It's a great joy of my life to take care of GJ. I thought you all were going to be far away when he grew up. I never imagined you would be here."

Later, I sat in the shade on our patio, listlessly staring at the stack of student research papers from my college environmental studies class. Halfway through the stack, I abandoned them. I gave what I thought was a reasonable and motivational assignment: identify an environmental problem in your home neighborhood, research it and provide alternative solutions, choosing the best one. After reading the first papers, I decided that I had a way to go with this class. But in the end we would get there.

Gary Junior, now four, played nearby in his sandbox with his toy soldiers, tanks and jet fighters. Based on his vocalizations, it was an epic battle.

Changing gears, I began stuffing Vietnam War newspaper and magazine articles I had begun saving several years before into a folder. Initially, I kept the articles for Gary to read when he returned home. But now, I thought more in terms of retaining the stories for GJ. He was too young to understand the war. With each passing day, it became more certain to me that Gary would not be coming home. After five years with no news of him, my hopes had diminished.

A flash of green in the corner of my eye zoomed to the feeder and began sipping nectar. Remaining airborne, the juvenile ruby-throated hummingbird went around the feeder with a blur of flapping wings, sucking from each of the yellow flower ports. I knew it was a juvenile because there was no white stripe at the end of the tail. My male hummers had disappeared about ten days before, now well on their way to Florida. Crossing the Gulf of Mexico awaited them. How will this bird that I am now looking at get to a place it has never been? I wondered. The bird went to my butterfly bush sampling the flowers and then flew away.

As I scanned the news clippings, the entire tableau of the war spread before me: JFK, LBJ, Nixon, The Gulf of Tonkin Resolution, Operation Rolling Thunder, Dow Chemical, napalm, the University of Wisconsin, teach-ins, demonstrations, Khe Sanh, Tet, Kent State, the previous year's release of the Pentagon Papers, Jane Fonda's recent *faux pas* ('Hanoi Jane,' playing with a North Vietnamese antiaircraft gun near Hanoi), and the failed raid upon the Son Tay POW camp.

Most distressing to me personally, the newspaper articles covering the July 14, 1967, missing in action status of Jack O'Shane, Doug Klepperson, and Gary Deale.

And worst of all—My Lai. It took several years for the story to emerge. Only after Seymour Hersh and others wrote about a government cover-up was the truth revealed.

One murderous day in that isolated village in Central South Vietnam showed all that was wrong about Americans in the Vietnam War and how depraved soldiers can become. An elusive enemy repeatedly struck American soldiers using ambushes and booby traps. Every single peasant became the enemy. The troops acting out of fear, revenge, disillusionment, grief and anger, with a sense of bloodlust, abandoned all morality.

And so it happened on the morning of Saturday, March 16, 1968, two weeks after GJ was born and eight months after Gary went missing. A group of one hundred soldiers of Charlie Company, assigned to Task Force Baker, with the Army's Americal Division descended upon My Lai and a slaughter ensued.

Now, four years later, the number of reported casualties range between 387 and 504, including up to 182 women and 173 children.

When encountered on the scene, soldiers reported that they had been ordered to kill. The command was, "Waste 'Em."

"GJ, who's winning?" I asked. I had let him decide on his own toys. Each time we visited a toy shop, he bought more soldiers. While I would have preferred that he buy toy fish or dinosaurs, I wasn't about to force my values on him. Most boys went the cowboy and pistol route, so I couldn't see much difference between that and soldiers.

"We are," GJ said, moving a tank forward. "Thanks to the Air Force. They turned the tide."

Good, I thought. At least he knows one marine biology term.

In Hawaii, Gary had told me that he had no direct role in the war in the south because American planes based in Thailand were prohibited by treaty from bombing in South Vietnam.

But, he had said, "I don't really know what happens in North Vietnam. When being shot at while dropping bombs at 500 knots, anything can go wrong." I believed him.

These four years after the massacre in My Lai, seeing news stories about the dead civilians sickened me. During the time after Gary had been shot down, the Vietnam War had become an anathema to me.

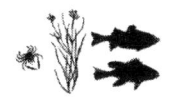

THE LIST

_____ 84

Allison Faith Deale
St. Martin Neck Farm, Bishopville, Maryland
January 4, 1973

AFTER HENRY KISSINGER, National Security Adviser to President Nixon, made his famous, "We believe that peace is at hand" statement in October, I hoped the Vietnam War would finally be over. The Paris Peace Talks had dragged on for tedious years. Soon I will know about Gary, I had thought at the time. Disappointment followed.

Before the Paris talks had even begun, it took what seemed like decades to design a table arrangement. Those participating in the peace talks appeared unable to resolve their differences. North Vietnam, South Vietnam, the nascent Communist organization in South Vietnam and the United States could not agree on the table shape and size.

With a self-imposed deadline of January approaching, President Nixon had decided to up the ante and force the reluctant parties to negotiate. He approved plans to unleash B-52 strategic bombers over North Vietnam.

Operation Linebacker II, involving over two hundred B-52s, began sustained bombing operations on 19 December, primarily in the Hanoi-Haiphong area. Gary had referred to missions in that area as Pack 6 strikes. Many facilities, held sacrosanct during the war, were bombed and flattened. Mines were dropped into Haiphong harbor, closing it to shipping.

Following TV news carefully, I identified the various kinds of airplanes to GJ as they appeared on the screen. "That's a B-52," I said, pointing. Being almost five, GJ had trouble with some of the words I tried to teach him. But he knew his airplanes.

"F-4, Phantom," he stuttered.

"Look, an F-105! That's the kind of plane your daddy flew."

"Daddy, daddy!"

I hugged him. "Yes, your daddy."

Each passing day, GJ looked more and more like a younger version of Gary. The Deale family line showed itself in his nose, chin and mouth. Now, even his gestures reminded me of Gary. GJ had never seen him. Sometimes, I stood silently in amazement, watching GJ strut about, just like his father.

After eleven days of bombing, the campaign stopped. Sadly, news reports stated that fifteen B-52s had been shot down during the raids. A total of ninety-two crewmen had been recovered by helicopter, were killed in action, or were missing.

I held my breath, hoping the deadlock would dissolve. By the end of December, the parties agreed to peace terms and the war appeared over.

IN MID-JANUARY, I received a phone call from Matt Foxe. "It's Matt," he said. "I have news."

My heart slowed with dread. Feeling dizzy, I sat on a chair overlooking the river. GJ came and stood beside me. I held his hand in mine.

"Where have you been? I've been trying to call you."

"Thailand. It was all hands on deck. I racked up a few more missions up North."

"I suspected that."

"I took a flight of four Phantoms over the Hanoi Hilton very low at 800 knots. If Gary was down there, we rattled his ear drums."

"Oh! Gary."

"Yes, Gary. Word is they're going to be coming out soon. First-in, first-out. Hanoi's supposed to provide a full and complete list of names, soon."

"Then we'll know," I said, grasping the MIA/POW bracelet on my arm. I looked at the engraving: LT. GARY B. DEALE, USAF, 7/14/67, NVN. As I turned the bracelet, I thought, Alive? Dead? Yes? No? I had purchased four of the bracelets one year before from Voices in Vital America; for Gary, GJ, Matt and myself.

"Yes, then we'll know," Matt said.

"I hope his name's on the list! He has to be there!"

"Would you believe it? Nixon turned the B-52s loose to force the North Vietnamese to return to the peace table. Not to win the war, mind you, but to bargain for peace. Who ever heard of such a thing? Nobody understands it. If LBJ had used the big boys back in 1965, this fracas would have ended long ago. What do we have to show for all this besides 58,000 dead?"

"Not much!"

"I agree. I'm in touch with my people. I'll let you know as soon as I hear anything."

"Thanks, Matt."

I sat in the chair sobbing. GJ put his arms around me, comforting me the way I did him. "Mommy, are you OK?"

I couldn't answer.

SEVERAL WEEKS LATER Matt called again. "There are almost six hundred people who are going to be coming out," Matt said. "The list provided by the North Vietnamese keeps shifting."

"Gary?" I asked.

"No. His name hasn't appeared on anything so far."

"How soon will they be free?"

"First group comes out in mid-February. Don't give up hope."

"I won't. Thanks, Matt."

Long ago, I had decided that Gary was dead. There had been absolutely nothing to tell me he was alive; no signs, no premonitions, no silver clouds, no name on a list. In my heart, I knew. I kept that decision to myself, not telling anyone. On this day, I wondered if I was wrong. Maybe he will come home.

ON FEBRUARY 12, the first group of 116 POWs departed Hanoi on four Air Force C-141 cargo planes. The men held prisoner the longest came out first.

As the men arrived at Clark Air Force Base in the Philippines, their images were captured by TV news cameramen. Each man appeared gaunt with sunken cheeks. A few were carried on stretchers. As the now free men approached the general officer greeting them, they saluted smartly and shook his hand. Now almost home, they smiled and nodded their heads, free at long last.

Over the next weeks, additional prisoners were released.

Matt called again on March 4. "According to the date he was shot down, Gary should have been released yesterday," Matt said. "He wasn't on the plane."

"Are you sure?" I gasped, fighting back tears.

"Yes, it's certain. Doug Klepperson was on the plane. I'm going to go see him as soon as he gets back to the states."

"Now what?" I asked, twisting the phone cord in my hands.

"We wait until the final group comes out. There could have been a big screw up over there with dates. Those creeps don't seem to be too well organized."

"I'll wait. But I'm losing hope."

"It doesn't look good," Matt said, sadly.

THE NORTH VIETNAMESE released the final group of prisoners held by them on March 29. A total of 456 Americans had been set free from North Vietnamese camps. Additional POWs came from camps in other Southeast Asia countries.

Matt's phone call came the next day. "It's over," he said. "Gary didn't come out. The North Vietnamese say they have no other prisoners. They also say they have no knowledge about anyone else still missing. The US gave them a list of men unaccounted for. The list of 2,583 names doesn't seem to hold any weight with them."

"Gary's gone," I said, flatness in my voice.

"Yes. I'm afraid Gary is dead. I'm sorry."

I heard the word dead. Now it was official, not something I just believed. "Thank you, Matt."

"I talked with Doug Klepperson. He says that he never saw Gary on the day they were shot down. None of the prisoners saw Gary in the camps or even heard his name mentioned. Doug went to the prison with Jack O'Shane, but O'Shane died from his injuries soon after."

"How is Doug?"

"Bad shape. The North Vietnamese beat the crap out of him. He says that torture is too kind a word for what they went through."

"Oh."

"I was thinking about that, you know, after these six years—maybe I'd better not say what my thoughts were."

"That Gary was better off being killed?"

"Since you put it in those words, yes."

"Poor Gary!"

"I'm sorry."

"Thanks, Matt." My waiting, for all of those years, now over.

AN UNGRACEFUL EXIT

_____ 85

Allison Faith Deale
St. Martin Neck Farm, Bishopville, Maryland
May 5, 1975

IT TOOK SEVERAL days for the stories and photographs to emerge. As I sat by a window in our cottage sunroom, scanning the newspaper, I glanced at the St. Martin River and just happened to see a bald eagle snag a fish with its talons. Good for you, I thought. Looking back at the paper, the pictures filled me with sorrow and shame.

Beginning as a slow moving invasion of the south by the North Vietnamese Army in early 1975, the military situation turned into a rout and then outright chaos. All of this, of course, in direct violation of the Paris Peace Accord signed in 1973. Not that anyone in the United States cared. The Vietnam War was history. No one in the nation wanted to resume fighting in Southeast Asia. Over the following months, the South Vietnamese Army fled the advancing Communists and the country collapsed into itself.

Orders came down through the American chain of command to begin evacuations in early April and events went wrong from the very beginning. On April 4, an Air Force C-5 Galaxy cargo plane carrying orphans crashed near Saigon killing seventy-eight young Vietnamese children and more than fifty American servicemen and women.

From that day forward, panic took over as South Vietnam gradually disappeared.

Near the end of April, the North Vietnamese army approached Saigon and began shelling Tan Son Nhut Airbase, causing the field to be closed.

On April 29, an immediate evacuation was ordered of all remaining Americans, numbering about 5,000.

I watched in horror as remarkable photographs of Vietnamese also trying to escape flooded TV newscasts: soldiers hanging from helicopter skids, hundreds of civilians swamping small boats, barges crammed full of children, and most telling, civilians clamoring to climb a ladder to a twenty-by-twenty foot rooftop, trying to board a small CIA helicopter.

During the chaos, mostly without American government approval or support, more than 150,000 Vietnamese soldiers and civilians fled the country.

So, this is how Vietnamization, Nixon's so-called "secret plan" to turn the war over to the South Vietnamese worked out, I thought. What his plan led to was a betrayal and abandonment of the South Vietnamese and national humiliation for the United States.

When I called Matt Foxe to discuss the situation with him, he had a two word description of Kissinger, the Paris Peace Accord and Vietnamization—"Balderdash and Bullshit."

In the end, more that 58,200 Americans and also probably, Gary, died for this, I thought, for nothing. All those many lives and all of that potential, simply wasted.

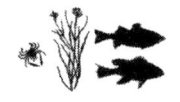

THEN

_____ 86

Allison Faith Deale
St. Martin Neck Farm, Bishopville, Maryland
July 14, 1977

THE LAST OF the 591 Prisoners of War held in South Vietnam, Laos, Cambodia and North Vietnam arrived in the Philippines on March 29, 1973, after implementation of the Paris Peace Accords negotiated by Henry Kissinger. In the end, President Nixon's secret plan to end the war took five years after his first election, during which time thousands of additional American troops died in Southeast Asia. To add even more irony, Nixon ended up resigning in disgrace over the Watergate cover-up in his second term.
 After the plane loads of prisoners had returned home, more than 2,500 men, including Gary, remained missing in action. In the intervening years, the North Vietnamese released the remains of several Americans killed during the war leaving a large number of men still unaccounted for.
 I talked with Lieutenant Colonel Doug Klepperson after he returned from the camps in Hanoi. He had not seen or heard of Gary after the North Vietnamese shot down their three planes on Friday, July 14, 1967. Doug had seen Major O'Shane, the other pilot, on the ground.

TEN YEARS AFTER Gary was shot down and more than four years after the POWs came home and in consultation with Colonel Matt Foxe, Amy West of DIA and the military,

I decided to officially have Gary declared dead. Once I had considered all the evidence and made the decision, which was totally up to me, the Air Force issued a Presumptive Finding of Death—Body Not Recovered.

I had presented my proposal to Gary's parents before deciding on a course of action. While they were saddened by my decision, they also had given up hope.

Many well-intentioned people still believed that the North Vietnamese held Americans in secret and darkness. I could not hold on to that dream, following rumors down overgrown trails in the jungle.

I had decided years before that Gary was gone—dead. While I didn't believe in spirits or the dark world, I always believed I would feel something if Gary were alive. I had sensed nothing telling me that Gary lived. All I felt was a big empty void.

ON JULY 14, ten years after he went missing, we held Gary's memorial service on our farm. I walked down the dirt lane on the arm of General Granger, the commander of the 4th Tactical Fighter Wing at Seymour Johnson. Dressed in a formal uniform with white gloves, the general set a slow, measured pace. A large group of friends, neighbors, family and officers from the base followed behind. Colonel Matt Foxe and Lieutenant Colonel Doug Klepperson would arrive at the appropriate time.

Walking by the corn and soybean fields at the edge of the pinewoods, I felt at peace. I held GJ's hand as we trod the dusty road toward a small area enclosed by a white wrought iron fence. Although nine years old, he didn't fully understand the process. To him, it didn't make sense to have a funeral without a body. He didn't understand where his father was. I didn't either.

Flags whipped and snapped in the wind.

Inside the enclosure, the chaplain and the minister from my church waited. An honor guard lined the path leading to the gate, while a firing detail stood at attention near the fence.

My mother and father and Gary's mom and dad stood behind me. The chaplain and minister said their words of comfort and recited prayers. Carmen and Ramon sang a beautiful rendition of the spiritual "Going Home." I wept as they sang those haunting words to the melody of Dvorak's *New World Symphony's* 2nd Movement.

Fingering Gary's dog tags, which he gave me in Hawaii, I remembered that short time in paradise, the last time I saw him.

During the service, I read and reread the engraving upon Gary's marker, GARY BISHOP DEALE, LIEUTENANT COLONEL, USAF, BORN 17 JUNE 1942, KILLED IN ACTION 14 JULY 1967, NORTH VIETNAM. The silhouette of an F-105 had been engraved at the top, above the writing.

Suddenly, they came out of the sun. Four F-105s borrowed from the Virginia Air National Guard and led by Doug Klepperson, headed directly at us. As they approached, the number 3 plane climbed up and away from the formation in the missing man pass. That plane, breaking from tradition, swept above in a great loop and again approached in afterburner, with deafening sound. Even lower this time, the F-105 swept over the graveyard and away. Matt Foxe offered his final salute, completing Gary's final mission.

Nearby, the firing detail raised their rifles and fired three volleys. I shook, startled at the loud cracks. Then, a lone bugler played his mournful version of Taps.

Ray Hurlock, a fellow professor and more than a good friend, had stood by my side over the past few years. I held his arm through the service. I was glad he was there. GJ bravely stood at attention, awed by the military trappings and especially by the flyover of the F-105s, the plane his dad loved.

I leaned down, gave him a hug and whispered to him, "You were very brave."

The firing detail sergeant fixed a shell casing into the triangularly folded flag and passed it to General Granger, saluting sharply. The general offered to hand it to me, but I motioned for him to hand it to GJ. "On behalf of the President and a grateful nation, I present this flag to you,'" General Granger said, passing the flag into Gary's son's hands. He stepped back and saluted.

How I wished my anguish would end with that ceremony, but I knew it wouldn't.

Negotiations were underway with the government of North Vietnam to recover the bodies of those missing in action. I hoped that someday soon Gary's remains would be returned home.

In Washington, there was discussion about a monument on the National Mall to honor the dead of the Vietnam War, more than 58,200 of them in all. I wrote letters and called my representatives in Congress, urging action. Those men, Gary among them, needed to be honored.

Ten years before, I had been young and wildly in love. Gary's death hurt me too much and aged me too fast. It also turned me into a cynic about our government and its wars.

The lesson I learned from Vietnam is that wars should not be caused by fantasy, accidents or someone's whim. Thousands of Americans died in Vietnam because of naïveté and stubbornness. As each day passed, I more strongly believed their deaths had been in vain.

PAYBACKS

Yuri Vaskilev, General Lieutenant (Retired)
GRU, Soviet Military Intelligence
Bagram Airbase, Kabul, Afghanistan
2 August 1987

YURI PACED THE parking apron, cursing and waiting. Two helicopters circled over the airbase and slowly went into hover mode, approaching the ramp. He turned his back to the downwash. His eyes watered in the blowing dust. Four attack helicopters, Flying Tanks, the pilots called them, had been sent to counter a raging ambush upon a truck convoy. Only two, he thought, this isn't good. What in the hell happened?

Eight years after the Soviet Union invaded Afghanistan, the war ground away. Entire Soviet Battalions had been chewed to pieces by the Mujahideen, the Afghan insurgents and holy warriors. Some said it had become a quagmire.

After the Americans began supplying the Mujahideen with Stinger shoulder-launched antiaircraft missiles over the previous year, Soviet helicopters and jet fighters had become sitting ducks.

Yuri and Sergeant Komarvsky had been called out of retirement and ordered to Afghanistan to test a flare dispensing system for the helicopters. Designed to counter heat-seeking missiles, the system was plagued with malfunctions.

As the rotors spun down, Yuri looked in vain into the passenger compartments, searching for Sergeant Komarvsky's face. He didn't see him.

Running to the first helicopter, Yuri looked into compartment. He didn't see his sergeant. As he neared the second one, the pilot crawled out of his cockpit.

"Sergeant Komarvsky?" Yuri yelled.
The pilot shook his head. "Missiles! Two helicopters! Kaput!" the pilot said, throwing his hands into the air. "The flares didn't work!"

"Fuck your mother!" Yuri yelled, grimacing to hold back the tears. He had worked with Sergeant Komarvsky for fifty years. The sergeant was his best friend. "Those fucking Americans!"

Later, Yuri rolled onto his cot. An empty bottle of vodka crashed to the floor. Visions of the sergeant, his body yet to be recovered from the wreckage, flashed through his brain. Yuri remembered all the damage he and his friend had done and the pain they had caused the Americans in Vietnam and other places. Paybacks are hell, Yuri thought.

THE WALL

_____ 88

Allison Faith Hurlock
Vietnam Veterans' Memorial, Washington, D.C.
July 14, 1992

MONTHS AFTER GARY'S service, Ray Hurlock and I were married. We had been together since 1976. The wedding early in 1978 was followed in December by the birth of our daughter, Christine. She was born eleven years after GJ. We built a new house on our farm, near where my parents lived.

GJ fulfilled his lifetime dream of attending and graduating from the Air Force Academy, following his father. The fact that Gary had graduated from the academy and had been an MIA for many years eased Gary Junior's entry.

Earlier this year, GJ began his Air Force career in heavy bombers by graduating from B-1 Lancer pilot training. He was assigned to Ellsworth Air Force Base in South Dakota.

RAY, CHRISTINE AND I slowly walked by Panel 70E, the short one at the east end of the memorial. I wanted to view the entire monument before searching for a specific name.

Waiting for ten years after the dedication, I had decided that the time was right for me to view The Wall. Gary had been dead almost twenty-five years. It was time to touch his name engraved in the black marble. While his body had not been recovered, and no one knew where it was, I retained hope that someday soon I would have closure.

Walking to the apex, where the east and west panels meet, I watched our reflections move along the black marble. As we neared the juncture, the slabs grew taller.

Finally, there we were at Panel 1E, the beginning of the war, covering the time period 1957 to 1965. That slab contained 132 lines with 660 names. Just to the left, Panel 1W covered 1972, to 1975, the end.

A volunteer explained that Maya Lin, the architect, planned the memorial so that the names of the dead from the beginning of the war were located next to the ones from the end, closing the circle. "There are 58,200 names here," the volunteer said, sweeping his arm from one end of the V-shaped memorial to the other.

After inspecting each of the 140 slabs, I sought out Panel 23E. About halfway down, I found my objective. While a volunteer did a name rubbing, I counted the lines. Panel 23E covered the time period from July 4, 1967 until July 25, 1967. Exactly 120 lines with 600 names.

I saw my reflection join with my real hand as I placed my fingers on the engraving—GARY B DEALE

PERESTROIKA AND GLASNOST

Yuri Vaskilev, General Lieutenant (Retired)
FSB Office, Lubyanka, Moscow, Russian Federation
21 November 2003

TEN YEARS AFTER the dissolution of the Soviet Union, Yuri decided to test the limits of *Perestroika* and *Glasnost*. Nearly six months after submitting a packet of documents to the Federal Security Service, he received a call to report to a certain office in Moscow. Yuri knew the building, the realm of the former KGB, very well. Sergi, his son, dropped him off in Lubyanka Square. "Go back to the *dacha*. Get out of here," Yuri said, slamming the car door.

Not knowing whether prison or a bullet to the back of his head awaited him, Yuri had arrived prepared for both. He wore his old dress uniform with rows of medallions, including his Hero of the Soviet Union Medal. If it were a bullet to the back of his head, Yuri welcomed it. Better that than the fate awaiting him, which gnawed at his lungs. He became sicker each day.

Yuri sat at a battered wooden table facing three stern-looking men. Their inquisition had gone on for an hour. It all came down the question of whether Yuri intended to embarrass the Russian Federation or the President, Mr. Vladimir Putin.

"I don't know anything about the President, Mr. Putin," Yuri said, slamming his hand on the table. "I haven't seen any confidential documents since 1989. The only secrets I know are how to grow cabbages, potatoes and beets."

"Why are you doing this?" the one with the tinted glasses asked.

"Because I have no time left. Because I want a pilot buried in Vietnam to be sent home."

The man smirked. "This has been approved. But I must go with you to the embassy."

"From the bottom of my heart, I thank you."

"Order us a car and driver."

Upon arriving at *Bolshoy Daviantinsky Pereulok No. 8*, the man with the shaded glasses cleared Yuri's path through the security ring. Handing Yuri the packet of documents, he stood aside.

Yuri looked inside the large envelope and inventoried its contents. The seven photographs, his hand drawn maps and the reel of 35 mm movie film were all there. Maybe this will help the Americans find this boy, Yuri thought.

As he approached the security booth, the marine inside jumped to attention and saluted. Yuri returned his salute.

"I wish to speak to the Air Force Attaché about an Air Force pilot killed in Vietnam in 1967. I have documents."

"Yes, sir. It will take a few moments."

The marine punched in a series of numbers on the phone and turned away from Yuri.

Moments ticked by, and Yuri wondered if anyone would respond. Maybe they no longer care about this boy in Vietnam, he thought. But I still care. This young pilot who had been in the ground in Vietnam for all these years was a soldier and deserved an honorable burial. After thirty-six years, maybe it doesn't even matter to anyone except me.

"Sir," an Air Force colonel said, stirring Yuri from his reverie. "Colonel David Sands," he said, saluting.

Yuri returned the salute. "I am General Lieutenant Yuri Vaskilev, my card."

"How can I help you, sir?" Colonel Sands asked.

"I have documents showing position American Air Force Officer, Lieutenant Gary Deale, buried near Hanoi, 1967. I check names list. I think still MIA."

"Jesus, above. Is this information authentic?"

"I was there. I saw with my eyes. I hold for thirty-six years. Yes, it is true. They approve," Yuri said, pointing over his shoulder at the FSB man. He handed the envelope to the colonel.

"Sir, on behalf of the United States, the Air Force and this man's family, I thank you."

"It is no bother. This boy should be at peace at home."

"I'll call you with the results when we've confirmed this."

"Please hurry. I have no time."

Later, as the car arrived at the lane to his *dacha*, Yuri thanked the men and invited them in for tea.

"We have to return to the city. It's Friday afternoon, you know."

Yuri walked his lane, taking shallow painful breaths of the clean country air. He smelled another hard winter approaching. Yuri looked at his *dacha* and his snow covered gardens, rejoicing that he had done this. His time was short. When the pain became unbearable, he would finish the job with his Makarov pistol. Then he would join his wife, scattered in his beloved gardens.

"Fuck your mother," Sergi, his son, yelled from the doorway, "they didn't shoot you."

PART 12

Finally, we must recognize that the consequences of large-scale military operations—particularly in this age of highly sophisticated and destructive weapons—are inherently difficult to predict and to control. Therefore, they must be avoided, excepting only when our nation's security is clearly and directly threatened. These are the lessons of Vietnam. Pray God we learn them.

—Robert S. McNamara, *In Retrospect*, 1995.

THE CHAIR

Suddenly the time came.
Surprisingly.
His number called
being so young.

His soul floats triumphant
not aware of the
earth reclaiming
bones and flesh.

A fleeting vision.
Radiant, she waits.
The anchor of his life
haunted by the empty chair.

From the combat diary of Gary Bishop Deale,
First Lieutenant, USAF, 12 July 1967

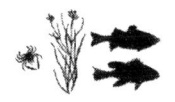

CON TE PARTIRO

Allison Faith Hurlock
St. Martin Neck Farm, Bishopville, Maryland
June 4, 2005

AS THE YEARS passed by, I continued to teach and conduct research. But with each passing semester, I had reduced my workload and devoted more time to farming.

After my parents died, Ray and I moved to the old farmhouse, which had been remodeled and reconstructed. Our daughter, Christine and her husband, moved into ours.

Our country, America, changed. For the first time, a mass casualty terrorist attack occurred on United States soil. I had watched as the twin towers fell and the hole was gashed into the Pentagon. Forty others had died when United flight 93 crashed into a Pennsylvania field.

While I had initially concurred in the decision to attack Afghanistan, over the past three years, my feelings have changed. Gary had told me, so long ago, that moderation in war was imbecility. Which is exactly the way the war in Afghanistan has been conducted. The war seemed to be a half-hearted, or as Gary would have said, a half-assed effort. As the years have gone by, it has been revealed that many of the best trained and most capable soldiers and marines were diverted away from Afghanistan.

Not even thirty years after the end of the Vietnam War, America found itself in another disaster. After the secretary of state made a speech at the United Nations in February 2003, using declarative sentences about WMDs and Iraq cooperating with al Qaeda, among other things, the United States invaded the sovereign nation of Iraq. It took only a few months for the full extent of the catastrophe to emerge. The president had led America into the greatest foreign policy mistake and disaster in our nation's history, or so many commentators said. I believed every word. I absolutely could not comprehend how America's leaders had fallen into this trap, totally ignoring the lessons of Vietnam.

The iconic image of the Iraq War, that banner on the aircraft carrier—MISSION ACCOMPLISHED—shames our nation. We know how the message from that little photo op turned out.

GJ is part of the war. Now on his fourth deployment to Diego Garcia since 2001, he flies his B-1 Lancer bomber on missions to Iraq or Afghanistan. GJ lovingly refers to his plane as The Bone (after B-1 or B-one). His participation troubles me most of all. He knows that I pray for him each day. Just as I did for his father.

Occasionally, an Air Force C-5 or C-17 cargo plane flies over our house descending into Dover, no doubt carrying another load of transfer cases toward the morgue. Why? I wondered.

ARRIVING HOME AFTER a Saturday afternoon matinee and an early dinner, Ray and I were surprised to see a Mustang convertible sitting in our driveway. In the fading light, I saw a man sitting on the front porch. As I made my way through the front garden, I recognized him. "Hello, Matt."

"Allison, Ray," Matt said, standing to greet us. "Your daughter said to make myself at home."

"I'm glad someone was here to welcome you," I said, hugging him. "What are you doing in Maryland? I thought you were home in New Mexico."

Matt looked all of his eighty plus years. I loved him like a father. But he had lived a rough fighter pilot's life, which was taking its toll.

We chatted for a few minutes filling each other in on what had happened since Christmas, the last time he had visited.

"I have news that I wanted to deliver in person," Matt said, touching my shoulder. "Yesterday I received a call from JPAC in Honolulu. They have positively identified Gary's remains through DNA."

"Oh, my God!" I collapsed, sitting heavily onto our porch swing. After taking a deep breath, I sighed, chin quivering. Staring at the stars in the darkening evening sky, my eyes filled with tears.

"Apparently, a Russian general turned over documents in Moscow a while back, which led to the crash site. JPAC did a dig late last fall based on maps and photographs the general provided. He died just after he handed over the info."

"I don't believe it finally happened," I said, reaching into my purse for a pen and paper. I began writing. In a state of shock, I didn't trust my memory for all the details.

"I don't either."

"What happens now?" I asked, jotting down the date and time. Russian General, I underlined.

"From what the officer in Honolulu told me, you should have the remains in early July. You need to start planning what you want done."

"Okay."

"I'll rattle the chains and make sure this moves along."

"Thank you!"

"Whatever you do, I'll be here."

I sat on the swing. I didn't know whether to cry or scream. I don't believe this, I thought. Years after I completely gave up any hope of ever knowing what happened to Gary, it finally happened. Now I knew.

THURSDAY, JULY 14, 2005, turned out to be one of those delightful summer days, full sun with low humidity. Stark white fair-weather clouds drifted by, riding the wind.

When it was time, I took Matt Foxe's and GJ's arms and followed the horse-drawn farm wagon carrying Gary's flag-draped casket down the farm lane toward our fenced plot. Doug Klepperson led a procession of Air Force officers and neighbors behind us.

Corn leaves rustled in the wind. A fresh sea breeze carried the scent of the ocean. Dust swirled ahead of us. A laughing gull flew by, making his "Ha, Ha, Ha" call. There was nothing funny, however, about what was happening.

Eight airmen carried the casket from the wagon to the grave. My minister and an Air Force chaplain said their brief kind words. When Carmen and Ramon sang *"Con te Partiro,"* my knees buckled. Ray strongly held my arm. Singing with alternating lines and harmonized chorus, Carmen and Ramon's version of *"Time to Say Goodbye,"* touched my heart.

Fingering Gary's dog tags draped around my neck, I recited *Fate and Chance*, one of his last poems that I had found in the combat diary. The one that told me that he had had a premonition of death in combat.

Fate and Chance

His number up,
there in the blue, time ran out.
A congruence of fate and chance
called him home.

Her laughter concealed the sorrow.
Pain washed away by tears.
A mountain of grief
eroded by the rains of time.

Four F-15E Strike Eagles from the 4th Fighter Wing at Seymour Johnson perfectly executed the missing-man formation pass. Shortly after, another plane approached. A B-1 Lancer bomber, from the squadron GJ commanded at Dyess Air Force Base in Texas, flew over the plot. With the variable-sweep wings extended, the bomber made a low speed pass. Then, as the plane began a turn to the left, the wings began to retract into the swept position. With the afterburners from the four engines roaring, the plane made another pass over the site and disappeared over the eastern horizon.

After the firing detail fired the three volleys and Taps sounded, the casket bearers folded the flag and handed it to Matt Foxe. He, in turn, gave it to me, saying the time-honored words, "On behalf of the President and people of the United States..."

I removed Gary's POW/MIA bracelet from my pocket and placed it upon the top of his casket. "This is yours," I said, "you're no longer missing."

After my guests retreated to our house for a catered lunch, I stood at Gary's grave, tears running down my cheeks. Carmen and Ramon's lyrics about saying goodbye echoed in my heart. As I turned, I saw GJ, Matt Foxe, Doug Klepperson, Carmen, Ramon, Ray and Christine standing there, waiting.

"He's home," I said, "at last, Gary's home."

AUTHOR'S NOTES

The Republic Aviation F-105 Thunderchief was planned and developed as a nuclear-strike single-engine and single-seat fighter bomber. A total of 833 planes were built on Long Island, New York. F-105 pilots lovingly referred to the production plant as the "Tank Factory."

Initial operational capability of the F-105D, the aircraft of this book, occurred in 1961. While the primary mission was presumed to be nuclear-strike, the F-105D had a conventional weapon capability and participated in live ordnance demonstrations during the period 1961 to 1964.

As the wars in Southeast Asia intensified, F-105D aircraft were deployed to Thailand from Japan beginning in 1964. Later, aircraft deployments arrived from Seymour Johnson Air Force Base, North Carolina, and McConnell Air Force Base, Kansas, as well as from other bases.

While other aircraft types flew combat missions, the F-105D bore the heaviest burden, being utilized in more than seventy-five percent of all attack sorties over Southeast Asia.

The first F-105D to be heavily damaged by enemy fire occurred over Laos on 14 August 1964. This same aircraft was later shot down over North Vietnam on 21 September 1966.

On 13 January 1965, the first F-105D to be shot down in combat occurred over Laos.

Operation Rolling Thunder, the American bombing campaign over North Vietnam, had an ominous start on 2 March 1965. Three F-105D and two F-100D aircraft were shot down over North Vietnam.

As the years progressed, ever increasing numbers of F-105s and pilots were lost in combat.

A total of 282 F-105s were shot down over North Vietnam, with an additional fifty-two over other

Southeast Asia nations. At least 205 aircraft of all types were shot down by Surfact-to-Air Missiles (SAMs), including thirty-one F-105s.

An additional sixty-three F-105s crashed for operational reasons: maintenance, engine failure, pilot error, mid-air collisions, or fuel exhaustion. Nearly half of the production run, a total of 397 F-105 aircraft, were lost in Southeast Asia.

The fly-away cost for each F-105D was $2,200,000. Other reports state a cost as high as $15,000,000. This price discrepancy is caused by differences in how research and development costs were amortized for the overall production run.

A heavy price was paid by the F-105 pilots. At least eighty-six were killed in action. An additional thirteen were killed in operational crashes. Forty-seven are listed as being missing in action. Another 105 became prisoners of war and were released by the North Vietnamese in 1973. Fortunately, 121 pilots were rescued by helicopter after ejecting.

During the time the protagonist in this story flew missions over North Vietnam from 22 February 1967 until 14 July 1967, at least twenty-eight pilots from the 355th Tactical Fighter Wing based at Takhli were shot down. Four were killed in action, five were listed as missing in action, seven were recovered by helicopter, thirteen became prisoners of war and were returned in 1973, and one prisoner of war died in captivity.

While the protagonist flew missions from Takhli, at least sixty-two pilots from the 355th Tactical Fighter Wing at Takhli completed one hundred counter sorties over North Vietnam. Of this total, fifteen were from

Gary's unit, the 333rd Tactical Fighter Squadron. These figures show that some pilots did indeed beat the odds.

I wrote *Delta Sierra* to describe the brutal conditions under which F-105 pilots flew up North. I regret any technical or procedure of flight errors. Likewise, I own and regret any errors in proofreading or copy editing.

F-105 pilots were only one component of those who fought, bled, and oftentimes died in Southeast Asia. The Vietnam Veterans' National Monument on the Mall contains the names of 58,300 airmen, soldiers, marines, and sailors who gave their all.

Each and every one of this Band of Warriors deserves our eternal gratitude and respect.

ACKNOWLEDGEMENTS

I began writing *Delta Sierra* in 1997 after having a dream which provided the spark for this project. Delayed by two major medical issues and one long distance move, I have finally finished with the assistance of many friends. Thank you kindly to each and every one!

My first structured fiction writing experience was in a non-credit course offered by Harford Community College at Bel Air, Maryland. Our instructor, Patricia Punt, pushed me down this path with these words, "Of all the people I have instructed, you are one who is actually going to do this." In the end, it took a while. But I did it.

Since then I have taken classes and attended writing conferences in several locations. Along the way, I met Maribeth Fischer, founder of the Rehoboth Beach Writer's Guild. Maribeth, a published author and accomplished teacher, has been an inspiration. She clarified and sharpened my vision of what this book was about, which greatly improved the final manuscript.

Over the years, I have been involved in several writing critique groups at Fallston and Riverside, Maryland, and most recently at Rehoboth Beach, Delaware. Bonnie Walker, Debra Siebert and the late Georgia Leonhart shepherded this book over the past ten years. Without them, I would still be lost.

I am grateful to Nathan Ostrow for the cover painting. Nate is a retired military illustrator and has painted many military aircraft, ships and vehicles.

For help with technical and aircraft related details, I obtained suggestions and comments from a number of F-105 pilots and others. These individuals graciously provided answers to all my questions even though they did not know me. I am amazed at the courtesy and patience offered by them. First and foremost, I would like to offer my heartfelt thanks to Brigadier General Al Lenski (USAF, Retired), Colonel George Acree (USAF, Retired), Lieutenant Colonel Gene Basel (USAF, Retired), Colonel David Brog (USAF, Retired), Lieutenant Colonel Ralph Stearman (USAF, Retired) and also to the late Brigadier General Ken Bell (USAF) and the late Lieutenant Colonel Michael Cooper (USAF). Each of these pilots went out of their way to describe their experiences of flying F-105s over North Vietnam. The late Colonel Jack Broughton graciously granted permission to use his name in the text. Maintenance and operational questions were answered by Lieutenant Colonel W. Howard Plunkett (USAF, Retired), Chief Master Sergeant John Forgette (USAF, Retired) and the late Master Sergeant Harold "Lem" Heydt (USAF).

Several aerial photographic interpreters assisted me in recalling procedures and light table minutia, among them Arthur Fry, C. E. "Ed" Comer, James Jacobs, Donald Shipman, Glen Gustafson, and the late William Dufrin.

Dr. William Kirby-Smith, Professor Emeritus at the Duke University Marine Lab, Pivers Island, Beaufort, North Carolina, took me on several boat rides on the Newport River Estuary and helped clarify ichthyology.

Jean Wheeler, C.R.N.P., a retired neonatal intensive care nurse who worked at Johns Hopkins Hospital, provided details and comments related to pregnancy, the birth process and care of infants.

I referred to the following while writing this book: *Pack Six* by Gene Basel, *100 Missions North* by Ken Bell, *Going Downtown* by Jack Broughton, *Thud Ridge* by Jack Broughton, *Roll Call: Thud* by John Campbell and Michael Hill, *The Republic F-105 Thunderchief: Wing and Squadron Histories* by James Geer, *Vietnam Air Losses* by Chris Hobson, *F-105 Thunderchief: Workhorse of the Vietnam War* by Dennis Jenkins, *Magic 100* by Al Lenski, *F-105 Thunderchiefs: A 29-Year Illustrated Operational History* by W. Howard Plunkett, and *When Thunder Rolled*, by Ed Rasimus.

A companion collection of poetry, *Cowboys and War*, written with the point of view and in the voice of Lieutenant Gary Deale, is also available.

The content of *Delta Sierra* was approved by the Publication Review Board of the Central Intelligence Agency. I thank the members of the board for their courteous and timely review of the manuscript and proof copies.

Lastly, I extend my eternal gratitude to my wife Jean for all her patience, proofreading assistance and encouragement over these years.

May 2018
Ocean Pines, Maryland

LARRY R. FRY is an Air Force veteran who served as an aerial photographic interpretation specialist. He is a veteran of the Vietnam War, having been stationed at Tan Son Nhut Airbase, near Saigon, South Vietnam, in 1962-63. Larry also served at Taipei Air Station, Taiwan, and Don Muang Airbase, Thailand. Later, he was employed by the Central Intelligence Agency as an imagery interpretation analyst at the National Photographic Interpretation Center in Washington, D.C., and also as an economic intelligence analyst at the headquarters in Langley, Virginia. He is a retired business education teacher. This is his first novel, having written two nonfiction books on family history/ genealogy and a textbook on computer programming. Larry and his wife Jean live on the Eastern Shore of Maryland.